JAZEI

JAZEI

a fantasy novel

Justin Murray

This book is a work of fiction. Names, characters, places, and incidents are entirely the product of the author's imagination. Any resemblance to actual persons, events, or locales is entirely coincidental, as well as deeply surprising.

DEDICATION

To my family, without whom this book
would not exist: thank you for listening to
what it was, for hearing what it wasn't yet,
and for helping it become what it could be.

TABLE OF CONTENTS

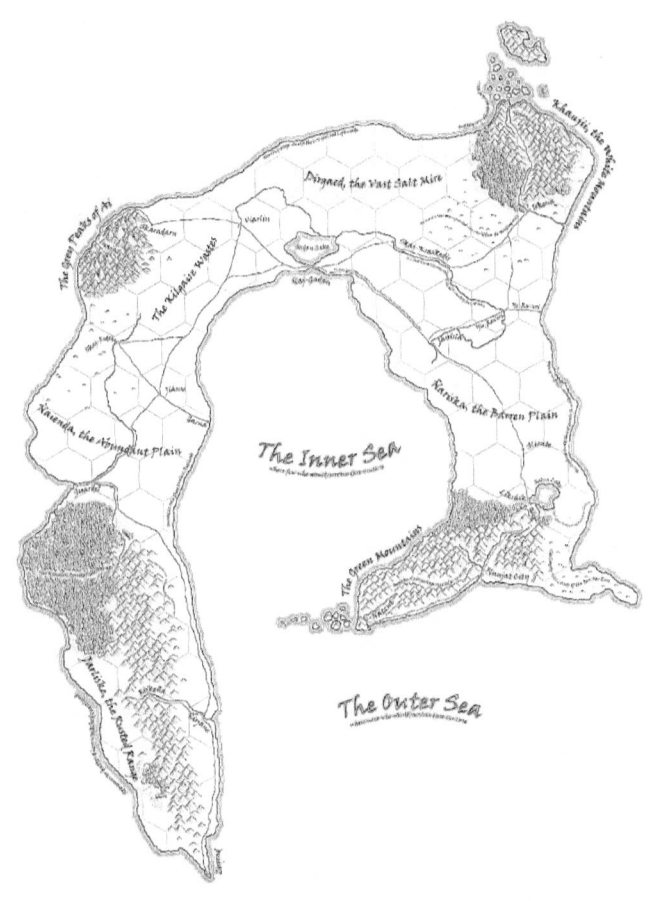

Sketch of a damaged tapestry: "[illegible]...Resplendent
Evikastan Topography with Ten League...[illegible]...the
Merchant's Guild to Ranton the...[illegible]"

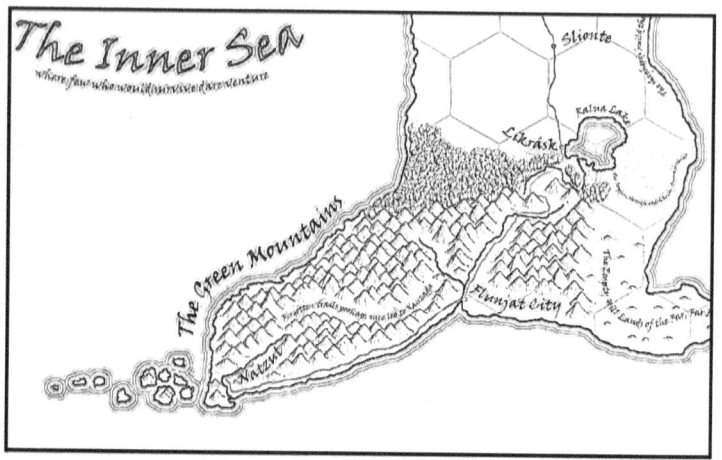

Detail: southeastern Jranjana

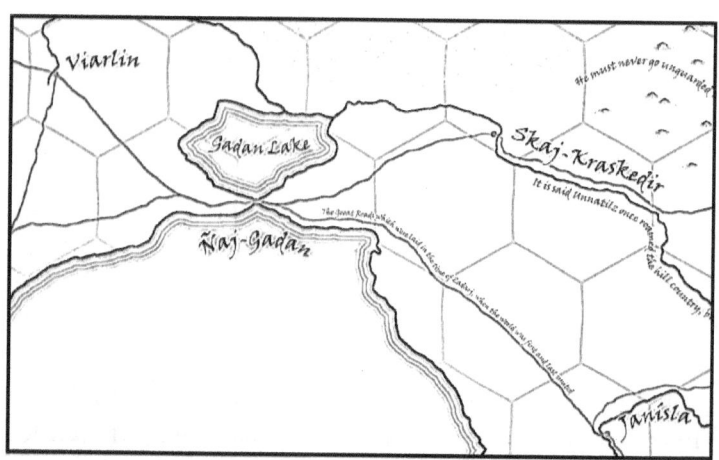

Detail: central Jranjana

High resolution maps and additional
resources available online.

JazeiBook.com

The song half-heard, each part with but a scrap,
Is whispered in the wastes beyond the map.

PROLOGUE:

Madness is the dissonance a sound mind cannot abide. Nothing can be noble and savage, nor can there be evil that is good, any more than the sky can fall upon the ground. And yet, from a high place of darkness, he looked down from the precipice and saw the sky. Madness.

And with that poignantly portentous thought, Lord Klanjad made himself laugh.

Well, not *laugh*, perhaps; it was more of a scoff, a single *pah* more like an acknowledgement of humor than actual mirth. What sentimental nonsense! Drifting off into poeticisms, caught up in the eerie unreality of the half-morning... How very soldierly of him! How very lordly! How Shadale would mock him if she knew; he smiled at the thought. "My, what an abstract morning you're having, Lord Klanjad," she would tease. And she'd be right to tease. The world is simple and sane; the sky is never on the ground.

Dismissing sentiment, Klanjad looked again. From his clifftop vantage, the fog-shrouded forest far below appeared like a looming, glowering storm, the shadowed trees within evoking the layered darkness of a thunderhead. Starlight sinking into the mist from above, blending the highlights and sharpening the shadows, furthered this resemblance to an unruly sky. Except that it was on the ground, and the sky should never be on the ground. It *could* not be so; even the charade was unnatural. Inconvenient, too, to anyone who wished to look out and see anything other than skies. Inconvenient, and perhaps even deadly.

"*Ah...*a striking morning vista, my lord."

Subconsciously, Klanjad knew this address was probably directed at him, but it didn't break through his reverie; the voice, somewhat nasal and flecked with peculiar humming emotes, came from behind him, and all Klanjad's thoughts were focused forward. Sneaky, that's how he would describe this nonsensical ground-sky. A forest and a fog have no business masquerading as a storm unless they have something to hide. He knew they were hiding something; he even knew *what* they were hiding. But though he knew the lie, he still could not penetrate it, for despite knowing what to look for, all that he could see was skies.

And that was why the soldiery could not be permitted to know what he looked for or how it hid from him: the superstitions of simple men can transform a stroke of ill luck into an omen of evil.

"My lord?" The nasal voice cut in again, this time insistent enough to stir Klanjad. "My lord seems, *hmm*, taken in by the view this morning."

And Jlak seems, *hmm*, taken in by how taken in his lord is by the morning, Klanjad thought, but he checked himself. He knew Jlak wouldn't bother him with simple pleasantries; he had something less useless to say, but he had to preface it with small talk because that was just Jlak's way. Being curt wouldn't help.

So...the morning. Klanjad glanced eastward to where the cliffs ran away, gradually lowering toward the forest-sky before disappearing in the distant haze. Beyond the haze, just a very thin smear of pinkness heralded the sunrise. "There's hardly much morning yet, Jlak. Eager for the dawn?"

"*Hmm*, well," Jlak answered, "I would hope that the sun might chase away a bit of that fog below, *em*, if we are fortunate. If the dawn would, *ahh*, but hasten."

"And what has our fortune to do with the fog?"

"*Hmm*, well, perhaps if were there no fog, we could see clearly what moves below. Perhaps? There would even be time, *ahh*, to move to the more defensible slopes without worry, maybe, if we could but see where our foes are."

Such truth, Klanjad thought. Nevertheless, he hesitated to confirm Jlak's analysis lest he provide an answer that might satisfy Jlak but discomfit many more. Ever since the mid-night, when a returning scout had indiscreetly announced that their enemy marched by starlight, the soldiers and entourage had been asking themselves why their commanders had chosen *here*, an unremarkable point along the clifftop road, to build their defenses. Why not follow the road to the east to where the cliffs were lower, where the path veered north and zigzagged its way down a steep slope to the forest below? A position there, a mere two-hour march away, would be nearly unassailable.

But the mid-night scout had been the last and only scout to return, and his information had come from seeing the enemy leave their camp at dusk. No word had come regarding the enemy's subsequent movement, and so there was no way of knowing whether they proceeded slowly or quick-marched through the night. If the former, they would likely reach the base of the cliff ascent just after dawn and would probably set up camp there, but neither Klanjad nor his brother, Ranton the King of Natzut, considered that likely.

Surely, they thought, the only reason for their foes to march through the night would be to ascend the cliffs before Ranton and his allies could occupy and fortify the clifftop. So they would have moved quickly, climbing the winding road even as the mid-night scout brought word of their march to the Natzut camp, and cresting the clifftop within the next hour.

Klanjad had estimated that Natzut's army would require three hours to assemble, form up, and march to the clifftops; their allies from Flunjat, King Kaevor and his comparatively disorderly army, would be even slower. Long before they arrived, their enemies would have deployed the bulk of their army—their numerically superior army, according to numerous reports—to the clifftop road, prepared their defenses, and even had about an hour to rest before the battle.

It was too risky. Ranton the King was unwilling to gamble on such a march, and King Kaevor of Flunjat concurred, so they had opted to spend the night fortifying their current position instead.

Klanjad could not but agree that his brother's choice was the most prudent one: to meet the larger army without securing a tactical advantage could be disastrous. Yet it needled him that they must sacrifice their chance at the clifftop position based on their own speculation, not actual information. What if, counter to all their reasoning, their enemies *hadn't* quick-marched? Or what if the scout's report, which no other scout had returned to corroborate, was inaccurate or misleading? A thousand second-guesses swarmed about Klanjad's head, driving him to stare relentlessly at the inscrutable fog on the forest below the cliffs. If he could only *see* something, any indication of what transpired below! But the sky was on the ground, and it hid what should have been visible, and all that he could see was obscurity.

"*Hmm*, my Lord Klanjad is *quite* taken by the view, *umm*, perhaps."

"Yes, Lord Klanjad has many things on his mind," Klanjad retorted irritably, then checked himself again. Jlak's curiosity and concern were both perfectly natural, and he had not done anything to deserve a caustic comeback. In his mind, Shadale teased him again: "Well done checking your temper; now try doing it *before* you say something unhelpful." Taking a deep breath, Klanjad sighed away his impatience.

Then, gathering his tact, he turned around to speak to Jlak directly. Jlak was a smallish, pigeon-toed, frail-looking figure with a lopsided way of standing, like a poorly-made puppet inexpertly dangled too low to the ground. Those who did not know Jlak often summarily judged him to be either pathetic or conniving. To Klanjad, however, he was the most loyal and trusted adviser anyone could ask for, and he deserved to be addressed with respect.

"You're right, Jlak," said Klanjad, meeting the man's eye. "The fog does prevent us from seeing...that which might be informative, perhaps even give us leave to move up. But be discreet: neither the fog nor our positions should be of widespread concern."

Jlak smiled. "No such concern shall be—*hmm*—spread wide. Naturally, my lord."

Klanjad nodded, satisfied. There was no risk of Jlak circulating secrets even after he'd been clever enough to deduce them: he was every bit as loyal as he was cunning. When they returned to Natzut, Klanjad planned to find Jlak an official role as an advisor at his side.

For now, though, Jlak's advisory role was unofficial. His real responsibility was logistics and engineering for the second regiment of the army of Natzut, and in this role he was currently overseeing the construction of a defensive fortification. "How goes the abatis, Jlak?"

Jlak indicated the forest behind them, where dozens of soldiers were making slow progress on the defensive structure. "The digging goes slower than the axing, my lord," he answered ruefully. "The ground is—*ahh*—frozen but a foot or so below the surface here. We should have the full line fortified within the hour, but—*hmm*—I fear our abatis may be neither as sturdy nor as deep as we might like."

Klanjad nodded. "Make of it what you can, but do not let them tire themselves overmuch. We need the defenses, but we will also need fresh soldiers to man them."

"Do we expect a hard fight, my lord?"

"One should never underestimate an enemy's strength. Nor...his numbers."

"His numbers, my lord? But—*umm*—surely, we and our allies together..."

Klanjad shook his head somberly as Jlak trailed off. Meeting the man's eye again, Klanjad finished quietly, "Be discreet. And let's speak no more of this now."

Jlak's eyes were wide, but he accepted Klanjad's dismissal and turned back toward the construction. After a moment, Klanjad also turned, continuing his futile attempts to peer into the impenetrable not-sky.

Nothing. No answers. No clues to their location, no reliable information about their numbers or their composition or their intentions... Who were these foes anyway? What possible enemy would—or even could—raise and deploy such an army to this part of Jranjana with so little warning? None of the northern kingdoms stood to gain from a war with Natzut and Flunjat, and none of the lesser cities and towns had either the incentive or the ability to rebel in force. And why now, when Natzut and Flunjat had already mustered and deployed their armies to suppress the rebellious Misk clans in the northern mountains? And who would outfit an army almost entirely in bronze, as the scouts had reported this army was equipped? Klanjad could not think of a single coherent explanation for any of it. It was infuriating, and it drove him to peer ever closer at the impenetrable prospects before him. In the face of the inscrutable, every unanswered question spawns speculation which, without guidance, quickly devolves into a hopeless search for sense in nonsense, harmony in dissonance.

A sound caught his ear. Something was going on, somebody was calling his name again. "My lord Klanjad!" What now? "My lord Klanjad, the king asks for you!"

Klanjad turned instantly. The voice belonged to a page, no older than seven or eight years, whose red face and breathless summons communicated his hurry. "On what account?" Klanjad asked, though he had already begun to move, grasping the startled boy's shoulder and steering him back the way he had come.

"My lord, an emissary has arrived and speaks to the king."

"From our foes?"

"I do not know, my lord. I did not recognize his garb."

Now striding alongside the page at a quick walk, Klanjad shrugged. "Well, no matter. Perhaps his garb did not recognize you either and will take no offense."

From the corner of his eye, Klanjad saw the baffled look the page gave him, and he forced himself to keep a straight face. Speaking nonsense to youngsters was one of the few real pleasures of seniority, he'd found: it did no harm, and it was nearly the only sort of mischief he could continue to allow himself in his role as a lord. Besides, the experience would serve the boy well; enduring absurdities was a key skill for courtiers, and for many others. Even for soldiers.

As Klanjad and the page approached the center of the camp, Klanjad was surprised that Ranton's royal tent—small, warm, and simple, according to the Jazei traditions—was empty. Instead, the emissary was being received in the lavish and luxurious tent of Kaevor, king of Flunjat, even though that king was away in the forest with his own army. Ha! Well, Kaevor probably wouldn't mind, he was a genial fellow. But for Ranton to be attentive to the stateliness of the tent... Apparently this emissary was from somewhere important.

The page stepped away as Klanjad ducked through the flaps into the tent, blinking as his eyes adjusted from faint starlight to smoky candlelight. Only two other men were within; one was Ranton the King of Natzut, Klanjad's brother, who said, "Thank you for your haste, Klanjad."

Klanjad smiled warmly. "What good ever comes of walking slowly?"

The brothers were much alike in appearance: both medium-tall, sturdily built, with the wispy white-blond hair and flashing emerald eyes characteristic of the Jazei race. Ranton, the elder, was the handsomer of the two: his glance was steady and his bearing kingly, whereas Klanjad's glance was often too bold—aggressive, even—and his brash bearing was that of a warrior, not a king. Both brothers wore traditional Jazei war attire—sturdy leather armor and leggings ornamented with accents of wolf fur—and both carried exquisitely-crafted Jazei longswords at their sides. Both, too, ignored the formalities of a lord greeting his king, sharing only an informal glance and grin before turning to the emissary.

He was like most Jranjanans: of average height with brown eyes, dark brown hair, and a medium-stocky build. He had a beard, a characteristic of the northern cities where the old traditions had been largely forgotten. He wore rather fine traveling attire and was armed only with a kirsk, the short ornamental greeting dagger all nobles carried, which was still intact. This was no messenger of war.

Klanjad mechanically drew his own kirsk, proffering it grip-first to the emissary in the sign of welcome. The other touched the pommel, accepting the salute. "Greetings from Ñaj-Gadan, Lord Klanjad," the emissary declared in the great ambassadorial tradition of blathering names. "I, Jaem of Iskena, bring you the best wishes of the Commune of Kings, and particularly of your kinsman Jendraski."

Klanjad, ever tactless, said dubiously to Ranton, "Jendraski is our kinsman?"

Ranton quirked an eyebrow, his royal substitute for a shrug. "A little Jazei blood runs in his veins, I think, but perhaps that is a conversation for another time. Jaem brings us tidings from the north."

"Let us hear them, then," said Klanjad.

Jaem bowed assent. "The Commune of Kings remains entirely focused, as it has been for fifteen years now, on repulsing the Droál invasion. So far, that war has been conducted principally in the southwest; however, several weeks ago our spies among the Droál reported that an army from Zirgrad was preparing to embark east across the Inner Sea."

"A perilous route," remarked Ranton, and Klanjad silently agreed. Any ships that sailed the Inner Sea remained close to the shores, for the waters beyond sight of land were treacherous. Though many ships had sailed those waters—

typically by accident—and survived, many more had been lost forever in that sea.

"The Droál," Jaem replied, "do not seem to find it as perilous. Their way of sailing is still a mystery to us, but they do not fear to venture far from shore on either the Inner or the Outer Sea. It is from the sea, in fact, that they come, though we do not know from whence they sail.

"To continue, as soon as the Commune learned of the Droál's movements, I was dispatched to bring you the tidings. Jendraski believes you have never encountered Droál, having thus far refused to join the Commune in repelling their invasion in the west."

Klanjad thought he heard a note of bitterness in the emissary's voice. Ranton certainly did, for he answered, "You've been told our reasons, I presume: it is our ancestral duty to suppress the ancient Flunjat Misk tribes, which we cannot do without strong garrisons. Besides, if we were not here, how should you now deal with a—Droál, was it?—incursion on this coast that you do not guard?"

The emissary nodded respectfully but did not pursue the topic. "I was bidden to warn you that these Droál are not like foes you have previously fought. They come in tremendous numbers with fanatical fury..."

Klanjad felt himself immediately bored by what sounded like stale, bard-standard dire warnings. "We have come from suppressing rebellious *Misks*—" he began impatiently, but Ranton waved him to silence.

"...and yet, their great strength does not lie in their numbers or their fervor," continued Jaem. "They are but humans—not even human magicians, but ordinary men—and yet they somehow command a strange kind of magic which all men can sense, and which affects the physical world. Without touching anything, they can cause things to move and shift and break, as though with massive, invisible hands. They can tear down structures and rip apart trees from a distance. They can stop a charge and hurl entire battalions to the ground in a blow."

Klanjad glanced at Ranton, and Ranton met the glance; there was skepticism in the elder brother's eyes, and outright rejection in the younger's. Magic that could be sensed by everyone? Magic could only be sensed by magicians, this was simply a fact—and no one, magician or not, could move things without touching them. "Do you mean to say," Ranton suggested, "that their entire army is composed of magicians?"

Jaem shook his head vigorously. "No, in fact the opposite: none of their men are magicians. At least, they are not the sort of magicians Jranjanans know; they are not like you Jazeiz are. Theirs is some other kind of magic, involving…involving a chanting invitation to magicians from other Strata… I am sorry, I wish I could explain better. I am not a magician myself and do not know how it should be described."

"Indeed," said Ranton, not revealing the doubt Klanjad knew he felt. "Is this, then, the threat we face today? These Droál and their…strange magics?"

"That…seems probable," Jaem answered hesitantly, "but I do not know. I came here from the south by way of Flunjat City, having sailed originally from Ñaj-Gadan to Natzut to find that you were campaigning against the Misks here in the north. I'm afraid I have little knowledge of what you face at present."

"Indeed," Ranton repeated courteously. "I thank you for your news, Jaem, but I seem to be a bit unclear on the specifics." Klanjad kept his face carefully unamused. Ranton continued, "Perhaps if we show you how we plan to defeat these Droál, you can advise us directly on what we should expect. Mayhap that will help my brother and I more clearly understand the…facts you describe."

Jaem recoiled slightly and held up his palms. "Sire, I am not a soldier, but a man of the court! I came only with a message, not with strategic aid."

Ignoring the man's protest, Ranton took a map of the area from a nearby desk and began to outline their strategy. "Here is a sketch of our current position; note here, the cliffs to the north, perhaps half a quarter-league from the road. The army is camped off this edge of the map, and we have built our defensive positions here, along this line from the edge of the cliff south across the road and another few stades into the forest. We, the army of Natzut, will defend these positions as though from a frontal assault; however, once the battle is begun, King Kaevor and the army of Flunjat will move from their hidden positions here, in the forest to the south, to attack the enemy on their flank." When Ranton had begun speaking, the emissary had been standing away from the map, alarmed at being asked to even look at it. But as Ranton continued to speak, pointing things out on the map, speaking clearly and seriously, the emissary gradually drew closer and leaned in, listening intently. "Once Flunjat has begun their attack, we will then push forward on our right flank—here, away from the cliffs—to join a line with Flunjat, which we will then roll north as we continue to push on the flank. If our left flank holds, or even if it gives way a little, we will press our enemies back against the cliff, forcing them to retreat back the way they came or be driven from the precipice." By this point, the emissary was fully attentive to Ranton's explanation. The king encouraged him, "You see? What do you think of this? How do you suppose a plan such as this may fare against these Droál magics?"

Jaem was silent for several moments. At last, he said hesitantly, "I am, as I have said, not a soldier, but…this does seem a good plan." He looked at the map again. "You are fortified here?" he said as he pointed to a place on the map. Ranton nodded. "You should tell your men to stand somewhat behind the barricades; the Droál's magic will likely destroy any structures, but the rubble and any surviving earthworks may still unsettle their infantry's advance. If your men are yet standing after the fortifications have been shattered, you may still gain an advantage this way." Ranton nodded again, at least appearing to take this advice seriously. "And your allies from Flunjat are here?" Jaem continued, pointing to another spot on the map.

"Here," Klanjad corrected him.

"Is their lot not particularly dangerous, isolated and away from fortifications?" Jaem asked. "If they are discovered by scouts or smelled by Unnatilz, then—"

"Unnatilz!" Klanjad barked as Ranton stiffened noticeably. "What's this now, they have Unnatilz with them?"

"A-at times," Jaem answered hastily, alarmed by Klanjad's reaction, "the Droál have been known to employ Unnatilz in their armies, as scouts or... But as for this particular army, I do not really know..." He trailed off as he realized neither Klanjad nor Ranton was listening to him anymore.

"The wind is in the east," said Ranton, half to himself, half to Klanjad. "Perhaps they will go unnoticed."

"But the wind is weak today, and the cataracts are to the southwest," Klanjad countered. "The breeze off of them will carry the scent right to the Unnatilz, despite the east wind."

"How much time do we have?"

Klanjad, who was nearer the door to the tent, leaned out and bellowed, "Has anyone heard word of the enemy from Kaevor? Or scouts? Anything!"

"No, my lord," someone called back. "There's been no—" Klanjad did not hear the rest or bother to identify the speaker before ducking back inside.

"No news means nothing," said Ranton at once. "Our foes could be minutes away, or Kaevor may have been already ambushed and overrun."

"Surely, this all seems a bit hasty," Jaem ventured in alarm, but no one listened.

Klanjad added to Ranton, "With Unnatilz in the field, any messengers on their own... Well, at least we know what became of our scouts!"

"Such truth," Ranton replied, nodding. "We can't rely on our runners, they're easy prey. Yet we must warn Kaevor. Will you go, brother? Warn Kaevor to fall back, with all haste."

"Of course," answered Klanjad promptly, but he hesitated as he turned toward the door. "Ranton..."

Ranton, deep in thought, did not immediately hear him. He muttered, "We may lose this fight. Our scouts and communications are useless, and they probably know everything about our positions by now! And if they caught any, interrogated any..."

"Ranton," Klanjad repeated, a little louder, and Ranton turned to him. "Shadale is with the entourage..."

Ranton met and held his brother's gaze for a moment, then rounded toward Jaem. "Have the Droál allied themselves with Misks? Have they?!"

"I..." Jaem seemed almost fearful of the answer he was about to give. "I do not know about their ties in the southeast, but Droál are not averse to Misk alliances. For many years, in the southwest, they have collaborated closely with Clan Eyjazinka."

"One above!" Klanjad swore, aghast.

Ranton swallowed hard, and when he spoke again there was a snap in his voice. "We will prepare for battle, immediately. I will tell the men to arm; any bulwark that is unfinished will remain so. We will dispatch the entourage into the mountains to the south for safety. Go with them, Jaem; be prepared to lead them if you must."

"Lead them?" Jaem gasped. "I— Who?"

"The entourage—those who travel with us to serve the army, but do not fight. Blacksmiths, cooks, wives... Get them moving, lead them if you have to, southwest into the mountains to safety."

"Sire!"

Ranton blinked, and when he opened his eyes, the emissary found himself transfixed by the king's glance—as firm as a glare, but as clear and direct as an order, and utterly inescapable. "I can spare none of my officers, Jaem," said the king in an even tone that rang with command. "I do not know what this magic you speak of may be, but regardless of that we are outnumbered, out-scouted, and we may even find ourselves facing Misks. I need every soldier and every officer here to ensure victory, but for the rest… I would have them seen to safety. If it comes to it, will you lead them?"

The emissary stood speechless, his wide eyes still locked to the unbending glance of the Jazei. Klanjad saw him shaking; he seemed on the brink of refusing, of crumbling in fear of the unexpected task before him. But he was caught in Ranton's unwavering stare, a stare that pierced through tact, ignored the euphemisms and excuses that customarily protect apathy, inaction, and cowardice. A man caught in that stare could either rise to the occasion or slink away in fear, fully awake to the honor or shame of their decision.

Taking a fortifying breath, drawing strength from the clarity of the challenge presented to him, the emissary straightened his shoulders and answered the king: "If it comes to that, Sire, I will lead them."

"Good," Ranton approved, releasing his stare and turning to Klanjad. "Shadale will be safe. Go now, warn Kaevor…"

Klanjad burst out of the tent at a sprint, slipping on the dew as he turned to run southeast into the forest. Once clear of obstacles, Klanjad called upon his skill as a magician and Faded, adding speed to his sprint and sharpness to his senses. The magic gave the world around him a slowness, but that was only in his mind. He sped through the trees, easily leapt over the nearly-completed defenses, and continued into the forest where Kaevor and his men were stationed.

Ordinarily, Klanjad would not have used magic with an enemy potentially so close at hand; if there were magicians in the enemy army, they could easily sense him and be alerted. However, there were probably Unnatilz with this army, and

Unnatilz would detect him no matter what he did. No one could elude Unnatilz.

Be he sensed nothing and he saw no one; in fact, nothing at all disturbed his journey. Unsettled, unsure whether he was overreacting or already outmaneuvered, Klanjad pushed himself to run faster. After just a few minutes, he stumbled breathlessly into King Kaevor's presence and was instantly set upon by the royal guard.

"Enough, enough!" boomed a deep voice as the stocky figure of King Kaevor thrust his way through his soldiers. "Can you not see the white hair? This is Lord Klanjad of Natzut!" The soldiers quickly backed away from the panting Jazei, muttering apologies, until Klanjad stood alone with the king. Kaevor, eyes aglitter with mirth, clapped Klanjad on the shoulder. "You seem in rather a hurry this morning, Klanjad. To what do I owe—"

"Fall back!" Klanjad gasped, still out of breath from his sprint. "Fall back away from the road. The Droál may be bringing Misks and Unnatilz with them. They will find you, they will know you are here!"

"Slow down, Klanjad," said Kaevor his mirth vanishing. "Misks and Unnatilz, you say? Among…who's bringing them?"

"Droál—the army we face, apparently they're called Droál."

"They have Misks?"

"And Unnatilz, yes. Maybe. Probably."

"My scouts have not returned; where and when did you get this information?"

"An emissary came, not half an hour ago."

"From these enemies?"

"*No*, from— He brought news of them, I will tell you all once you prepare and *fall back*, you must—"

He stopped, for there was suddenly no more to say, and nobody was listening. *Something* was happening to the east; Klanjad had felt it and, it seemed, so had everyone else.

It was magic, certainly, but unlike any other magic Klanjad had ever known or imagined. An ordinary magician using magic could be sensed as he was, and he could be seen to Fade, and other magicians could know him by his magic. But something entirely different was happening to the east. It seemed as though dozens—or perhaps hundreds—of magicians had materialized at once, a crowd of magic that did not *begin*, but simply *appeared*. And everyone, magician or not, could feel it.

The shared sensation drew everyone's eyes eastward just in time to see the commotion begin. Flunjat's army was deployed near the river where the trees were sparse, and they could see all the way to the eastern extreme of the army. There was a pause, then a hiss and rumble as of a rockslide, and suddenly they saw the soldiers on the far eastern flank being hurled bodily into the air. Some unseen force tossed armored men about like storm-blown leaves; they screamed and flailed as they flew, smashing into trees, landing hard on the ground, or raining down on their comrades. The inexplicable *crowd-sense*, the shared perception of impossible magic, was overpowering.

"I feel it," said Kaevor in a stupefied voice. Klanjad knew that Kaevor was not a magician and could not sense normal magic; he should not be able to sense magic at all. "I feel it," he repeated. "What does this mean?"

Klanjad was speechless. He had not believed it, he had not even *considered* what it might mean if Jaem had spoken the truth: "Without touching anything, they can cause things to move…as though with massive, invisible hands." This could only be the force he had spoken of, this…strange magic. What could this *mean?*

To the soldiers of Flunjat, it meant that the day was lost before it had even begun. Ambushed, flanked, and confronted with a magic that defied all belief and explanation, Flunjat's army instantly disintegrated into a rout. Shaking off their astonishment, Klanjad and Kaevor began bellowing at the fleeing soldiers, haphazardly trying to rally them, but their efforts only added to the confusion, for the terrified soldiers would not be rallied. Instead, Klanjad was forced to defend himself against his routing allies who, panicking, struck at anyone and everyone in their way.

Between the frantic faces fleeing past, Klanjad caught confused, fleeting glimpses of a horde behind them. From this distance, it looked as though a great wave of dark, roiling gold was pouring forth from the denser forest at the edge of the clearing. As the wave approached, individual soldiers became distinguishable: human heavy infantry clad in banded bronze armor with brimmed helmets on their heads and short, sturdy spears in their hands. The bronze Droál advance was swifter than the steel-grey Flunjat retreat, and the line where the forces met turned red with the blood of Klanjad's allies.

Men; only men! The nature of the fight instantly changed for Klanjad: no time to fret over strange magic when there were men to fight! Fading with his own magic, Klanjad pushed through the panicking Flunjat soldiers, throwing them aside as he alone counter-charged the advancing Droál army. As he charged, he loosed the Jazei war scream—a high, open-throated, inhuman screech—and hurled himself at his foes.

He hit the Droál like a rampaging bull, his magically-enhanced speed and strength smashing right through their line. Those he hit directly fell, and their comrades stumbled and scattered; they had been at ease, recklessly pursuing a rout, and were totally unprepared for a counterattack by a Jazei magician. Seeing their enemies falter, Kaevor and his elite guard let out a cheer and rushed in to join the fray.

Fourteen men—a Jazei, a king, and twelve royal guards—were overmatched beyond all hope, but for a few impossible moments, there seemed a chance that they might be able to hold back the bronze tide. Perhaps the Flunjat soldiers, freed from close pursuit, would rally and return to the fight; perhaps Ranton had heard Klanjad's war scream and would come—

The *crowd-sense* returned, and the strange magic crashed through the place where Klanjad stood. With his own magic's speed, he watched in horror as it approached: the invisible wave ripped up everything, soldiers and fallen from both sides, and even scored great gouges into the ground itself. Then Klanjad too was flung off his feet, tumbling backward as though caught in an invisible landslide.

...

Everything was heavy, and dizzy, and stuck. He gave an uncoordinated heave, yanking his leg out from under...somebody. Somebody's armor had caught on his leg, tore some skin, and there was blood. His blood? Lots of people's blood. The blood was slick and fresh; that was something, at least. It made it easier for Klanjad to drag himself out of the heap of broken men.

He rubbed his eyes as though he would wipe the dazedness from them. What had happened? There had been the fight...and the strange magic...and now, all around, there were only the dead. Not so many dead—it had been a rout, not a massacre—but more than enough; Flunjat's army had been crushed.

Flunjat... Where was Kaevor? Klanjad glanced at the heap of bodies beside him. No, he didn't see Kaevor in there. He did, however, see the ivory hilt of his sword, and he instinctively reached for it.

The moment his hand touched the sword, Klanjad's thoughts began to clear. The fight here had been lost, so Kaevor was likely dead; but if not, he might have fled back toward the Natzut position. Back toward Ranton, with the overpowering Droál magic at his heels...

Alarm banished the last of the sluggishness from Klanjad's mind. He sprang to his feet and sprinted back westward, not even pausing to sheathe his sword. As he ran, he tried to organize his thoughts, tried to comprehend the many disasters of this thrice-damned morning. There must be a way to salvage the situation; Ranton and he would have to contrive a new plan. But Ranton didn't know about the Droál magic; like Klanjad, he would never have dreamed that Jaem's explanations on that topic could be real! He had to be warned, he would need to be ready if they were to have any chance of defeating the Droál now.

Despite being unsure of how they would prevail, despite what he had seen, Klanjad could never truly conceive of defeat until the moment he dashed up to the fortifications and saw defeat before him.

Jaem had been right; the Droál had torn easily through the fortifications without so much as faltering. Not a single bronze-armored corpse lay on the road near the gate they had built, and a scarce few lay in the ditches before the splintered fortifications. But the dead of Natzut lay everywhere: twisted on the ground, crushed under boulders and logs, or suspended in the few standing trees like macabre marionettes. Behind these, the shredded remains of the royal tents swayed limply in the drifting morning mist.

It was... It was decided, then? Just a few moments, and an unthinkable magic, and hundreds of lives lost...and they were defeated? It was over? Klanjad shook his head in disbelief. It could not be, they could not be defeated! Where was Ranton? Ranton would never have allowed this to happen. But if it had happened, then...

A high, roaring Jazei war scream tore through the morning. Klanjad instantly recognized the sound: Ranton! He still fought, he still lived! But something was wrong, for the scream was too loud, too long, too wild. Klanjad had never heard such a sound from his brother before.

Advancing cautiously this time, he moved in the direction of the sound—northwest, through the trees behind the ruined battle line. This area had been the scene of intense fighting only minutes ago. The soldiers of Natzut had been driven back through here, and the dead and dying from both armies lay strewn about the forest floor. Here and there, the copse showed signs of damage from the Droál's inexplicable magic: even the forest itself could not stand against them.

Pushing through the underbrush in the densest part of the forest, Klanjad suddenly found himself at the edge of an unnatural clearing where even full-grown trees had been torn up and thrown into each other or tossed off the cliff to the north. Here the last of the battle was being fought; Ranton stood alone, frozen like a wolf at bay, surrounded by at least a dozen assailants in heavy black cloaks.

With a shout, Klanjad began scrambling across the debris to help his brother. His shout caught the attention of Ranton's assailants and of everyone else in the area, but Ranton himself gave no sign of recognition or even of having heard. Another moment he stood there, perfectly still, then moved faster than Klanjad had ever seen.

Two foes were slaughtered in the blink of an eye, and their comrades skipped backward to save themselves. But Ranton had already flung himself in the opposite direction, slashing madly at his foes on the opposite side; one more fell. Klanjad, still approaching through the debris, was both elated and troubled. This fighting was too wild, the magic too chaotic. Ranton had been a paragon of discipline and control for years. Was he simply exhausted?

Seeing Klanjad's approach and Ranton's ferocity, the black-cloaked assailants retreated a little to assess the situation. Klanjad used the space to move nearer to Ranton, preparing to fight alongside him. Ranton swiped menacingly toward his enemies, screamed his new, overlong, disturbing Jazei scream, then rounded on his brother.

Years of training together, of sparring together, of simply being brothers had made Klanjad and Ranton nearly able to predict each other's movements. Klanjad reacted on pure instinct, flinging himself out of reach even as his mind failed to comprehend what was happening. As he fell backward out of the sword's path, his shocked eyes found his brother's face.

There was no recognition there; the familiar green eyes reflected nothing of the brother he knew. Instead there was only...madness.

Klanjad landed hard on his back, still in shock, but Ranton had already whirled his mad fury back toward his black-cloaked foes. Using some strange magic of their own to enhance their movements, they skipped out of range before him, staying out of harm's way as they waited for...

Klanjad knew it would come even before he sensed it. The *crowd-sense* formed again, only this time it was much stronger than before. Klanjad, Ranton, and their black-cloaked foes were all hit and hurled backward by the force of the strange magic. Klanjad found himself tumbling and skidding over the battlefield; he screamed in pain as a passing rock ripped a chunk of flesh from his left shoulder.

The strange magic had flung Klanjad toward the cliff's edge, and he skidded to a halt only a few yards from the precipice. He struggled to his knees, clasping his torn shoulder and casting about for his sword, but it was not near him and he couldn't have wielded it effectively anyway. He was hurt, he was winded, he was dizzy—and worst of all, he was afraid.

Raising his eyes, he saw that Ranton had regained his feet faster than their black-cloaked assailants. Though his sword had been knocked away, Ranton was pouncing from foe to foe, seizing them as they tried to rise and smashing them brutally back into the ground. He was heedless of the strange magic that had just overpowered them all, nor did he react as the *crowd-sense* formed once again overhead.

The magic pounded downward, crushing Ranton to the ground; however, instead of dissipating, this time the presence remained, pinning him. Ranton struggled, howling incoherently and foaming at the mouth, but the strange magic was too strong even for him. In anguish, Klanjad called his brother's name aloud. No one replied.

While Ranton continued to thrash and the few surviving black-cloaked assailants picked themselves up, Klanjad saw that they were no longer the only ones in the clearing. A small procession, men shrouded in deep blue robes, had emerged from the trees to the south. They moved ploddingly, as though they were focused not on walking, but on something else that lent an ominous, deliberate rhythm to their steps. Faintly, Klanjad thought he could hear the sound of chanting.

As the procession loomed nearer and Ranton struggled madly against the strange magic's hold, Klanjad struggled in agony against himself. The chanters did not look much like warriors, but these must be the workers of the strange magic; even if he hadn't been injured, Klanjad had no idea how to fight them. Suddenly, one of the figures turned its hooded face toward Klanjad and raised a hand to shoulder height.

Klanjad did not know what the figure planned to do, but he feared it. He could not fight them, not like this; he was wounded, unarmed, and facing a magic he could not begin to understand. The battle could not be won, so he had only one option before him: abandon the fight. Abandon those who could not retreat. Abandon Ranton.

And Klanjad turned, scrambled forward, and slid himself over the edge of the cliff.

PART I

The truth they sake, and so to seek
    Dispatched they Taeve, legendary scout.
        "Go ye," said they, "to find the place,
        And, hidden in the battle trace,
        Seek news of what Zadarj did face
And what destruction did he wreak.
    Go now, and be these rumors true, find out."

Turned Taeve Swift like horse in lane
    And flashed across the prairie like a gale.
        For dusty day and dusky night
        She flew her unrelenting flight.
        And thus by second morning's light
She came upon the withered plain
    Uncovered by the dawn's emerging pale.

In rim-fire ends the waning night,
    The sun enkindled early on its path.
        So painted in a burning hue
        The land that lay in Taeve's view
        Was glazed withal in rusty dew.
But not all red was born of light:
    Steeped here the draining dregs of a bloodbath.

—*The Song of Rage*, verses 12:14. Excerpted from
Canticles of Zadarj, a collection from the third century of
the Silvered Court, inspired by the memories of the
Wanderer.

CHAPTER I:

Kenlin had never been to the summit. He couldn't see it from here—the shape of the mountain was such that, from the rocky outcropping on which he currently stood, lower shoulders hid the true peak from his sight—but he knew it was there. *Yes? And? There is no cause to attempt going up there. I wouldn't even be able to see the valley as well as I can now, and that was the only reason to come up here at all. Besides, Adanedi would never make it to the top.* Kenlin glanced down toward his friend, who was still struggling up the mountainside below. Then, with a sigh, Kenlin turned from the hidden heights above, flicked his white-blond hair from his eyes, and looked out over the valley they had come to survey.

Through the center of the valley ran a little river, now in late summer hardly more than a stream, around which was scattered a patchwork of young forests and overgrown fields. Faint traces of regularity still visible in the patchwork proved that this valley had once been inhabited and farmed, but the inhabitants were all gone and the farms had been long-since abandoned. Sixteen years ago the Bronze Invaders had sacked the city of Natzut and massacred its inhabitants, and the few survivors they left behind lived almost exclusively in Irnaji.

With his eyes, Kenlin followed the little river southeastward toward its mouth, where it would join the mighty Kirai only a few short leagues from the sea. Kenlin couldn't see that junction—the valley narrowed to the east, forcing the river to pass below an imposing cliff face that blocked Kenlin's view of what lay beyond—but the Kirai valley he knew very well. *Home.* Well, in a sense, at least. Technically speaking, Irnaji was home for Kenlin, as it was for Adanedi and everyone else Kenlin knew. Less technically, however, Kenlin felt more at home in the wilderness around the town than he'd ever felt in the town itself.

But the wilderness lived and thrived on its own, whereas Irnaji required constant effort from the young and the able-bodied to survive. This, in fact, was why Kenlin, Adanedi, and six other young men had come to this valley. These eight lads were the town's best hunters, relied upon for meat and pelts alike, and some weeks ago they had followed an elk herd into this valley only to discover that the area had been claimed by a ferociously territorial pack of wolves. There needn't have been conflict—there were plenty of elk in the herd for both hunters and wolves—but the wolves had taken the initiative. After two ruined hunts and a direct confrontation where one of the lads was nearly mauled, it was clear to the hunters that the wolves had no interest in peace. *So be it. They won't share their territory, yes? Alright, then; we'll just take it.* So this time the hunters had come in force, all eight on a single hunt, and this time they hadn't come for elk. *We have to find the wolves, track the pack to their den, then kill them all.*

And that was why Kenlin and Adanedi were on this mountain: while the other lads scouted parts of the valley in pairs, Kenlin and Adanedi had climbed up here to assess the land, look for any signs of the wolves they could see, and note locations worth scouting tomorrow in case nobody found a trail today. Well, to be accurate, so far only Kenlin had climbed up here to do those things; Adanedi was still climbing. Glancing down the slope again, Kenlin could see his friend doubled over panting with his hands on his knees. *Still? Come on, Adanedi.* "Hey! How's it coming down there?"

Adanedi shook his head without raising it and panted something in reply, but at this distance and over the wind Kenlin couldn't hear him. "What?" Kenlin called. This time Adanedi looked up, tilting his head at the question and eying Kenlin with a sort of bemused exasperation. He didn't try speaking again, but after a moment he gestured a response. He pointed first down the slope below him, then up to where

Kenlin stood, then he made a balancing motion with his hands before pointing down at his own feet. Kenlin nodded and waved, biting back a grin. He understood his friend perfectly: on the journey from where he'd started to where he was going, Adanedi reckoned he'd more or less made it to where he was.

With a chuckle, Kenlin turned again toward the valley. This was why he preferred the wilderness to Irnaji, and all the other lads felt the same. Out here they could be young. Out here they could *do* things, try things, and all the excitement and joy to be had in life was in the context of the attempt. In contrast, people in Irnaji never did or tried anything unless it was absolutely certain that it wouldn't make their lives worse. As a village, their collective objective was nothing more than to continue existing, and anything that might disturb their subsistence was just too horrible to be considered. Lazaeddi, Kenlin's mother, had told him once that this was a result of the sacking of Natzut. That memory—the death, the chaos, the fires and the screams—still caused many in Irnaji to cling desperately, almost pitifully to whatever life they could scrounge for themselves. No such desperation afflicted Kenlin, however; he'd been more than three years old when Natzut was sacked, but like most other lads his age, he didn't remember any of it.

In fact, in Kenlin's case, he hadn't even been in Irnaji during the sacking. Where exactly he and his mother *had* been was unknown—Lazaeddi refused to speak of it—but before the arrival of the Bronze Invaders, no one in Irnaji had ever seen her or her white-haired son. Then, a few moons after Ranton the King had left with the city's army to fight Misks in the north, the Bronze Invaders had arrived from the sea. The city of Natzut was built into the side of a mountain, walled on all sides with only a single, heavily reinforced gate in the west; it had been thought to be impregnable. But the fortifications were as nothing to Bronze Invaders; they stormed up the switchback road, smashed the reinforced gate, and slaughtered the overmatched garrison left in the army's absence. They even made brief assaults on the keep, an ancient and immeasurably strong fortress high on the mountain above the city, as well as on the lightless Dwarf tunnels connecting Natzut to the Underground Empire. But after being repelled from both these assaults, they used whatever power had smashed the gates to collapse the indestructible tunnels, bringing down half the mountainside and the unconquerable keep in the process. Then they began an unopposed massacre, slaughtering the populace with sword and fire for ten days on end. Then they left the way they had come—by sea—thinking to themselves that only the dead remained.

But though they had massacred every village and settlement they could find, something very small and unimportant had been overlooked: Irnaji. Really more of a slum of Natzut than a village in its own right, Irnaji was built on the western edge of the same alpine shelf as Natzut. However, it was outside the walls, and since there was no gate on that side of the city, Irnaji was only accessible by either scaling cliffsides around the walls or by crawling through tiny sewers beneath them. Thus this slum, populated only by those who had absolutely nowhere else to go, was completely overlooked by the Bronze Invaders, who completed their massacre and departed without ever having known it was there.

Nor were the villagers of Irnaji the only survivors: no massacre can be that thorough. In the days after the sacking, isolated cries—mostly from small children emerging from tiny hiding places—echoed through the smoldering wreckage of Natzut. These cries eventually brough villagers from Irnaji into the city, looking for whomever they could find, and one of the people they found was Lazaeddi, her white-haired son at her side, scrounging for food in the ruins of the dead city.

That had all happened before Kenlin could remember, but ever since that time he and his mother had lived in a tiny hovel on the edge of Irnaji (which was yet another reason to prefer the wilderness). The mystery surrounding their origins, and particularly surrounding Kenlin's white-blond hair and emerald-green eyes, had of course fueled salacious gossip for years. White-blond hair and green eyes were Jazei features, which led to the most popular theory holding that Lazaeddi (whose eyes and hair were both deeply, richly brown) had been a "well-liked" handmaid in the keep in the time when it was ruled by a Jazei lineage. Lazaeddi refused to discuss this rumor, which the gossips interpreted as an admission that it was true; but as for their part, Kenlin and has friends suspected that blond hair and green eyes were simply more common in general than old stories would have had them belie—

"*Heya!*"

The shout came at the same time as hands landed heavily on Kenlin's shoulders; he jumped up and forward and nearly sent himself tumbling off the mountain. "One above! Adanedi...!"

Having finally finished clambering up the slope, Adanedi had used what remaining breath he had to scare Kenlin, and now he had none left over with which to laugh. "Oh!" he gasped, wheezing from trying to laugh and breathe at the same time. "Oh!"

Now recovering, Kenlin was chuckling too, though not nearly as much as Ataland. "Don't *die*," he said, eying the way Adanedi was holding his sides. "Scare me off a cliff, then kill yourself laughing: you have the greatest plans."

"Mirth murder-suicide...best way to go..." Adanedi quipped between gasps, collapsing to a seat on a rock and still clutching his sides. "Oh... Oh, that was good. That's what you get for climbing up here so fast. Lost in your thoughts again?" Kenlin shrugged. "That's fair. If my thoughts were as directionless as yours, I'd get lost in them too. Oh, One above... I need to breathe."

Damn you, Adanedi. Kenlin was still chuckling intermittently as he waited for his heartbeat to subside. "Well, I'm glad you finally made it," he said. "How was the climb?"

Adanedi laid down on his back, puffing. "I won't lie to you, it's been an uphill battle," he said. "At first, you know, when I was looking up at the slope, I was feeling a pretty low; but now, honestly, I think I rose to the occasion."

"'Rising to the occasion.' Damn you, Adanedi, I was going to use that one."

"Yes, well that's you, isn't it, always a step behind? Struggling to keep up?"

"Ha! Such a low blow! And here I thought you were finally on the high road."

"So I am," Adanedi replied, his tone waxing flamboyant, "and rising by the minute. Indeed, after such an ascent, to stand high and straight seems only right, wouldn't you say? For when one comes to such a height, staff in hand, he towers above all the world, a veritable pillar of manhood!"

"Evidently we climbed different mountains and are on *very* different high roads."

"Well, that would explain how you got here so fast."

"Also, I see no sign on you of a staff, in hand or otherwise."

"Ooh, a low blow from you too, then?" Kenlin chuckled but declined to further escalate. By now, despite his verbal flourishes, Adanedi had begun to catch his breath. "And you? While I was busy making great strides, have you had time for anything other than thoughts? Spotted the wolves?"

Kenlin shook head. "No, no spotted wolves. I did look a bit, and I've gotten a sense for the valley, so I have...some thoughts. Look for yourself; what do you see?"

With a groan, Adanedi sat up, then spent several minutes staring at the landscape below. His eyes traced the river beneath the cliff, the fields and copses opposite, and the rough slopes beyond that sharply demarked the valley's edge. "I see nothing interesting. You saw the same?"

"As I said, I've gotten a sense of the place. If pressed, I reckon could guess at where the wolves might be."

"That sounds definitive. So where might you potentially hazard a guess that these wolves could possibly be?"

"Look there," Kenlin pointed, ignoring the ribbing. "That copse over there is denser than the others, probably older, so that might be worth investigating. They might hunt out in that meadow you can just see in the distance. And to the east there, on the other side of the valley, that ravine dug into the mountainside; that'd make a good rendezvous for them, so that's *certainly* worth a look."

"I see," said Adanedi with a twinkle in his eye. "So what you're saying is that they're in the forest, or they're in the fields, or they're in the mountains. Is that about right?"

Kenlin answered deadpan, "That's my best guess, yes."

"Well, I'm convinced. Seems like a waste that we sent the others out, really."

"Well, they're in the forest and the fields and the mountains, too. I'm sure they'll catch up."

"Jokes aside, I think we've discovered the least efficient way anyone could possibly look for wolves. What's our plan here?"

Kenlin looked back to the landscape before him. Across the valley below, three pairs of their fellow hunters were plodding about looking for direct signs of the wolf pack they were hunting. "We could join them, I suppose," Kenlin suggested slowly, scratching his chin. "We have what we came up here for, and if we don't find the wolves today we'll know good places to look tomorrow, so…I suppose we climb down the mountain."

"Is that it, that's our plan? We climb up, then we climb down again?"

"We could stay up here and keep looking, but only blind luck would help us actually *see* the wolves from here. Is it odd to look for blind luck to help see things?"

"Probably, but every now and then you do stumble on something," Adanedi replied with a half-grin. Then he sighed,

"Well, if somebody down there finds the wolves today, then this whole excursion was useless anyway."

"So were the other two excursions. That's why we sent out four pairs, Adanedi: we hope that one pair will find something, but we can't know which one."

Adanedi sighed again. "I know, I know. But...perhaps we shouldn't be so quick to give up. I guess you have a 'sense' for the landscape, but *I* don't yet..."

"And you're not so keen on hiking down the mountain right now," Kenlin said with a knowing grin.

Adanedi affected umbrage. "I'll have you know," he said with his nose in the air, "that I hike downhill with the best of men! In fact, I—"

He broke off at a faint sound, and both of them turned their ears toward the valley. After a moment, the sound came again: a far-off howl, enough like an animal's to avoid unduly alarming their quarry, but not alike enough to fool an attentive listener. It was a signal from one of the hunting teams that they had located the wolves and that the other hunters should come to them.

"Ha!" Kenlin crowed. "Downhill with the best of men, yes? Well, here I am. Shall we?"

Adanedi sighed. "Damn you, Kenlin."

. . .

By the time Kenlin and Adanedi descended their slope, nearly an hour had passed and whoever was still howling the signal was growing hoarse. Someone else had to take over the howling soon, but even *he* was growing hoarse by the time Kenlin and Adanedi finally found them.

Dzan and his brother Ijki had been the ones who found the wolves. They were sitting atop a bare rock hillock, Ijki periodically howling at the top of his lungs while Dzan massaged his throat ruefully. The others had gathered at the base: Vaai, Jranzak, Kahand, and Graddij.

"It seems we're expected, Adanedi," Kenlin said brightly as the two of them stumped up to the hillock, the last to arrive.

"Finally," croaked Dzan. He reached out and slapped his brother Ijki on the shoulder. "You can stop bawling now," he said, gesturing toward Kenlin and Adanedi.

"Finally," his brother echoed. "I wouldn't have looked so hard if I'd known I'd have to yell about it for an hour afterwards."

"Sorry," said Adanedi seriously. "We came as fast as Kenlin could make it. So you found them?"

Dzan nodded. "Up there a ways," he said, pointing eastward toward the mountainside behind him. "We didn't want to make them feel threatened by our shouting."

"They were at the ravine, then," Kenlin surmised, recalling the layout of the valley. "I wonder who might have predicted they'd be there, Adanedi?"

Adanedi rejoined easily, "Probably someone who was taking in the sights while everyone else was doing things."

"So you saw the ravine," Ijki interrupted, his appetite for repartee sullied after two hours of yelling. "Good, we think that's their rendezvous. We saw signs and some pups, but we couldn't get close for fear of disturbing them. Any good approaches?"

Kenlin considered. "The slope above the ravine looked shallow, so they probably can't see it from inside. I couldn't get a good look at the gorge's mouth, but if it's narrow, we might could block them in."

Dzan nodded. "It's narrow enough that we were thinking something similar. A few men with spears and spikes at the mouth, the rest on the ridge with bows."

"Maybe add torches to the spears and spikes, but I like the idea. How many are there?"

Dzan shrugged. "It's hard to say for sure. We saw about four pups without getting a good look, so if there are one or two more pups and again as many adults..."

Adanedi whistled. "Twelve, maybe more. That's a big pack."

This pronouncement brought the conversation to a brief lull as everyone dumbly bobbed their heads in agreement with the obvious. As the silence began to be tedious, Kahand, the self-appointed balladeer of the group's hunting exploits, intoned, "With plenty prey, their pack is growing strong; methinks they've held this valley far too long."

"Such truth!" Kenlin declared over the ensuing chorus of snorts. "So we have a plan. Adanedi, pick two and prepare to block the ravine's mouth once the pack returns for the night. The rest of us will be on the ridge above, waiting for your signal. Before sundown if possible; we'll have an easier time if we can see what we're shooting at."

"I'd almost rather *not* see," remarked Graddij a little sadly. He was the youngest of the hunters and often expressed sympathy for their prey, despite the teasing this earned him from Vaai and Jranzak. When Kenlin looked at him quizzically, he shrugged. "The dark might give them a sporting chance, don't you think? Or at least make it easier for me to stomach it."

Vaai was preparing a derisive retort, which Kenlin silenced with a look. Speaking very seriously, he replied, "The darkness might make it easier to kill, but not to kill well. In the dark, you shoot wildly and you hit poorly—limbs and guts instead of vitals. That you didn't witness your kill might make you feel better, but it doesn't change the fact that your quarry died a slow, frightened, and unnecessarily painful death. Comfort by way of ignorance isn't worth it. I think you don't want to die that way, and I know I don't; so when we kill, we kill consciously, cleanly, and quickly."

Graddij shrugged, convinced but not consoled. "I know, except now you've made it feel weird. You make hunting sound like etiquette."

"Of course there's an etiquette," Adanedi interjected, winking. "Everything kills everything else, that's nature's way; but killing politely is what separates men from beasts."

. . .

This is a day for successful hunts. The wolves come home with slow feet and swollen bellies; happy for them to die satisfied.

Fourteen in all Kenlin had counted: eight adults and six pups, nearly three wolves per bowman. "Don't rush," Kenlin had told his comrades, "and place your shots carefully. They may become riled when the fire comes and the arrows follow, but they can't go anywhere. Take the time to shoot well, or take the time to shoot again."

The sun was behind the mountains by the time the wolves, the blockers, and the bowmen were all in the proper positions. The fading light was still enough to see by, but time was running out. The hunters on the hillside above the ravine waited restlessly, bows and nerves strung tight, waiting for Adanedi's signal.

Kenlin was the first to spot the glow of torches as Adanedi, Kahand, and Graddij rushed from the cover of the forest to the mouth of the ravine. Adanedi had evidently evolved the plan since the afternoon; he and Kahand were carrying a large tied bundle of brushwood while Graddij followed with three long sharpened sticks and a torch. When they reached the mouth, Adanedi and Kahand threw the bundle to block the narrow passage, then stepped away. Graddij handed them each a sharpened stick, then kindled the bundle.

"Get ready," Kenlin hissed to his comrades, "but don't shoot yet. Once that fire's big enough, I'll signal."

The others didn't indicate their agreement, nor did they need to. With coordination born of long companionship, the five of them silently stalked forward, taking up positions on the very edge of the ravine with Kenlin at the front. Dzan, Ijki, Vaai, and Jranzak nocked arrows and chose targets as Kenlin carefully watched the growing fire. *When the flames reach waist height, that should be enough to deter the wolves. Not yet…almost, my hand is up, draw your bows, yes…almost…now!*

Kenlin dropped his hand, and four arrows took flight. The wolves, distracted by the fire, were completely unaware of the hunters and barely twitched at the dull *thumps* of the bows. In that first volley, every arrow found its mark.

When retelling this story later in Irnaji, the hunters would tell it as though the shot wolves immediately collapsed to the ground, implicitly still wearing comical expressions of dull surprise. But such near-instant kills were quite rare; none of the four wolves struck by that first volley toppled immediately. The impacts made them stagger, but then they bolted forward with a yelp, sprinting madly about in terror, desperately trying to run away from the deadly spikes embedded in their bodies. The other wolves did not understand and scampered fearfully away. The ravine's floor turned to bedlam.

Kenlin now joined his fellows, nocking an arrow and peering into the confusion below for a target. In a moment, the confusion abated somewhat as the wounded wolves began to slow and collapse, and their uninjured comrades eyed them with concern. Then *thwack!* Another five arrows sped into the ravine, another four wolves staggered and bolted, and chaos reigned again.

Only two adult wolves remained unharmed, and Kenlin chose one of these as his next target. The creature was toward the back of the ravine, trotting back and forth, staring up. Unlike its pack mates, this wolf was not panicked; it had spotted the hunters and recognized them as the source of the threat, and now it paced to and fro, to and fro, as though it were trying to plan a counterattack.

With an arrow nocked but not drawn, Kenlin watched and waited for the wolf to pause. Suddenly, the wolf spied Kenlin as well, and it froze in its tracks. As Kenlin drew his bow and aimed, the wolf's eyes fell full upon him; against the dimness of the ravine the eyes burned a fierce, vivid green.

For a fraction of a moment, they locked eyes; then, exactly as Kenlin loosed his arrow, the wolf sprang to the side. There was no way up that ravine slope, so the wolf dashed away in search of another fight. As Kenlin snatched a new arrow, the wolf charged through its panicking comrades and they scrambled out of its way. It sprinted headlong toward the fire blocking the ravine's exit. Kenlin drew his new arrow: the wolf would halt when it couldn't find a way around or over the fire, and then he would kill it. But he was wrong: at a full sprint, the wolf sprang *into* the burning brush—and crashed through!

The tangle of branches caught around the mad wolf's legs, and the force of its leap sent both wolf and bonfire tumbling away from the ravine's mouth. The wolves remaining in the ravine turned at the sound; the few who weren't immediately cut down by arrows sprinted toward the now-open escape. The last few wolves streamed out past Adanedi, Kahand, and Graddij as the mad wolf disentangled itself and rose to its feet.

Flames now licked about its fur and smoke rose from its hackles. The other wolves fled past it toward the forest, but this one would not flee. *Now* it could reach its enemies, and it turned its rage and bared teeth on the hunters.

As Kenlin ran along the ravine's top toward a better vantage, the three hunters on the ground moved quickly to defend themselves. They spread into a semicircle, holding the wolf at bay with their sharpened sticks. It seemed momentarily stymied by this tactic; then, with a snarl audible even from Kenlin's position, it turned and sprang away. Graddij and Kahand visibly relaxed, but the flight was a feint. As suddenly as it had turned away, the wolf cut to its right, outside of the hunters' semicircle, and before they could reposition, it had leapt for Graddij's throat.

Graddij's terrified scream echoed off the mountains as he toppled with the raging wolf tearing at him. Fearful of accidentally stabbing Graddij, Adanedi and Kahand swung their sticks overhead and broke them across the wolf's back; the beast ignored them. Graddij screamed again as Kenlin, finally reaching his vantage point, bellowed, "Move!"

As Adanedi dragged Kahand out of the way, Kenlin drew his arrow past his cheek and aimed to where Graddij and the wolf thrashed together on the ground. Both were moving, both were struggling, both within half a yard of each other. Kenlin hesitated. *This is a bad idea.*

He took a shallow breath and released it slowly, trying to place his shot just perfectly. *Stop moving!* The wolf changed grip, biting hard, and Graddij screamed once more. From the ground, Adanedi shouted, "Do it, Kenlin!"

There is a time for good ideas, and there is a time for good shots.

CHAPTER II:

Graddij's howls of pain had stopped once the arrow was removed, but they still echoed off the cliffs in Kenlin's mind. His reckless shot had found its mark, burying itself in the muscle of wolf's shoulder. But the heavy bow had thrown the arrow too hard; it had passed right through the shoulder and continued on into Graddij, piercing his neck on the side, well behind the throat, and emerging again at the nape. In some ways, the shot had had its intended effect: it had distracted the wolf from Graddij while Adanedi found another, bigger stick to beat it to death. However, as the animal had writhed and struggled, the arrow had been wrenched and twisted tortuously in Graddij's neck.

Once the wolf had been killed and the arrow broken off, Kenlin left Kahand and the others to recover the pelts while he and Adanedi carried their wounded companion back to camp. There, where Kenlin had access to his herbs and bandages, he had removed the remainder of the arrow the only clean way: by pushing it all the way through. Even with poppy tea, that sort of pain was torture.

In the hours since then, the stars and the moon had emerged, and the other five hunters had returned with whatever was salvageable from the wolves. Graddij, after a brief nap, had recovered his spirits and was alternating between genuinely thanking and playfully teasing Kenlin. "Honestly, this is probably the only chance I'll ever get to say this in my life, so let me say it clearly: thank you for shooting me."

Kenlin gave a sort of noncommittal chuckle but kept his eyes on the hide he was cleaning.

"Really, it was quite a good shot," joined Ijki. "From that range, under those conditions, and managing to hit two targets with a single arrow..."

"Oh, come now, it wasn't like that!" interjected Vaai, grinning. "I'm sure Kenlin wasn't *aiming* for both of them. If he had been, he might have gotten Kahand and Adanedi too!"

Kenlin smiled gamely and shrugged as the rest laughed. "Well, what can I say?" But he didn't really feel like saying anything.

The laughter subsided into a silence. After a moment, Adanedi said seriously, "With all things considered, it really was quite a shot, Kenlin. It got that wolf's attention; you probably saved Graddij's life."

Kenlin grunted, still keeping his eyes on his work. "Two thumb-widths higher and I would have taken his life, not saved it. At that range, that's a breath's difference. A breath for a life."

"Then breathe easy, Kenlin," Graddij said, "for I'm still alive."

Kenlin said nothing.

"Don't go spoiling the mood, Kenlin," Adanedi admonished. "Time enough for that later. So everything didn't go exactly as planned, so what? When does it ever? We should be celebrating!"

"We should be cleaning hides," Kenlin said quietly.

"How very festive," Adanedi replied, now with a hint of real annoyance. "You're joy itself tonight, aren't you? Come, let it go! Let's have some pleasant conversation—that isn't about anything that happened tonight."

"If not about tonight, how about once upon a time?" said Graddij. "Anyone have any fun stories to tell? Kenlin? Any tales?"

Telling and hearing tales was a favorite pastime among the hunters; and, as was appropriate for hunters, they could all spin a good yarn. Kenlin, however, was exceptionally fond of old legends and folk tales, the sort that one could only hear from the village elders while helping them with something. Quite recently, Adanar the weaver had told him one that he liked. "Have I told you all the story of Leiver and the Mad King?"

Adanedi shrugged. "Not sure. There are so many Leiver stories, I lose track. It doesn't sound familiar, though."

"Let's hear it and find out," Graddij said, and the rest of the hunters chorused their agreement. Kenlin hesitated for a moment: he was usually cautious when telling stories, for he was leery of imposing on uneager listeners too polite to make a fuss. But they were asking now, and even if they were primarily asking in order to cheer him up... *Well, then, all the more reason to give them a good, fun, cheerful tale.* He began.

> "In a far northern city there was once a mad king who ruled with the whim of the blowing winds. His city cried out in sickness and hunger and chaos, but the mad king paid them no heed, preferring to pursue his own pleasures. It is said that his halls were hung with the finest silks, that his fountains spouted and gushed quicksilver, and that he kept a hand-picked harem of the most beautiful women in the land.
>
> The mad king could not be bothered with managing his nobles, tending to his people, or catching criminals. However, in one duty the king excelled: if a criminal were brought before him, he would dispense punishments with a wholly inappropriate eagerness. So much pleasure did he gain from this 'dispatch of justice' that he held court every day to judge those brought before him, and he never gave a sentence except for, 'Keep him imprisoned for three days to contemplate his fate, then behead him in the square.' The mad king did not care for guilt or innocence. 'What is the purpose of a court except for beheadings?' he asked his court; but everyone in court fancied keeping his own head and so declined to enlighten the king as to the higher calling of jurisprudence.

It happened that one day, a man was brought to the court who was of small stature and bright eyes, accused of being a cutpurse. The mad king, complacent as a cat, sat on his throne and said, 'Tell me your name, convict.'

'I am Leiver, so it please your majesty,' said the little man, looking back at the king.

'Do not look directly at my majesty,' demanded the king, 'lest I find you disrespectful.'

'But, your majesty,' said Leiver, 'your clothes are so fine; if no one is to look at them, what is their purpose?'

'They adorn my person,' said the king, 'and glorify my appearance.'

Leiver said conversationally, 'I would have thought, you being the majesty and they the clothes, that it was *you* who glorified *their* appearance.'

'A most apt observation,' said the mad king, and he turned to his court. 'It shall henceforth be known,' he said, 'that the king adorns his clothes, and glorifies their appearance. So say I, your king.' Then he returned his gaze to Leiver. 'Now, witty convict, I proclaim that you shall spend three days and three nights in my dungeons, after which you will be beheaded in the square. What say you to *that?*'

'I say it is a fine ring your majesty wears,' said Leiver, for he had caught sight of the king's signet ring and fancied it. 'It would look well with my rings.' And so saying, Leiver held up his hands, and all could see that he wore nine rings, one on each finger, but the tenth finger was bare.

'Very well then,' said the mad king, speaking to his guards. 'Cut off his fingers and bring me his rings, that they may look well together with my signet ring on my hands.'

'But it is known,' said Leiver, 'that the king adorns and glorifies the appearance of his attire. Thus, were the king to wear *my* attire, would it not be I who, in consequence, should be glorified?'

'That is so,' agreed the king, and turned back to his guards. 'Do not bring me his rings or his fingers. He shall have to glorify his own attire; I will not do it for him. Now, away with you, witty Leiver; in three days' time, thy head shall adorn and glorify my walls.'

And with that, Leiver was led away to the dungeons. But Leiver did not fear to die, for he still wore but nine rings, and it was well known to him that he would die with a ring on every finger. So he went cheerily to his cell, and straightaway fell asleep.

Near midnight, Leiver was awakened by a creeping chill, as though the dead of night itself had crept into his cell and crawled into his bed. Leiver sat upright and peered into the darkness to find a pair of bright red eyes glaring back at him.

'I am the ghost of Vazhim, the first prisoner of this cell,' came a voice through the darkness. 'I was wrongly condemned to die because I defended the honor of my family and challenged to a duel the man who wished to elope with my sister. Now, terrible is my wrath for the injustice of my execution, and I return each night from the dead to visit my vengeance on the world.'

'That sounds a fairly prolific enterprise,' said Leiver solemnly. 'If you have been dead for some time, given all of every night, I imagine your vengeance must have visited a fairly large portion of the world so far.'

'Alas, I cannot,' said the spirit. 'My wrath was born in this cell, and it is to this cell I am bound, as I was in life, until my vengeance is spent.'

'And when will your vengeance be spent?' inquired Leiver.

'Not until my captors, the head jailor and the mad king, lie dead of my doing will my spirit rest quietly. But until that time, I will satiate my fury on what small prey I am allowed.'

'So, so,' said Leiver. 'It is a good plan, that. However, you should know that I, too, am sentenced to die in three days, and for petty reasons. I suppose you could kill me now, and that would count somewhat toward your vengeance; but would not your vengeance be better served by leaving me alive to pine and grieve over my impending doom?'

The spirit looked at him. 'What you say is sensible,' it said doubtfully, 'except that you appear to me to be neither pining nor grieving.'

'An insignificant point,' said Leiver. 'If we decide that that is the way to proceed, I can commence pining and grieving at your discretion. Then, after I have spent three days more or less in abject misery, you might either kill me yourself or leave the king's men to complete your vengeance on me.'

The spirit pondered this, then replied somberly and with an air of embarrassment, 'Your thoughts are sensible and good, and you inspire me to new levels of wickedness. I humbly admit that you are a crueler person than I and, given the opportunity, would make a far more terrifying vengeful spirit.'

'Not at all,' said Leiver soothingly. 'Come, I will show you that you are the more terrifying of the two of us.' And so saying, he commenced banging on his cell door until the guard came to investigate. Peering through the window in the door, Leiver asked the guard, 'Tell me, good sir, do you find me terrifying?'

'Not in the slightest,' said the guard, 'for you are a little man.'

'Very good,' said Leiver. 'Now, if you would just look at my friend here...' And so saying, Leiver stepped aside so that the guard could see into the cell to where the spirit was standing. At once, the guard screamed in terror and fled from the dungeon. Cheered by this reassurance, the spirit began to converse with Leiver, and they talked merrily far into the night.

By and by, near the approach of dawn, the guard who had fled in terror brought the head jailor to Leiver's cell; at the sound of their approach, Leiver went to look out and see who came. Said the head jailor, 'What's this I hear, that there is a spirit in your cell?' for he could not see the spirit in the cell because Leiver was in the way.

'I have no spirits in my cell,' said Leiver innocently. 'Step inside and look, if you wish.'

And so the head jailor unlocked the door to Leiver's cell and stepped inside, whereupon he was immediately set upon and consumed by the vengeful spirit as the guard ran screaming from the dungeon again.

'My vengeance is half-accomplished thanks to you, Leiver,' said the spirit happily. 'Yet now I fear I must depart, for I cannot abide the light of the morning.'

'Be of good cheer,' said Leiver heartily, 'and come back again tonight; perhaps your vengeance will be accomplished in full.' And so as the first of the sun's rays streamed into the cell, the spirit departed; and Leiver, finding the jailor dead, the guard gone, and the door unlocked, walked out of his cell and proceeded up into the castle.

It happened that, as Leiver was wandering about the castle, he came into a room where two noblemen were discussing a plan to overthrow the mad king. When they saw that Leiver had overheard their plans, they drew their swords to slay him; but Leiver said, 'My friends, are you so quick to do away with me? You must know that I have been sentenced to die and have as much reason as any to wish the king deposed.'

'We cannot risk that you betray our plans,' said one of the nobles. 'Tonight, our men will overwhelm the castle while the king is at the feast; with so little time left, we cannot make certain that you mean us no ill.'

'But why would I have come here except to share in your plans, to help you?' said Leiver.

'You may be a spy for the king,' said one.

Leiver answered, 'If that were the case, why would I have walked into this room such that you saw me? I would instead have simply stood by the door and listened to your talk without you ever knowing.'

'You might have come here by accident, intending nothing,' suggested the other noble.

'Come now,' said Leiver, 'I am convicted to die, and I have obviously escaped my cell; yet I have not left this most navigable of castles, but instead sought you out to share in your plans. Why ever would I do such a thing if I did not wish to assist you?'

'Your words sound truthful,' said the first noble, 'and yet I am nervous.'

'As you should be,' said Leiver, 'for it is a dreadfully dangerous task you have set yourself to, and frankly your plan does not seem like it will work. You say that you will attack while the king is feasting; but is the king known to be a good host?'

'No,' said the first noble, 'it is his custom to rudely wander away from the feast with no explanation.'

'I see,' said Leiver, 'and is the king a great warrior?'

'I know not,' said the second noble, 'but he is of Jazei descent, and their warriors are ferocious beyond compare.'

'And so,' said Leiver, 'might it not be disastrous if he should wander away from the feast, discover your men and their assault, and enter the fray before his guards are defeated?'

And the first noble said, 'It is true, this could ruin our plans.'

'Tut, tut,' said Leiver. 'Come now, I will help you prevent this from happening. After the feast has begun, I shall ensure that the king is distracted until your guards have overtaken the castle, at which point the king will have to surrender.'

'How will you accomplish this?' asked the second noble.

'I will attend the feast,' answered Leiver. 'But I must have a disguise.'

'I will provide you with a disguise,' said the first noble.

'Very well,' said Leiver solemnly. 'Remember, my friends, the great reasons for which we do this.'

'For the benefit of the kingdom,' said the second noble helpfully.

'Precisely,' said Leiver. 'It is an honorable task to which we set ourselves; we must not fail.'

Later, as the sun was beginning to set, Leiver attended the king's feast in disguise. All the fine folk of the kingdom were there, from the high-ranking officials in the army to the overseers. Leiver walked and talked among them freely, chatting amicably until at last one of the scheming nobles told him that the guards were fighting, and so the king must be distracted. Nodding, Leiver walked straight to the king, knelt, and kissed his hand.

'Do I know you?' said the king, looking at the disguised Leiver with suspicion.

'It would surprise me if you remembered me, my lord,' said Leiver, 'as we have not met in many years. You were not yet king when last I came here from Zirgrad, bearing the tidings of my lord to your lordship.'

The mad king squinted at Leiver even more suspiciously. 'I think I know you,' he said.

But Leiver could make no reply, for at that moment, one of the castle guards came at a run and said to the king, 'My lord, I bring urgent news, the castle is—'

'Your majesty!' gasped Leiver. 'Did you not see? That man just stole your signet ring!'

And the king looked at his hand and, finding no signet ring there, drew his kirsk dagger and with it slew the guard. 'I thank you,' said the king to Leiver, 'for spotting this treasonous pickpocket. Will you help me now to search the body and recover my stolen ring?'

'Indeed, my lord,' said Leiver, 'I can help you find the ring, for in fact it was not this guard who stole it at all. I stole it when I kissed your hand, and here it is!' And with that, Leiver reached into his pocket and produced the king's signet ring.

Then did the mad king recognize Leiver, the prisoner he had convicted the day before, and his wrath was terrible to behold. He reached again for his kirsk, but Leiver slipped away and ran from the feast room, the mad king giving chase. All about the castle the king chased Leiver, until at last they were far from the feast and Leiver turned down the stairwell to the dungeon. Then the mad king stopped at the top of the stairs and laughed. 'You have nowhere else to run, criminal Leiver,' mocked the king.

'There is only one way into or out of my dungeons, and you have passed through it for the last time.'

Leiver called back, 'There may be only one way into your dungeons, but there is another way out. Follow me, and I will show you.' Then Leiver turned, ran through the dungeons, and ducked inside the cell in which he was originally imprisoned. The king followed, his dagger raised high above his head ready to slaughter Leiver; but as he stepped inside, he froze where he stood and his mouth fell open in terror, for before him stood Vazhim the vengeful spirit. The mad king turned to flee, but the spirit gave a cry of joy and set upon him, consuming the king where he stood until no trace of him remained.

Then the spirit turned to Leiver. 'My wrath is sated and my vengeance accomplished, Leiver,' said the spirit.

'Truly?' said Leiver politely. 'That is wonderful news, and I must congratulate you on such an accomplishment.'

'And I must thank you for your aid,' returned the spirit with a smile. 'You are without a doubt the most efficient bait to have ever assisted any vengeful spirit.'

Leiver bowed low. 'I am flattered and honored.'

Said the spirit, 'The time has come for me to depart; I can sleep now, knowing my death is avenged.' And so saying, the spirit vanished.

When Leiver emerged from the dungeons, the two nobles confronted him and told him that the conquest of the castle had been successful, thanking him for his part in distracting the king. When they asked what had become of the king, Leiver said, 'He followed me into the dungeons, but he left by another exit.'

'How then?' said the first noble. 'There is a second exit to the dungeons?'

'Not anymore,' answered Leiver. 'When the king left through the exit, the exit left with him.'

'Your words to us have always been sensible,' said the second noble in confusion, 'and yet now you speak nonsense.'

'And such is the reason,' concluded Leiver, 'that I so rarely tell the truth.'"

There was an appreciative ripple of laughter as Kenlin finished his story. "I definitely had not heard that one before, Kenlin," Adanedi said with an approving nod. "I like that one."

Vaai was interested in continuity. "So, does this story offer any clues? What do we think: does Leiver get the rings?"

"Yes," said Kahand exasperatedly, "as I've said before, Leiver *always* gets the ring."

"Leiver *never* gets the ring," Jranzak retorted. "This story proves it! Even if he still had the ring at the end (which we don't know), it was a *king's signet*, so they would never have let him keep it. That's why he always starts the next story with nine rings, finds one he wants, but never gets to ten: he *never* gets the ring."

"I'm not so sure, Jranzak," Dzan countered. "He's got that prophecy, or whatever it is, that he'll die with a ring on every finger. So if he finds a new one he wants, rather than going to ten, wouldn't he just swap it out for one he doesn't like so he always stays at nine?"

"Also, which story is 'next?'" Ijki added. "I didn't think the Leiver stories had any real chronology to them. They're not *true*, are they? Leiver wasn't a real person."

"I like to think he was," piped up Graddij. "I'm sure he didn't do all the things in all the stories, of course. But he's like the Wanderer, isn't he? Just because he shows up in an absurd number of stories doesn't mean he wasn't real."

This assertion was greeted by a lot of skeptical *hmm*-ing. Kahand voiced his doubt: "Even if the Wanderer is real—and I'm not sure I believe it—he's a Faery, and Faeries live forever. I think the Wanderer has far better odds to be real than *Leiver* does. And as for the rings, I agree with Dzan, he just cycles them out. Why else would every Leiver story introduce a new ring that he wants?"

Jranzak opened his mouth and left it that way, apparently for want of a reasonable comeback. Adanedi came to his aid. "If we're considering that Leiver keeps the new rings from every story, do we ever *know* of a ring that he kept? Or, actually, he always starts every story with nine rings; do we know of any stories where he has *eight*?"

Kenlin hadn't volunteered his opinion yet, but at this point everyone automatically looked to him as the expert on Leiver stories and the number of rings therein. Kenlin met each of their eyes individually, enjoying the suspense. Then, with an air of mystery, he said, "If I *do* know such a story, I think it'll have to be a story for another night."

"Oho!" said Adanedi melodramatically, "and he shoots down both sides at once! A fitting end to his evening, no doubt." Kenlin groaned, and the rest of the group laughed once they recognized the joke. Adanedi continued, "Well, lads, I can't speak for you, but I've been done cleaning hides for a while now. Time for me to sleep, I think."

"Actually, I think you just volunteered for the first watch, jester," Kenlin retorted with a grin, and the others laughed again.

But Vaai, it turned out, was the least sleepy of the group and was happy to take the first watch. The conversation quickly split into small groups, and then into pairs. Before long, only Vaai tended the lowering fire as the rest of the hunters drifted off to sleep.

CHAPTER III:

Vaai's enthusiasm for being the watchman wore off quickly, and by the time he shook Kenlin awake he looked both bored and exhausted. Kenlin himself felt refreshed, so he got up without any further urging and looked about. Vaai had let the fire burn down so that only a few glowing coals remained. Kenlin hesitated, then shrugged; it was a warm night anyway. Let the fire die.

He collected his bow, then sat on a rock and looked out across the valley. They had camped near the top of the cliff by the river, overlooking the valley. At the cliff's foot, the gurgling water wended gently by, glistening in the moonlight. Across the water lay a sandy beach and, beyond, a thicket of heather stretched a few hundred yards before ducking beneath the shadowed awning of a forest. Kenlin breathed deep: for all the wolves and winds and wildness, the mountains were peaceful in the summertime. And tonight, not even the howling of wolves shattered the night's restfulness. As the minutes stretched on into obscurity, he learned to hear every sound in the valley: the fluid chuckle of the river below, the call of an owl in the trees behind him, the quiet rush of the wind through the heather.

And...talking. The fire was cold by the time he heard it, but the unnatural sound brought Kenlin abruptly out of his reverie. There were people talking somewhere nearby, people who had not been in earshot a moment ago. He frowned; sometimes wild men of the mountains traveled through the lands he knew, speaking to one another in their strange languages. But right now it was the middle of the night, brightly moonlit though it was. Who would be out wandering now?

Kenlin listened harder; the voices became clearer. He could hear two people talking, a man and a woman, but he couldn't yet make out what they were saying. After a moment, Kenlin finally spied two figures making their way along the shore of the river below, skirting the heather to their left. They soon drew near enough that Kenlin could understand their talk.

"...still say it's a fool's errand, Father," said the woman's voice. "No one has been in Natzut in sixteen years—no one useful to us, at any rate."

"If it's a fool's errand, then I'm a fool," said the man, "for it is my errand. I've told you, Ranja, the Commune is on dying ground. It'll not be more than a few years before the Droál sit on the threshold of Ñaj-Gadan; the wastes won't stymie them forever. And once they have a foothold across, then what? They'll be able to reinforce and resupply at will. Should we just stand at the front, engage them where they're strong, and trust in the strength of our own obstinacy? No. No matter what happens, we must have an avenue of retreat—the more, the better. And if they have to venture into a mountainous wilderness to attack our stronghold..."

"So, in need of a secure retreat, we return to a city and fortress that has already fallen to the Droál once?" The girl's voice was heavy with sarcasm.

This evidently annoyed her father. "You forget that, when Natzut fell, it was defended by two hundred archers and fifty spearmen who were expecting to welcome home a friendly army, not to repel an unfriendly one. With a proper garrison and a knowledge of Droál capabilities, we could hold Natzut indefinitely. You also forget that, when the War of Men and Misks turned against us, it was Natzut that kept the Jazeiz safe for years; and of the five kingdoms Zadarj established, it was Natzut's kingdom—*our* kingdom—which best endured. Natzut is strong."

Hearing this, Kenlin hurried to Adanedi's side and shook him awake, shushing him as he began a groggy question. "Come see this," Kenlin whispered, tugging on Adanedi's arm.

When they reached the cliff's edge, the girl's voice was saying, "...not really what I'm questioning. What I want to know is why we are scouting? Why did we not simply come with masons, ironmongers, soldiers..."

"Because, Ranja," said the man, exasperated, "it's possible—though unlikely, I think—that the Droál have realized Natzut's strategic value. Well, I'm certain Skralade has realized it, but I don't think the Droál would give him the resources to occupy the city as it has so little direct value to them. They can't attack anything from Natzut, so why bother? They won't see the necessity of keeping us from returning. But, if by some ill fortune they have set up an outpost or, One forbid it, taken up residence in the city... We can't waste men on a full settlement expedition without at least knowing what awaits us."

"Better to waste time—your time, Father—on a scouting expedition to one of the most remote corners of the world? Come now, you can't really expect me to believe this was your *first* plan."

Her father didn't answer immediately; then, wearily, "If you must know, Ranja, I *did* ask for a full expedition; and as I'm sure you've guessed, the arguments I've been telling you are the same excuses the Commune gave me. The Viarlin delegates claimed to have knowledge that Natzut is uninhabitable, and Jendraski won't overrule them without a trustworthy report to the contrary. So here we are, reporting. Now are you satisfied?"

"Not the word I would choose," the girl replied a little sullenly. "As you said, I had guessed as much, but... It's just incredible that the Commune would *still* be so pigheaded toward you. So ungrateful."

Her father did not answer this. By now, the pair had reached the river's beautiful beach, directly across from where

Kenlin and Adanedi sat watching them. The man paused, looked about, and said, "This will do for a few hours' rest. Are you tired?"

"I could keep going, if I must," said the girl. "I'm not really sleepy, but I wouldn't mind sitting awhile."

"Alright. First or second watch for you?"

"First. As I said, I'm not really sleepy."

"Very well."

As the father and daughter set about building their campsite, Adanedi whispered to Kenlin, "Who are they?"

"I have no idea," said Kenlin. "By their talk, I'd guess they don't live near here. But just before I woke you, they were talking about old Natzut, and the man called it 'our kingdom.'"

"He—what?" Adanedi said, startled. "You think he might be the old king—Ranton, was it?"

"Don't know, can't recall that I ever saw him. Somebody at Irnaji would know, though."

The pair on the shore had by now set up a very simple camp; the daughter was kindling a fire as the father laid down to sleep. Adanedi frowned. "I don't understand. If he's the king, and he's alive...where did he go? And why would he come back after all these years?"

Kenlin answered, "Well, didn't you hear? The Drool have forgotten that Natzut has a value, even though...somebody-or-other told them it does; and though they have forgotten perhaps they haven't forgotten, so a Commune can't waste men on an expedition until they have a report that contradicts their other report that told them not to waste men on an expedition."

"Oh, right, of course. I forgot about all that. Really clears it all up, that does."

For a little while, they both studied the pair of strangers on the shore. The girl had lit a fire, and by its light she was now idly examining a dark stone pendant that she wore. Her hair was as black as the night, and it gleamed in the firelight even at this distance. She had unbound it after kindling the fire so that it fell loose behind her back; from what Kenlin could see, it was not quite straight, but was a little twisted and so light that it fluttered about itself in the faintest of breezes. *Like my own hair, very light and wispy, although mine's short and blond, not long and black.* On a hunch, Kenlin looked very narrowly at her face, but it was no use: he could not see from this distance whether her eyes, like his own, were emerald green.

Remembering that the royalty of Natzut had been Jazeiz, Kenlin turned his attention from the girl to her father. He was asleep on his back just outside the firelight; Kenlin thought he saw light-colored hair, perhaps even blond, but at that distance and dimness it could just as easily have been grey. The man's clothes were even less indicative: he wore a light traveling cloak over some sort of furred tunic with no obvious trappings of station.

Still seeking some clue about who they were, Kenlin turned his attention to the pair's belongings. Their packs were nondescript canvas bags, a little small for mountain travel but otherwise unremarkable. Their most intriguing possessions, by far, were their weapons. The father carried a longsword, but because he had lain it beside him beyond the firelight, Kenlin couldn't see it very well. The daughter carried... "Adanedi, any guess what that thing is?"

Adanedi took a moment to consider. "It's an odd thing, for certain. Some kind of spear?"

"No, I think it's an edged weapon. See how it curves there? It looks like a big, slightly curved knife on a stick."

"Maybe it used to be a battle axe, and then they lost the axe head and all they could find to replace it was a big knife."

"... That is certainly a theory."

Silence seized them as they both saw it at the same time: out in the heather behind the travelers' camp, something moved. For a moment they struggled to see distinct shapes in the darkness; then, as their eyes forgot the fire they had been staring at, the situation became clear. There were six—no, seven figures cloaked in deep blue or black creeping toward the travelers' camp.

"What's this now?" Adanedi whispered even more quietly than before. "This is new."

"Too early to say," Kenlin replied. "At a guess, I'll wager it's the beginning of a very friendly encounter."

"I'll take that wager."

The seven cloaked figures advanced slowly, taking great pains not to make a sound above the rustle of the night. As the seconds became minutes, Kenlin found his attention drawn more and more to the seventh figure, who seemed to be hanging back behind the others. Something about that one seemed odd. Perhaps his cloak was just a shade darker than the cloaks his fellows wore; but there was yet something stranger about him. *He's...he can't know where I am, and he's all the way over there; and yet, I feel as though he's watching me.*

After a moment, all the figures stopped and the other six turned toward the seventh, perhaps in response to some quiet signal that Kenlin and Adanedi could not hear. The seventh gestured some instructions to the others; they then huddled together, apparently speaking quietly amongst themselves, while the seventh figure retreated a short distance from the group. Kenlin and Adanedi shared a puzzled glance.

Whatever it was the huddled six were doing, it gained energy over the next minute; shoulder to shoulder, they bobbed their heads and bodies in unison, as though they were silently singing a ritual song. The seventh, meanwhile, had circled part way around the camp and was watching the travelers intently. He reached his hand into his cloak; what he drew forth glinted sharply in the moonlight.

"This is getting much too friendly," Adanedi hissed in alarm. "Kenlin, should we do something?"

Kenlin was already stringing his bow. "Yes, rouse the lads," he said shortly. Staying low on his hands and toes, Adanedi scuttled away to do so.

The huddled six were now nearly hopping with frenzied energy, and the seventh was utterly focused on the travelers' camp. It still wasn't clear to Kenlin exactly what was happening, but it was obviously accelerating. Had he understood what he was seeing, perhaps he would have acted differently: he could have thrown a rock or shot an arrow or tried to send the warning some other, quieter way. Be he did not know. He could not have known. He knelt atop the cliff with an arrow on his bowstring and shouted, "Ambush! Ambush! They're behind you!"

The huddled six were far too enthralled by their ritual to be interrupted, but the girl, her father, and the seventh ambusher all jumped at the shout. The ambusher turned his cloaked head toward the clifftop, and Kenlin's sense of being watched increased tenfold. The girl also immediately looked to the clifftop, scanning for the source of the shout; but her father, startled from his sleep, had instead looked straightaway into the heather. From the riverbank where he lay, he could not possibly have seen any of the ambushers through the foliage, yet he looked directly toward where the seventh was crouching. *He can sense that one too!*

For a breath of a moment after Kenlin's shout, no one seemed sure what to do. Then the seventh ambusher sprang into action, crashing through the heather toward his companions, calling out instructions and gesticulating toward both the camp and the cliff. The girl and her father both snatched their weapons, and the girl turned toward the clifftop and screamed, "Run! Run away!"

But the huddled six were no longer silent: a strange, rhythmic chanting filled the air. Kenlin did not understand, but it obviously meant something to the girl's father. "Out of time. Brace yourselves!"

Atop the cliff, Adanedi and the rest of the hunters crowded up behind Kenlin, still stringing their bows and shaking sleep from their eyes. Kahand began, "What's the emergen—" but he cut himself off as every eye was suddenly and involuntarily drawn to the riverbank below.

There, at the edge of the heather, was a crowd. To say that a crowd had formed would not truly describe the sensation. There was nothing to see and nothing to hear, no one had gathered and there were no more people than there had been a moment ago; and yet every one of the hunters knew, without a doubt, that an invisible *something* had amassed between the travelers and the ambushers. It was the feeling of being watched, or of someone standing too close, or of an unwelcome *almost* touch. But this feeling was far clearer and stronger than any of them had known before. It was not a sense that *something* was wrong, or that *someone* was near: it was a certainty that *they*—an invisible but undeniably present *they*—were *there* on the edge of the heather.

As suddenly as it had appeared, the crowd-presence charged forward toward the father and daughter. The pair crouched low and held their weapons close, bracing for a physical impact, until the presences were upon them. The force of the invisible charge lifted them off their feet and hurled them, along with their packs and debris from their camp, into the river. Then as it had come, so did the crowd-presence disappear—into nothing.

The entire conflict was over within two heartbeats, and not one of the lads was certain what had happened. "Did you see what I saw?" Graddij uttered in an aghast whisper, and everyone murmured replies that no one listened to. Half of the hunters were staring into the river, trying to see what had become of the travelers; the other half looked at the huddled six, still in their frenzied chant. But Kenlin's eyes looked to the seventh ambusher—and the seventh ambusher looked, and pointed, back at Kenlin.

We're next! His instinct outstripping his comprehension, Kenlin began to move before he really knew why. He flung himself wildly away from the cliff's edge, colliding with his companions behind him. They yelped in surprise and fell in a heap, but Kenlin continued to scramble backward, grabbing at their clothes as if to haul them away from the precipice. *We're next!* "We're next! Get away from the—"

But it happened again: that inexplicable crowd-presence reformed above their heads, paused for the briefest of moments, and crashed downward.

Everyone was hurled violently to the ground. Kenlin felt his head smack hard against the dirt, but he somehow kept his grip on somebody's shirt—Adanedi's. As the world swam before his eyes, he reached back, grabbed a root, and weakly tried to pull himself and Adanedi further away from the cliff. But the crowd-presence reformed above, hovered, then pounded down with ground-shattering force.

And the ground was shattered. First came an ear-splitting chorus of crackling as the battered rock began to fail. Then came a horrific creaking of stone against sliding stone, the cliff's dying screech. Then the screech became a roar as the entire clifftop crumbled into a landslide.

Some of the lads had been knocked senseless by the crowd-presence; they slid away without a sound. Some of the lads were still aware, and they screamed in terror as the roaring landslide pulled them down and swallowed them. Kenlin clung desperately to the root in his left hand, to Adanedi's shirt in his right; there was nothing to do but hold on.

And then he was dangling. Though the ground beneath them had crumbled away, they had not fallen with it. Kenlin looked up: his root was from a tree that still held doggedly to stable ground, keeping Kenlin and Adanedi from falling. He looked down: in the ruin below, the screams of the fallen were being overcome and silenced by the pounding of falling boulders.

Kenlin felt his grip on Adanedi slip. "Stop flailing!" Adanedi did not answer and continued to wriggle, and after a moment Kenlin understood. His grip on Adanedi's shirt had kept him from falling, kept him alive; but now the shirt had been pulled up tight around his throat. The very grip that was keeping him alive was choking him to death.

There was no chance of Kenlin being able to pull Adanedi up. He tried, heaving upward with his right arm, but his muscles overstrained and failed; he wasn't nearly strong enough. He tried to swing Adanedi closer to the cliff wall; Adanedi clawed at it, scrabbling for a grip, but the newly-bared stone was too sheer. Adanedi then grabbed for Kenlin's foot, but his arms were impaired by his stretched shirt and he could not grip properly. Then, abruptly, his attempts to find a hold stopped as both his hands went toward his throat, and he began to thrash and writhe.

Kenlin shut his eyes, fighting the pain in his arms, fighting the weariness in his hands, but most of all fighting panic. Adanedi was choking to death in his grip, but if he dropped him... He glanced downward hoping perhaps the river ran beneath them, but there was only the jagged refuse of the landslide more than twenty yards below. Kenlin shut his eyes again. *That can't be my only option. There is no option!*

Adanedi's thrashings grew weaker and weaker, and Kenlin felt his grip on the root slip very slightly. He squeezed his eyes shut, then opened them and looked down one more time. *There!* A small patch of dirt that had settled together, mostly free of stone, not quite under them but perhaps... Adanedi's movements were slowing. *Enough; do it!*

With a rasping yell of exertion and anguish, Kenlin swung his friend out over the abyss and let go.

The instant his hand was free, Kenlin scrambled back atop the cliff and began prowling along the precipice, looking for a descent. He looked down—there was Adanedi, he had fallen on the smooth spot, but it was hard to see in the darkness—was he moving? *I have to get down there!*

The new cliff face was sheer where they had dangled, but a short distance away was a more gradual descent. Kenlin nearly threw himself down the slope, sliding recklessly over jagged edges and unstable ledges. He was heedless of the scrapes to his hands, the cuts to his legs, and the constant risk that a single mistake would pitch him off the steep slope to his death. His only focus was on reaching Adanedi. Within a few moments, he was there.

But it was all for naught. The soft-looking patch of dirt had been a lie, just a thin sprinkling of dust over unyielding rock. The force of Adanedi's impact had been enough to blow the settled dust away, and blood and bone were streaked across the newly-exposed stone. No, he was not moving; Adanedi was dead.

Kenlin understood death. He had seen it too many times—as a healer, as a hunter, and even once or twice as a friend—to mistake it for anything else. He stood stock-still. Then he took a step back. Then another step. His eyes could not mistake it, and his actions could not change it; but his mind, wholly focused until now on saving Adanedi, struggled to fully recognize it. *Adanedi is dead.*

Yelling. People were yelling. High, savage screams and panicked shouts in strange languages bounced off Kenlin's unhearing ears. He couldn't listen to them now, he had to focus on this. He had to understand this, accept this. His overstrained right arm throbbed, and his hand trembled. Adanedi was dead.

Stop yelling! Like a fire set by lightning, Kenlin's shock turned to fury as the voices continued to echo around him. He whirled toward the sound; it came from the other side of the river. Kenlin was now no more than four yards above the water's surface, but he was still high enough to see into the heather on the other side.

A fight was underway there. It seemed the travelers had survived being flung into the river; and while the ambushers had been distracted with Kenlin and his friends, the travelers had climbed out of the water and attacked. At a glance, it looked like the chanting six had borne the first brunt of the assault; only one of them remained alive, struggling to defend himself from the girl. But Kenlin's eyes sought the seventh ambusher and found him; he was on the other side of the clearing, locked in a dizzying flurry of combat with the girl's father.

Kenlin watched as they fought, his eyes locked on the seventh ambusher. *Him. He did it.* The same single-minded focus that had tried and failed to save Adanedi returned, but with an entirely new nature. *He's the one. Let them kill him; I will watch him die.*

Even with such focus, it was difficult to see what was happening in the fight between the man and the seventh ambusher. They moved incredibly swiftly, the man in erratic bursts and the ambusher in a steady flow. Suddenly, the man sprang into a long, fast lunge, stabbing deep into the ambusher's cloak. He'd killed him! But no... The cloak did not topple like a man but collapsed like an empty sack. The seventh ambusher wasn't dead. *He's vanished!*

"Ittarshil!" Kenlin heard the man curse, and he adopted a wary stance as he looked around for his opponent. Kenlin, too, scanned the heather. *Where did he go? And how did he get out of that cloak?* But a sudden scream—not of fury or fear this time, but of pain—guided his eyes to what he sought.

Somehow, in no time, the seventh ambusher had moved all the way across the clearing to where the girl had just felled the last of the chanting six. Apparently having left his sword with his cloak, he had attacked the girl empty-handed, disarmed her, and now held her from behind by the hair and jaw, ready to break her neck.

The girl's father had also heard her scream and came crashing through the heather, but he stopped abruptly when he saw his daughter's peril. "Kill him, Father!" the girl yelled, but her assailant twisted her neck slightly and she screamed in pain again.

"Enough, Skralade," said the girl's father, taking a step back and lowering his sword. "We will talk."

A quick flash of annoyance momentarily flavored Kenlin's fury. *Talk! Goatshit. Listen to the girl, kill him!* But the father didn't seem ready to provoke harm to his daughter, and the ambusher was considering his options. They were at an impasse.

Angry and impatient, Kenlin looked about for something—anything—he could use to intervene. Half-buried in the ruins of the cliff around him were many items that had been in their camp. He saw a shredded bedroll, a wolf pelt, a hand he did not stop to identify...and a bow! It wasn't Kenlin's bow, but it was nearby and had survived the fall intact, string and all. Now all he needed was...broken, broken, *there!* An unbroken arrow.

As Kenlin knelt to string the bow, he glanced again across the river. *No progress.* The girl had twisted slightly in her assailant's grasp, and she hissed something at him in a strange language. He gave her a slight shake, prompting an angry shout from her father; but still the impasse held.

Kenlin stood, nocking the arrow on the now-strung bow. The seventh ambusher was speaking to the father in a cold, thin, and very stern voice: "Lay down the weapon, Jazei, and then we will talk."

You're talking now, idiot. From irritation to impatience to fury, Kenlin's emotions were spinning ever wilder. As he took aim at the ambusher, he found himself unconcerned that the girl was in the way. *After all, no matter who I hit, I'll break the impasse.* Nevertheless, he took his time aiming lest he miss altogether. It was surprisingly difficult to aim at this ambusher: it must have been some trick of the darkness, but the man was very hard to see compared to the others, as though he were somehow translucent.

The father was trying to maintain the impasse. "I think not, Skralade," he said to the ambusher. "If I put down my sword, you'll just kill her and flee before I can retaliate."

The ambusher was not impressed. "Enough, Jazei. You know me, and you know well that I can Vanish unharmed no matter the case."

Can you, now?

This time, Kenlin's aim was nearly perfect. The arrow hit the ambusher on the right arm just below the shoulder, causing the arm to spasm and loosen its grip. Quick as a hare, the girl twisted out of the weakened hold and flung herself to the side. An instant later, her father had lunged forward with inhuman speed, thrusting his sword into... But it couldn't be. *He's vanished again!*

It was absurd—people do not simply *disappear*—but there was no other possibility. Kenlin did not believe for a moment that the ambusher had simply dodged out of sight somehow; *no one is that quick*. And, as if to confirm Kenlin's suspicions, the father stepped forward, stooped, and picked up the arrow that had, moments ago, been embedded in the ambusher. *That's it, then. That bastard has some sort of magic, and he used it to vanish. Animal! Coward!*

And it seemed the girl's father felt the same; though Kenlin could not understand the words, the sentiment in the man's shout was clear: "Skralade! Jirdali, ladi jalj-na valecoi, uien datejira-y-toirie ha, Skralade!"

CHAPTER IV:

"Aaaaaaaaarrr*raaAAAA!*"

The wildest throes of anger—anger without outlet or satisfaction—bring with them every sort of childish impulse: maturity is no vessel to contain such a tempest. Kenlin strode wildly about, as aimless as furious, to keep his feet from stamping; and his hands throttled and wrung the grip of the bow, because without occupation they certainly would have flung it or broken it. Yet the more he constrained his fury, the more furious he became. A thousand incoherent invectives, blames, curses and damnations engulfed his mind until he could not even hear his own howls of anger and anguish.

"Can you hear me? Who are you?"

"Yes, I can hear you!" Kenlin snapped back, not even fully aware who he was snapping at. "Who am I? I'm the man with the bow, and the shout, and the— We... We were... And who are you?!"

"I'm the man with sword, *boy*, and—"

"Father!"

At the girl's reproach, her father took a moment to compose his response. "I am Gealvind," he said evenly. "And with me is my daughter, Relshine."

Though still whirling, Kenlin's mind focused just enough to reject this nonsense. *You called her 'Ranja' earlier; I'm not that stupid.* "The pleasure's all mine, I'm sure, *Gealvind.* I'm Leiver, if it please you. And while we're on the subject of names, who was that *dog* you were fighting, and *where did he go?*"

"He's gone, don't worry about him." It was the girl speaking now. "And, though it would please me, I don't think you're really Leiver."

Don't give me banter, give me answers! Ever more incensed and increasingly mistrustful, Kenlin began to look about for another unbroken arrow. "Well spotted, *Ranja*, my name's not Leiver. Why are you lying to me? *Who in the Depths are you?*"

"Calm yourself, boy! My questions first. You know of her? But you don't know of me?"

You're quite thick, aren't you? "I don't know," Kenlin snapped back curtly, "from what I've heard so far it's hard to say. Is your name, 'Father?'"

"Oh, you were listening—ah, you were camped up there, I suppose." *Brilliantly deduced.* "A local, simply encamped nearby." He sounded like he was reassuring himself. After a moment, he said, "Well, whoever you are, you have our thanks for the warning. But... If you don't know who we are, why get involved? Why shout?"

Despite the headiness of his anger, this question struck Kenlin as strange, and it was even stranger that he didn't have a ready answer. *Why did I shout? And what if I hadn't?* Alternate possibilities played out in Kenlin's mind, scenarios in which the travelers died and the ambushers were victorious...and their conflict had remained their own. *Why did I involve us?* Simply pausing to question, to doubt, sapped the energy from Kenlin's fury; he felt drained. "I... I did it without thinking," he said at last, and it was the most truthful and horrible thing he had ever said.

The pair across the river didn't reply immediately, but Kenlin's anger didn't rise again. Their question, and his answer, had filled him with an unspeakable hollowness. Overcome, he sat down on a rock and closed his eyes, breathing shakily.

The travelers had taken a moment to confer among themselves, after which the girl called out, "I know it's not much to offer, since you already know it, but...my name is Ranja. Pleased to meet you."

A gesture; small as it is, a gesture. Very well. "I'm Kenlin," he called back without turning to face them.

The girl's father didn't bother to give his own name—*No such gesture from him.*—but Kenlin didn't care. *They don't matter. They won't stay. Soon they'll be gone, the sooner the better, whereas we... I...* Unwillingly, Kenlin's eyes were drawn back toward the shadowed, shattered silhouette where Adanedi had landed. *One above...* Kenlin was not one to weep easily, but the great hollowness within threatened to consume him. He bit his lip and squeezed his eyes tight to keep it inside.

Noises from behind disturbed him: the rustling of gravel across the river, another strange, watchful sensation, and then the loud *thump-thump* of a heavy landing very near. He turned, then fell off his rock in surprise and sudden fright. The father was *here*, on this side of the river, standing not two yards from where Kenlin sat!

"Be calm, boy," said the man, displaying his empty palms; he had left his sword on the other side of the river. "I just had to see—"

"How did you get here?" Kenlin interrupted as he regained his feet, tense as the bow in his hand. "And *why* did you get here? Who are you?"

The man was staring very intently at Kenlin's face, and for the first time Kenlin got a good look at him as well. He was roughly Kenlin's height and very powerfully built, with close-cropped blond hair and strongly-defined, coarsely-shaven facial features. Eye color was impossible to make out in the darkness, but Kenlin felt sure that they were emerald green. After all, even the enemy, the seventh ambusher, had said it: *He is Jazei.*

They stared at each other for a long time as a sequence of confused, incredulous, and even wondering expressions crossed the traveler's visage. His study of Kenlin seemed to be confirming something that he could not bring himself to believe. Several times, he opened his mouth to say something, then closed it in silence. At last, he asked, "What was your mother's name? Was it Lazaeddi?"

The absurd, impertinent question had momentarily rekindled Kenlin's irritation, but only until the man correctly answered his own query. "You know my mother?" Kenlin asked, shocked.

The man nodded very slowly, as though he were still fully comprehending his conclusion. "Yes, I know your mother. Or I used to know her, long ago. Back then, I was Lord Klanjad, and she was Queen Lazaeddi of Natzut, the wife of my brother Ranton the King, your father."

. . .

"Come on, boy, keep the pace up."

In the morning half-light, Kenlin knew his expression couldn't be read. That was good; he didn't want his new companion to see what might be written there.

For Kenlin's thoughts were still whirling— *They're dead, how are they all dead?*—but he wasn't allowed time to control them. Klanjad and Ranja, the pair Kenlin's warning had saved from the ambush— *They died to save them.*—had quickly decided what to do in a cryptic conversation full of things they both implicitly understood. Kenlin was not given a say. "She's staying here," Klanjad had told him brusquely. "You and I are going back to Natzut. Yes, now, the moon is bright enough. I need to see the city...and speak to Lazaeddi. Let's go."

And so for several hours Klanjad had driven the pace, a relentless pace but only such as could be sustained in the semi-dark, leading the way back to Natzut along old paths he evidently knew very well. He did not know the location of the little raft that now served as the only ferry across the Kirai, so Kenlin directed him to that, but otherwise Kenlin followed while Klanjad led. "Keep moving, boy, come on."

Yes, it was good Klanjad couldn't see Kenlin's face. *Does he think I lag behind because I'm tired? Well, I am; yesterday was a hard day on its own, and the night...* A flash of emotion, a maelstrom of horror and terror and anger and grief, suddenly overwhelmed Kenlin's thoughts. *No time for that. No time for anything. What in the Depths is this Klanjad so hurried about? Does he think that seventh ambusher might come back, perhaps with reinforcements?*

Yes... The seventh. Kenlin could see him in his mind; another flash of emotion coursed through him. *Yes, he might come back, and then what? Then they could kill him! But they couldn't kill him before. Then maybe I could kill him. But no; he wouldn't give me the chance to use my bow, and hand-to-hand he fought this Klanjad—this Jazei—nearly to a impasse. I could never...* With his left hand, he touched his right arm where it still ached from having failed to pull up Adanedi. *Adanedi...* Emotion came in a wave this time, not a flash, and for a moment Kenlin's feet failed him. He paused, left hand still touching his right arm, breathing deeply.

Klanjad noticed. "What's happened? Why are you stopping."

Back off. Aloud, however, he merely said, "Just give me a minute."

In the half-light, Kenlin couldn't see Klanjad's face either. He heard the older man take a breath as though to speak, then release it without having said anything. *Thank you.* They stood in silence for only a few seconds longer as Kenlin gathered himself. Then he said, "Alright. Let's go." They began to move again and Klanjad continued to lead, but he didn't admonish Kenlin to keep up the pace anymore.

As the half-light strengthened toward dawn, their path took them southwest along the Kirai to the old main road. Years ago, this road had been Natzut's principle vector of trade, bringing food from farmers and fishermen and trade from abroad into the city, then bringing out Natzut's exports, jewels and worked metals stemming from their trade with the Dwarves, to the little riverside harbor towns from which they would be shipped to the world. Then, sixteen years ago, the

Bronze Invaders had sailed into those same harbor towns, then marched up the mountainside along this very road, switchback by switchback, to the unbreakable gates of Natzut.

As Klanjad and Kenlin passed through the broken gates, Klanjad's eyes turned to the wreckage as though pulled against their will. The gates themselves were hardly visible anymore; the ash which had settled among the ruins had long-since turned to dirt, and shrubs and trees had taken root wherever they could. As he looked around, Klanjad's steps slowed almost to a stop. Kenlin asked quietly, "Would you like a minute?"

"No," Klanjad said without hesitation, shaking his head. "No." But he didn't resume walking quickly either. After a pause, he asked, "As far as you remember, you've only ever seen it like this?"

The city? Kenlin hesitated, then gave a small shrug. "There was less green here when I was younger." Klanjad didn't reply. After another pause, Kenlin said, "And you? As far as you remember, you've never seen it this way, yes?"

"Many times," Klanjad replied, a hard edge to his voice. "So many times, in so many places. Here was the first place I saw it; there was no green at all the last time I was here."

So he'd come back after the sacking; he must have simply failed to find Irnaji, like everyone else. Kenlin watched as Klanjad's steps slowed even further; the older man wouldn't let himself stop, but his eyes were on everything but his path. Kenlin just stopped; he too was seeing the overgrown ruins as though with new eyes. "I guess it's greener now than it's ever been," he said quietly.

"Yes, it is," Klanjad snapped abruptly, now with an even harsher, sarcastic edge to his voice, "and there will always be fools who comfort themselves with hollow bromides like that. See how life continues! See how beauty returns! Can what's lost even be counted as missing after brambles and weeds come to claim it? That upturned soil from the landslide by the river will have exactly such greenery soon."

While saying this, Klanjad had turned toward Kenlin as though expecting him to recoil or retort. Kenlin did neither; he held himself very still. "Yes," he answered. "I know."

Surprised, Klanjad eyed the younger man with a hard stare. "And does knowing that will happen change anything for you?"

He held himself very, very still. "... No."

Klanjad waited for Kenlin to elaborate; Kenlin said nothing. After several moments, Klanjad jerked his head in a gesture somewhere between an unsure shrug and a satisfied nod. "*Hmm.* Good." Then, stepping quickly again, he resumed his journey into the ruins of Natzut. After another few moments of stillness, Kenlin followed.

. . .

To reach Irnaji, they had to traverse the ruined city from west to east. Klanjad led the way initially, his eyes looking this way and that as his countenance became darker and darker. Once they reached neared the eastern walls, however, Kenlin led the way; evidently Irnaji had been too small and insignificant for even a lord of Natzut to know it was there.

Kenlin led the way down into the sewers, long-since washed clean for a dead city produces no filth, then out under the eastern wall to the small, stony outcropping where Irnaji precariously perched. Klanjad muttered something incredulous, amazed that he'd never known this was here, but Kenlin wasn't listening. *Damn. They're awake. I had hoped they wouldn't be awake yet.*

The sun was barely peering over the mountains to the east, but already the earliest-rising villagers had emerged from their huts and begun the day, cooking food, carrying water. *They will see me. They will have questions.* But Kenlin didn't want to talk to them; he felt sick.

Klanjad had quickly scanned the faces he could see, but he didn't recognize them. "I don't see you mother. Where is Lazaeddi?" he asked.

But before Kenlin could reply, the voice of a young girl scarcely beyond childhood cried out, "Kenlin? Hey, Kenlin's back!" Kenlin's heart sank further; it was Saije, Adanedi's little sister. *No, Saije, please... I don't want to talk to you, and you don't want to hear the things I will say.* But her shout drew attention; now everyone who was already outside was looking at Kenlin, and some who had still been inside their huts were coming out, eagerly anticipating the return of brothers, cousins, sons... *What can I possibly say to you all?*

As the growing crowd drew near, volleys of questions started pelting Kenlin's ears. "Where's Adanedi?" "Who is this?" "Are my sons not with you?" "Getting back this early, Kenlin? Did something happened?" *"Klanjad?"*

From the corner of his eye, Kenlin saw Klanjad's head snap up at this last question. He quickly scanned the crowd looking for the speaker, and just as quickly he found her. "Lazaeddi," he said, so quietly that likely only Kenlin could hear him over the noise of the crowd. "Then it really is true."

Lazaeddi said nothing; she was staring at Klanjad in utter shock.

But the crowd, still focused on Kenlin, was growing more and more concerned. Kenlin's countenance told those who knew him that something was wrong, and the longer their volleyed questions remained unanswered, the more worried they became. "Kenlin, what's happened? What's wrong?" "Did somebody get hurt? Is Adanedi okay?" "Who have you brought with you, Kenlin?" "Kenlin, where is my boy?" "Kenlin..." "Kenlin?" "Kenlin!"

"Enough!" Kenlin hadn't meant to shout—it wasn't right, they didn't deserve that from him. The crowd fell silent instantly; even Klanjad was watching Kenlin, waiting for him to speak. *But what can I say?* His eyes fell on Saije. *What could I tell you? Of the ambush? Of the landslide? Of how I dropped*

your brother to his death because I wasn't strong enough to keep him alive? But silence was no answer either; the longer he hesitated, the more frightened she became.

"Adanedi's dead," Kenlin said flatly, meeting his sister's eyes. Then, looking up and around the crowd, he said just as flatly, "They're all dead. Everyone. I'm the only one left."

A shocked, horrified pause gripped the crowd. "What? They're *dead?*" "No, no, *no...*" "Wait, Graddij too?" "Not my sons, Kenlin, you don't mean—"

"Please!" Not a shout this time, but still loud and forceful; the crowd was silenced again. *One above, restrain yourself!* Kenlin took another deep, slightly shaking breath. "Please... I'm sorry. I'll... I'll tell you, I have to tell you, but this is..." He shook his head as though to clear it. *Control your mind.* After one more deep breath, Kenlin looked at his mother and gestured to Klanjad. "He wants to talk to you." Then, turning to the rest of the crowd, he said, "I'm sorry. They're dead. If you... If you want to..." *Control yourself.* "... I'm going to the stream, to wash my face, and... If you want to ask me questions, that's where I'll be. Please don't come all at once, but... I'm sorry. It's too much."

He had run out of thoughts, and he'd run out of words in which to put them. Without waiting for a response and without looking again to his mother or to Klanjad, Kenlin stepped forward, gently pushing through the crowd, and walked away toward the mountain stream that ran near the village.

Chapter V:

Mothers feel the pains of their children. As Lazaeddi watched her son walk away, she felt the turmoil she knew he kept locked within, restrained. Even without knowing what had happened, she felt every press of the weight that weighed on Kenlin now, and her heart ached to rush to him, to comfort him as she had when he was a baby. Yet despite the turmoil and the weight she felt on her son's behalf, her eyes remained unwavering and her shoulders remained unbowed. So, she saw, did his. "Good for you," she whispered inaudibly.

As the crowd began to break into frantic huddles and panicking disbelief, Klanjad approached Lazaeddi. "My lady," he said perfunctorily, then followed her eyes toward Kenlin. "I was curious to see how he was going to handle this. Actually, I'm still curious to see that. Your son deals with tragedy strangely."

Lazaeddi turned to Klanjad. Rough-cut blond hair, Jazei green eyes, taller than she was but not quite so tall as Kenlin or Ranton... He looked just as she remembered him from so many years ago. "Kenlin keeps his mind restrained," she answered simply, "as he must. His father...is the same."

Klanjad did not miss her choice of tense. His countenance darkened and he shook his head: "He *was* the same, you mean."

"Yet you're alive, so——"

"No. I'm sorry, Lazaeddi. Ranton is dead, and has been for sixteen years." She felt a tiny pang of grief, but it was little more than an echo; she had already grieved this loss for too long. She started to ask a question, but Klanjad quickly said, "This is not where we should discuss this. Can we speak in private?"

His abruptness was as jarring as it had always been. She'd found it annoying in her youth, but now it almost made her laugh. "Very well, Lord Klanjad," she said, surprising herself with her own formality; Klanjad's sudden reappearance had evidently taken her back to the high court of Natzut. "Follow me, then."

Her home, little more than a drafty hut, was on the near edge of town only a few dozen yards away. As they walked to it, Klanjad commented, "Like his father... I don't think Ranton would have handled all this that way."

They had reached Lazaeddi's hut and, without ceremony, ducked inside. Within, Lazaeddi turned to Klanjad and raised an eyebrow. "What is 'all this,' and what is 'that way?'"

Klanjad nodded his head in the general direction of the mountains from which he'd come. "His comrades were all killed, as he said. Without going into too much detail, there was an ambush intended for Ranja and I. Kenlin intervened, and his friends were all killed."

The sympathetic pain Lazaeddi felt for Kenlin twisted tortuously in her heart, but her bearing did not show it. "And how did my son react to this that surprised you so much? What was it you expected him to do?"

"Hard to say, Lazaeddi," Klanjad said with an impatient shrug; he had evidently not intended for this topic to turn into an entire discussion. "Some men facing loss don't believe it, or fall into hysterics, or just go numb. Kenlin... So far he's swung randomly amongst a few different kinds of reactions. I just find it strange; I can't imagine Ranton being so...erratic." That made Lazaeddi smile a small, slightly wistful little grin. Klanjad saw this, and he frowned. "You disagree? He was a bit wild when we were young, I'll grant you that, but by Kenlin's age he had himself under very strict control."

As does Kenlin, Lazaeddi thought. Aloud, however, she said, "You loved your brother, and your admiration will always be a part of your memory of him. I was his wife, and I knew my husband well; there was much about himself that he did not share broadly."

Klanjad's eyes narrowed. "The years have made you no less cryptic, I see."

"Nor lent you a modicum of delicacy," Lazaeddi returned coolly.

Now it was Klanjad's turn for a small smile. He chuckled, his eyes dropping from hers. "No," he said quietly, shaking his head. "No, the years have not been delicate."

Lord Klanjad and Queen Lazaeddi had never been particularly close; he'd found her unpleasantly cold and austere, whereas she thought of him as unrefined and a bit of a blunt instrument, despite Shadale's influence. But his laugh now had eased the tension in the room, and One above, she wanted answers! "What happened, Klanjad?" she asked, barely keeping an imploring quaver out of her voice. "The last courier said the Flunjat Misks were defeated, but then...*they* came. They destroyed everything, and no one ever came back. What happened?"

At these questions, Klanjad's expression had darkened instantly. "I did come back," he said after a moment. "I didn't find this place—I would *never* have imagined this was here— but I tried to warn Natzut, I came back just after..."

"... After?"

Klanjad shut his eyes and sighed. "After we routed the Misks, another army suddenly appeared in the region. Do you remember the Droál?"

"Is that a...diplomatic entity?"

"Ha! In a sense. It's the empire that invaded Jranjana just over a decade before Natzut fell. The Commune of Kings sent us missives about them from time to time."

"I have some vague recollection of that. That was all only happening in the west, though, yes?"

"Yes, well..." The more he recounted, the darker Klanjad's mood and expression became. "An important detail the Commune forgot to mention was that the Droál were allied with certain Misk clans, and apparently Clan Flunjat requested aid from them. They arrived after we'd already defeated the Misks, but I don't think they cared; they weren't really trying to help the Misks, they just wanted to fight our army out in the field instead of a city. Well, we fought them, and they crushed us—with ease. Much of the entourage escaped into the mountains and dispersed in the region, but Natzut's and Flunjat's armies were slaughtered almost to a man."

Lazaeddi knew—the answer was obvious—but she had to ask anyway. "And Ranton?"

"... Yes, he was killed by the Droál."

She hadn't been expecting his hesitation as he answered, but she couldn't help noticing it. A dangerous chill entered her voice: "Are you lying?"

"No, Lazaeddi," Klanjad answered just as coldly, "I'm not lying. The specifics aren't important. They killed him."

Lazaeddi's eyes narrowed questioningly, but Klanjad plowed ahead with his narrative. "After the battle, I made my way back to Natzut as quickly as I could, but... It was over. I even looked for you briefly, but I...didn't spend long after I saw what they'd done to the keep."

"The rockslide?"

"Yes, it looked like they brought down half the mountain. How did you survive?"

"There was a cellar that remained intact and was covered in rubble when the rest of the keep collapsed; Kenlin and I had been sheltering there. The rubble kept us hidden from the killers they sent through the ruins, and later I managed to dig us out and brought Kenlin down the mountain." Hearing this, Klanjad gave an approving nod, but he couldn't quite hide a tiny grin of surprise. "What's funny?" Lazaeddi asked.

"I'm impressed," said Klanjad, shaking his head. "You digging, you climbing down a mountain..."

"I'm his mother."

"I know. I'd just never imagined you doing such things."

Deciding to interpret this kindly, Lazaeddi gave a sad smile of her own. "The years have not been delicate."

"No. Nor have they been informative, it seems." Klanjad's quick change in tone caught Lazaeddi by surprise; now he sounded almost angry. "Not for Kenlin, anyway. He didn't know you were the queen, he didn't recognize my name at all, and so far he hasn't even shown any understanding of the fact that he's Jazei. What have you told him?"

Taken aback though she was, Lazaeddi responded perfectly evenly. "Of his heritage? Nothing."

"Why in the *Depths*—" Klanjad growled furiously, but Lazaeddi cut him off.

"Why didn't I tell him? Why would I have told him? And *what* would I have told him? What was he to be king of, the dead? Or Irnaji?"

"Royalty be damned, Lazaeddi, he is Jazei!"

"He is blond-haired and green-eyed," she answered coolly, "and you and I both know that *Jazei* means far more than a color palette. What would that legacy mean for him here? How could his heritage do anything but complicate his life among these people?"

Klanjad was not mollified. "Ignorance and isolation... Such a life. Do you think Ranton would have chosen that for his son?"

"And to think you believe I chose this," Lazaeddi said in a low, frigid whisper. "To think you believe I wanted any of this for him. I didn't kill my husband. I didn't ruin my home. And I didn't leave behind my jewels and my silks and live in a hovel for sixteen years out of *choice*. In a terrible situation, I did what was mine to do. How *dare* you second-guess me."

Her eyes were locked on Klanjad, and he returned her gaze with equal ferocity. So they stayed for a moment—a moment that could have been any of the dozens in which they'd clashed, queen and lord, in the high keep of Natzut so many years ago. Then Klanjad blinked and, with another shake of his head, looked down. "What's done is done," he said grudgingly.

Lazaeddi gave him no reply.

"So you never told him he is Ja— of Jazei descent," Klanjad said after a moment, returning to his usual brusque demeanor. "And he never reached any such conclusions on his own? His hair? His eyes? Is he stupid?"

"Hardly," Lazaeddi said, resisting the urge to roll her eyes, "but there was little need for him to speculate about his parentage when the whole village was so eager to do it for him. Some people guessed rightly at first, of course. But no one here had ever seen me, and 'queen and prince' is rather a grandiose rumor to hold onto without confirmation; I merely had to ignore it for the townsfolk to replace it with more plausible alternatives."

"Such as?"

"Most assume he's a bastard," Lazaeddi answered with a wry smile. "He probably thought the same; I never told him otherwise. As for the rest, they find it easier to believe I was a handmaid...favored by some lord than to think the queen and prince would ever deign to live in Irnaji."

"'Favored by some lord?' Then the rumor is that *I* fathered Kenlin?"

The thought clearly annoyed him, which Lazaeddi found strangely amusing. "Among those who remember your name, I assume you'd be thought a candidate," she said lightly.

Klanjad looked disgusted, but he muttered to himself, "I suppose they probably don't remember I was married."

Ah, so that was his concern: he didn't like the implication that he'd been unfaithful. To her own surprise, Lazaeddi found this touching; a little extra warmth crept into her voice as she said, "I'm certain that's true. If they didn't know me, even when I stupidly introduced myself with my own name, they surely never knew about Shadale. And even if she hears about it, I doubt she'll mind; knowing her, she'll probably find such an absurd rumor funny."

But Lazaeddi stopped suddenly. Klanjad's expression had fallen, not to darkness or anger this time, but to something much deeper and more painful. Reviewing her words, Lazaeddi hazarded a guess: "Have I used the wrong tense again?" Klanjad merely nodded. Lazaeddi closed her eyes; another pang, another echo, but this one lasted a little longer: she hadn't grieved for her friend as thoroughly before. "I'm sorry." He did not answer. "If I may ask... In the battle?"

Klanjad shook his head. "In childbirth," he said very quietly. "She was pregnant when she insisted on accompanying the campaign."

Lazaeddi, of course, had known that. She had even guessed who Ranja was when Klanjad had mentioned the name earlier, for Shadale had told her what names she had liked. Lazaeddi didn't mention any of this, though. "I'm sorry, Klanjad."

Without looking up, Klanjad gave a small shrug. "The years..."

She nodded. "There have been many." For a few moments, neither spoke. From outside the thin walls of the hut, Lazaeddi could hear the frightened voices of the villagers. Now and then, she could make out words: Kenlin, Jazei, children, death. She sighed. "And this year, I suppose, will be even more indelicate than most."

"Yes, it will," said Klanjad, taking the cue. "I came here on a scouting mission on behalf of the Commune; I didn't expect to find anyone. But somehow Skralade—a Misk, a great enemy of mine—was informed of my mission long enough in advance that he could set up an ambush of Droál. By sheer luck, Kenlin saw the ambush and warned us, and we were able to fight them off. But Skralade escaped, which means he will return, and this time he won't only be coming for me."

Lazaeddi's heart sank; she could already guess where this was leading. "He saw Kenlin?"

"I don't know if he saw him, but he certainly heard him, and I'm sure he sensed him. Your son is a magician, Lazaeddi; I sensed him the instant I tried, and presumably Skralade did the same. He will come back, and if he finds people to interrogate, it will not take him long to learn of the blond-haired emerald-eyed boy who was the only one of his friends to survive."

She knew it; this was what Klanjad had come to talk to her about. Swallowing hard and struggling to keep her expression calm, she asked, "So Kenlin must be gone by then?"

"I think everyone must be gone by then."

"Every— The whole village?"

Klanjad nodded gravely. "Anyone still here when Skralade returns will not survive the interrogation; he won't have come for them, but he will not spare them. You, especially, *cannot* be here when that happens. For you, death would be the better option. If they find out who you are, they might take you prisoner."

"I see. In that case...where shall we go?"

"Anywhere. If I were you, I would take the old coast road to Flunjat, then look for a new place to settle east of there, where the mountains grow more gentle. I will take the mountain roads up the Kirai, as far from the seaside as possible."

"Why take separate paths?"

Klanjad hesitated, wearing the expression he used to make when he was about to make a joke he knew she wouldn't like. He caught himself this time, though, and said diplomatically, "Neither of us are young anymore, Lazaeddi, and you were never a woman of the wilderness. The coast road is not easy, but it is nothing compared to the mountains. Also, if I were travel with you and the village, that would almost guarantee that Skralade would attack us. So large and slow a convoy would be impossible to defend, and so near the sea it would be very easy for him to attack."

"I think you're deluding yourself, Klanjad, if you believe the entire village will just pack up and evacuate purely on your say-so. There are some here far older than you and I, and even some of those younger will never leave Irnaji."

"Then they will die here," said Klanjad with an apathetic shrug. "I know Skralade. He'll want to know where Kenlin came from, and now that he knows there's something to find, he *will* discover this place. Anyone who remains here will be killed, but those who leave by the coast road will at least have a chance. If his real targets are far away in the mountains, hopefully those on the coast will be of no interest to him."

There it was: the comment Lazaeddi had been waiting, and dreading, to hear. "'His real targets...' So you think that Kenlin will go with you?"

Klanjad nodded, meeting Lazaeddi's eyes. "Yes, he will. There is no other option. I...understand why you thought he would live out his days here, and that knowledge of our family's heritage would only complicate his life. But all that is over. He is known, at the very least, to be a human magician, and one way or another Skralade will soon learn that he is Jazei. He cannot stay as he is. I will take him and train him as we were trained. He cannot hide anymore from the world we live in, but at least I can teach him how to fight it."

"Then we live in a world that is hostile to Jazeiz?"

"Ha! We live in a world that is disintegrating, Lazaeddi. Jranjana as we know it clings to life by the might and will of its last strong kingdoms, which have yoked themselves together as the Commune. They are not our enemies, but they are hardly the best of allies. Those who hunt us are different: Misks and Droál alike hate us as they hate nothing else. There is nowhere in Jranjana where their hatred will not pursue us."

"I see," Lazaeddi said with a sigh. She closed her eyes, forcing herself to accept. "I understand. And when Kenlin understands, he will choose to go with you."

"That will make it easier," said Klanjad dispassionately. "As I said before, though, there is no other option. His choice is not really the issue."

"Don't try to force him," Lazaeddi warned, and something in her voice caused Klanjad to look up sharply and meet her eye. "Don't lead with coercion; he will not take it well, and in the long term it will not work. Just tell him what he must know and answer his questions. Then he will choose."

"I see. And you're sure he will choose correctly?"

Correctly... The word almost made her laugh. Instead she simply smiled—sadly, bitterly, resolutely, proudly—but on the outside, merely cryptically. "He is my son. He will tell you what he chooses to be."

. . .

In the spring, the stream that ran past Irnaji was a torrent. It was barely a trickle now, but it was cold and clean on Kenlin's face. He had seated himself on the opposite side of the streambed from the village, and the water formed a line that all who approached knew, instinctively, should not be crossed. It added a certain clarity to the situation. *This is where I sit, splashing myself occasionally, and answer questions; that is where they stand and ask.*

So it had been for an hour or two, but the one who came now did not stand. Klanjad strode directly to the stream and dipped his hand in; then, satisfied with the temperature, he unceremoniously sat down and laid back in the shallow water, catching his breath at the coldness.

Kenlin eyed him, but did not begin the conversation, and Klanjad was equally silent. And the silence dragged on for minutes. *Here we sit idle, in the trailing and leading shadows of disaster. My friends are dead, his daughter is alone in the wilderness, he insists that we will soon be pursued by...Misks, and perhaps whatever else ambushed them. And yet here we sit, oblivious to urgency, unable to broach a conversation because neither of us have any idea what this conversation sounds like.* And Kenlin laughed aloud. *Simply recognizing the strangeness just adds to it!*

Klanjad raised his head and shot Kenlin a puzzled glance. "What is funny?"

"Nothing," Kenlin answered with a flippant, airy shrug. *And the nothing is funny. Ha!* "This is a good conversation for today."

Evidently Klanjad didn't follow. Narrowing his eyes uncertainly, he asked, "What conversation?"

"Exactly! What conversation? What sort of conversation can there even *be* on a day like this? Most days, I only have old conversations, the same ones I've had for the past ten years or more. But today I've had new conversations. 'Your sons are dead.' 'Your brother will never come home.'" He paused, frowning slightly. "I haven't liked these new conversations." *No...* Then, looking at Klanjad again, he said more brightly, "And now there's you! This is a far better conversation we're having now, I like it much more. Wouldn't you agree, Klanjad? Or should I instead call you 'Uncle?'"

Klanjad took a few moments to consider before reply slowly, "*Uncle* is an awkward moniker; just 'Klanjad' is probably clearest. And no, I'm not sure I'd agree that this is a good conversation."

"You'd rather have a conversation *about* something, yes? Very well; what would you like to discuss?"

Again, Klanjad took a moment to consider. He opened his mouth to answer, then changed his mind and instead asked, "Are you always this way? You are very strange to talk to. Are you trying to be straightforward, or are you just...strange?"

That question is rude, isn't it? I suppose I should be offended. I'm not, though; maybe I am strange. Taking a breath to catch his flitting thoughts, Kenlin said aloud, "I'm not trying to be strange. I do sometimes succeed without trying, but... I am trying to be straightforward. Strangely straightforward, perhaps." *That wasn't helpful.*

But to Kenlin's surprise, Klanjad was grinning now. "I can respect that," he said with a satisfied nod. "Perhaps we really are kin after all. So, following your example, I too shall be strangely straightforward: this village must be abandoned, and you must come with me, for we—you, Ranja, and I—are the last true Jazeiz in Jranjana."

"Why?"

"Why..." Klanjad was caught off-guard. "Why what?"

Kenlin's flippant mood was passing, but it still took him a moment to articulate his thoughts. "Why... Actually, 'why' to everything you just said; but most importantly, why do you say that I'm Jazei? Because of how I look?"

Klanjad sighed wearily. "No, there is more to it than that. We Jazeiz are a race, a bloodline, a tradition—a family, if you will, especially now that there are only three of us. Of course, blond hair and emerald eyes do make it easy to identify a Jazei, but those details do not *make* a Jazei. Also, not all Jazeiz have had the hair and the eyes: my daughter Ranja has black hair, and even Zadarj himself had one blue eye."

"Again, then, why? Why do you say that I'm one of you?"

"Your father was Jazei, the greatest in the last two centuries. And he was my brother. Since he did not live to teach you himself, I owe it to him to pass on his legacy."

Kenlin bit his lip for a moment, choosing his next words very carefully. "That—my father's legacy—means less to me than you would like it to, I think. I have no memory of the man, and nothing I've learned, either from the village or from my mother directly, has made him into anything more than a word to me."

At the mention of Kenlin's mother, Klanjad looked annoyed. "Yes, her *discretion* on this topic has really been such a great help to everyone," he muttered.

Yes, Mother... "She has been more reserved than even I thought she was, it seems," Kenlin said quietly.

"She's always been that way," said Klanjad brusquely. "I never understood her and she never liked me; if Ranton hadn't married her, she and I would have had nothing to do with each other. That's all in the past, and it's unfortunate that it makes the present more complicated, but it is what it is. You are Jazei—by heritage, by legacy, by family—and I intend to teach you what that entails. Your father would have wanted that."

"He probably also wanted to do it himself, and to be alive while doing so." *Careful.* A sudden darkening of Klanjad's expression told Kenlin he was on dangerous ground, but he didn't want to provoke his uncle. "I'm not trying to be dismissive, Klanjad. I understand that the wishes of 'your brother' are important to you, but 'my father'..." *Careful.* Kenlin paused to rephrase what he'd been about to say. "I can't think about it that way. It doesn't help me to know that *he'd* want me to go with you; why should *I* want to go with you?"

Klanjad frowned thoughtfully, studying Kenlin's face. "*Hmm...* What do you know of the Jazeiz?"

Kenlin knew what he'd heard in stories: stories of warriors, stories of commanders, stories of kings, conquerors, liberators, legends... "The stories, I suppose."

Klanjad nodded. "Would you like to learn the truth?"

The truth... What do I really know of it? Kenlin turned his eyes to the horizon, thinking. He thought of the ambush, of the strange power that had thrown Klanjad and Ranja into the river, the same power that had then crushed the hunters and collapsed a cliff, yet the Jazeiz had returned and fought back and killed their attackers—*almost* all of them. He thought of the fight between Klanjad and the seventh ambusher, of the speed and power he'd seen—so dimly and at such a distance—as the Jazei had overwhelmed his foe and would have killed him if he hadn't taken a hostage. He recalled a few moments later, a strange sensation and Klanjad's sudden appearance across the river from where he'd been moments before. He must have leapt the river, perhaps using magic to do so; what strength that must have taken! Kenlin's right arm still ached a bit; idly, he gave it a loosening shake.

Klanjad noticed and nodded toward the arm. "Were you hurt?"

"I'm alright." *I am fine.* A strange, familiar eagerness was building with him. He could not see precisely where it would lead from here, but he knew the direction. *Yes, I am fine. But I can be better.*

"Yes," he said at last, looking his uncle in the eyes. "I will learn."

Chapter VI:

Ranja sometimes wondered whether, in the dark, her eyes glowed like a cat's. She couldn't remember when this thought had first occurred to her, and she wasn't really certain she even *wanted* glowing eyes. Still, it was something to consider.

She frowned. People always told her she had exactly her father's eyes, and his eyes didn't glow at night; but then of course she didn't have *exactly* his looks. For one thing, he had the wild, wispy blond hair of the Jazeiz, while her hair was a bit more lush and was raven black; her father said it reminded him of her mother. So if she didn't have his hair... Ranja peered into the opening of the water skin beside her, but she couldn't see any dazzling green eyes glowing amidst the reflected darkness of the cave around her. But then, this was hardly a proper mirror. Why hadn't she ever bothered to check in a proper mirror? Ah, well, perhaps someday she would ask somebody whether her eyes glowed or not. If she was bored enough.

And *that* was really the problem: she was bored with sitting in this cave, waiting for Father and...Kenlin, she supposed...to return. Naturally, Father *would* bring Kenlin back with him; he would want Kenlin to help with the war. They would go north, Kenlin would be introduced to Jendraski... Yes, she knew how it would be, for it couldn't be any other way. She laughed a little, imagining Kenlin's confusion at all this. Apparently, he hadn't realized he was Jazei until yesterday (rather stupid of him, she thought, but she tried not to judge), and now he would suddenly be expected to step into the shoes of the ancient Jazeiz, a living legend in a time that desperately needed such symbols. She wondered what Kenlin would think of the fact that to half the world he symbolized the best and mightiest of humanity, while to the other half he was a fiend from their darkest tales. For her part, she relished the polarized passion with which people viewed her; far better to be loved and hated than to be simply ignored.

Languidly, Ranja glanced toward the mouth of her sanctuary cave and was startled to see that the light was becoming quite clear outside. How? She supposed she must have fallen asleep—stupid, careless thing to do in a cave in the mountains. She quickly tied her water skin closed, strapped it onto her pack, then picked up her glaive—a pole-arm consisting of a long haft and a short, single-edged blade which together were a few inches taller than she was—and made for the cave's mouth.

Force of habit made her creep up to the edge of the cave, on her toes and ready to move at the slightest disturbance. Constant sensory vigilance, this was one of the many costs of having been born without magic. She could have sensed the presence of Misks easily if only... But that was an aggravating thought, and not worth dwelling on.

And of course, the idea of there being an ambush waiting for her outside the cave's mouth was absurd—the Misks didn't know she was hiding here, and they couldn't have sensed her anyway because she wasn't a magician—but she knew she should be wary nonetheless. For a moment, she pictured herself as a fish, ready to dart away to safety at the slightest motion in the water around her, but she suppressed that thought: she didn't like picturing herself as a fish.

After confirming that no ambush awaited her (of course), Ranja began making her way to the cliff top near where Kenlin and his friends had camped just before the ambush. Before leaving, her father had told her to hide and wait until the second dawn, find a place where she could see the beach on which they had been attacked, and ready an arrow. He had given her Kenlin's bow, then departed without specifying what exactly she was supposed to be shooting at. Perhaps he had thought it would be obvious.

She glanced over her shoulder to where she could see the bow tied to her pack. It was an ordinary hunting bow, short and thick, a fairly primitive design, but it was well-made and sturdy. She didn't know what kind of wood had been used to make it, but it was far stouter than any bow she had ever bent; it had taken nearly all her strength and weight to string it.

Strapped to her pack next to the bow was the sword that Skralade the Misk had dropped in the ambush. It was a simple design, guard-less and forward-balanced like most Misk swords; it was a little heavy by Misk standards, though still quite a bit smaller and lighter than her father's sword. She shook her head and shrugged; why someone with a Misk's strength would choose to use such a light weapon was a mystery. Still, it seemed a good enough blade, and she had decided to save it to give to Kenlin, because of course Father would want to train him in combat. She thought about what she knew of Kenlin—a hunter bred in a mountain village with no exposure to combat—and again she laughed a little. Training *him* should be entertaining.

When she reached the cliff top, the sun had not yet passed over the mountains, so she re-strung Kenlin's bow and sat down to wait. Presently, she caught sight of a disturbance in the field behind the beach; someone was walking there. By squinting, she was able to discern that the distant figure had blond hair, but it was not cropped close like her father's, nor did he hold his left arm as her father did. She tensed immediately: had Kenlin come to find her alone? But why hadn't her father come?

As Ranja watched Kenlin's approach, she became increasingly alarmed. Kenlin was stepping very warily, glancing about him every few steps. He was uneasy; something was amiss, probably the same thing that had detained Klanjad. Had they been ambushed? Then her father certainly would have sent Kenlin north while staying to draw the attack himself. But then why was Kenlin wary here? Why bumble in like this, crashing loudly through the heather in broad daylight, and yet still seeming wary? Unless...

She deduced what was happening even as the events began to unfold. She stood and nocked an arrow just when Kenlin froze in place, evidently having heard or sensed something. At the same time, a thick patch of brush a few feet away from Kenlin began to shake violently, and someone screamed. Ranja raised the bow, her eye on the brush, but after a second's silence Klanjad stepped into sight cleaning blood from his sword. The Misks had obviously left one of their number to watch the beach while they continued their search elsewhere. Klanjad had anticipated this and stealthily hunted down the sentry, using Kenlin as a diversion while Ranja covered them both from range. Ranja couldn't help but smile: the Misks were right to fear her father.

As she unstrung the bow and tied it back onto her pack, Ranja glanced at the cliff face leading to the river below. It was about twenty-five yards down; it might take more than an hour to climb down that safely, exhausting herself and likely mangling her hands and feet in the process. She scoffed to herself: what a waste that would be when the alternative was so much easier. She was somewhat upstream of the landslide from yesterday, and here the river ran deep beneath the base of the cliff. Ranja glanced down once more. Of course, she told herself, it was a completely needless risk to jump from here, chancing any number of improbable dangers. In fact, she reasoned with herself, there was really no good reason at all to jump off this cliff. Then she took her pack, tossed it over the edge, and leapt after it without the slightest hesitation.

The first time Ranja had ever jumped into water far below, she had been absolutely petrified, but that was quite a few jumps ago. She knew she would hit the water with a painful slap to the soles of her feet followed by the disorienting roar and swirl of the water around her, but there was no fear anymore. She knew all the costs and she knew all the risks, but it was worth it just to feel the wind around her.

Then with a crash and a splash, she hit the river. She let herself hang limp in the water for a moment, reorienting herself, then snatched her pack from where it floated beside her and swam for the shore where her father waited.

But when she reached the beach, she found that Klanjad was not waiting for her; Kenlin was. As she opened her mouth to ask why, Kenlin waved frantically for her to be silent. Ranja couldn't decide if she was offended or simply confused, but one of those emotions must have shown on her face because Kenlin made a hopeless shrugging gesture that seemed to say, "Don't ask me, just go along with it."

Now Ranja was annoyed; why was *he* relaying commands to *her?* But she set her jaw and waited in silence, still kneeling in the shallows, until she spied her father returning from...whatever he had been doing.

"Hello, Father," she called to him.

Klanjad flapped his hand as though her greeting were a fly that he would swat. "What was that?" he snapped harshly.

Ranja was stung by his tone, but answered as quickly as she could, "My jump?"

"The *timing* of your jump," Klanjad snapped again, now standing close by and quite obviously angry. "I hadn't signaled that the Misks were gone, yet you moved and gave away your position. What if they had left two sentries? That would have been the smart thing for them to have done, and you would have alerted the second that we were aware of them."

If Ranja had initially been hurt, she had forgotten it now. She snapped back, "They wouldn't have left two sentries unless they had enough Misks with them to leave two behind and still scout forward with enough to pose a threat to you, which is unlikely. And if there had been two sentries, they would have been fools not to remain in sight of one another, so they would have already been alerted to us when you killed the first." She was speaking off the top of her head, yet she still made a fair point; if she hadn't been so angry, she would have been quite pleased with herself. "In that case," she continued, "my jump would have simply served as a further diversion, making the second sentry wonder about the complexity of our ambush and buying you time to locate and kill him."

Out of the corner of her eye, Ranja saw that Kenlin looked impressed, but Klanjad was having none of it. "And you were thinking all this when you jumped, were you?" he said coldly.

"No," she retorted, "I was just thinking I was glad to see you."

Klanjad drew in a deep breath and released it very, very slowly; then the tension eased away from his countenance to be replaced by something akin to weariness. "It's good that you're safe, Ranja," he said quietly. "But there might have been more of them. You always have to think."

And he turned away without another word. Furious, Ranja stood up and began slapping at her clothes, dashing away some of the water they had absorbed. When Kenlin stepped into the river and tried to get her pack for her, she nearly slapped him too.

Though a quick twitch showed that he was startled, he did not pull away. This surprised Ranja. Would he have just let her slap him, or could he somehow predict that she would catch herself? Forcing herself to stand calmly, when Kenlin again lifted her pack and offered it to her, she took it with all the grace and dignity she could muster. "Thank you."

Kenlin grinned, clearly amused by her abrupt decorum. She forced her countenance to remain impassive. He nodded toward the cliff across the river. "That was an impressive jump. Very bold of you. Good men have died from such a fall."

It took Ranja only a moment to piece together the significance of his comment, but formulating an answer was not so easy. Before jumping, she hadn't even considered that this was the same cliff that had taken the lives of however many of Kenlin's friends. After a moment to collect her wits, she managed, "Yes, well... I got to decide when, and how, and whether I fell. Not everyone is so fortunate."

Kenlin nodded amicably, as though his question had been nothing more than polite conversation. Then, indicating Klanjad with another nod, he asked quietly, "So, he seems convinced, but I don't know enough to say for myself: could there really have been more of them, or was he just overreacting?"

Ranja had no idea what to say. He was *direct*, this cousin of hers. But Klanjad had overheard Kenlin's question and answered it himself: "There most certainly could have been more of them. And I overreacted."

Kenlin seemed unsure how to answer that. Ranja knew not to even try; for what it was worth, that had been her father's best attempt at an apology.

CHAPTER VII:

Throughout their day's journey north, Kenlin had the chance to observe, in ever more detail, the dynamic between Klanjad and his daughter. The father's behavior continued as it had begun: *he is wholly obsessed with preparedness.* And consequently, Klanjad was well prepared. They walked through streams to hide their tracks, they detoured over laborious hill trails just to gain a view of who might be following them, and they trekked for an extra hour into twilight because Klanjad had not found the perfect, un-ambush-able campsite in which they could rest. Kenlin would have thought it all quite excessive except that, immediately after the first ambush (as evidenced by his instructions to Ranja), Klanjad had already devised a new ambush of his own to counter his enemies' response to the failure of their first ambush—and he had been right to do so. It was a bit dizzying.

Ranja, however, didn't seem to be dizzied by any of it. *Unsurprising, presumably she's spent much of her life getting used to her father's antics.* But she was more than simply unfazed. She had that most classic talent of a good daughter: a perfunctory mastery of her father's obsession. The menacing, ambush-filled world—which her father spent most of his energy fortifying against—was simply *the world* to her; and the malevolence of life was still a cause for preparation, but not for concern. *I suppose it's her aspect, more than her behavior, which differs from her father's. It isn't that she disagrees with his preparations, and it isn't that she doesn't believe in the threats. I think she just finds the whole business rather dull.*

But she acted the good daughter, she never complained, and there were no more spats like the one on the riverbank. The three of them returned to the Kirai valley, then journeyed northeast along the valley's axis until the sun was well below the mountains to the west. By the time they finally stopped to camp, both of the men, who had spent the majority of the last two days trekking at speed, were exhausted.

But Ranja, who had spent no small part of her recent time waiting in a cave, seemed to have energy to spare; and with nothing better to spend it on, she began to prod Kenlin for conversation. "So...you're Kenlin."

Kenlin gave a weary nod. "That's what they tell me. And in the sense that you mean it, it's a new idea to me, too."

That intrigued her. "So you really never knew? You never realized that you were Jazei?"

One above, this again? Kenlin shrugged. "I don't think it's a question of *realization.* I assumed that my father had been of the royal family—everyone did—but that didn't really mean anything. Maybe it mattered when I was too young to remember or care, but... In Irnaji, *Jazei* is just a word out of legend. I'm not a legend; I'm Kenlin. So regardless of who thought my father was what, it's been a long time since I was anything other than Kenlin."

"That's unusual," Ranja commented, sounding almost impressed. "The Jazei legend is entrenched deep enough in most people's minds that, very often, there's little that can overcome it."

Kenlin cocked his head. "Yes? You speak from experience?"

As though in retort, she cocked her head identically. "Yes and no. To most people in the broader world, we tend to be Jazeiz first and individuals second. When I want to, though, I can make an impression of my own."

Interesting. "So, that's a 'yes,' then, not really a 'no' at all." Ranja reacted to this, withdrawing slightly, but Kenlin hardly noticed. "I think it's hard to not be an individual in a place like Irnaji, though. You don't meet people for the first time very often; you two excepted, it's probably been years since the last time I 'made an impression.'"

Ranja listened still with a slightly reserved expression on her face as though she was unsure what to make of Kenlin. She nodded, but let the topic drop.

After a moment, Klanjad said, "This talk of Kenlin's village reminds me, Ranja, that your aunt had a gift for you. An heirloom, of sorts." From his pack he withdrew a book, bound in leather, neither tall nor wide but thick as a flagstone. Kenlin had seen this book among his mother's possessions whilst growing up; but although she had taught him to read Jazeskri, neither of them had been able to comprehend that book.

Ranja, however, took the book with interest, and after only a moment's look at its pages, she caught her breath. "Father, is this..."

"The *Diary of Franvaz*, brother of Zadarj and our forefather," Klanjad completed. "Not the original, but a copy—perhaps the last complete and unmodified copy in the world. Lazaeddi saved it and brought it down with her when the Keep was destroyed."

Ranja did not reply, but her expression as she turned back to the pages was more than enough answer for her father. For the briefest moment, Kenlin saw some of the stony hardness fade from his uncle's face, as though it were gently illuminated by his daughter's delighted glow. Then he noticed Kenlin and seemed to recall that they were not alone; the moment passed.

Very touching. Not very welcoming, though. I seem to remember hearing that I would be invited to learn Jazei truths. Yes? Kenlin waited for a minute or so to be included in the conversation, but neither Klanjad nor Ranja said anything. *Alright, then; I suppose I'll have to bring up my questions myself. Politely, if I can.* "It's wonderful news that this artifact was saved. I don't know what it would have meant if it had been lost."

Ranja shot him a quick and unfavorable glance. "You're being glib," she said, "but this is very serious and very true. Do you know what this is?"

Off to a good start. "No, I don't," Kenlin said, perhaps more bluntly than necessary. "It seems there's quite a lot that I don't know. I'd like to, though. Who was Franvaz and what is his diary?"

Ranja narrowed her eyes further, eyeing him with a disfavor bordering on mistrust. Klanjad's expression was more difficult to read; after a moment, he answered, "Franvaz was the first king of Natzut, Zadarj's brother, and the founder of our line. And his diary...well, it's that book that Ranja has."

How unhelpfully succinct. But he suppressed his irritation and asked on: "And what's the significance of the book?"

Klanjad took another brief pause before answering, as though he were double-checking that his answer was as scant and tepid as possible. "Like I said, it's an heirloom, mainly. An heirloom of the Jazeiz, of our kingdom, of our family..." He trailed off with a shrug.

This won't do at all; I will not be kept to the side like an eavesdropper as they confer comfortably between themselves. This could have been easier, they could have been open without confrontation. But if I must be—

"During the War of Men and Misks, Natzut was established as a stronghold of the Jazeiz by Zadarj himself, the greatest of the Jazeiz." It was Ranja who spoke, preempting Kenlin's demand for an answer. In a tone and a manner that could only be described as *level*, she continued, "After the war was won, Zadarj bequeathed kingship of Natzut to his half-brother, Franvaz, who was the founder of our lineage. Franvaz's diary is one of the few original sources of knowledge about Zadarj and the founding of the Age of Men. It would have been an immeasurable blow to history if the text of his diary had been lost forever."

Thank you, Ranja. Thank you for making this easier. But to maintain the conversation's momentum, Kenlin restricted his gratitude to a single quick nod of appreciation, to which she did not react. "So... My mother taught me letters well enough, but even she couldn't make out what was in that book."

Ranja's controlled, even expression only permitted the subtlest of shrugs. "It's written in the language of Misks, ironically. I suppose she must have never learned that language; it isn't studied commonly."

Kenlin nodded again, this time to further the topic. "It seems peculiar that an early patriarch of the Jazeiz would write his own diary in Misk. The stories tell that Misks and Jazeiz have been foes forever. In fact, wasn't there a Misk at the ambush two days ago? Are the Jazeiz not fighting Misks even to this day?"

A sort of glimmer had appeared in Ranja's eye: a glint of comprehension, but not necessarily of cooperation. "Well, you must understand that the Misk language was considered the language of permanence, even among humans during the War. Though Jazeskri—the common speech, you know— was spoken by almost all humans, most written documents from that time used the Misk language and script."

I think I'm being toyed with. But he persisted: "That's fascinating. But despite any similarities in record-keeping, Misks have always fought the Jazeiz, yes? Are they as much enemies today as they ever have been?"

The glimmer in Ranja's eye had developed fully into a gleam of mischief, but Klanjad interrupted. "If you have real questions, boy, just ask them directly. If you keep trying to...*navigate* the conversation, she's going to lead you around in circles, and we'll be here all night." Ranja shot her father a glance that was equal parts sheepish and self-satisfied, but said nothing.

Alright, then. "Seventeen years ago, the Jaz—our family ruled the city of Natzut. But I grew up as a presumed bastard in a village on the edge of a ruin; and you, after so long an absence, returned in the night with nothing but your daughter, your weapons, and your enemies. I don't understand how any of that happened, so to start with, can you please explain…all of that?"

"Seventeen years in a single question, to start with," Klanjad remarked drily. "That's probably too tall an order for tonight. Any chance you could narrow that down?"

Ranja stifled a giggle; Kenlin ignored her. "Very well. Let's start with this, then: why did Ranton the King—my father—die?"

Klanjad's countenance revealed little, but he had been so inscrutable for these past minutes that Kenlin noticed even the most subdued flickers of emotion: surprise, apprehension, weariness, sadness. The elder Jazei hesitated, then answered, "He is dead because we fought the Droál when we did not know what we were fighting. And so we were beaten, and so he was killed."

I will drag you along one sentence at a time, if I have to. "Why did you fight them without knowing what you were fighting?"

"Well…we were already in the area in response to a minor uprising. A very minor uprising, to be honest, our presence was more of a show of strength than a real *fight*. But then the Droál arrived and threatened Likrásk—a city north of the mountains—and since we were already nearby, and we responded."

Don't keep giving me morsels for answers; I will not accept them. "So you intervened just because it was convenient? Because you happened to be in the vicinity?"

"Yes, just so simple—" Ranja chimed in sarcastically; but at a sharp look from her father, she cut herself off.

Klanjad took his time before answering: "Sometimes people do things like that, don't they?" *What does he…? Oh.* Kenlin had no reply, but Klanjad didn't wait for one. He continued, "In our case, though, it wasn't quite that simple, no; we didn't fight them because it was convenient. We fought them because it was our duty, and we were expected to fulfill it. As the Jazei kingdom in the southeast of Jranjana, we were still regarded as a sort of protector, even if most of the cities no longer acknowledged us as their sovereigns; and because of that regard, we enjoyed a privileged relationship—diplomacy, trade, there was even a sort of unofficial military vassalage— with every other domain in the region. So when our protectorate was threatened, we responded."

"How did you respond? What exactly happened?"

Klanjad sighed deeply, bowing his head. *Perhaps this was the very topic he has been so reluctant to approach.* As he sat, Ranja gave her father a concerned, almost commiserating look; and she cast an equally dark and accusing glance at Kenlin, though only for a moment. *What is she annoyed about now? I want answers, and it seems like I might finally be about to get some.* And after a moment, his uncle seemed to rally, gathered his thoughts, and began to speak. "For me, that day began on a clifftop, looking out over a stormy fog on a forest..."

CHAPTER VIII:

Kenlin listened, transfixed, to every word of Klanjad's tale, and with every new detail his interest and his energy grew; the past two days of exertion seemed to fall away from him like caked mud in the rain. But the telling had the opposite effect on Klanjad: his face became drawn, his manner grave, and his voice harried and weary. By the time his tale neared its end, it seemed to Ranja as though Kenlin were draining the life from her father, extorting from him—under a sense of obligation—the one story in the world that caused him the most pain.

But, ever stoic, her father pressed on to the very end: "By the time I returned to the fighting, it was far too late. The Droál had overwhelmed Natzut's army; and Ranton, trying to fight them all alone, had driven himself mad with magic. I tried to help him—I tried to save him—but I was thrown away from the fight and injured, and he was overwhelmed by the Droál's strange magics. And then there was nothing I could do, so..." Ranja half-expected Kenlin to prod her father verbally, but he didn't; he just fixed that horrible *driving* stare of his on Klanjad until, at last, the elder Jazei finished. "So I left him. I slid over the edge of the cliff onto a ledge below, feigned my own death like a coward. I abandoned Ranton. I fled."

Klanjad fell silent. The weariness—the total emotional exhaustion—was plain to see on his face. Surely, Ranja thought, Kenlin must be satisfied *now*, now that Klanjad had relived the most hateful day of his life just so that Kenlin might be *informed*. Surely—

"But you would not have stayed on that ledge for long." Kenlin's query crushed the silence, crushed any hope for an end to the painful memories tonight. "You couldn't have, you would have to know. After he was overwhelmed—after you were defeated—what happened to Ranton?"

Ranja couldn't bring herself to look at her father, for she knew how much this memory tormented him. She had seen him steel himself many times; she had watched him swallow the turmoil in his heart; she had heard the cold, flat, emotionless declaration of his answer: "Ranton was taken by the Droál, bound in iron, thrown into an oaken cage, and burned alive."

The subsequent silence was too short by far. Much too quickly, much too easily, Kenlin followed up with another question. "Burned alive? That seems…a bit extreme. Is that typical for the Droál, or was it done especially because my father was Jazei?"

In spite of herself, Ranja nearly snorted at Kenlin's assessment that burning alive was, "a bit extreme." Evidently, her father did not look favorably on the remark either, for his response was frigid: "The Droál often burn their captives alive; it is a sort of religious devotion of theirs."

Kenlin nodded and proceeded almost without pause, "And the binding in iron, is that a part of their devotion?"

Ranja caught a breath and prepared to lambast Kenlin with it, but Klanjad answered first: "No, the binding was because Ranton could not be restrained otherwise. He was…the greatest and strongest magician I have ever known; and in his last madness, he was stronger than ever."

"Madness…from magic, you said," Kenlin continued, apparently blind to everything except his own insensitive curiosity. "In fact, you said he'd driven *himself* mad with magic…"

Ranja could bear it no longer. "Well, I think the time has come for at least *some* of us get some sleep," she declared coolly but loudly, throwing a meaningful glare toward Kenlin in the hopes that *something* would get through to the oblivious buffoon. Turning to Klanjad, she continued, "Father, I've had the most rest for the past two days, so I'll take the first watch. You both should sleep; but if *anyone* wants to ask me about things, I'll be awake, just outside the firelight and perfectly happy to talk."

"If he has more questions, Ranja," her father replied without favor, "then I'll answer them. Don't come charging to my rescue when I haven't called for aid."

But Ranja's intrusion had finally cut through Kenlin's single-mindedness. He looked at Ranja, then at Klanjad, then back to her, then back to her father. "Thank you. I think she's right, though," he said, with a sudden and absurd air of propriety. "I've learned a lot tonight. I will, *um*... There are many nights ahead of us. Ranja, I might bother you for your thoughts if I can't get to sleep, but... Yes. Thank you."

"Well phrased," Klanjad said, deadpan, "very eloquent. I won't argue, though; I've had enough for tonight. Wake me for the third watch." And with that, he turned away and immediately began laying out his bedroll.

It was about as formal a *goodnight* as their camp ever had. Ranja, still desiring to separate Kenlin's inquisitiveness from her father, stepped out of the firelight and seated herself on a comfortable rock nearby. Kenlin, however, did not follow her immediately. Instead, he remained where he sat, staring into the fire, and it was not before many minutes had passed—Klanjad had long since closed his eyes—that he stood up.

She did not react as he came out of the firelight near her; she did not react as he sat down opposite her; and she did not react as the silence between them grew more and more unbearable. This, she realized, was his game: his tolerance for awkward silences was high, and he could force a conversation simply by creating awkwardness and outlasting it. Well, he would not outlast *her*; and if he wanted her to give him answers, then he would have to ask directly.

He was watching her as the silence wore on; and though the darkness made it uncertain, she thought she saw a sort of appreciation, bordering on respect, in his gaze. When the silence between them was beyond unbearable—it was unproductive—Kenlin said, "I'm sorry."

The apology caught her off-guard, but she did not let herself show it. Cocking her head a little, she replied, "Sorry? For what?"

"For whatever has offended you. For...pressing too hard, I think. For pushing when you think I should have held back."

"*Hmm.*" She was now more wary than angry, but she still had to resist the temptation to give a snappish retort. "*Offended* is probably not the right word. Just...*overwhelmed*, maybe."

"You, or your father?"

"Both: he from his memories, and I by proxy. You too, I'd imagine, are somewhat overwhelmed, though you don't seem so. Telling these tragedies isn't easy for him; hearing them can't be easy for you."

In the distant firelight, it was hard to tell if his shrug was forbearing or merely indifferent. "Well, not much has been *easy* these past three days. And tragedies make for some of the best stories in hard times, yes? Tales of other people's disasters can help distract us from our own."

What a clueless, tactless fool! "Very true," she replied icily, "provided the disasters really are *other people's.*"

Kenlin held up his hands, palms forward. "That's fair, and I've already apologized for that. But still, you have to see that they aren't *my* disasters. And for that matter, are they *your* disasters, other than—what was your word—by proxy? You can't actually *remember* the story he told, can you?"

"Now you're just being outrageous. Am I only to care about things that happen to me personally? That story—that *painful* story—happened to my father. And to your father! Do blood and kinship mean nothing to you?"

Her temper must have shown through in her voice, for Kenlin visibly pulled back. There was a long pause as Ranja breathed herself back to calm, and Kenlin chose his reply with great care. "Blood and kinship, it seems, are things about which I have much to learn. I guess there are many, many things I have to learn about." Then, as though to himself, "*New* thoughts, lots of new thoughts."

"That's reasonable," said Ranja, once again speaking coolly. "And it's reasonable, I suppose, that lots of new thoughts should bring lots of new questions. And I did say that I'd be glad to talk, so... Are there more questions that you want answered tonight?"

Still preoccupied, Kenlin shook his head slowly. "Not tonight, no. I already have enough to think through for now. I'll have more to bother you with tomorrow, though, and the days after. How many days after?"

"You mean, how long will we be traveling? Initially, I think we're heading for the Flunjat River valley via the high roads, so...fifteen days, perhaps, if I remember the maps correctly. And we'll be going on from there, so..."

"...many days," Kenlin finished, nodding. "No need to rush, then, there'll be plenty of time for more questions. Thank you. Do you mind if I take the watch now?"

"I've been on for no more than half an hour, Kenlin. You should sleep, and I'll wake you in a few hours for your watch."

He shook his head with a quiet laugh. "I won't be able to sleep with all these new thoughts. I'll wake you a bit early for your watch, if you insist; but give me some time to quiet my mind before I have to take my rest."

Although she still was not inclined to do him any favors, his request was not unreasonable; and given the promise that he would wake her just as soon as he began to yawn, she retired to her bedroll.

Six or seven hours later, she was awakened by the dawn. Kenlin still sat where he had been all night, wide awake and watchful.

· · ·

For one so frustrated by my forwardness, she is rather forward with her frustration. I suppose she couldn't have done it much better—no childishness, no yelling, just a cold and unambiguous airing of concerns—but that it should bother her to begin with... Did she expect that I wouldn't have questions? That I would be content to wallow in ignorance?

No matter. However she feels, she's civil at least; and Klanjad, happily or not, does give me answers. A dim and strange light, but enough to learn by.

And so much to learn! I suppose it was silly to ever think it would be simple, but the scale of it... I never knew how much I didn't know; even what I've learned tonight I could never have imagined two days ago.

... Has it really only been two days? Two days...

So he actually was a Misk, that one; and Jazeiz kill Misks, not just in stories and ancient times but also recently, from what Klanjad has said tonight. Interesting. But it wasn't Misks that killed my father, apparently, nor...others. Droál, is that what they called them? Droál, evidently, are allied with Misks—I'll have to ask about that later—and it is they, not the Misks, who provided the force that defeated the Jazeiz so many years ago after the Misks had already been vanquished.

Interesting.

But they can be fought. Indeed, Klanjad and Ranja both fought them—and killed all except the Misk, no less! How? I will ask. I will ask about everything. Klanjad has spent the past sixteen years fighting Misks and Droál, and I will learn every scrap of knowledge he can teach me. And Ranja, too; presumably she has knowledge she'll be willing to share.

Or perhaps not: she didn't seem much interested in Klanjad's narrative, though I suppose she's heard it before. She was, however, keenly and repeatedly fascinated by my unfamiliarity with the Jazeiz, and the Jazei lineage, and the Jazei heritage, and the Jazei abilities... Well, maybe I can ask her about that, then. She herself is considered a Jazei, yes? Despite the black hair? Yes, I remember, Klanjad mentioned *that in Irnaji, and she's probably the last person I should ask about that particular topic.*

Or is she? I'm being hasty, going too fast, thinking too many new thoughts... I need to slow down. She was right, I was too overbearing tonight. I mustn't seek out conflict with them, for we face a long road together. Fifteen days, she said—half a moon until we reach even the first turn in the road. Plenty of time; no need to keep blundering forward this fast.

It's just been a very fast two days, hasn't it? Very fast. So fast. So fast that I'm forgetting. Did I forget... Do they all yet lie unburied?

Enough! There is time, but not for that. No. I have too much to ask, too much to learn, too many new thoughts to think. Yes, now is the time for thinking new thoughts, specifically new thoughts. Unless... Are they waking up? How long have I been thinking already?

Though the full dawn had not yet come, the pink glow of the first light was gleaming from the mountaintops around them. Ranja stirred first; and at the sound of her movement, Klanjad's eyes opened as well. The two of them looked at each other, then at the brightening scenery around them; then they both turned to Kenlin with matching expressions of exasperation.

One above! Have I accidentally watched the whole night through? Well... Alright, then. "Good morning!" Kenlin crowed, donning his cheeriest smile. "I have questions!"

CHAPTER IX:

In the southwestern lands beyond the desert, where the air is always warm and dry and the sun never hides but to make way for the moon, the dying king called his sons to his side. 'My death is woeful,' said he, 'for I cannot but think that the ruin of our kingdom is upon us, unless I forge an agreement between you two.'

The king first turned to his elder son, whose name was Mitakotta. 'You will make a fine king, my son,' the old man said. 'You are strong in word and war, and your mind is ever upon the ruling of the kingdom. The city sleeps peacefully knowing that you will do whatever is necessary to keep it safe. But alas! Your reign alone would mark the end of our kingly line; for you will never take a wife, my son; and should you ask, no woman would have you.' And he spoke the truth, for Mitakotta was a harsh and unyielding man, and had no interest in affairs of the heart.

'And you, Kadrim,' said the king to his younger son, 'I have no doubt that you will find love, for you are fair and true and sweet of words. Of women you know something, and of romance a little; but of the world you know nothing. No, my son, you are no king fit to rule my kingdom; and though your heir would be assured, your rule would fail even before you died, and you would bring ruin upon the city.

'Therefore, it must be that you will share the throne, one king for ruling, one for siring. Mitakotta, you must rule as you see fit, governing the kingdom and protecting its cities and towns. However, understand that when you die, kingship will pass to the children of your brother.'

'So be it, Father,' answered Lord Mitakotta.

'As for you, Kadrim,' said the old king, 'you sit on the throne so that your children may sit there: to you I leave a title, not a kingdom. Defer to your brother in matters of law and war and attend to the lot which is yours:

to find a suitable queen, and with her to provide for the future when your brother has gone.'

'I understand, Father,' said Lord Kadrim.

The king said, 'Then I may die in some semblance of peace,' and breathed his last breath.

And so a second crown was forged, and the brothers Mitakotta and Kadrim rose to the throne. And while King Mitakotta attended to the affairs of state, Kadrim began his task of finding a wife.

But though he attended many feasts and danced many dances, and though many women envied each other of his favor, he loved none of them. His brother said to him, 'Surely one of these women will suffice?'

But Kadrim always answered, 'I do not love any of them, and they do not love me.'

Mitakotta, not comprehending, would ask, 'But surely they are all capable of producing heirs? Is that not the purpose of this search?'

But Kadrim would shake his head, for he knew that Mitakotta could not understand that which he sought.

And yet for years his search remained fruitless, and he grew discouraged and despaired of ever finding love.

Then one day, as he was hunting in the fields to the south of the city, his hunting party was set upon by lions; and though the hunters fought against them, Kadrim's horse panicked and he found himself being carried away from his men, away to the south and into the forest of the Faeries.

In the trees of that nameless wood, Kadrim wandered wantonly until after the sun had set, until at last he came upon a sheltered vale by a pool of water, whereupon he said to himself, 'I shall do no better than this place tonight, even if I wander until morning. Perhaps, when I wake, I shall find what I seek.' And so saying, he lay down upon the ground and slept.

Perhaps the forest heard him—strange are the ways of the Nameless Forest of the Faeries—for it did indeed bring to him that night the thing which he sought.

While he was sleeping, a young woman clad in rags, her beautiful face curtained with sleek hair that hung down below her lovely waist, came from within the forest. Happening suddenly upon the sleeping King, she screamed in surprise and he awoke. Yet he did not see her, for she stood in shadow, and so he was yet startled when she said to him, 'No Faery are you.'

'Nor are you,' he replied, for he could not sense her magic. 'May I ask who you are? I do not see you.'

Though in her mind she was still wary of him, the young woman was curious about this stranger who, even come upon in the wilderness without warning, remained well-spoken; and she did not deny to herself that she found him very comely. She stepped into the light and revealed her beauty to him, flushing when he caught his breath. 'You may call me Shaéde.'

King Kadrim was immediately taken with her surpassing beauty, and for a moment he could not speak. He then stood and touched his fingers to his lips as a sign of respect, for if he drew his kirsk he worried of frightening her. 'Lady,' he said, 'I cannot but betray this with my actions, so I must confess immediately that you are the most beautiful woman I have ever met. How came you here?'

'My father searched here for the Faeries,' she told him, 'throughout my youth. Then, many years ago, our camp at the edge of the forest was set upon by bandits, and my mother and I fled into the forest whilst my father and brother fought them. When we could no longer hear the fighting, my mother returned to try to find my father, leaving me in the forest; but she never came back to me. When I had been alone for some time, I began to cry, and I was heard by the Wanderer.

'I cried the harder and asked him to return me to my parents, but he soothed my tears and told me that it could not be done. Then he kept me beside him for some time, staying in the forest and teaching me the ways of the woods. And here I have lived ever since; and though I have never seen the Nameless Capitol, I call this forest my home.'

The King was dumbfounded, and knew not what to say.

She spoke again: 'But what of you, traveler?' she said. 'From whence do you come?'

King Kadrim opened his mouth to speak, but found that he did not want her to know of his position lest she be frightened, or intimidated, or feel somehow that he was too important or dangerous for her. So he said, 'Lady, I have no name to give you. What name I had is of no importance to me anymore.'

'Indeed?' she laughed. 'And what is that you seek here, nameless man?'

But all thoughts had left the King except for Shaéde and her beauty, and he answered, 'Truthfully, I have forgotten.'

'Perhaps we may find it together,' she said lightly, 'for I know this forest better than any other human.'

'O, I do not come from the forest,' answered the King, 'but from the plains beyond. Yet perhaps we might search there together.'

She pondered for a moment, then said, 'The Nameless Forest is the place for the nameless man. When you tell me your name, I shall guide you from the forest.'

And many moons passed as she showed him the myriad wonders of the forest, which he had never imagined; and he told her of the wonders of the cities and the plains, which she could not recall. And they became lovers, and their love grew until one night as they lay together, she asked him, 'Will you deny me anything that I ask?'

'Nothing, my love,' he replied. 'If it is in my power to give, it is yours, as I am.'

She said, 'Then tell me your name.'

And Kadrim worried, for he did not know how she would react; but he said, 'Then I must tell you that I am Kadrim of the Jazeiz, king of all the lands watered by the two rivers.'

And she was alarmed, for she could not understand how this could be. 'If you are a king, then how came you to be here?'

'Whilst I was hunting, our quarry turned upon us and I was taken into the forest by my frightened horse. But I have not thought of such things since you found me in the glade.'

But she persisted, 'Yet if you are a king, must you not return to your kingdom?'

And he answered, 'The affairs of the kingdom are in the hands of my brother, a better king than I. Still, I must return someday, for when our lives are spent, it must be my children who rule.' And he hesitated, for he did not know how he should ask her to return with him to his kingdom.

But she was troubled in her heart, for she wondered at his hesitation and was disturbed by his kingly status. When Kadrim had been silent for a long time, she said, 'I once told you that, when I knew your name, I would guide you from the forest. I shall do so. Return to your kingdom.'

Kadrim asked, 'Will you not come with me?'

But she could not imagine leaving the forest; and so, though it pained her nearly more than she could bear, she answered, 'I will not. I will remain here, in my home.'

And he was aggrieved. Yet he thought to himself, I shall tell my brother Mitakotta of all that has happened; then I shall return and, if I cannot convince her to leave with me, we shall live out our lives together here, and deliver our child to the city as king when the time for that arrives. So he said to her, 'My heart, I truly cannot fathom my life without you; for I must produce an heir for my kingdom, yet I cannot bear the idea of doing so with any other woman. If you will but wait for twelve days near the forest's northern border, I will return to you; for it may be that we can yet be together.'

And she, also, was sick with sorrow; and though she scarcely dared believe in what he said, she agreed to wait for him near the forest's edge for twelve days.

The next morning, she showed him to the edge of the forest, and straightaway he went to find his brother Mitakotta, in whose hands the entire kingdom had been left.

When he arrived at the palace, all were astounded that he yet lived, for they had long ago assumed him to have died; and when Mitakotta saw him, they greeted one another with the utmost warmth.

'My brother,' said Kadrim, 'I must tell you that I have at last succeeded in our father's last mission to me; I have found a woman I love, who will produce the next king. However, she resides in the south and waits for me in the Nameless Forest, and I must return to her ere ten more days are past.'

Mitakotta answered, 'As glad as these tidings are, they cannot be acted upon now, for there is unrest in the south. The ancient Misk clans have arisen against us and have sent an army northward to attack us. Even now, I muster an army from within the city to meet them on the field of battle, after which I will muster the entire kingdom to crush them in the mountains; however, you must not risk yourself by venturing forth to the south, for we are Jazeiz and cannot hide from Misks.'

'But if such is the danger,' said Kadrim said in alarm, 'then she, waiting near the forest's edge, is in danger just as great.'

Mitakotta said, 'Send a squad to fetch her if you wish, but they may all be caught and slain by the Misks.'

But Kadrim replied, 'Even if they could make the journey in safety, she would elude them. She will not come forth for any but me.'

King Mitakotta, though he was not inclined to be sympathetic, explained, 'Remain in the city; it is not safe for a lone Jazei outside the city now, and we cannot spare an army with which you could ride to rescue your bride. If you are right, and she is so clever, perhaps she will evade them and you can go to her when the Misks have been driven back.'

'But she might be taken,' protested Kadrim, 'or she might be driven away from the forest's edge by the presence of the Misks and I might never find her again.'

With a cold look, Mitakotta simply answered, 'Remain here.'

Within days, Mitakotta departed with a glorious army to face the Misk horde in the south, but Kadrim was uneasy. He could not bear to leave his love in the forest, in peril she could not possibly realize and with no word from him. At last, he decided that he must go to her; and he ordered the garrison, who had been left to guard the city, to muster and ride forth with him to the Nameless Forest.

When they arrived, Kadrim ordered his men to remain at the edge while he ventured into the forest. When he had passed beyond hearing of the edge, Shaéde appeared from the trees around and they embraced.

'My love,' he told her, 'you must return with me, if only for a short while. A host of Misks has come north from the mountains, and I cannot trust the forest to protect you without trying to do so myself. Return with me, and we can go where we please once the Misks have been defeated.'

She agreed, smiling and saying, 'I, too, have a reason that I should return with you; from our love has sprung the heir it was your duty to produce.'

And they rejoiced together as they returned to where the soldiers were waiting to bring them to the city.

But the battle against the Misks had gone ill, and away to the east of the forest, King Mitakotta had been driven back and forced to retreat to the city with scarcely a hundred men alongside him. The Misks, depleted though they were in number, followed even to the gates of the city. But Mitakotta, finding the city's garrison gone, asked, 'What has become of the soldiers who were to guard the city? Their duty is at hand!'

But the gatekeeper told him, 'My King, thy brother departed not three days ago to the south, leading the garrison away with him.'

Then did Mitakotta's wrath blaze terribly, and he ordered his exhausted, wounded men to take posts atop the walls, where they did all they could to repel the Misks when they attacked. But when the gate was splintered and thrown open, Mitakotta stood alone in the breach against the Misk host, holding them back for hours without rest until Kadrim came up behind with the city's garrison. When the Misks saw themselves thus flanked, they said to one another, 'We must return to our clan in the south and fight another day, for we cannot hope to win as we are now.' And so they departed, and Kadrim brought the guard and Shaéde his bride into the city.

But the wrath of Mitakotta was dreadful to behold, and he confronted his brother, saying, 'You have disobeyed me, even going so far as to leave the city completely unguarded in a time of war. You have shamed our line and nearly destroyed everything this kingdom, and our lineage, hinges upon.'

And Kadrim said gravely, 'For what I have done, there can be no apology or forgiveness. But I did what I had to do, and would do so again if the need arose. I could not abandon my love to the Misks, or to the thought that I might never return to her. But rejoice, brother, for the city is not lost and our lineage is now assured, for see! My love bears the heir which was the duty our father left me.'

Then Mitakotta was silent for a long time. At last, he said to Kadrim, 'Come; we must speak alone.'

They went to a balcony of the keep; below them, the city lay sprawled, surrounded by the fields which stretched away to the horizon in the east and the shadow of the Nameless Forest in the south. Then Mitakotta said to Kadrim, 'Did you mean as you said, that you believe you were right to lead the garrison to the south to retrieve your bride?'

Kadrim answered, 'I do believe so.'

Mitakotta pressed him, 'And you would do it again, should the need arise?'

Kadrim replied, 'My love is more important to me than a hundred kingdoms. To protect her, I will do anything and everything in my power.'

Mitakotta gestured to the kingdom as seen from the balcony. 'Look! You see my bride. This is the duty left to me by our father, this kingship. You understand, brother? You understand that I must do whatever is necessary to protect my bride's safety?'

'I understand,' answered Kadrim.

'Then you also understand,' said Mitakotta, 'that I am sorry.' And so saying, he threw Kadrim from the balcony.

When Mitakotta returned into the palace, Shaéde asked him, 'Where is my love Kadrim?'

Mitakotta looked at her unflinchingly. 'I killed him,' he said.

And she cried out in terror and sorrow, and she refused to believe him; but she could no longer deny it when she saw Kadrim's body brought back into the palace. In despair, she begged Mitakotta to kill her as well.

But he refused her, saying, 'It is your lot to live, for your child is the future of our lineage. You will remain at court and bear this child, after which you may do as you please: kill yourself, return to your forest, I care not. But you will fulfill your duty, just as he has fulfilled his and I have fulfilled mine. Now retire, for this talk distracts me from my other tasks.'

And with heavy heart, Shaéde allowed herself to be led away.

It was not a Leiver tale that ended with a quip and a ripple of laughter; as Ranja finished her story, neither Kenlin nor Klanjad spoke up to fill the ensuing silence.

It had now been more than half a moon since the three Jazeiz had left Natzut, journeying east and north through the most rugged and desolate mountains in southeastern Jranjana. Their progress had been slower than anticipated because of the disused state of the high roads, but Kenlin did not mind:

the longer the journey, the more he learned from his companions.

Klanjad, unsurprisingly, was a very direct sort of teacher. When asked a clear question, he would give clear information—usually. His understanding of events beyond the mountains was vast and detailed, and his knowledge of the Droál was (according to Ranja) unmatched in the world. But though he was usually willing to answer almost any question, every now and then something in the conversation would send him into a pensive, *closed* sort of mood. He would then answer as shortly as possible and, if pressed, would soon walk away to seek solitude. Initially, Kenlin had assumed that Ranja would hold him to blame for these bouts of despondency, but it soon became apparent that even she didn't always know what would trigger the mood.

On most questions, and particularly those related to recent history, Ranja usually deferred to her father and would only interject if she felt some important part of an answer was being neglected, or if she had questions of her own. On the subjects of history and legend, however, her father deferred to her and consulted her when he felt a historical perspective would be apropos. In these instances, she would constrain herself to details that were directly relevant in order to keep her responses tight and clear. The only times Kenlin had seen her become open and expansive in her answers was in the evenings, like this evening, when she was either telling or discussing a story.

And she knew *many* stories, far more than Kenlin knew. Kenlin's repertoire mostly comprised folk tales, with only a few legends based in history. Ranja knew many folk tales as well, but she seemed to prefer legends and histories. The tale she had told tonight about Kadrim and Mitakotta was, apparently, based on real events that had occurred nearly five centuries ago.

As his thoughts came back around to the story, Kenlin finally broke the camp's silence. "So that was all true, then?

Those two brothers really did exist, and one killed the other...?"

Klanjad shrugged dispassionately, continuing to stare into the fire. Ranja answered, "It's probably not *all* true—stories need fine details that history can't be bothered with—but the main happenings were all historical events, memories of the Wanderer. Mitakotta and Kadrim really were two brothers who shared the throne of Guardél for several years, and Kadrim really did perish before his son was born. Whether or not Mitakotta killed him, we can't be sure. Most stories say that he did, but other versions say that Kadrim died fighting Misks when he and his bride returned to the city."

"*Hmm.* That doesn't quite have the same narrative spice to it. But the Misk army was real, then? Mitakotta and his brother fought an uprising of Misks, just as my father and Klanjad did sixteen years ago?"

Ranja made a dubious face and glanced at her father, who gave a low laugh. "Ranton and I never faced a Misk uprising like *that.* The most we ever had to put down were small and ragtag war bands, nothing historic. The event in that story was the Eyjazinka Uprising of 2541, the worst such event since the War of Men and Misks."

That war was already familiar to Kenlin. Two thousand years ago, Misks had ruled Jranjana without challenge, partitioning the land according to clans. Of the Five Species who now inhabited Jranjana, only four had been known at that time: Misks, who had been dominant; Unnatilz, whose primeval hunting society had never led them to seek conquest; Faeries, who had never been known to have any political agenda whatsoever; and Dwarves, who lived underground and had, at that time, almost no interaction with surface dwellers. That had been the Age of Misks, the first age in Jranjana's recorded history.

But nearly two thousand years ago, the first humans had appeared in Jranjana and had quickly been absorbed into the inter-clan wars of Misks. Kenlin gathered that Misks were, on an individual basis, far stronger and more dangerous than men; but while women can theoretically bear one child every year, she-Misks carry their children for a decade or more before giving birth. Thus, the Misks had forced the fast-growing human population into slavery, at first mostly as conscripted soldiers but subsequently for other purposes. Dissident humans were killed, dissident clans were eradicated, and before long every Misk clan in Jranjana considered humans only as slaves.

These conditions had persisted until the arrival of the first Jazeiz inspired a great human uprising, beginning the War of Men and Misks. After more than a century and a half of fighting, the Misks were finally defeated by humans under the Jazei commander Zadarj the Djinn-slayer. Rather than choosing to exterminate Misks from Jranjana once and for all, Zadarj had chosen to banish them to remote territories in mountain ranges all around Jranjana. As added protection against resurgent Misks, Zadarj had established kingdoms ruled by Jazeiz to oversee—and, when necessary, overpower—each of the banished Misk tribes. Five such kingdoms had been established: Natzut, Iskena, Skaradarn, Kirjane, and… "Guardél was one of the five Jazei kingdoms, yes? So the Misks didn't just *happen* to be mustering nearby, it was Mitakotta's responsibility to repress that rebellion."

"True," said Ranja drily, "but I think that's rather a lot of detail to put into a story."

"That's fair; but it does add to the story when you have some notion of the context. And on that note, what causes these Misk rebellions in general, and that one in particular? Weren't the clans all decisively defeated at the end of the War of Men and Misks?"

This was something of a mixed question, half about history and half about world affairs, but Ranja clearly felt that her father should answer it; so both she and Kenlin turned expectantly to Klanjad until, after a moment, he looked up and noticed them. "You both know the answer to that last question," he remarked a little impatiently. "Of course the Misks were crushed at the end of the War. But despite Zadarj's relatively merciful treatment of them, their hatred from that war remains very, very strong."

"I'm surprised they ever deigned to surrender to humans, if they hate us so much," Kenlin commented leadingly.

Klanjad chuckled again, recognizing the lead and taking it anyway. "Ha! It's much easier to stand by your spite when your life isn't in jeopardy. I suspect the opponents of the surrender became much less vocal while they were cowering beneath the Sheathless Sword. Even so, the surrender might not have been considered if Lakradaz, erstwhile chieftain of Eyjazinka, had still been alive. But after their loss at Kilgáire, where he and a huge number of Eyjazinka males were killed, his widow Relshine became the *de facto* clan leader, and it was she who surrendered to prevent the annihilation of her clan.

"But," Klanjad continued, darkening, "whatever the reason they chose to surrender at the time, Misks have resented it ever since. And periodically, a faction within a clan—usually young males—will become aggressive and deluded enough to try to fight their way out of their mountain enclaves, thinking… I suppose they might think they can conquer fertile land in the plains, or that they might capture some humans and reinstitute slavery, or some such. Different rebellions have different aspirations, but all have the same fate: all are crushed on the battlefield and sent running in fear and shame back to their enclaves."

This proclamation hung in the air for a few moments, unchallenged. Then Ranja ventured, "In the case of the 2541 Uprising, there was a bit more going on than in many other revolts. Perhaps because of their central importance in the War of Men and Misks, Eyjazinka had always been watched more closely than any other Misk clan and, as a consequence, had never once risen up in the five centuries since the War. But after five centuries of relative peace—however involuntary—Eyjazinka had built up quite a population for a

Misk clan. Perhaps they were feeling cramped in the valley to which they were confined, or perhaps there were other factors, but the tensions between Eyjazinka and Guardél were already running very high in the early twenty-sixth century. It was probably only a matter of time before the Misks went to war; but the final push came from Uzkrendid the Bastard, a half-Unnatilz who incited the uprising to serve his own bizarre agenda."

Several parts of that sentence were completely new to Kenlin. "Interesting. A half-Unnatilz, you say? And the other half human? So crossbreeds are real, yes?"

"Oh yes, crossbreeds are very real. Human-Unnatilz crossbreeds are not all that uncommon; crossbreeding with Misks is exceedingly rare; Faery crossbreeds are purely theoretical; and Dwarves, I couldn't begin to guess."

"Perhaps this is a silly question, but...*why?* Aren't Unnatilz brutish, and simple of speech, and overwhelmingly orange? Are there just not enough human women for some people?"

Ranja let out a little *Pah!* of laughter. "It isn't just men who crossbreed; it goes both ways, and not always voluntarily. But in the case of Unnatilz, certain circles regard it as a sort of deviant adventure, wild and forbidden. You've heard the expression, 'Nobody's been to Garna?' Well, it turns out that quite a lot of people have been to Garna. And Uzkrendid was born in Garna, so...that's how *that* works."

"So Garna was also involved in the Eyjazinka Uprising, allied with the Misks? Or was it just Uzkrendid?"

"It was mostly just Uzkrendid. Garna is the only city Unnatilz have ever inhabited, and it's always been politically neutral. Uzkrendid wanted to turn it into something more powerful, like human kingdoms; but his ideas never took root in Garna, and he and his followers were eventually hunted out of the city. His involvement with Clan Eyjazinka was to incite them to revolt against Guardél, presumably in the hopes of weakening both sides so that Garna could grow into the void.

But the Eyjazinka Uprising was smashed, Uzkrendid was driven into exile, and his efforts did nothing for Garna except to damage its reputation and neutrality. His name is a curse in his home city, even today."

Kenlin nodded slowly as the details began to align in his mind. "And what became of Eyjazinka? Is this the same Clan Eyjazinka that is currently allied with the Droál?"

"There is only one Clan Eyjazinka," Klanjad uttered, and the sudden severity of his voice startled both Kenlin and Ranja. They waited for him to continue, but he remained silent.

The somber mood has come for him again, I see. Eventually, Kenlin broke the silence. "The Droál are humans, yes? It seems peculiar that Eyjazinka, of all Misk clans, would ally themselves with humans."

Klanjad shrugged. "Enemies of enemies. Both seek to destroy the current kingdoms of Jranjana. Both hate the Jazeiz."

Kenlin could see his uncle's endurance for the conversation waning, so he pressed all the harder. "It makes sense that the Misks would hate us; but why do the Droál?"

Ranja could probably answer this just as well as Klanjad, but Kenlin caught her eye and nodded toward Klanjad indicatively. She scowled at him, then answered anyway. "Without knowing where the Droál come from or what their history is, it's hard to be sure what grudge they might have. Perhaps they were originally inhabitants of Jranjana and became enemies of the Jazeiz at that time; or perhaps they encountered Jazeiz on whatever land they now come from, and that's where they learned to hate and fear us. The only thing we can be sure of is that they *do* hate and fear us. We are the monsters in their legends and the villains in their folk tales."

"That's intriguing. Do you really think there might be other Jazeiz in the Droál homeland?"

"No," Klanjad cut in even as Ranja opened her mouth to respond. "The Droál myths refer quite definitely to our history and to Zadarj himself: though he is not given his real name, many characteristic details are described, including his sword Vraníl and his legendary Rages. If those myths didn't come from first-hand knowledge, then they must have come from Clan Eyjazinka. They've been retold for many years throughout the Droál homeland, warping and shifting, but many unmistakable markers remain intact: *we*, the Jazeiz of Jranjana, are their demons."

I might as well try my luck. Kenlin asked, "How do you know so much about their stories?"

At this, Ranja shot Kenlin a wide-eyed and *very* exasperated look. But Klanjad suddenly laughed and looked up with a quick, insincere, madcap smile. "I had them all to a party, where I plied them with pleasantries and polite conversation. They may have said more than they meant to; there was mead, and plenty of cake, and the festivities went on and on and on." Then he excused himself, stood up, and walked briskly out of the firelight.

His footsteps soon faded to silence, whereupon Ranja said to Kenlin, "Once again your tact and discretion do you *such* credit. *Yes*, don't protest, I know you have questions, you need answers, so much to learn, and *la-de-da*. But you shouldn't press him so, not when he's exhausted. Even you must see that you'd get more answers if you were just a bit less overbearing."

"Not tonight, I wouldn't have," Kenlin countered dismissively. "I didn't bring about that mood, he got there on his own while you and I were talking. And you know perfectly well that, once the gloom sets in, it's only a matter of time before he walks out of the conversation. You're just upset because you, too, want an answer to my last question, and you've never gotten one either."

"You're quite right," she retorted, affecting sudden modesty, "I have a long history of not learning about Father's actions against the Droál; so as something of an expert in the field, I can tell you that blurting out inquiries is the very best way to continue not learning anything. He didn't give me a real answer the first thirty times I blurted about it, and he hasn't answered any of your blurting so far. I feel that a pattern is emerging."

So snippy. "Alright, then. If blurts are so ineffective, how would you recommend I ask? If I ever try to sidle up to a topic subtly, he spots me and mocks me for it. And if he doesn't, you do."

"Maybe you're just not subtle enough."

"Very funny, Ranja, but I'm being serious. If I'm not to ask directly, how should I ask?"

She shrugged and sighed heavily. "Obviously I don't have all the solutions; otherwise, I'd have my answers. I guess I don't really know how you *should* ask; I just know a lot of ways you *shouldn't*. He won't give in to pressure, and he won't fall for trickery. As on other topics, I suspect it's simply best to convince him that, for some practical purpose, you *need* to know."

"For a practical purpose? Meaning we need to know, before we have the knowledge, how said knowledge would be useful?"

"More than useful: *essential.* And that's the crux of it all, isn't it? I can't know what I need the knowledge for without at least some knowledge of what I don't know."

"Ha! Wisdom for the ages." She threw a pebble at him; it flew wide, probably by intent. Kenlin continued, "But why is this subject so special? He doesn't enforce this sort of information rationing on other topics."

She laughed. "Oh, but he does! Think of the answers he has given you in these past weeks. He tells you of kingdoms, of alliances, of wars and battlefields and armies; but he avoids particular events, doesn't talk about strategic deployments and strengths, and never elaborates on his own activities. The knowledge he does give you, you need *now* in order to build on it. You'll need such context for when we reach the Commune. Similarly, he talks of weapons, and how to use a sword, and when to hold and when to give ground; but he doesn't speak of the old trainings, of the Jazei traditions he won't have time to expose you to, or—so far—of magic at all. Don't you see?"

Kenlin did see, but he was neither encouraged nor entirely convinced by the sight. "That's not all we've discussed these last weeks, surely. What about all the history we've discussed, and the stories I've learned?"

Quirking an eyebrow, she lifted one finger and pointed to herself. "That comes from *me*. Certainly, Father joins in the discussion when he thinks it's interesting. Occasionally, he even volunteers information when it has utility, as he did earlier tonight when he talked about Droál legends featuring Zadarj. But by and large, *I* have been the one telling stories and answering your questions about legend and history. If it were only the two of you, he would minimize those answers, or just fail to give them."

A long silence followed this remark. *It is strange. I had never thought that the conversations were being steered; but now that she's mentioned it I can't think otherwise. How, in all these weeks, has he not told me aught of magic? And why have I not thought to press? Early on, I recall that I did ask directly; but my inquiries were always deflected into other topics. To "provide context."*

Ranja was watching his silence. "You seem disturbed."

"Confused," he muttered, "might be a better word. He has specifically avoided teaching me anything real of magic, hasn't he? That's..." *...not good. I don't appreciate that at all. Wasn't his promise from the very beginning to teach me of what I could be as a Jazei?* "Why would he withhold that information?"

Ranja shrugged, unconcerned. "'Withhold information' sounds very conspiratorial. I doubt Father's 'withholding' anything from you, as such; he just doesn't think you need to know it."

"I didn't realize that was his decision to make, without discussion," Kenlin replied evenly.

She shrugged again. "He has the information, hasn't he? You can ask for it, but he'll only give you what he thinks is appropriate. Even when he's not in that...openly closed mood, Father's very careful of saying overmuch." Kenlin's face must have shown his dissatisfaction, for she continued consolingly, "You mustn't take it as a sign of mistrust, Kenlin. Father doesn't tell me any of these things either. Everything I know of the old traditions—of magic—I learned from other sources."

"Why would *you* ever need to know anything of magic?" Hearing his own words aloud, and seeing Ranja's reaction, he instantly regretted having not phrased that differently. "I mean... Sorry, what I meant was—"

"No need to clarify." Her voice was suddenly very even, with only a hint of restrained coldness. "I know because I value knowing; so whatever Father won't tell me, I try to learn some other way. And those traditions, in particular, are an important part of our heritage as Jazeiz."

"But I thought you couldn't use magic."

Now with a definite chill: "They're *Jazei* traditions, Kenlin."

He had no wish to provoke her further, so he averted his eyes from her icy stare. After a moment, the tension around the fire relaxed a little. Ranja reached for her pack to fetch her bedroll. Kenlin debated—*Is it even worth asking?*—but ultimately he decided to venture it. "So, these teachings that Klanjad has avoided telling me... You do know of them?"

Levelly, "I know some, yes."

"In that case, why haven't *you* told me about them?"

She eyed him for several moments, running her tongue across her teeth as though she were tasting each of several responses. Finally she said, "I haven't told you because I agree with Father. You don't need to know yet. You're not ready."

And that was the end of the evening's conversation.

CHAPTER X:

The next day began as had the one before it, and the one before that. Kenlin (who had been condemned to the third watch since his accidental triple watch at the start of their journey) allowed the sunrise to wake his companions. They broke their fast with cured meat and berries, then rolled up their blankets, smothered the fire, and resumed their interminable trek through the mountains.

But a strange silence soon settled over their party: Kenlin wasn't asking any questions. Ranja broke into the silence, asking her father something or other about the ridge before them. Kenlin did not mind. The old road here was wide enough for three, but he allowed his companions to outstrip him by a few paces, leaving him space to ponder.

The conversation from the evening before had haunted him through the whole night and into the morning. She had said it so lightly—"...he'll only give you what he thinks is appropriate..."—as though she considered that sort of concealment perfectly normal. *But of course she does. She agrees with him, she said as much!*

That comment, too, had stuck in Kenlin's mind— "You're not ready."—and it rankled more than he cared to admit. She might have said it just to be mean, as payback for his rudeness about magic; but it was also seemingly a sentiment that she believed. And Klanjad certainly believed it, if his sly reticence throughout their journey was any indication.

"They say when the birds stop chattering, it means a storm is brewing," Klanjad called, looking back without stopping. "What's wrong, boy? Empty of questions, or full of answers?"

"*Hmm*? Are those not the same?" Kenlin deflected with a shrug.

But Klanjad, it seemed, was in a lighthearted mood. "Well, perhaps they are. Is a question nothing but the absence of an answer? And vice versa? At a glance, that *seems* reasonable considering that, once an answer has been given, it is beyond question."

"Yes," said Kenlin without listening. '*Not ready.*' *What does it mean to be 'ready' to know something?*

"However, I would contend," Klanjad rambled on merrily, "that a world where a question is merely an unanswer has no room for curiosity. For if an answer is but a morsel of knowledge, and a question is the absence of that, then would not the ill-informed be invariably full of questions? And in such a world, what is there to distinguish the curious from the ignorant?"

"Sure, indubitably."

"Ha, 'indubitably!' Doubly indubitable, daren't you doubt. And additionally, we mustn't allow ourselves to overlook the oxymoronic impact of the absent—intellectual or actual, as applicable. Ironic, I deem, to ascribe impact to the uninvolved where impact, assumedly, is associated with input. Although, implicitly, the absence of expected input eliminates impact expected; and if the absence of impact be input also, then the inattentiveness of the unaccustomedly insensible inflicts, in fact, an impact analogous to that expected of the attentive."

This onslaught of gibberish would have been enough to cut through Kenlin's thoughts even if Ranja, laughing, hadn't started applauding it. *What is he on about? None of that is worth parsing.* So he simply repeated, "As I said: indubitably."

Ranja looked as though she were concocting a rejoinder, probably full of nonsense and assonance, but Klanjad stopped walking and turned to face Kenlin directly. "You seem out of sorts, Kenlin; and on this morning, I find that I'm awash with sorts. Can I lend you some?"

Kenlin took a deep breath, centering himself, and allowed a perfunctory chuckle at the wordplay. "I'm not out of sorts. And I'm not out of questions. If anything, I'm overfull of questions."

"How ominous," Klanjad replied lightly. "Are these standing questions or walking questions?"

Alright, then. "Let's stand. What does it mean to be 'not ready' to learn something?"

A knowing look appeared on Ranja's face, but Klanjad merely grinned. "Don't tempt me to repeat my question-and-answer spiel."

"Please don't. I'm being serious. How can someone who wants to understand be 'not ready?'"

Some of the frivolity faded and was replaced by Klanjad's characteristic caution. "*Not ready* is a variation on *should not know.* Are you asking why, in general, knowledge might be kept from someone?"

Enough indirection. "I'm asking why, in particular, knowledge of magic might be kept from me."

"Ah." Comprehension flooded Klanjad's expression as he nodded slowly and cast a quick look at Ranja. She met his eye, but otherwise did not react. Turning back to Kenlin, he answered calmly, "We are in the middle of the mountains, half a day from the Flunjat River valley, many days from Likrásk, and moons away from Ñaj-Gadan. Plenty of time for such tellings later."

Kenlin didn't blink. "Why not now?" And, when Klanjad didn't reply immediately, Kenlin continued, "Am I not ready?"

From beside the conversation, Ranja made a quiet *huff,* but Klanjad seemed not to hear it, and Kenlin refused to acknowledge it. He kept his eyes locked on his uncle while the older Jazei considered the question. Finally, Klanjad concluded, "No. No, I don't think you are ready."

Something in Kenlin's mind—his pride, or perhaps something darker—bridled at this, but he kept his answer calm and civil. "Why not? What does it mean for me to be 'not ready?'"

Klanjad quirked an eyebrow drily. "It means that you should not know now, and implies that there will come a time when you should know."

It was almost imperceptible—she only gave the tiniest of satisfied nods—but Kenlin saw it. Quick irritation flashed through his mind: *Who is she to keep this from me?* But again he ignored her and said to Klanjad, "How will you know when that time comes? How will you know when I'm ready?"

Klanjad answered, as drily as before, "Right now, you don't need it. Someday, you will. That is how I will know." And he turned as though there was nothing else to say.

"True, I don't need it right now," said Kenlin, refusing to move so that Klanjad had to turn back to face his reply. "Nor will I need it tonight. Nor tomorrow, probably. And, if they ambush us in camp one night before I *need to know*, then perhaps I'll never need it."

Klanjad was unimpressed. "If they manage to surprise us again, and we're not lucky enough to be warned, I doubt it will matter whether you know of magic or not."

"We needn't necessarily be lucky in order to be warned. I don't know very much of magic, but tell me this: could that ambush have taken place if *you* had been on watch?"

In the corner of his eye, Kenlin saw Ranja stiffen. Klanjad glanced at her, then turned back to Kenlin without favor. "Make your point."

"As I said, I don't know much of magic; but I do know that magicians—trained magicians, at least—can sense other people who use magic, and can know them by their magic. I remember, the instant you awoke on that beach, you looked toward that Misk who was ambushing you. You sensed him, you knew he was there. And if I were trained in magic too, then would not two out of three of our watches be immune to such an ambush?"

At the words *two out of three*, Ranja shifted noticeably. Kenlin looked at her this time and gave a little shrug that he hoped was ameliorating, but perhaps she did not interpret it that way.

Klanjad scratched his chin, considering. "That is not a bad point," he said after a pause. "But then, neither are the points in favor of delaying your study of magic. Only a fool tries to run before he can walk."

"I'm not a child, Klanjad. I can walk."

"Can you? Can you walk? When the magic fills you with strength and speed, when your legs pull twice as strong, twice as fast as ever they did before, when your mind suddenly struggles to accelerate to keep pace with your newly-empowered body... Can you walk then? I'm not so sure."

Despite Kenlin's mounting frustration, this was far too intriguing to ignore. "What do you mean, when my legs pull faster? Is that what magic feels like?"

Klanjad gave a heavy, resigned sigh; then, glancing at the climbing sun, he gestured toward a shaded copse beside the path. Kenlin couldn't help feeling a touch of triumph, couldn't help stealing a glance at Ranja's face. She ignored him completely and followed her father to the shade.

When all three were out of the sun, Klanjad began his explanation. "For lack of time for the usual ritualism, think about it in this way: magic magnifies you. It doesn't allow you to do entirely new things, as such. All those old stories about men flying, reading minds, moving things without touching them...those are all just stories. Misks can do *some* other things, and nobody really knows how much Faeries are capable of. But for humans—for Jazeiz—magic is much more confined. You will do the same basic things with magic that you do without, but you will do them 'better.' Any movement you make will be enhanced. If you run, you will run faster; if you jump, you will jump higher; and if you flail about wildly and over-extend your elbow, with magic you might very well break your own arm. Do you see?"

"No. What? I might break my elbow with magic?"

"As an example, yes. Think about it. If you swing your arms about now, there's very little risk of injury: you've used those arms your entire life, and you know very well how to move them without damaging yourself. But imagine I suddenly grabbed your arm and flung it about, following the same motion but adding all my strength into it. That motion, which before was safe because it was familiar, is now unfamiliar and much more powerful. Unless your mind was ready to counteract the unfamiliar force, your arm might behave unpredictably: it could snap to hyperextension, or twist your shoulder unnaturally, or swing forward and hit you in the face."

"I see."

"So then imagine the damage that even simple mistakes could do with magic. What might happen if you rolled your ankle while sprinting at the speed of a diving hawk? What if you lost your balance while jumping the height of a tree? And how much worse would your flailing be— Yes you do, don't deny it, your current martial style is almost entirely flail-based. You're improving, but at present you're still an uncoordinated clod with a sword in your hand. You will have a hard time convincing me that adding magic to this mixture will make any of us safer."

At Klanjad's description of Kenlin's swordsmanship, Ranja had suppressed a snort and turned away. *What have you to laugh about, girl?* More heatedly than he'd intended, he said to Klanjad, "This, then, is why I'm being held back from magic? Out of a crippling fear of pratfalls and slapstick?"

This time, Ranja couldn't suppress the snort, but Klanjad was not amused. Curtly, he ordered, "Packs down. You too, Ranja. Both of you, draw your weapons, leathers off." They both obeyed slowly, Ranja with an air of growing alarm that, privately, Kenlin shared. *What will this demonstration prove? I already know she can best me; that's one reason I know I must learn more! And why take the blade leathers off?*

However, he dutifully removed the thick protective leather from his sword's blade and readied himself to spar. But before they could begin, Klanjad gave another order: "Now trade weapons."

That was a complete surprise. For the past few weeks, Kenlin had been learning to use his sword at least well enough to avoid hurting himself; but Ranja's weapon, a polearm that she called a glaive, was wholly mysterious to him. She had let him try it once for a laugh (and with the blade leathers on), and he had immediately become entangled with it before accidentally thwacking himself with the haft. Asking him to spar with such an unfamiliar weapon was beyond reckless. *But then, I suppose that's his point.*

Ranja, however, was having none of it. "Father, this is ridiculous. He hasn't a clue how to use a glaive. I appreciate the point you're trying to make, but it's not worth bleeding for convincing rhetoric."

If he wants to see that I'm committed... "Give me the glaive, Ranja," said Kenlin stonily. "I'm willing to risk it."

"Then you're an idiot," she spat venomously. And, rounding again to Klanjad, "I'm not sparring bare steel with him unless I'm allowed to kill him, especially if he has the glaive. Between me holding back and him having no idea what he's doing, *I'd* probably be the one to get hurt. I absolutely refuse to die proving a point about bad ideas; that's just too ironic for my taste."

"Then I'll spar him." And with a quick movement that drew a cry of surprise from Ranja, Klanjad snatched her glaive and threw it, flatwise, at Kenlin. Caught completely off-guard, Kenlin dropped his sword and barely managed to catch the glaive before Klanjad was upon him, attacking empty-handed.

In the corner of his mind that was still thinking clearly, he realized Klanjad was not trying to injure him: he was slapping, not punching or grappling. *He's proving his point that, if I don't know my weapon, I'm more of a menace to myself than to my enemy.*

I'll take that trade. Kenlin's instinct, under attack and clutching a weapon he didn't know how to use, was to drop the weapon and fall back into a protective hunch, but this second line of thought had other ideas. Rather than retreating, he drove his right shoulder forward and pulled the weapon down in a slashing motion, as he would a sword. Of course, it wasn't a sword, and the haft's slashing motion did little more than brush over Klanjad's clothing. But despite the inefficacy of the attack, Kenlin surged forward as though he were stepping into a real advantage.

A moment later, he was on his back in the dirt, his hands were empty, and Klanjad's face swam before his dazed eyes. "You've got grit, boy, and nobody can deny it!" Klanjad crowed in a tone that was not unlike respect. "Are you really that committed, or are you just stupid?"

"Stupid!" Ranja shouted angrily, snatching her glaive up from where Kenlin had dropped it. "Both of you are completely stupid!"

Kenlin was still dazed. "What happened? Did I win?"

In spite of himself, Klanjad howled with laughter at this. "Did you win!" he repeated, helping Kenlin to his feet. "You're disarmed, on the ground, on your back, and slapped silly. And you know something? Mayhap you really did win!"

"Father, no!" Ranja snapped in outrage. "The only thing that's been shown today is that neither of you are capable of approaching this topic intelligently."

"Maybe not to your standards," Klanjad countered, still chuckling. "But you can't deny the boy's as good as his word. Fighting unnecessary battles with unfamiliar weapons might be a terrible idea; but put him in the situation, and he'll do his damnedest to make it work."

"And that's what, some sort of meathead virtue?" retorted Ranja furiously. "The intelligent response to an idiotic situation is avoidance. Why are we still having this conversation? You've explained—quite eloquently, if I may say—why teaching him magic at this moment is a bad idea.

And now you've demonstrated—quite undeniably, if I may say—that he's so single-mindedly thick that, given a bad idea to start with, he's guaranteed to see it through to the point of maximum stupidity. All told, everything indicates that we were right to think what we thought from the beginning: he's not ready, and teaching him magic right now is perhaps the most reckless thing we could possibly do."

"You have quite a lot of opinions for somebody who's so uninvolved in this decision," Kenlin rejoined hotly. *Get out of my way!*

"He's not wrong, Ranja," said Klanjad, no longer laughing. "Why are you stepping into this?"

For a moment, she seemed affronted by the question, as though insulted that her involvement needed to be justified. But a moment later, the full force of her rhetoric was back. She flung out a hand toward Kenlin. "Just look at him now, look how he stands! His weight is on his heel, all on the left leg, knee locked. Even his fingers are flexed back, braced against his hips as he stands there, arms akimbo, glaring at me. See how his head lolls back now, either from dazedness or arrogance, stressing the spine; and when he's winded, he puts his hands on his knees and hunches over, as though he's lost his breath in the grass and must bend down to find it."

This is absurd. "What are you trying to prove, Ranja? What difference does it make how I stand?"

Klanjad broke in, "It is how you stand, but it's also representative of how you move. She is not wrong either, Kenlin. Unless you move more fluidly and stop placing such strain on your joints, you *will* rip yourself apart with magic."

"As I said before, I'll risk it. How can I learn to move with magic except to learn magic?"

Ranja said coldly, "You can learn the same way I learned: with discipline, hard work, and time."

Kenlin snapped. "The way you learned *what?* You can't use magic, Ranja! I'm sorry for your jealousy, but the fact that you just can't do it won't stop me from becoming a real Jazei."

He hadn't meant to say that, not at all, but there it was. *Real Jazei.* The words had every bit as much impact as he might have imagined. Instant silence fell over the conversation. Klanjad physically stepped back. Kenlin stood his ground. Ranja stood still as stone for several minutes, meeting Kenlin's eye but doing nothing except to control herself. The silence soon became uncomfortable, then unbearable, but still she did not move.

And then, finally, she spoke. Her voice was soft, but her tone was like a rope stretched taut, holding back a terrible force. "Perhaps you're right," she said, almost whispering. "Perhaps I shouldn't try to help." Then she turned—not whirled, not stormed—and walked away down the path.

Klanjad watched her until she turned out of sight. Then he sighed, shook his head, and sat down in the grass. Kenlin wasn't sure whether he should sit, or stand, or seek his own solitude. "So... What happens now?"

Klanjad threw up his hands. "Well, as you've demonstrated, Kenlin, you can do as you please. I doubt you could have handled that conversation any worse; so do whatever you like, it can only be an improvement!"

Kenlin shrugged. "I could have been less rude. But I wasn't wrong."

"To imply that my daughter is not truly Jazei," said Klanjad, a dangerous low in his voice. "Don't *ever* imagine that you are the arbiter of that title. I've told you from the beginning that we are a *family*; so if you value your membership, I advise you to never question hers again."

Kenlin felt that part of himself bridle once more, but he ignored it. "I didn't mean it that way. But it is true that she can't do the things in the stories."

"Neither can you. Neither can I, for that matter. And that's the trouble with you, Kenlin: to you, *Jazei* is still just a word from a story. You like stories, and that makes you think you know something. But the stories are full of half-truths and misunderstandings. *Jazei* is a kinship, but it's not a birthright.

Think of it as a standard, a family tradition of driving ourselves beyond our limits. We judge ourselves more harshly than the world judges us; and right now, you measure up *far* shorter than Ranja does."

"I know! That's what I'm trying to remedy!"

"And you'll tear down anyone who stands in your way, will you? No restraint? Have you always been so aggressive?"

The word *restraint* summoned a memory to Kenlin's mind, and he heard the word in his mother's voice from her many urgings throughout his childhood: Restrain yourself! Speaking slowly, he answered Klanjad, "I'm not always unrestrained, no. But I suppose I haven't...tempered myself recently."

Klanjad quirked an eyebrow. "Then consider doing that before you make yourself insufferable. There is a hastiness—no, a violence—that runs in our bloodline. From the ruthlessness of Gealvind to the Rage of Zadarj, our heritage has always been aggressive. Given proper direction, that aggression can drive you to greatness; but it can also drive you too far too fast. Controlled ambition: that is the Jazei way."

Kenlin nodded, forcing himself to internalize this. *Too much, too fast; restrain yourself.* Then he gestured down the path where Ranja had disappeared. "Control, I suppose, is her specialty."

"And ambition; together, she would say, they make *discipline*. Do not underestimate Ranja. She has spent her entire life crafting herself into what she is; and your relentless impatience earns you no respect from her. You want everything to be given to you at once, and you're not totally in the wrong: we don't have as much time as Ranja or I would like. But keep in mind that nearly everything you want to do fast, she has done *right*. And she did it on her own, for I was not there to guide her or force her to learn. I would start teaching her magic today if she could use it, and it's nothing but a cruel joke of nature that she can't."

Kenlin nodded again, slowly. "I take it, then, that you will not start teaching *me* magic today?"

"No, I will not. She is right, the risk of injury is too great, and any injury here in the mountains would almost certainly prevent us from continuing to travel. But you've made your point as well. The sooner you can learn magic, the better; so as we travel, I want you to start preparing."

"By...moving fluidly, yes?"

"Fluidity in both mind and body; temper yourself, as you said. Magic is as much a strain upon the mind as upon the body. Just as a flippant motion with magic could break your body, a flippant mentality could break your mind."

Kenlin frowned. "Can you elaborate? I don't know what a 'flippant mentality' is."

"Then let me be clear: a reckless, damned-be-the-consequences attitude *will not work* either for learning or for using magic. As you learn, your limitations will not always be obvious to you, but the price for overstepping them is *dire*. To Fade—the form of magic that you will use—requires the simultaneous cognizance of a stratified existence, which is something like being many places at once. We will discuss the details another time, but for now just know that it is extremely taxing. Magicians who overstep their abilities can suffer a number of afflictions, including a broken mind."

"Broken in what way? Does this happen frequently?"

"You never tire of details, do you? It's impossible to predict whether or how the mind will be broken until it is. They say some minds become feeble, or childlike, or merely strange. Some minds lose the power of language, or of movement. In the case I saw, he became violent—horribly violent—perhaps because it was the demands of the fight that drove him beyond his limitations."

"He?"

As harsh as Klanjad's tone had been, a markedly different darkness now filled his voice. "Ranton, your father. Recall that I told you he drove himself to madness with magic? This is how it happened. In his last battle, Ranton was faced with the magic of the Droál, an unnatural and powerful technique that they call *Necromancy*. Ranton tried to oppose them directly, for until then he had never met anything stronger than he was. But he pushed himself too far, attempted magic that was too strong for him, and the strain of it broke his mind beyond recovery. The last time I saw him, it was but a monster in my brother's body."

A long silence followed the conclusion of this story. Klanjad seemed to be struggling to endure the darkness that always came with this topic. Kenlin forced himself not to press. *He's right, I've been overbearing. Ever since the clifftop, I have pushed—him, her, myself—as though the world would end at Midwinter. I should slow down, collect my wits, find a pace I can maintain; this artificial urgency cannot last.*

Kenlin's preoccupation prevented the silence from feeling awkward. After a few minutes, Klanjad recovered his spirits enough to speak again. "Well! That's a morning well-spent infuriating each other. Come, no doubt Ranja's waiting ahead, eager to continue your conversation."

That seems likely. "I suppose we'll find out. But, to summarize, before that I must work to show that I can move and think fluidly, as you describe. When I have done so, then you will teach me magic?"

Klanjad chuckled drily. "I make no promises except to watch, over the coming days, to see how you improve. Never lock your joints; never land heavily; never absorb force with a bone that you could instead absorb with a muscle. I'll provide correction when I see something obviously wrong. But if you want to work from an example, study Ranja. Her movements are flawless."

"Very well. But…sorry, I have to ask: *why* are her movements flawless? Why would she go to the trouble of learning all that when she'll never be able to use it?"

Klanjad shrugged. "That is simply her way."

CHAPTER XI:

The following morning, they crossed the high pass—"Mind your left knee, Kenlin, you've locked it again."—and descended into the Flunjat River valley. From a rocky hilltop the day after that, they glimpsed the ruins of Flunjat City away to the south—"Don't hunch your back so, it strains the spine."—but their path lay along the road to the north. Kenlin looked back several times for any signs of the people of Irnaji, whose seaside road should have brought them to Flunjat City; but it was too distant to discern anything useful, and—"If you whip your head about like that with magic, you will certainly break your own neck."

Kenlin breathed deep, nodded humbly, and turned back to the road.

The critiques and corrections persisted for several days and were so frequent that they precluded almost any other conversation. By nightfall, Klanjad was weary of talking, Kenlin was frustrated from listening, and Ranja...

After the argument about magic, Kenlin and Klanjad had found her waiting for them half a league down the road. She had been sitting on a boulder by the roadside, reading from the Diary of Franvaz. At their approach, she had looked up, answered her father's greeting in kind, and calmly rejoined their journey; but her air of untouchable, haughty poise told Kenlin that she had neither forgotten nor forgiven his words to her.

And so a pall had settled over their company. There were no more stories, legends, or histories by firelight. Kenlin and Klanjad conversed a little, and Ranja spoke when spoken to, but for the most part she sat with her back to the fire, reading her book. And the days were so full of movements and corrections that they were no cheerier: Klanjad critiqued, Kenlin tried harder, and Ranja looked on in judging silence.

Kenlin knew she watched him, and that she saw every minute mistake he made, even when Klanjad did not. Her scrutiny added an extra sting to every error. *Does she revel, vindicated, each time I show that she was right to call me unready? Revel, then; enjoy your victory while it lasts.* But whether she really extracted joy from his failures, her taciturn expression did not tell.

For she would never comment, never smile. Though she made no effort to hide her observation, she never gave a hint of her conclusions. Initially, that had surprised Kenlin; he had expected her to join in her father's criticisms, or at least to have some fun at his expense. But she showed no inclination to either help or hinder him; she simply watched, as though from a great distance. Kenlin sometimes wondered if she knew that, just as she was watching Kenlin's movements, he was studying hers.

And her movements were, as Klanjad had said, flawless. Kenlin had noted her graceful, loping gait early in their journey, but only now did he recognize the depth of her control. There was never a locked joint, rigid stop, or heavy landing. Like a cat or a dancer, she flowed from each posture into the next; and even when a movement was sudden, it still seemed tapered and clean. Given that she was naturally unable to use magic and no amount of study could change that, her dedication to moving like a magician was baffling. And humbling.

So Kenlin breathed deep, nodded humbly, and determined to improve.

As their journey continued, their progress was swift, but the mountains were vast. On the fourth day from the argument, Klanjad's corrections began to come more slowly, and still the road stretched on. On the sixth day, hours passed without a word, neither correction nor conversation, and *still* the road stretched on. Kenlin knew, of course, where they were going—a lakeside city north of the mountains called Likrásk—and that Ranja had estimated it would take them at least eight days yet to reach it. Nevertheless, having lived his entire life in a single valley system, the sheer magnitude of the world continued to amaze him.

The Flunjat River valley—named, like so much else, after the Misk clan that once dominated the region—meandered north by northeast for nearly twenty leagues from its outlet before taking an abrupt turn to the east. Here the river was less meandering, the valley narrower, and the hamlets even more scarce for ten more leagues while the river dwindled to an exuberant stream. Finally, on the eighth day since they had entered the Flunjat River valley, they left the river and began the long and arduous climb to Skilé Pass, a high saddle that, according to Klanjad, was the last pass before they left the mountains.

The idea that they were reaching a change in their journey excited Kenlin; and, though he was unable to penetrate Ranja's taciturnity, he assumed it excited her as well. Not Klanjad. The higher they climbed, the darker and colder he became. By the time they reached the pass, he was so broody as to be nearly oblivious, and Kenlin had to ask Ranja directly in order to learn that the river in the valley before them was called the Naj and would, eventually, lead them to Likrásk.

Curiously, however, the road did not immediately descend from the pass to join the river. Instead, it followed a high shoulder of the mountains for a few leagues, refusing to descend until the geography absolutely forced it to. Klanjad drove the pace through this area, pushing them to cross the pass and continue along the road well into the night. When at last he allowed them to stop, he ordered Ranja to take the first watch and Kenlin the second, while he himself would take the third. This was so unusual that, despite their recently chilled relationship, Ranja asked Kenlin a favor when she woke him for his watch: "When you wake up Father, wake me up too. I want to see where he goes."

It was a small favor to ask, and Kenlin was just as curious as she was; so, when the time came for his watch to end and Klanjad's to begin, he surreptitiously shook Ranja's shoulder on his way back to his bedroll. They waited for many minutes, pretending to sleep while Klanjad kept watch, occasionally looking at the sky. Kenlin had almost decided that nothing would happen after all when, at last, Klanjad stood, took a small torch from the fire, and left.

A moment later, he was out of sight; and a moment after that, both Kenlin and Ranja had risen to follow. Ranja picked up another burning stick from the fire, but Kenlin shook his head and pointed to himself. *He'll see us for certain if we take light, but we don't need it; I can follow his trail without it.* She frowned, looking very skeptical, but nevertheless she smothered her torch and allowed Kenlin to lead them into the darkness.

It was early, early morning now, heralded by not so much a lightening of the sky as a weakening of the stars. The forest was dense, but life as a hunter had taught Kenlin to move stealthily through such terrain. Ranja, despite her best efforts, had not as much relevant experience. As she crunched through yet another shrub, Kenlin smiled broadly into the darkness. *Well, I've finally found something I do better than she does.*

But despite her crunching, they still proceeded quietly enough to avoid alarming Klanjad. Now and again, Kenlin would catch a glimpse of the older Jazei's torch, or hear him forcing his way through the undergrowth ahead. In this way, they continued for the better part of an hour as the black sky slowly gave way to a deep, majestic blue. Increasingly, they had to scramble over fallen trees, as might have been knocked down by a great storm or avalanche.

Then a clearing opened up before them, across which Klanjad's torch had stopped moving. Kenlin strained his eyes, trying to see what the older Jazei had stopped for, but the darkness was too deep for him to see anything other than the light of the torch itself. *If I could get closer...* Tentatively, he stepped out into the clearing, keeping his shoulders below the height of the grass, moving soundlessly on his hands and feet. Then he gave an involuntary *hiss* and pulled his hand back as something cold and sharp cut into his finger.

"Shhh!" Ranja hissed angrily, oblivious to the irony.

A harsh chuckle came from nearby. "Too late for that." From the shadowy grasses—nowhere near the torch ahead, which must have been wedged upright somehow—Klanjad rose, a silhouette in the gloom. "Understandable," he said, a note of disappointed criticism in his voice. "Unwise, and very poorly executed—but understandable."

"You weren't exactly subtle, Father," said Ranja with only a hint of startled flutter in her voice. "What did you expect us to do?"

"This. Mind yourself on the ground there, Kenlin," he added as Kenlin rustled carefully through the grass looking for what had cut him. "There are many old blades here, and not all will have rusted away."

Ranja caught her breath suddenly; and a moment later, Kenlin had put it together as well. "This, then... Here? I thought it would be north, further along the road."

"No, this was the place. We would have fought them nearer the descent if we had had time, but... Come, the light is growing. Come to the clifftop."

A paler blue was now filling the sky, and the deep blue, displaced, had fallen upon the ground. Klanjad extinguished the torch and guided them by the growing half-light, leading them around the densest parts of the woods until, at last, they arrived at the edge of a cliff.

A silence, almost reverence, gripped Kenlin and Ranja as they waited for Klanjad to speak. At length, he said quietly, "This is where that day began for me. I stood here, and Jlak stood there—about where you're standing, Ranja—and we spoke of the day we thought would come."

After a brief silence, Kenlin asked, "Jlak was a friend?"

"He *is* a friend. He survived that battle—one of the few—and found me after the Droál had departed. You'll meet him soon enough; he lives in Likrásk now."

"Ah, that's who we're going to meet, yes? I had wondered why we were going to a city when we've been so carefully avoiding every village and hamlet for the past half-moon."

The light was now sufficient that Kenlin could see Klanjad shrug. "We are Jazeiz. Everyone we talk to will remember our faces, our hair, our eyes. And they will tell all their friends, who will tell their friends; and eventually, somebody's friend's friend will be put to question."

"And yet, now we're going to a city?"

"It's a risk, I'll grant you. We'll disguise our hair and try to remain inconspicuous, but it's a risk nonetheless. But in this case, I think it's a risk we'll have to take. Once we reach the prairie, we'll no longer be able to avoid at least *some* human contact unless we shun the roads altogether; so sooner or later, Skralade will know that we're in the area. If we go to Likrásk, he's almost certain to find out we're there within a few days. But if we can purchase horses and depart quickly... And I doubt Skralade will be able to put together an ambush on a moment's notice anyway: Droál presence in the southeast is still very limited. That may have changed, of course, over the past few moons; but if it has, or if they've made any other significant movements that I need to know about, Jlak can tell me."

"I see. Skralade... That's that Misk, right? Your nemesis, or some such?"

"*Nemesis.* How dramatic. Your word or Ranja's?"

"Ranja's."

"Hey!"

"I thought as much. It's dramatic, but it's actually not far from the truth. Skralade and I have 'known' each other for a very long time. We just can't seem to be rid of each other, though not for lack of trying."

"Right." *Right.* "He's the one who led the ambush. He's the one who killed—"

"He's killed quite a lot of people, Kenlin," Klanjad said abruptly, snapping Kenlin back from the sudden darkness in his voice. "Your friends were not special in that regard; such is the nature of war. I'll grant you, though, that small-scale ambushes in the mountains are not usually Skralade's style. He must have had intelligence of my journey and wanted to be there personally to see me die. It's rather flattering."

"And a little intriguing," Ranja interjected. "I wonder what the Droál have been doing this past season such that they could spare Skralade for an entire moon or two."

"A good point," Klanjad agreed. "Presumably the impasse over Kilgáire still holds, so perhaps they've just decided to consolidate their strength for a while. They'd certainly be unwise to attempt any campaigns without Skralade's support and guidance."

Ranja nodded as though this was obvious. *Interesting.* "I didn't realize this Skralade was so important. He's a great leader of the Droál, then?"

Klanjad chuckled. "Well, strictly speaking he's a great leader of Misks, not Droál. Skralade is the chieftain of Clan Eyjazinka, with whom the Droál are allied. The Droál could never have achieved their current success without Eyjazinka's assistance, and they owe many of their greatest military accomplishments to Skralade himself. So I suppose, in a practical sense, he *is* a great leader of Droál. In any sense, he is a great enemy of Jranjana, and of the Jazeiz."

"*Hmm.* A pity, then, that I didn't aim just a little higher."

Klanjad seemed momentarily confused, then laughed. "That's right, you *did* shoot him, didn't you! You should feel honored: few have drawn Skralade's blood and lived to tell of it. But even if you had shot him in the neck, or somewhere similar, he still would have survived. I smashed his knee in combat once, and he was still able to Vanish away despite the pain."

Yes, I remember. "That's what he did after I shot him, yes? Vanish? Is that some sort of Misk magic?"

"Correct and correct. This is not the time for details, but the magic of Misks is to disappear from one location and reappear in another. The technique is called *Vanishing*, for obvious reasons. Skralade is an exceptionally talented magician for a Misk; I've seen him Vanish through pain, through distraction, and even multiple times in rapid succession, all at a moment's notice. It makes him very dangerous to fight and almost impossible to kill."

"On the whole," said Ranja drily, "he's someone worth avoiding."

Klanjad nodded. "Such truth. I don't know what sorts of spies the Droál have in the region. Jlak, hopefully, will be able to give me better intelligence of that; but in the meantime we must assume that, sooner or later, our presence will be noticed, and we must do everything we can to postpone and prepare. Kenlin, you and I must keep our hair covered, and we must all try to keep our green eyes lowered. I'll buy cloaks, and perhaps hats, as we approach the city, and we'll do what we can to conceal or disguise our weapons. We'll enter the city by the west gate instead of the south, then proceed directly to Jlak's home. With any luck, we'll escape the notice of whatever spies are present for at least a few days, and we'll be riding north by the time they realize we were there."

By this time, the stars had all but vanished from the bluing sky, and the orange light in the east, though still pre-dawn, was strong and clear. Kenlin, who had seen many sunrises from mountaintops, knew the sun itself was still nearly half an hour away. Ranja, who had seen fewer, kept looking expectantly at the horizon, searching for the first glimmer of fire. But as the moment approached, Klanjad suddenly seemed eager to be gone. "Come, let's return to camp, eat, and be on our way. We still have many leagues to travel before we are out of the mountains."

Ranja frowned, disappointed, but Kenlin voiced his surprise. "Go now? Did you not bring us here to see the dawn?"

Klanjad had already turned away; but, after a pause, he said over his shoulder, "I came here again to see the morning, but not the dawn. I have never seen a sunrise from this point, nor do I want to. This place... It is a place of sadness, and loss, and tragedy, and beauty; but I never want to remember it as a place of light."

CHAPTER XII:

"And inevitably," Ranja muttered, wrinkling her nose, "there *must* be an east wind as we approach from the west, mustn't there?"

Klanjad's face was blank, but his voice carried a note of stoicism. "Try to be at peace with it; it will only get worse when we actually enter the city."

"It smells like every fish I've ever gutted, all at the same time," said Kenlin, sniffing the air in revolted fascination. "So, Likrásk is a fishing town, yes?"

"They do quite a lot of fishing," Klanjad confirmed. "Ralua Lake is the largest lake in Jranjana, save for Gadan itself, and there are many delicacies that can only be caught here. Years ago, fine salts from Flunjat City were brought here by the cartload to cure fish for shipment all over eastern Jranjana. But now that the salt mines lie abandoned, and luxuries like imported fish are ever more dearly bought... Well, we shall see what has become of the city."

It was the morning of the fourth day since their clifftop conversation in the mountains. From there, the road had brought them down the cliffs, into the forest, across the Naj River, then alongside it for several leagues until the forests began to thin among the foothills of the mountains. As Klanjad had predicted, this had proved a much more populous region, and soon they could hardly walk for half an hour without encountering either a homestead or another traveler.

From a peddler, Klanjad had bought three cloaks and two cloth hats, under which the Jazeiz concealed themselves as best they could. Apart from this trade, however, they had kept to themselves on the road and avoided conversation with anyone they encountered. In this manner, they had progressed without incident from mountains to forested foothills, and finally to the undulating grasslands surrounding the surprisingly pungent city of Likrásk.

And now, as they approached the city itself, Klanjad became more tense and wary by the moment, and Ranja followed his lead. Though they kept their heads slightly bowed to hide their emerald eyes, they were watchful of everyone, every face, every cloak, every pair of shoes that they encountered on the road. Kenlin, too, was trying to remain inconspicuous, for he fully understood the seriousness of their situation; and yet, glancing at his uncle and cousin, he struggled not to also find the humor. *Do they expect to see someone they know? Or do they think to identify a spy by the expression on his face? But perhaps I shouldn't be so quick to poke fun; after all, they know far more of such things than I.* For a moment, he considered whether he, too, should bow his head and surreptitiously glower at passersby, if only for consistency's sake, but that seemed a little too frivolous for the occasion.

So instead he attended to their surroundings, for there was much to see as they approached the city. Kenlin had assumed that, like the ruins of Natzut, the city of Likrásk would be entirely encircled by a sturdy stone wall, but it was not so. Well before they had reached the walls, the roadside became cluttered with an undisciplined sprawl of ramshackle dwellings, many of which were little more than scrap-wood sheds. This slum stretched for nearly a quarter-league outside the west gate of Likrásk; and within that area, the city's overwhelming fish smell was mixed with the stink of masses and masses of people. *So many! I never really understood how small Irnaji was until now, though Irnaji was never so squalid. But then, why do I think that? Irnaji was a village of hovels, no better constructed than the least of the shanties I see here. Ah, but Irnaji was never so clustered, and never so coarse; and we had hides, and colors, and murals in crude paints, and at least a little dignity, and at least a little pride. These people...*

Even the city's fortifications, when the travelers finally reached them, seemed degenerate. Though the defenses of Natzut had been smashed ever since Kenlin could remember, even their ruins yet showed how mighty they had been. But these walls, though intact, stood in such an obvious state of neglect that they seemed even weaker than ruins. The very guards at the gate did more to symbolize apathy than to defend their city. Their helmets lay in the dirt, and their spears leaned against the stonework; and while traffic passed unnoticed to and from the city, the guards focused all their watchfulness on a cup of dice.

"Don't, Father," said Ranja quietly. Kenlin glanced at his uncle; the older Jazei was glaring at the oblivious guards as though their mere existence offended his military sensibilities. "Don't," Ranja repeated. "We shouldn't attract attention."

"Perhaps they have information," Klanjad growled, his stare still fixed on the guards. "They might could tell us if they've spotted Droál hereabouts."

Kenlin very much doubted that information was Klanjad's real interest in these guards, so he was relieved when Ranja replied, "They don't look like they've done much spotting recently. And anyway, even if they had information, it's too late for us to use it. Our dice are cast." Klanjad grunted a reluctant consent, and they passed through the gate without stopping.

Inside the walls, the city looked just as neglected and decrepit as it had on the outside. The buildings were of wood that the damp air had turned a murky grey. Dull green moss gathered on the shingle and thatch of the roofs. Though the construction here was better and taller than it had been beyond the walls, the two-storey dwellings were clustered more tightly than ever. Each building seemed to lean against the others as if it were too weary to stand on its own, and without the support of its neighbors it might accidentally stumble into one of the narrow alleyways that wound around it. Kenlin thought they looked like a crowd of very old men leaning on one another, waiting to collapse. "What a dejected city," he said to no one.

Ranja nodded, seemingly without thinking. Klanjad smiled sadly and bitterly. "This is what I expected to see here, the gentlest of the effects of the Droál invasion: this is simple poverty. The same malady has taken hold of cities throughout Jranjana, especially in the west where the Droál actually hold dominion. Here you see poverty distilled, without anything to confuse the image; but in the west, it is mixed with the fear, oppression, slaughter… This, here, is the beginning. In the west is the middle. And the final gift of the Droál is Natzut: massacre and fire."

Natzut. Behind Kenlin's eyes, memories of the ruined city formed into an image. *I have seen these streets, or others very like them, somewhere in Natzut. There was stone there, not wood and dirt; and there was clear air, not like the stink and filth here. But apart from these, the two places might be the same.* And for a moment, he saw them thus. His mind's eye remade the world around him in stone, cleared the air, and filled this would-be Natzut with such people as he saw before him. Shuffling men who watched their feet, weary women with hunched shoulders, shy girls who averted their eyes, and boys who peered keenly out of dirty faces… *These people are the skeletons I saw whilst playing with Adaned—with Adanedi and the others as children. That boy there, who watches us now with such curiosity: I found your bones, boy, in the overgrown wreckage of a smithy in the second circle of Natzut. I never thought of it before, but who were you, boy? Before you burned?* And with that, the scene in his mind warped into a consuming fire. Blasting heat befouled the imaginary mountain air as the inferno burned off the fantasy, charring away the stone and leaving only the wood standing, while the people in the streets continued to shuffle about, oblivious. In a moment all was gone and Kenlin stood again in Likrásk, but he was no longer certain that he had ever really stood in Natzut.

They walked on. Klanjad led them only a little way down the main road, ducking into an alley within a few hundred paces of the gates. But the alley was only a hundred paces or so long, and soon put them onto another large street. They stayed on this new street only very briefly before Klanjad led them into a second alley, which took them back to the first large street. *What is he doing? Is he lost, or...? Ah, he looks back as we enter the alleys. He is ensuring that we are not being followed.*

Kenlin could not imagine how Klanjad managed to keep his bearings—they never followed a large road for long, and each dirty alley looked very much like the next—but they never seemed to lose their winding way. After nearly half an hour, they found themselves on a broad street in what was clearly a more affluent district. Though the buildings here still looked bland and geriatric, they were better constructed and had space between them. In front of each house, a wrought-iron fence imprisoned a small plot of tangled, dying bushes and flowers. "Why do they keep their dead plants in the front?" Kenlin asked.

Ranja stifled a giggle, but did not deign to reply. Klanjad said, "It's another sign of the times. People take great pride in their houses, and in prosperous days these gardens are well-tended and beautiful; but now they are ruined, and no one even has the time or will to pull them up."

"That's rather poignant of you, Father," Ranja commented with a little smile.

Klanjad shrugged. "If there's a chance you'll face danger in a city, it's worth noting what sort of city it is and what kinds of people inhabit it. People write their own stories on the world around them; learn to read the world and you can read the stories. The stories here are all of weariness and misery."

They continued on this road for only a short while before Klanjad turned aside, stepped through one of the dead gardens, and knocked on a door. Kenlin looked at the little sign that hung over the doorway: *Architect.*

The first knock went unanswered. Klanjad knocked again, louder. After a moment, the door opened to reveal a boy of perhaps thirteen years. "Can I help you, sirs?" said the boy with practiced politeness.

Kenlin was a little taken aback—*Does Jlak have a son?*—and Klanjad seemed similarly confused. "Is Jlak within?" he asked.

The youth was clearly prepared for this question and answered instantly, "Master Jlak is busy in his drawing room in the afternoons," the boy said, and the word *master* clarified everything to Kenlin: *He's an apprentice.* The boy continued, "But I can give him a message for you, and he'll be happy to see you tomorrow morning."

Klanjad paused at this, regarding the boy thoughtfully. Then he said, "Go tell your master that a former soldier is here to see him. And tell him now; neither he nor I will wait for the morning."

The boy hesitated, looked at each of them in turn, his eyes lingering on their faces. Kenlin met his gaze without favor. *I don't like his curiosity; we are too much at risk here. I don't like him thinking so much about us.*

Oh, don't be silly; the boy's just compiling a description to relay to his master.

And might that be Jlak, or some other master?

Enough. If Klanjad does not have these concerns, then neither should I. And if he does, then he will also know what to do. But all the same, as the boy finally acquiesced and disappeared behind the door, Kenlin felt uneasy. Klanjad's expression was difficult to interpret, but Ranja seemed to share Kenlin's discomfort: "Would the Droál assign a spy to watch Jlak?"

"They might," Klanjad said uncertainly. "It's hardly common knowledge in Likrásk, but neither is it a secret, that Jlak once served in Natzut's army, so they might spy on him in the hopes of catching me. If Jlak were brought to Skralade's attention—which I doubt would happen, but it's possible—

then I'm certain Skralade would *insist* on having him watched. But even then, they would post Khardalesh nearby to watch; I looked for that, but I saw no one. But an apprentice as a spy? I haven't seen it before, but…"

"…but that might be a reason for them to try it," Kenlin pointed out.

Klanjad frowned at him. "I'll thank you to finish your own sentences, if you please. We won't let the boy leave the house until Jlak has confirmed that he's trustworthy. If he is, then we have nothing to worry about."

Kenlin asked, "And if he isn't?"

To that, he received no answer.

Kenlin was on the brink of repeating the question—a bit louder—when the door opened again, this time wide enough to admit them. Standing inside the doorway was the most pathetic-looking weasel of a man that Kenlin had ever seen. He stood no taller than his apprentice and had spindly arms and legs, a small and hairless head, large brown eyes, and an off-balance posture; but the smile with which he greeted Klanjad was the smile of a real friend. "My lord," he said, bowing his head, "it has been—*hmm*—far too long."

Klanjad's face lit with a smile as warm as the one he received. "Far too long," he echoed. Then he waved his hand as Jlak reached for his kirsk. "No formalities, Jlak, or at the very least not here. You know I've never cared for such things, and at any rate your knees do not look as though they could survive much bending."

"Such truth!" said Jlak, with a sort of cheery ruefulness. "The years steal away what we don't watch carefully. *Hmm*— but here is Lady Ranja! Welcome, welcome, my lady, I— *em*—apologize that I do not greet you properly. And here is one that I do not know," he said, looking at Kenlin curiously, almost as though he thought he recognized something in him. Then he waved his hand—a quick, twitchy sort of flail—and said, "But, *ah*, we will make full introductions in a moment. Please won't you all follow me?"

Throughout this effusion of pleasantries, Jlak had been joyfully beckoning the Jazeiz through the doorway into his home. They now stood, with Jlak and his apprentice, in the foyer—a spacious and tasteful room, but somewhat dim and very still—as Jlak began to lead them further into the house. Klanjad did not move. Evidently Jlak understood, for he immediately stopped and looked expectantly at Klanjad, who said, "I see you've found yourself an apprentice."

Comprehension flooded Jlak's face, but he immediately covered it with a smile and said, "Indeed I have, and now I must apologize for failing to introduce him. This is Jiaján. *Hmm*, he's a diligent lad, and excellent with charcoal, though I can't always be entirely certain what—*ah*—designs he has in his head. He's a good student too—*em*—always looking for new insights among the things I've filed away; but it's about this age, I think, when boys begin to seek—*hmm*—deeper meaning in the world, if you understand me."

All three of the Jazeiz understood perfectly. Klanjad glanced at Ranja, who acknowledged with a quick nod. He then looked to Kenlin, who met his gaze blankly. *What is our plan here? I have no idea what you're wanting me to do.*

Jlak continued, "I think, however, that I shall require the boy's services late into tonight. I'm, *ah*, sorry Jiaján; I shall give you an extra evening free sometime when we are not so busy. But tonight, I would like you to stay in; we must entertain our guests."

Jiaján opened his mouth, then shut it again with a snap, as though to cut off the escape of an unconsidered response. After a brief pause, he said, "Of course, master. But if you please, some people—my friends, I mean—will be gathering in Lakeside tonight, and I told them I'd be there too, and they will not know what's become of me. I'll not be longer than an hour; may I go to tell them what's happened?"

Jlak frowned, "In Lakeside? You—*hmm*—had not mentioned this before now. And don't your friends live in Mongly?" As he said it, he met Klanjad's eye for a moment.

Klanjad nodded slowly, then looked again toward Ranja; she flexed her fingers. *What are they going to do?*

Jiaján, who seemed oblivious all this, still pleaded with Jlak: "It's only a little gathering, master; I didn't think to mention it, as you've never *asked* me to tell you before. Please, master, it won't take lon—*gah!*"

He got no further, for without warning Ranja had hooked her right arm around his neck from behind, her elbow just below his chin, and with her left hand she pushed his head forward, cutting off the blood flow through his neck. Kenlin started, felt his feet twitch forward and a cry of protest rise in his throat, but he caught himself. *And what would you do? They are strong, they understand. Learn!* So he watched as the boy put up a surprisingly furious fight for a few seconds, then went limp.

As she lowered the body to the floor, Jlak told Ranja, "*Ahem*, very neatly done, my lady," like she had just recited a lovely poem.

Kenlin was very actively controlling himself. "Is he dead?" he asked, trying not to shout.

Jlak smiled, as though he found Kenlin's question naïve or charming. Ranja simply shook her head. Klanjad answered, "He is merely unconscious. Help Ranja bind him."

Still tense, Kenlin asked, "He is a spy, then, yes? We know that now?"

Klanjad shrugged. "Well enough for me."

Kenlin looked to Jlak, who elaborated hesitantly, "I am not sure, but—*um*—I do not think it worth the risk to yourselves to let him leave the house. I must credit Lord Klanjad for reminding—*hem*—me to be suspicious; my old disciplines grow weak through disuse, it seems. The boy will remain bound here until you are gone, after which I will decide what is to be done with him."

That was not quite the reply Kenlin had hoped for, but there was nothing for him to say about it. He knelt down to help Ranja bind the boy; she waved him away and continued the task herself.

Klanjad asked Jlak, "How long have you had this apprentice? Is he new as of the last few moons?"

"*Hmm*—not at all," said Jlak, shaking his head. "He has been my apprentice these two years, so I, *em*, can't imagine that he's *entirely* theirs. But about a moon ago, I noticed that he started to take a much greater interest in my clients, studying their, *ah*, faces and asking me questions about them. Others in the guild have told me of similar behavior from their apprentices. I thought little of it at the time, but I now suppose that someone—*hmm*—went about and bribed the city's boys to bring them information."

"That would be many eyes and ears for a rather small price," commented Ranja as she finished binding Jiaján's wrists. "It would not take much coin to buy information off of bored youths."

"Many, many eyes and ears," Jlak agreed. "Which means—*ah*—that they probably already know that green-eyed folk have entered Likrásk. Though perhaps we have prevented them from knowing precisely where you have gone."

Klanjad chuckled wryly and said, as though to himself, "Well struck, Skralade. Well, if that's to be the way of it... Ranja, watch the street and tell me if anything alarms you. Kenlin, put that boy somewhere and block the door. Jlak, you and I shall go to the sitting room; there, we shall sit."

Chapter XIII:

After locking the bound and unconscious Jiaján in one of the house's bedrooms, Kenlin followed Klanjad's and Jlak's voices to the parlor, where the two sat in conversation. As he entered the room, Jlak turned and looked up at him so strangely—like a man seeing the ghost of a dearly-beloved father—that Kenlin immediately tensed and stopped. Jlak stood and took a few quick steps forward, his eyes still locked on Kenlin's face. Then, overcome, he knelt, drew his kirsk dagger, and proffered it grip-first to Kenlin.

Kenlin looked at the kirsk, then at Jlak, then at Klanjad. "I seem to be missing some context," he said.

"Sire, forgive me for not recognizing you," Jlak said, his head still bowed and a torrent of emotions running through his voice. "Now—*hmm*—that I look, I see that you are your father's son; but I did not think, *ah*, I had never allowed myself to believe you might yet live, sire."

That he was technically the reigning king of Natzut had, of course, occurred to Kenlin, and Ranja had even teased him briefly with the title of *majesty*. However, meeting someone who not only greeted him as a king, but actually paid him unsolicited homage on that account, was wholly unexpected. It felt weird and invasive, as though someone had sneaked up on him and tried, without permission, to place a crown on his head.

Noticing Kenlin's awkward hesitancy, Klanjad chided, "Touch the pommel, Kenlin—the peace greeting, remember."

Kenlin did so, then took the old architect by the elbow and helped him to his feet. As he rose, Jlak said shakily, "Your father—*hem*—was a great Jazei, and I was proud to call him my king. Would that his reign had been longer, and that he had lived, *ah*, to see you as you are."

"That...would have been something," Kenlin managed, for lack of anything worthwhile to say. It was obvious that their meeting was profoundly meaningful for Jlak, and for his sake Kenlin wished to say something kind. But for himself, the long-suffering loyalty of a faithful retainer was just bizarre, and he had no idea how or whether to accept it.

Naturally, Klanjad felt compelled to exacerbate the awkwardness. "Yes, that would, indeed, have been something," he agreed, deadpan, as Kenlin and Jlak seated themselves. Then, "So, you secured the apprentice somewhere?"

Kenlin nodded. "I put him in a bedroom, up the stairs and to the left. The key was in the door, so I locked him in."

Klanjad frowned. "Does the room have windows? Could he throw himself out of one?"

"He's a tied-up boy, Klanjad."

"That is *not* what I asked."

As Kenlin wavered, unsure whether this question was thorough or simply insane, Jlak offered, "I doubt the boy would be able to—*em*—escape that way, my lord. The window in that room is small, leaded, and high off the floor; *um*, it is enough for a little light, but not for egress."

Klanjad accepted this answer with a perfunctory grunt and a dissatisfied glance at Kenlin. Turning to Jlak, he said, "Back to the topic at hand. You were telling me what you've heard of Droál in the region."

"In the region," repeated Jlak, nodding accommodatingly. "*Hmm*. It is difficult to be sure, my lord, that they are doing anything, *ah*, differently now than at any other time. They maintain, as always, a quiet presence— sightings here and there, a negligible religious following, *hmm*, and such—but I have heard little to indicate any abnormal activity."

"Yet you suspect that they've bribed the city's youths to bring them information," Klanjad observed. "That can't be typical."

"It is not," agreed Jlak, "but only since your arrival have I—*em*—had any reason to suspect their hand in that. Which is a statement in itself, I suppose: life in Likrásk remains so—*hmm*—unaffected that even I have grown unsuspicious. That is what they wish, I think. Wholly absorbed by trivial local affairs, obsessed, *ah*, with our own impoverished misery, we—the southeast, from here to the hills north of Slionte—remain almost entirely uninvolved. Inert."

In his mind, Kenlin heard an echo of his own voice: *not my disaster.*

Klanjad asked incredulously, "So then, nothing important has changed? You've heard of no garrisons, no Unnatilz in the area, no sightings of Misks...?"

Jlak's mouth betrayed no smile, but his eyes twinkled knowingly. "Is, *um*, my lord disappointed to hear that his enemies have not prepared him a party?"

The unexpected cheekiness made Kenlin laugh aloud, and even Klanjad chuckled. "Not disappointed," he said after a moment. "More...skeptical, I suppose. I find it hard to believe that Skralade could know I was in the southeast, but not leave more to watch for me than a few idle boys."

"Ah, be not affronted, my lord," Jlak replied, his mirth succumbing to the seriousness of the situation. "*Hmm*—I have heard nothing to convince me that the Droál have increased their presence in the area, but that does not mean that they should be disregarded. If the city's urchins *are* working for them, then they will know, *ah*, very soon that the Jazeiz have entered the city. And when they do, such forces as they have to hand are sure to seek you out."

"What sorts of forces might we expect?"

Jlak considered for a moment. "This is—*em*—naught but speculation, as I have so little information about the Droál in the area; but if they felt the need to fight you, I would expect them to send mercenaries. We know them to be abundantly funded, and the use of locally-recruited, *hmm*, 'talent' would allow them to mobilize a significant force without paying the costs, in currency and secrecy, to maintain it."

"Hardly worth the trouble, at that point," Klanjad remarked. "Paying human mercenaries to kill me is a poor investment, and Skralade knows better. If that's the only force he has in the area, he won't even bother to attack us; he'll just try to keep track of us until he can set up an ambush that at least has a chance of succeeding."

Kenlin frowned slightly. "I thought Misks could disappear and reappear wherever they wanted. If that's true, why wouldn't Skralade just bring an army of Misks to attack us as soon as he knows where we are?"

Initially, Jlak seemed a little worried by that prospect, but Klanjad said, "I think we needn't worry about that. The specifics are more complicated than this, but as a rule Misks can only Vanish to places they have been before. So, if you wanted to ambush someone by Vanishing a platoon of Misks to attack them, then every Misk in that platoon would need to already have been to the site of the ambush. I very much doubt Skralade has a platoon of Misks who have already been to Likrásk." Klanjad sighed, then nodded as though acquiescing to his own circumspection. "Nevertheless, even a few Misks can pose a deadly threat, especially if accompanied by a handful of mercenaries. It is never safe to underestimate your enemy, especially if your enemy is Skralade. We should leave as soon as possible and continue northward. Jlak, what is the latest news from Ñaj-Gadan?"

Jlak shook his head and shrugged. "It has been many moons—perhaps, *em*, even seasons—since new tidings arrived from the north. As far as I know, the front still lies over Kilgáire, and—*hmm*—neither side seems to be preparing any campaigns to cross the wasteland. The Commune, I think, is focusing on defense for the time being, fortifying their positions and rebuilding their armies."

"Excellent!" Klanjad exclaimed, sounding relieved. "That was their plan when I left them three moons ago, but you can never be sure with them. Jendraski still wants to try to liberate (his word) Jiánse again; and a moon before that, the Viarlin delegation was babbling about trying for peace!"

At this moment, the door opened abruptly and Ranja stepped into the room. Jlak immediately rose, presumably to offer her a formal greeting, but the urgency in her manner forestalled him. She glanced only briefly at the other two in the room before addressing her father: "There are Khardalesh in the streets."

The atmosphere in the room changed instantly. "What? Outside, here?" Klanjad asked in alarm.

Ranja nodded. "Even since we've arrived, I believe I've seen two, and there might have been more that I couldn't identify. One was walking with a child, who I suspect was trying to spot us for him. They didn't seem to take particular note of this house, at least not yet. But they certainly know we're in the city, and I think they know, to within a few streets, where we actually are."

"That," said Klanjad, looking very grave, "is troubling."

Kenlin knew this was not the time for such questions, but he couldn't help himself. "What are Khardalesh? I've heard you mention them before, but——"

"They're spies," Ranja cut him off brusquely without looking at him. "They're an order—or a specialization, if you like—of Droál who live among us in disguise and perform a variety of clandestine functions."

"Will they attack us?"

Ranja merely shook her head. After a moment, Klanjad glanced at her and, seeing that she would not elaborate, did so himself. "Khardalesh fight rarely—and poorly, for they do not train for it. On their own, Khardalesh are not much of a threat, but they are almost never on their own. And for there to be *several* of them, and so actively prepared that they're *already* out in the streets looking for us..."

Ranja said quietly, "He is here, Father. Skralade has something prepared for us."

He is here... Skralade, the Misk, the seventh ambusher... Surprised at himself, Kenlin shook away this sudden reverie.

Klanjad looked grim. "Yes, I think we must assume it's him; any lesser assumption might set us up for a nasty surprise. We have to leave, as soon as possible. Ranja, do you think we could avoid notice if we left, in disguise, right now?"

Ranja quirked an eyebrow skeptically. "I doubt it. As they're already in the streets, walking out would be a game of chance, and there's little we could do to skew the odds in our favor. If we want any real hope of escaping undetected, we should wait for nightfall."

With a weak but valiant attempt at a smile, Jlak said, "Will my lords at least—*hmm*—be staying for dinner?"

Klanjad met his friends eye, and once again Kenlin caught a glimpse of that surprising warmth that he had only seen from Klanjad on a few occasions. He said gently, "Not this time, Jlak. With any luck, our departure tonight will be uneventful; but if we're unlucky, then I'd prefer not to run for my life with a hearty meal in my stomach. We'll take some bread and water before we go, but there won't be time for us to digest a proper meal before we must leave you."

"Leave him?" Kenlin blurted out in surprise. "Why are we leaving him? Won't he be coming with us?"

Jlak smiled politely, as though he appreciated the sentiment but thought it a bit naïve. "I have—*hmm*—never been a fighting man, sire. In your father's army, I oversaw the building of temporary barracks, bulwarks, and fortifications, but I stayed far from the fray. There is, *um*, very little that I could contribute to your escape."

Kenlin frowned. *Is he intentionally missing my point, or is he really not thinking of himself at all?* "So your plan is to remain here instead, yes? To stay in a house that we visited, in an area that the Droál know we went? If this Skralade is as clever as I've heard, then he must know that we weighed the risks before coming to the city; so will he not ask himself why

we took the chance? Who we came to see? And if anyone—
anyone—knows that you were once a soldier of Natzut, will
not Skralade's investigation inevitably lead him to you?"

As he had said this, a hint of an approving grin had
appeared on Ranja's face, but she turned away before Kenlin
could be sure he'd seen it. Klanjad's face, however, had broken
into a broad smile, and he laughed, "And he even *explains*
himself with questions, always another question! You just
might live long enough to become a fine Jazei, boy!"

Jlak was grinning too. "I see you've learned quickly, sire,
to play our—*ah*—dangerous game." Then he turned to
Klanjad. "My lord, it seems my, *em*, prospects here are
somewhat diminished of late. It has been many, many years;
but may I have permission, lord, to march with you once
more?"

. . .

There was much to do, but there was far too much time
in which to do it: night comes slowly to the flatlands. They
meticulously planned their escape, for there was still light.
Then they scoured the house and collected anything of value,
and there was still light. Then they slept a little, then they
talked a little, then they ate a little, and *still* there was light
outside. *What is prolonging this never-ending day? Is it
because there are no mountains to narrow the sky? Or is it just
my fancy, born of impatience for nightfall?*

They ran out of tasks and conversation long before they
ran out of daylight. Ranja might have helped pass the time
with a story, but she was in no mood to tell one and Kenlin
was unwilling to ask her. Eventually, they each found their
own ways to keep their hands busy. Klanjad sharpened,
cleaned, and oiled his sword, over and over. Ranja fiddled with
the hafting of her glaive, or restlessly wandered from room to
room. Jlak checked and rechecked every drawing and
document in his study, occasionally adding one to his pack or

consigning it to the fireplace. Kenlin pulled out all his arrows, arranged them on the floor, and began sorting them according to...

This one's a little short; that one's a little long; this arrowhead is off-center, I'd better fix that; warped shaft; split nock; and who did this awful, crooked fletching? This isn't my work, this arrow must have been Graddij's.

These aren't my arrows. Ranja collected these, she must have scavenged them from the bottom of the landslide. From among those who made them.

Gently, he placed Graddij's arrow on the floor next to the others. They all lay neatly here: so straight, so even, so clean. Unbroken. Kenlin did not tense or tighten—that time had passed—but he felt a heavy weight settle upon him: heavy but precipitous, like an alpine snowbank ready, at any moment, to avalanche.

Another thought struck him: *With whose arrow did I shoot the Misk, Skralade, at the ambush by the river?* But he couldn't be sure which it might have been, or whether that arrow was even among these. *Ah, but they said Skralade is here tonight. I suppose we will try to avoid him if we can. If we can't, though, then whose arrow...?* He looked over the arrangement before him and, after a moment, selected one. This arrow was flawlessly crafted, long and sturdy and balanced and true. *This is one of mine.* Idly, he ran his thumb along the stone arrowhead's rough, razor-sharp edge; and then he pressed down hard.

At the sound of the parlor door opening, all three Jazeiz looked up abruptly. Jlak leaned in: "*Hmm*—my lords, it is time." The Jazeiz stood, gathered their belongings, then joined him in the hallway.

With just a hint of a grin, Klanjad asked, "I take it you've drunked the boy?"

Jlak replied in kind, with a twinkling deadpan, "I have indeed, my lord. He took to it well; I—*em*—suspect this was not his first brandy, though it was probably his finest."

Despite the tension of the situation, Kenlin chuckled. Their plans for Jiaján were, by far, the goofiest part of the entire escape. The boy had initially presented the Jazeiz with a bit of a problem, the simplest solution to which was obvious, if unpleasant. That would have been Jiaján's fate, despite Ranja and Kenlin's discomfort, had Ranja not proposed that they allow the boy to escape with a false report about their destination. At her suggestion, Jlak had untied the boy, apologized, and "let slip" that Jlak and the Jazeiz would be occupied elsewhere in the city for a few days. He'd then given the boy brandy until his mind and fingers were clumsy, then tied him again with a tight but uncomplicated knot. The knot would hold him until the drink wore off, by which time the Jazeiz would be gone from the city. The boy would then free himself, "escape," and presumably carry his false report back to the Droál. It was a brilliant solution, without a doubt; but it was also so immensely silly that Kenlin couldn't help smiling every time he thought about it.

Ranja, however, didn't seem to like him smiling at her idea. "I'm glad it amuses you so, Kenlin," she hissed at him coldly. "It *will* work, though."

He protested, "Of course it will work, Ranja, that's not… It's not that I think the *idea* is amusing. I mean, it is amusing, but—"

Ranja's eyes were narrowing even further, but Klanjad reprimanded, "That's enough, you two. Kenlin, get that foot out of your mouth, you'll need them both to leave this city. Remember the plan. Move silently in single-file: me, Jlak, Kenlin, Ranja. We will try for the north gate first, then consider the west gate depending on what we find. We will favor stealth over speed as long as we are undetected; if the alarm is raised—or if I sense Misks, who will also be able to sense me—we will continue at a run. If we are ambushed, you three are to press forward while I deal with the ambush; and if we are separated for that or any other reason, we will regroup in two days where the south road enters the forest.

And, should any of us fall, they're to be left where they lie. Understood?"

They all understood. They were all ready. They left the lamps and the fire burning as they followed Klanjad out a ground-floor window and into the alleyway darkness.

Alley by alley they crept, darting across broader streets, keeping their bodies low. In the mountains, Kenlin had thought poorly of Klanjad and Ranja's stealthiness; but here in the city, far from brush and dry twigs, they were every bit as quiet as Kenlin. Even Jlak, who was comparatively elderly, moved with surprising grace and stealth. That was good, because Kenlin had never felt so keenly the need for absolute silence. Every noise seemed threatening; every light seemed too bright to hide from; and, as they crept arduously from shadow to shadow, every minute seemed to last eternity. Their progress was tedious and torturously slow. *Surely, we must be caught if we linger so; but then, just as surely, we must be caught if our haste makes so much as a sound.*

Jlak, who was in front of Kenlin, suddenly stopped and touched Kenlin's shoulder. Kenlin froze, reaching back to tap Ranja and warn her to stop. Trying to see what was causing the delay, he peered forward toward where Klanjad waited at the end of the alley, then bit back a curse.

The alley opened to the north onto a larger street between two warehouses. Down this street, faintly visible in the moonlight, a sentry—presumably a Khardalesh Droál—walked toward them. In the man's hand was a leash that restrained a Kilgáic war dog, which was sniffing the air suspiciously. Though Kenlin knew little of trained dogs, he could guess what would happen: the dog would sniff out anyone it came close to, and it would bark, and the escape would be discovered. *Dogs! How could we have forgotten about dogs? And what could we have done even if we'd remembered?*

Kenlin almost fell over as Ranja elbowed past him. When she reached Klanjad, she began to mime something to him, pointing first to the dog and sentry, then to Kenlin, then to herself and up to the buildings that loomed above them. Klanjad seemed to understand, but shook his head, then pointed to himself and the buildings above. Ranja shook her head, indicating her glaive, then pointing again at herself and the buildings above. After a moment's hesitation, Klanjad nodded.

Immediately, Ranja handed her glaive to her father and stood up, relying on the alley's deep shadow to conceal her. As quietly as possible, she began to climb, bracing herself against both buildings and using whatever holds she could find. When she was a little above head height, Klanjad handed her the glaive, then signaled Jlak and Kenlin to go back down the alley. When they had retreated far enough, Klanjad whispered to Kenlin, "Use your bow. When she kills the sentry, kill the dog. Make it silent."

Moments later, the dog and sentry had come very close to the alley where they were hidden, and the dog had certainly caught their scent. Dragging the sentry to the alley's entrance, it sniffed the ground where Klanjad had been crouched, then sniffed the sides of the buildings, but it did not look up to where Ranja hid in the shadows above. The sentry who held the dog's leash was peering warily into the alley, but he seemed to see nothing either. When the dog tugged at the leash, the sentry stepped forward.

One step...two steps...the dog was becoming ever more excited, probably aware that its prey was close. Suddenly, Ranja thrust downward with her glaive, stabbing the sentry through the throat. Immediately, Kenlin loosed an arrow, which pierced the dog through the eye. With a quiet, gruesome gurgling sound, the sentry collapsed to the road. The dog fell silently.

As quiet as the conflict had been, for a moment Kenlin felt certain that an alarm would be sounded. That moment passed; then another; then Ranja dropped to the ground,

Klanjad crept forward again, and Kenlin and Jlak both released quiet but audible sighs.

Ranja stabbed the dying sentry again up through the chin, putting a stop to that awful gurgling sound. Then she and Klanjad picked up the body and carried it back into the alley. Kenlin flattened himself against a wall to let them pass; as they did so, he whispered to Ranja, "Well done, that worked well." She ignored him. Concealed in the darkness, he threw up his hands. *Still? Still resentful? What does she want of me?* But he remained silent; this was not the time for such questions.

They were now very near to the north gate, and so they resumed their painstaking journey with renewed energy. Within a quarter-hour they had reached the end of an alley that opened onto the road leading through the gate. Peering out, they could see that the gates were wide open and lightly guarded; the guards were alert, fully bedecked in their livery, standing in a line across the road and staring watchfully out of the city. For a moment, Kenlin felt a rush of hope. *An opportunity! But no… Real guards on a night watch would not be alert unless they knew something was going to happen. If something were going to happen, it would either be from within the city, in which case the guards should be facing the other way, or from without, in which case the gates should be closed,. Also, if Skralade is as clever as Klanjad says, he would never leave the gates free of his own men; likely, those are all mercenaries in stolen city livery, and if we attacked them they would be quickly reinforced by Misks. This is worse than simple heavy guard; this is a trap.*

Klanjad turned to face the rest of them, and his face was grim. "Not good. This gate is much too dangerous, but we're running out of time. They'll soon miss the sentry we killed, and they'll know we're out and about. When that happens, Skralade will probably abandon caution and enter the city himself, using magic to detect us. Come, we will try for the west gate, but we must move quickly. Follow me."

They turned south, then west, now moving much more quickly at the cost of a little noise. They no longer confined themselves to alleys, but padded along the edges of larger streets and only ducked into alleys to avoid sentries. In his head, Kenlin appreciated the haste, but his heart leapt into his throat every time one of them kicked a pebble or startled a cat. *This cannot go on. If we keep this pace for long, sooner or later someone will certainly find us, or at least find our trail. We have to end this soon.*

But Likrásk was a large city, and the west gate was a long trek from the north gate, even at a stealthy jog. They pressed on, but Kenlin's agitation grew with every step. *Should we have just tried our luck with the north gate, even if the west turns out to be less guarded? Or could we not just scramble over the walls? I can see the walls from here… But no, there are sentries on the walls, and in the towers as well; they would catch us scrambling. If we cannot escape undetected, we must at least be able to escape at a run.*

Suddenly, a prickling sensation crawled up Kenlin's neck—a sensation that felt unsettlingly familiar. Klanjad's head snapped up. "The Misks have entered the city," he whispered. "Still quietly now, but stay close. And be ready." Rising from his stealthy half-crouch, the Jazei broke into a medium run, the rest of the group trailing behind him.

West two streets, south one, then west again, and there! There were the gates before them, closed and lightly guarded, showing no signs of the sophisticated ambush that had been prepared at the north gate. For the briefest moment, Kenlin dared to hope that it just might be that easy.

It was difficult to see into the deep shadows beneath the gate, but suddenly there appeared to be a few more men than there had been a moment ago. The sense in Kenlin's neck intensified dramatically: *Misks!* There was a commotion—the Misks were rallying the gate guards, whom they must have bribed or hired beforehand—and, within moments, the Jazeiz found their way barred by six alert, armored soldiers and two

Misks. And as they stepped out of the gateway shadows, Kenlin recognized one Misk's moonlit face: *Skralade.*

"Remember the plan: break through, then go!" barked Klanjad as he drew his sword. Then he Faded and sprang forward, charging straight for the Misks. For a moment, Kenlin and Jlak wavered, torn between obeying Klanjad or helping him. Ranja did not waver: dropping her pack and hefting her glaive, she threw herself into the fray to aid her father. After an instant more of hesitation, Kenlin followed her, and Jlak rushed after.

Klanjad's wild charge had scattered the soldiers before him, and he was now engaged in a furious fight against both Misks. Ranja, coming after, attacked the scattered soldiers. Those she attacked fell back, but the others quickly rushed in to encircle her. As one soldier prepared to attack Ranja from behind, Kenlin loosed an arrow; it hit the man squarely in the back, only for the stone arrowhead to shatter against his metal armor. The arrow's impact nonetheless caused him to stagger, and he and two others turned from Ranja to deal with Kenlin and Jlak. Kenlin instinctively reached for another arrow, but that wouldn't do. *There are too many, too armored, too close.* As clumsy as he felt using it, he drew out his sword as his eyes grew wide, fixed on the spear point plunging toward him. *One above! But I'm not ready...*

And in that moment when his mind abandoned him, he felt a sudden and strange ease, a macabre freedom. There was no thinking; instinct and training took over where thought had left off, and he saw himself bat away the encroaching spear, dart past its effective range, hew madly at its wielder—an inept and glancing blow, but enough to bloody the man, to make his face blanch with fright. They locked eyes for an instant, and the soldier's terror awakened in Kenlin a mad, thrilling elation. No words came with it: only a faint sound of high, cackling laughter.

It was lucky for Kenlin that both his opponents used spears, and used them none too well, allowing him to control the fight through range and aggression alone. The laughing elation added nothing but energy to his already wild sword swipes; and yet, mere moments later, he stood over his wailing, dying foes, splattered with their blood—and none of his own.

Shaking the laughter from his mind, he took stock of the rest of the skirmish. Klanjad remained locked in frenzied combat with the two Misks, but Ranja had already felled two of her foes and was more than a match for the last. Jlak was hard-pressed: armed with only a dirk, he had slipped past his enemy's spear, but the younger man had grappled him and both had fallen to the ground. Kenlin stepped forward to help, but at that very moment Jlak managed to bury his dirk in his opponent's thigh. As the man howled in pain, Jlak twisted like a snake and stabbed again, this time through the neck.

A feeling of triumph was building in Kenlin's chest, though Jlak looked only tensely relieved as he scrambled to his feet, but neither triumph nor relief would last long. Klanjad's fight had careened close to Kenlin and Jlak, and one of its participants was suddenly kicked free of the fray. *Skralade!* The Misk staggered toward Jlak, who turned in alarm and raised his dirk, but Skralade twisted mid-stride to deliver an unbalanced upward swipe. The blade contacted just below the shoulder, and the Misk's unnatural strength chopped right through the arm. Jlak dropped to his knees with a scream. He was still screaming as Skralade, with a magician's speed, recovered his footing and beheaded him.

Instantly, the laughter was back in Kenlin's head, but it was a different color now. This laughter echoed red, a crazed and ecstatic frenzy that laughed, not for joy, but for sheer madness. And as Jlak's decapitated corpse toppled to the dirt, Kenlin felt the laughter, and the fury, and the entire force of his hatred focusing on the killer: *Skralade!*

Kenlin bounded forward and hacked furiously at the Misk, who sidestepped the grand swipe with ease and bemusement. Caught in the momentum of his own attack, Kenlin lurched forward and threw his shoulder against the

Misk, trying to knock him off-balance. The Misk merely turned out of the way, and Kenlin staggered past, tripped, and tumbled to the ground. Skralade stepped toward him, still wearing a look of bemusement, and Kenlin swiped viciously at his feet; the Misk hopped back. Their eyes met for a moment, the Misk's wary amusement contrasted with Kenlin's burning hatred—*I've seen your moonlit face before, bastard!* But Skralade, unconcerned, simply leveled his sword for a lunge. Yet the lunge never came, for Skralade had to spring back again to avoid a new onslaught: Ranja, having killed the final soldier, had come to Kenlin's aid.

Focus replaced amusement on Skralade's face; there would be no reckless swipes from this one, for he now faced a real, known threat. She pressed her attack, forcing him to retreat as he batted aside her glaive. Then he suddenly advanced, trying to push through her glaive's range. She danced nimbly backward and swiped at his shins.

Then Kenlin saw, clearly at last, the deadly magic of the Misks. Skralade tossed his blade—swiftly, gently, and straight—over Ranja's head. She instinctively ducked, though the throw would not have hit her, and uncertainty filled her face. Then the Misk Vanished, and Ranja screamed in surprise and sudden fright. She tried to turn, but he was far too fast; he reappeared behind her, caught his sword, and sliced open her back behind the shoulders.

As Ranja crumpled, the fury burst forth in Kenlin more terribly than ever before. He opened his mouth with nothing to say, and no words came out. Instead, he released an open-throated, rasping, high-pitched and terribly loud screech. The sound echoed off the buildings, filling the area—Kenlin thought he could hear it in his head, mingling with the mad red laughter in his mind. He had never screamed like that before, but somehow that scream fit his fury, and it felt *right*.

Skralade wheeled, instantly alarmed by that scream. Still screeching, Kenlin thrust himself to his feet and hurled a handful of dirt into the Misk's eyes. Skralade leapt back, but he could not avoid it all, and he began to blink furiously as his vision blurred.

Yet he was not so blinded that he could not see the battlefield. His men were all dead or dying upon the ground, Kenlin was still on his feet, and Klanjad had just killed the other Misk. Recognizing defeat, Skralade flung his sword at Kenlin—throwing wide in his blinded state—and Vanished.

Even as the scream faded from Kenlin's throat, it still echoed in his mind with the laughter, and he felt everything at once. "He's gone again!" he cried, and it was a curse, a cheer, an enraged howl, a crow of triumph. "Coward! He's Vanished again!"

There was no answer, and the sudden quiet was deafening. Kenlin turned toward Klanjad, and his emotional tempest instantly ceased as his heart froze in fright. The older Jazei was on his knees beside Ranja, his hands on her back trying to hold her flesh together. But his fingers kept slipping in her blood, and the long, deep gash would open wide again. Glimpses of white bone gleamed amidst the blood filling the wound.

"If one of us falls," Klanjad intoned in a haunted voice, speaking to no one, "he is to be left where he lies, and the rest go on. We must go on." But he made no move except to try again to hold his daughter together.

The fright, which had begun overpowering, now mixed into Kenlin's berserk emotional maelstrom, but he wrenched himself back under control. "We can't leave her, Klanjad. Stay here, I'll go find help..."

"We cannot stay here," said Klanjad, still in a voice of emptiness, still hunched over Ranja. "Even now, Skralade has gone to the north gate to fetch every warrior from their ambush there. There is no time for help." His head shook slowly, unable to comprehend the very words he was saying. "There is no time for help. There is time enough for fleeing, and for dying."

"*No.*" It wasn't a denial, it was a refusal. "She *will not die here*, Klanjad! She has time yet, if I can close the wound and stop the bleeding..."

"I've told you," snarled Klanjad, his wrath flaring abruptly, "we must go on *now!*"

"So you'll just leave her here?" Kenlin bellowed back, knowing and despising his uncle's logic. "She isn't dead yet, I can help her!"

Klanjad looked up, and for an instant in his eyes Kenlin glimpsed an endless, frozen sea of fear that seethed and frothed beneath the ice that covered it, keeping it down. That sea was deep, and filled with many monsters. But then the glimpse was gone, and the ice returned with a snap to Klanjad's voice. "Carry her, then. I will protect us as we flee. Then save my daughter."

Kenlin's instinct was to refuse—everything Alalan, the old healer in Irnaji, had taught him about healing advised against moving the deathly wounded—but there were no options. To stay in Likrásk was the most certain of all deaths.

Klanjad picked up Ranja and put her in Kenlin's arms. She had lost consciousness, and it was difficult for Kenlin to keep her balanced while still trying to hold the wound closed. He would have made some sort of makeshift bandage, but there was no time: already the prickling sensation was growing stronger again, heralding the arrival of more Misks. Klanjad snatched up Ranja's glaive, Faded, flung the gate open, and led the way out of the city. They ran for almost half a league, pausing only for Klanjad to grab a torch from a nearby fire pit, then staying on the road until the city's slums were well behind them. At last, Klanjad stopped and pointed directly north into the grasslands. "Keep running," he said. "Find safety and take care of my daughter. I will catch up to you."

Kenlin fled into the field, but after several minutes he paused to look back. A red glow in the south marked where, to cover their retreat, Klanjad had set the grasslands on fire.

CHAPTER XIV:

Nothing, nothing will do! I cannot run in the dark, I can't risk stumbling as I carry her. But there is nothing here, and I must find a place to tend to her soon. How soon? Pausing for a moment, he moved his right hand from Ranja's wounded shoulders to touch the side of her neck. Her heartbeat was clear, but too fast, and her skin was becoming cool to the touch. *Too soon.*

From the darkness behind, Klanjad came crashing through the grass in wild haste. "What's happened? Why have you stopped?" His tone was the closest Kenlin had ever heard it to panic.

But panic was useless. "She lives yet, Klanjad, but she's bleeding cold. I need to clean the wound and close it, we have to stop moving her until the bleeding is under control."

"What, here? Now?"

"No, but we must find somewhere. *You* must find somewhere. Run fast, use your magic, I don't care what it brings down on us. I need light, fire, water, cloth...*damnation!*"

"What?! What is it?"

In the darkness, Kenlin couldn't see the dread on his uncle's face, and Klanjad couldn't see the despair on Kenlin's. "I need my pack, Klanjad. I dropped it in the fight, but it has my needles, catgut, all my herbs..." He trailed off; what else could he say?

Klanjad was silent for several moments, and even though moments were costly, Kenlin did not begrudge him these. At last, he said, "Go, take her somewhere. Anywhere. Do all you can, and *do not wait for me.* I will find you when I have what you need." Then he Faded—as the magic made his body translucent, he appeared for a moment as a spectral figure lit through by the wildfire behind him—and raced away into the darkness.

Grinding his teeth in frustration, Kenlin turned back north and began again to jog across the plain. "My apologies for killing you, Ranja," he growled aloud, talking only to keep himself from screaming. "I should have picked up my pack when we fled, but I didn't realize I'd dropped the damn thing until just now. And now Klanjad's gone back to get it, so I suppose I've killed him too. Sorry for that. And...for the rest as well, Ranja, I'm sorry for all of it. For pushing out of turn, for speaking brusquely and standing by it, for generally being an ass... I am sorry." But Ranja, limp and cold against his shoulder, did not respond.

Every minute was a day and every step was a league, but he plodded doggedly on. At last, a tiny unlit cabin loomed before him in the darkness. *It'll have to do.* He stumbled up to the sturdy wooden door and, for lack of a hand with which to knock, kicked it violently. Through his mind flashed a conversation—Who are you? What is so urgent? Why should I let you in at night?—that he did not have time for. He lifted his foot higher, steadied himself, and kicked again.

The door didn't give way immediately, but a sharp wooden *crack* told him that its latch wouldn't hold. Another kick, and then one more knocked the door wide open; Kenlin barged through. Inside, it was too dark to see anything at all, but from somewhere in the room he heard terrified breathing.

"Don't be afraid!" Kenlin called into the darkness, trying to sound as reassuring as a blood-soaked armed intruder could hope to be in the middle of the night. "I'm here to save a life, not to harm you. I'm sorry to wake you and to break into your home, but she's dying. Please, if you have any kindness, any mercy in your heart, give me light!" As he said this, he had lain Ranja face down on the dirt floor and put his hand against her neck: *Faster, weaker, colder.*

He hadn't really expected his plea to the resident to be accepted. The breathing remained terrified, but then came the sound of movement. Several things rattled and clinked in the dark; then there were sparks; then a tiny flame in a tinderbox revealed a withered little hand and a crooked nose. The hand took the flame, put it on a candle, held it high. As the light filled the room, Kenlin looked at the old woman with the purest gratitude of his life: "Thank you."

The old woman made no reply. Her eyes studied Kenlin intently, traveling over his hair, his eyes, his blood-stained clothes... Then she settled on Ranja, focusing on the ghastly wound. Without a word, she turned, shuffled to the hearth, and began adding kindling to the fireplace.

She is Alalan, I am sure of it. Somehow, the old healer is alive and with us tonight, acting through her, helping me. Whether or not the old woman was really a healer by trade, she seemed to know exactly how to help. As soon as the fire was lit, she brought two pots of water, giving one to Kenlin and setting the other to boil. She then produced a clean garment, which Kenlin cut into rags; they added most of the rags to the boiling pot, and Kenlin used the rest to clean the outside of Ranja's wound.

Only now, as he cleaned the blood and dirt away, could he really see what a horrible wound it was. The cut was bone deep from shoulder to shoulder, and it looked as though the sword had even nicked her spine. Thankfully, blood was not spurting uncontrollably, but that was the only good news. A gash this deep and this destructive would require two layers of sutures; the procedure would be slow, challenging, and—for Ranja—unimaginably painful.

The water on the fire was just beginning to boil when Klanjad staggered through the open door. The old woman started to her feet in alarm (although, strangely, she still did not scream), but Klanjad hardly spared her a glance. He seemed no bloodier than before, but he was physically shaking with exhaustion and frenzy. His sword, unsheathed and bloodstained, was still in his right hand; in his left he held Kenlin's pack. Dropping it beside Kenlin, the older Jazei gasped, "I had little time to look, but this is what I could find."

Kenlin was already rummaging through the bag, inventorying. *Needle, catgut, yarrow, poppy, bitterleaf...* "It's enough, Klanjad. Well done."

Klanjad nodded, but his eyes were fixed on Ranja. "How is she?"

Kenlin chose his words carefully. "Just now, she's not dire, but every moment will be a new lifetime tonight. Be ready, for I will need you."

A quiet gasp from the floor caught both of their immediate attention. Ranja, who had remained mercifully unconscious until now, was stirring at last. Kenlin's heart sank: *Too soon, too soon!*

She was trying to move, probably to roll over; but the moment she called on her arms to do anything, her entire back seized up and she cried out in pain. "Don't!" Kenlin said loudly, placing his hands gently but firmly to hold her in place. "Don't move, you'll only make it worse. Your shoulders are badly hurt. I'm trying to help, but... Oh, I wish you hadn't awakened yet! I have to clean inside your wound, and the pain teas aren't ready, but I don't think we can wait. This is going to hurt."

"Why... Why would you tell me that?" Ranja moaned, her brow already knit from the pain.

"Because, however much it hurts, you cannot move your arms," Kenlin said earnestly. The old woman tapped his shoulder again, this time to offer a thick wooden spoon. Kenlin nodded his thanks, then offered the spoon's handle to Ranja. "Bite down on this, and scream through it; and if the pain becomes too much, you can kick your feet from the knee down, but that's all. No matter what happens, you *cannot move your arms.*"

She nodded, her eyes shut tight, and took the spoon between her teeth. As Kenlin positioned himself to pin her left arm down, Klanjad knelt by her right side. Kenlin said, "When she starts to thrash, can you hold her arm still?" Klanjad looked him in the eye without answering; then he reached down and gently held Ranja's hand between his own. Shaking his head, Kenlin took one of the still-steaming rags that had just been boiled, wrapped it around his fingers, thrust it into the wound, and began to scrub.

Pain—every pain at once, heat and trauma and abrasion and fright—erupted from her in the most agonized scream Kenlin had ever heard. Her face contorted, her jaw clenched so tight that the wooden spoon began to splinter, within moments her feet began kicking frantically against the floor— and through it all, no more than a tremor passed through her arms and shoulders. Even when Kenlin pressed in, reaching with his fingers to pluck out debris, though she redoubled her screams her shoulders hardly shuddered. For a full minute Kenlin scrubbed the wound clean while Ranja screamed and kicked and held herself perfectly still. Then Kenlin withdrew his hand—"There, it's over, that part's done!"—and Ranja's cries slowly diminished to growls, then to whimpers.

When she had fully quieted herself again, she spat out the spoon and asked weakly, "*That* part's done? There's more?"

Kenlin sighed, "Yes. There's a lot more, though none of the rest should hurt quite like that. I have to sew your wound closed, Ranja; it's too big for a bandage alone. The pain teas should be ready now," he continued, glancing at the old woman, who confirmed with a nod, "which should make it more bearable. But I won't lie to you. Tea or no tea, this next...long while...will be very unpleasant."

She made no answer, but he could see that her eyes tightened and she swallowed hard. He gave her poppy tea to drink, which she drank without complaint, and she barely hissed when he pressed a bitterleaf poultice onto the wound. But when these were done, she cracked an eye and watched Kenlin preparing his instruments. He saw how her gaze lingered on the needle—not with fear, but with dismal, overpowering misery.

Kenlin shrugged helplessly; "I'm sorry, Ranja, but I have to do this." She nodded, never taking her eye off the needle and looking more miserable than ever. Kenlin sighed, but there was nothing else he could do. The needle was threaded; it was time.

The first stitch was muscle to muscle, pulling the severed shoulder back together. To accomplish this, Kenlin first had to stick his fingers into the wound and move the skin out of the way, exposing the surface of the muscle. He then pierced first one side of the gash, then the other with the needle; then he tugged upward on the catgut to drag the halves of flesh together, tying a knot to complete the stitch. As he sat back to wet his fingers and needle again with bitterleaf pulp, Ranja let out her held breath with a tortured gasp. "Was that *one?*" she asked shakily. "How many more like that?"

Kenlin looked at the rest of the wound, severed muscle under severed skin stretching across the width of her back: "Dozens." She groaned pitifully and turned her face away. With nothing else to offer, Kenlin said, "I know this is almost impossible, but... Try to think of something else. It would be best if you could sleep; but if not, try thinking of a story or a history or something. It won't lessen the pain, but..." *But what?*

The second stitch was much like the first: she was clearly in agony. But the third stitch seemed a little less tortuous. By the fourth stitch, she had found a story to distract her, and she hardly whimpered at all. On the fifth stitch, she began to speak in the feeble half-whisper she could manage.

Before the passage of time, One was all, for as yet no entities had arisen in distinction within the Greatest Existence. One's Thoughts were still—images of life displaying Thought without perception and shape without form. Then said One, "There would be more if my

Thoughts were to come apart, and to see one another and become distinct. I will make Form, so that my Thoughts may be distinct; and I will make the great Perception, such that my Thoughts may be aware." So One created time, which is the great Perception; and he created Form, in latter days called the Gap, the framework for shape, through which time might pass; and through this union of Perception and Form, the Lesser Universe—the world that is constrained—came to be.

Throughout the Lesser Universe played many of One's Thoughts. They enjoyed the Lesser Existence, sharing Form and Perception amongst themselves, ever growing and changing. Many of the Thoughts became as worlds, and some of these became gardens for other Thoughts; these were the Strata, where many Thoughts together could share in the Lesser Existence.

Other Thoughts begat thoughts of their own, and ever strove to fully experience the Lesser Existence. The study of Form and Perception was ever their delight, and they modeled their own thoughts on the Thoughts they encountered around them. In this way, they flourished and were glad.

But one of the beings was most diligent, and learned many things about the nature of the Lesser Existence; for he had seen quickly, written in the nature of Perception and Form, that there must be a Greatest Existence beyond such limitations. Passion filled him, and he yearned for the Greatest Existence, even when it became clear to him that the Greatest Existence was the domain of One alone. So he studied fervently, imbibing the secrets of the Lesser Universe, until at last he approached Indistinction from the Lesser Universe, but was not destroyed. Then he said to himself, "See! I am as the Lesser Universe is, and yet I am not the Lesser Universe; I am apart, distinct, and so must be beyond. I will overreach my bounds, I will stretch out my hands, and I will achieve the Greatest Existence— of which, clearly, I already partake." He took to himself the name *Other*, and he called behind him a host of other Thoughts that shared his desire for the Greatest Existence, though they did not share his understanding and so were not as great as he.

Other lead his allies to confront One, but no matter where they sought they could not find One; for they sought him hither and thither, among every distinction that Other could imagine, but they could not grasp the Greatest Existence, existence indistinguishable, wherein One could truly be found.

But One looked upon Other, and he understood their quest; and so One manifested himself within his own Thoughts to speak to Other directly. "Woe to you," said One, "for you seek that which cannot be found by your seeking. Though you fancy yourself unbound by the Lesser Existence, you are nonetheless tied to it; and though you think to attain the Greatest Existence, that which you seek is merely your destruction. None shall ever attain the Greatest Existence, for I alone so Exist, and am Greatest. In coveting the Greatest Existence, you wish simply that you were me; but the very distinction which defines you thwarts you."

Other replied, "If my doom is futility, then grant me my destruction. If such is the price of escape from the indignity of the Lesser Existence, I will gladly sacrifice my distinction for the moment of destruction in the Greatest Existence."

But One replied, "Your request betrays your ignorance. Such a thing cannot be, for there are no moments in the Greatest Existence, which lies beyond Perception and Form. You cannot become as I am, for the Greatest Existence does not *happen*; it simply *is*. But you have created your own doom. You remain distinct from the Lesser Universe because, while you share all its secrets, you work ever *against* yourself, but the Lesser Universe works *with* itself. You remain bound in Perception and Form, yet by your distinction you have consigned yourself to exist in the Least Universe—the world that ever destroys itself—and there will be your habitation for all eternity."

And so saying, One cast Other into the Least Universe, which is sometimes called the Deepest Sea, along with his brethren; and many more Thoughts came to join them, for as time marched on, ever more followed in the path set by Other, seeking the Greatest and finding, thereby, the Least.

Kenlin sat back on his heels and took a moment to breathe deeply, wiping her blood from his hands. Klanjad, who still knelt with Ranja's hand in his, looked from the still-open wound to Kenlin: "Is that all? Is it over?" Ranja opened her eyes and looked up, hopeful.

Kenlin shook his head wearily. *I have sutured the muscle, but now I must sew the skin.* "Not over. Halfway."

Klanjad's face fell, but Ranja gave a bitter chuckle. "That's convenient," she said, her voice weaker than ever but still clear, "as my story, too, has another half."

Such spirit! "Ranja, if the story helps you, it helps; but if you could sleep—"

"If you could stop stabbing me with needles..."

"... Alright, then. So, what next?"

As time passed, the Thoughts filling the Lesser Universe continued to evolve and advance; some Thoughts were as worlds that grew ever more detailed and complex, and some Thoughts were as beings that filled the worlds or strove to understand the Lesser Universe. Four of these beings were very dear to One, who looked on with favor as they allied together to create a new thought of their own, a world that would abide as they deemed it. The names of these four beings were Vaikya, Kralinos, Daguar, and Gadan, and the name they gave to their creation was Jranjana.

But Other, ever bitter from his defeat, saw the favor with which One regarded these four Demiurges; and with a mind to vengeance, he became determined to destroy Jranjana and ruin the vision that the four shared. Other knew that his power was limited outside his domain in the

Deepest Sea, but he was cunning. Stretching out his influence, Other spoke to Gadan, whose task it was to craft the seas. "So shameful," said Other, "to be consigned by your so-called friends to craft the oceans, the mere basin in which the glory of the entire world will bask. Such a waste that you should spend your skill on that which must only be subordinate, sloshing endlessly about the feet of your peers' work."

Gadan was not so easily fooled, and he bade Other begone; but discord was sowed, and Gadan began to suspect his companions of disparaging the seas of Jranjana. The agreements they had made were broken, the craft was compromised as the oceans rose above the mountains and mingled with the skies, and the entire fate of their creation was jeopardized. "What happened," said Kralinos in despair, "such that this chaos comes of our careful planning? There is discord in the nature of our project, where no discord should be. In what did we fail?"

Then Gadan repented of his suspicions, and he told his brethren of Other's words and temptations. "I became fearful," said Gadan, "that you were not honest with me; and so fearing, I became dishonest with you."

"It is well to see, and to speak freely," replied Vaikya, the eldest of the four. "Be not pained, for we are brothers again. But now we must turn our attentions to Jranjana; for unless we mend that which is discordant, it may be that our creation will be destroyed entirely."

So the Demiurges devoted themselves wholly to the creation and maintenance of Jranjana, soothing the world's turmoil and reestablishing the order that had been lost. But so great were their attentions, and so unrestrained were their efforts, that in the end they immersed themselves wholly in their creation, losing distinction until they themselves were the essence of Jranjana, a part of their own creation.

Then was One aggrieved, for he had loved the Demiurges as they were; and though he loved Jranjana as their image, he wept that the four had been destroyed in its making.

And though he had failed to destroy Jranjana, Other rejoiced in One's distress. As a final act of cruelty, Other again reached out his influence to Jranjana. From sea, land, mountain, and sky he crafted the Djinn—the mockeries— in the likenesses of Vaikya, Kralinos, Daguar, and Gadan. Their wills were enthralled to Other, and they walked Jranjana as his puppets for One's torment.

But One, to Other's bewilderment, was moved rather to pity than agony. He freed the Djinn from Other's domination, binding them instead to wills from within Jranjana; for he said to them, "Your mere existence is abomination, a dance staged upon the tombs of those who were great. It is not right that you should dance to the music of Other, but neither is it right for you to make your own dances. You will dance to Jranjanan music and be bound to the world you were made to mock. So let your wills be bent to the trifles of Jranjanans—crown, collar, cincture, bracelet—that you may serve this world until you are wholly spent and may seek peace at last.

"And you," said One, turning to Other. "It is not good that you exert such influence upon worlds apart from yourself. Do you attempt to increase the holdings of the Deepest Sea? Even as you extend your hand to take what you wish, you work ever against yourself. Your very aim is conflict and wanton misery to all; it would be better for all, not least of all you, if you simply did nothing. Be still, be content, and never again extend your hand to Jranjana."

Then did Other return to his domain, seething and still pondering how, despite One's decrees, he might hope to destroy Jranjana at last.

Kenlin tied the final stitch less than a minute after Ranja finished her story. There was still much to do—the surface of the wound must be cleaned again, then salved, then bandaged—but for a few moments he allowed himself to pause and breathe deeply. Very gently, he touched the side of Ranja's neck once more; her skin was still cool to the touch, but her heart had slowed its hasty patter. With a sigh of relief, he said, "I think we've come through, Ranja; I think you've survived."

The barest hint of a smile told him she had heard him, but she said nothing and did not open her eyes. Whether from the mounting effects of the pain teas, or from her story, or from pure exhaustion, the tension of acute pain had at last eased from Ranja's face. *Maybe now, finally, she can sleep.*

Klanjad, still holding his daughter's hand, muttered thoughtfully, "That was quite a story."

In spite of his exhaustion—or perhaps because of it—Kenlin laughed aloud at this. "Such truth! Seventy-odd stitches worth of story, that was. And she kept telling right through all of it, pain and medicine and weariness alike!"

Klanjad, too, grinned a little. "She felt she had to finish it, once she'd started. She wanted you to hear it."

Yes, I was afraid of that. "She didn't tell all that for *my* benefit, surely. I told her not to exhaust herself—"

"And she ignored you, as is her wont," Klanjad interrupted, taking his turn to chuckle. "I think it did help her with the pain, especially at first. But she chose that story very particularly, and she chose it for you. That's the story of the creation of the world, as Faeries tell it; and traditionally, that story is the first thing taught to aspiring young magicians."

Kenlin nodded slowly at the significance of this. "So…she thinks I'm ready to learn now, yes? Do you agree?"

Klanjad quirked an eyebrow. "Well, ready enough to be getting on with; and I think tonight proved that we can't afford to keep delaying. But many other things have also changed since that morning near Flunjat when you first asked. You have worked hard, and you move much better now, though I think we can still expect plenty of injury as you begin learning magic. But your injuries will no longer pose a threat to our journey, for we won't be journeying much for a while. As important as it is that the Jazeiz return to the Commune, Ranja will need time to convalesce, and we cannot hope to travel safely until she's well enough to move on her own again.

So we'll flee into the wilderness, find a secluded hamlet in which to hide; and while Ranja recovers, I will teach you of magic."

Ranja seemed to have finally fallen asleep, and Kenlin did not want to wake her; but he gently touched her hand with his fingertips and whispered, "Thank you." Very slightly, her fingers shifted and raised, returning the touch.

But there were more pressing matters, and Kenlin turned back to Klanjad. "You say we'll flee into the wilderness," he said, "but we really *cannot* be moving her in this condition."

Klanjad shook his head. "Staying isn't possible, Kenlin, and you know it. Even now, Skralade is gathering every resource he has in the region to begin the hunt for us. By morning they will be combing the fields, and the dogs will surely find our trail. They will find this cottage no later than midday. We must be gone—and leave nothing that might tell them where we may be going."

A sudden chill, threating to become outrage, fell on Kenlin's heart. "I hope you're not suggesting what I think you're suggesting."

Klanjad answered gravely, "So do I." Then he turned to the old woman, who was now seated on her bed, watching them. "My lady," he said with a courtesy—almost reverence—that Kenlin had never heard from him before, "I can never thank you enough times, nor in enough ways, for what you have done for us tonight. I'm afraid my kin and I cannot stay here even until the dawn. But tell me: in what few hours we have, is there anything at all we can do to repay your kindness?"

The woman, who was very elderly indeed, simply smiled at them. After a moment, she raised one finger and tapped it on her lips. Then, hesitantly, she pointed to her eye.

This clearly meant nothing to Klanjad. He said warily, "I don't understand. What are you saying?"

"I think she's saying that she cannot say," said Kenlin, finally comprehending. "She is a mute."

The old woman nodded with a sad, almost apologetic little smile, and she tapped her lips again. Then she pointed to Kenlin, and once more indicated her eye.

Kenlin hesitated. "My eye? You ask...oh!" He and Klanjad exchanged a glance. Kenlin gave an abrupt, quick nod; and after a moment, Klanjad replied in kind. Turning back to the woman, Kenlin said, "Yes. We are Jazeiz."

At that name, the woman's eyes grew wide, and it seemed as though a bright glow shone from within her face. She clasped her hands in apparent delight and, unable to contain herself, wobbled to her feet. Kenlin stood and stepped forward, unsure what she was doing but prepared to catch her if she became unsteady. But no sooner had he stepped close than she reached up suddenly, put her hands around his face, and pulled it near to hers.

From so close, even in the firelight, Kenlin could see her eyes well: they were dark brown, like those of most people, but age had filled the pupils with thick, silvery clouds. Yet from so close, even in this firelight, she could see past those clouds and look, for a moment, into the emerald eyes of the Jazeiz. So they stood, eye to eye, for nearly a minute. Then at last, the old woman released Kenlin's face and sat down again. Her eyes were shut now, and a peaceful, contented smile lighted her face.

Kenlin, too, sat down again, but his mind was very troubled. *That was not comfortable, not at all. Is the legend of the Jazeiz truly so powerful to her that merely to see us— no, to have us break into her home in the middle of the night—could bring her such joy? Whose eyes did she see when she looked into my face? Not mine, not really; there are no legends of Kenlin.*

There will be.

This reply, though still in Kenlin's mind, came as a complete surprise. While it was a thought, it was not like his other thoughts; in fact, it was so different that he wondered for a moment whether it was even his *own* thought. It seemed coarse and alien, as though spoken in the guttural voice of a stranger. *There, I hear it again, the same thought-voice! But not speaking now: just a distant, indistinct cackling.*

Klanjad was watching Kenlin's face and saw his disquiet. "The weight of the legend is heavy," he said quietly, "especially when it catches you unawares. Heavy weights make powerful weapons, if you can wield them. It is a gift of sorts, an ambient inheritance from a thousand years of who we have been."

Kenlin, still disturbed, muttered, "But *I* haven't been."

Klanjad clicked his tongue. "Someday you may have to decide just how significant *you* really is. Consider it carefully." Kenlin shot him a perplexed glance, but Klanjad continued, "Not now, though; now is not the time for considering anything other than sleep. Rest, Kenlin, if only a little. I will keep watch for an hour or so; but after that, we must prepare to be off. I will find some way for us to move Ranja, and we will depart before the sun rises."

Kenlin was almost afraid to ask: "And what of our hostess?"

They both looked at the old woman. She still sat on the bed, leaning on the wall behind, with her eyes closed. In her exhaustion, she had fallen asleep thus, with the blissful smile still on her face. After a pause, Klanjad said, "I think we needn't worry. I'll leave a few dinels for damages and for thanks, but I don't think we need to buy—or otherwise ensure—her discretion."

Kenlin nodded, satisfied and very relieved. "Before dawn, then. And what of our foes? What if they find us again?"

"Then we'll have to fight for our lives again," Klanjad replied with a shrug. "But as long as we leave early, hold a good pace, and don't draw attention, I think the odds of such a fight are low."

"That's a relief."

Ha! That's a pity!

What?

PART II

A heavy step; a looming hush;
    Swift Taeve, shut-eyed, loosed a fearful cry
        And whirled, and scrambled quick away
        When, towering there, to her dismay
        The shadow of the great Jazei
Framed black against the dawn-light blush.
    He stopped, and stood, and stared with mismatched
eye.

No birds to sing, nor crickets creak;
    Alone they waited on the wild of death.
        But though Zadarj stood caked in gore
        And thus had stood three days or more
        'twas she who quavered him before.
A ghoul he seemed, a demon freak
    Whose undead presence choked away her breath.

Yet calm was he, at peaceful ease,
    And undisturbed by that which she abhorred.
        Concerned him not the passing time,
        Nor heed he paid to blood and grime;
        He wiped not off the gory slime
Nor spurned the reek of rot disease.
    Implacable, unbending Jazei lord!

—*The Song of Rage*, verses 17:19. Excerpted from
Canticles of Zadarj, a collection from the third century of
the Silvered Court, inspired by the memories of the
Wanderer.

CHAPTER XV:

"We have time enough to discuss this now, right, Kenlin? Ranja will be alright without us for a while? I can begin teaching you of magic later if you need to remain close to her."

"It's been five days, Klanjad. If she didn't die on the cart, and she didn't die on the mule, and she didn't die on the boat, then I hardly think she's going to die on the pallet. She'll be fine as long as she doesn't try to get up, or something similar."

"She's not an idiot, Kenlin."

"I know; that's why I don't worry. And you say we're safe from attack in these swamps?"

"Well, the wetland will deter Unnatilz, and the vast emptiness of this region should make finding us impracticable without them. Then, even if we are found, semi-dry, wooded little hillocks like this one are reasonably defensible, at least against a small force like a search party."

"So...safe, or unsafe?"

"We can never *truly* be safe, Kenlin. We must always be wary. But so long as we keep that in mind, we are as safe here as I think we could hope to be."

"Then that's exactly how safe Ranja is. If that's not enough for you, we can postpone this; or we could simply stay near her while you tell me the basics."

"No, I am content. She needs rest, not prolonged conversation."

"True. But it does feel a bit thoughtless, Klanjad: I think she'd *very* much like to be a part of this."

"Well, feel free to include her—on your own time, and when she's well enough for the discussion. For my part, I'll not taunt her with knowledge she can't use; but what she asks you, and what you answer her, are not my concern."

"In that case, I suppose we'd best begin. Should I have my sword?"

"No. I'm afraid today will exclusively be a day of sitting and talking. Respectively, in fact: you sit, and I'll talk."

"But you're already sitting."

"And you're still talking. I'll be skipping as much of the mysticism and pageantry as possible, but even the bare essentials of magic will require a fairly lengthy conversation, so *sit.* ... Better. Now, do you remember the story Ranja told you the other day?"

"About One, and the Thoughts he had, and Other, and...the rest of that?"

"Exactly. That story outlines the Faery conceptualization of Jranjana, the gods who created it, and the other worlds that exist around and alongside it. This Faery tradition—this metaphysics, for lack of a better term—forms the basis of how we describe and discuss magic."

"That became very dense *very* quickly."

"Yes, and there's more. In the context of that story, you can consider any entity to be a 'Thought,' and every coexistent collection of entities can also be considered a 'Thought.' In a sense, a 'Thought' as used by that story is a unit of being. So you and I would both be considered 'Thoughts' of One's, as would every other person, and as would Jranjana. Jranjana, however, is a special kind of 'Thought' which we refer to as, 'the world.' In a way, it is simply a context of existence in which other entities can interact on a mutually observable plane."

"I got lost at 'context of existence.'"

"Don't worry about it overmuch, it isn't necessary (or possible) to gain a *specific* understanding of these things. I'm simply trying to define the idea of a *world* for you: it is a 'place' that multiple entities can inhabit and perceive in a consistent way. When I was struggling to grasp this, Ranton described it to me as, 'a language of being, through which multiple individuals express existence in a way that can be mutually recognized and conducted in a contained environment, protecting us from being overwhelmed by the complexities of the undiluted Lesser Existence.' Was that helpful?"

"No."

"Yes, it didn't help me either; but ultimately, all that's needed is a general understanding in order to proceed. So by now, you should have a rough idea that worlds—Jranjana and others like it—exist, and specify existence within themselves. We generally call these worlds *Strata*. There are many of them, each different from the others; but all Strata allow magicians to *be* inside of them, providing that shielding from the 'undiluted Lesser Existence' that Ranton mentioned."

"Klanjad, before we continue, can you give a quick definition of *magician*?"

"Obviously, a magician is someone who can use magic. Why some people are magicians and others are not, I have no idea."

"That's...unsatisfying."

"Ask Ranja about it, if you have no tact whatsoever and feel the need to speculate. She has heard the metaphor of the languages and has some ideas, none of which have any practical applications. So... Where was I?"

"Strata."

"Oh, yes. There are many Strata that allow magicians to *be* within them. In fact, it is possible for a magician to *be* in multiple Strata at the same time. This is the process we call *Fading*, which is the foundation of how humans use magic."

"Can you give a quick definition of *magic*?"

"That is the point of this entire conversation, Kenlin; and no, the definition will not be quick at all. *Magic* is the name we give to any conscientious interaction between a thinker and the Strata, principally where the thinker derives some advantage. There are several forms of magic: *Fading* is the form that humans use, while the magic of Misks is called

Vanishing. Faeries can Fade just as humans do, but like Misks they are also what we call 'creatures of magic.'"

"Can you define—"

"I will define it in my own good damn time. Right now, we're discussing *Fading*, which is when a magician exists in multiple Strata at the same time. In a sense, it's like being in several places at once, except that the other places are different sorts of both *being* and *places.* Fading is accomplished by 'recognizing existence' in multiple Strata—essentially speaking multiple languages of existence simultaneously. A principle component of this is visualizing the other Strata and placing yourself in the visualization, but the sensation is difficult to describe. When you Fade, you will see both Jranjana and the Strata to which you Fade at once, as though painted on top of each other; as you seem faded to the world, each world will seem faded to you. These visual components are essential aids in Fading; I will teach you the complete process in the coming weeks. By Fading, we magicians are able to take advantage of the multiple physical existence. By recognizing an extension of our physical existence, we are able to recognize and access the physical attributes of the recognized extension—principally, strength. You can think of it as…duplicating yourself in the other Strata, and those duplicates would then be able to lend their strength to yours as you are in Jranjana."

"So, if I were to Fade such that I…existed…in three Strata besides Jranjana…"

"Colloquially that's *Fading to four Strata*, or just *Fading to four*: one for Jranjana and three others."

"Alright. So if I were to Fade to four, would I be four times as strong as I am now?"

"Something like that."

"And you say I could 'lend the strength,' from the other Strata to myself as I am in Jranjana. Could I also lend my strength from Jranjana to one of my Faded selves in another Stratum?"

"In theory, certainly; but why would you want to? We live in Jranjana, and we have to exert concentration and effort to remain Faded; when we relax, we return naturally to Jranjana alone. For this reason, we only Fade in order to gain one of the advantages of magic for some purpose in Jranjana. We have no agenda in the Strata we Fade to; those Strata are strange to us."

"Do these other Strata have 'native' inhabitants of their own that we might encounter if we Fade there?"

"Some do; the Faeries, in fact, seem to spend a lot of time exploring such Strata. But I've never heard of anyone but Faeries doing that, and I imagine that a sentient population would make Fading to such a Stratum difficult because of the added complexity of visualizing such a population. Faeries do as they please, but we other creatures concern ourselves with Jranjana, and it would be an unnecessary complication if we were to encounter beings from other Strata while we were simply trying to Fade. Many Strata are bleak and empty wastelands; most magicians find these the easiest to Fade to."

"And can we see other magicians in these Strata? For instance, if I were to Fade and you were to Fade right now, would I see you in another Stratum as I see you here?"

"Not as such, no. Recall that Fading is mainly actuated by how we place ourselves in the perceptions we create; thus, in order to see you in another Stratum, I would have to visualize that Stratum as it was and as it contained you, insofar as you were there... You see how quickly this becomes so intractable that I'm not even sure how to express it. Let me say this: I have never encountered another human or Misk or Unnatilz magician in any other Stratum except Jranjana. I have heard rumors that Faeries have ways of doing such things— of detecting magicians through other Strata, finding them and perceiving them and communicating with them—and I have seen things that make me believe those rumors. But encountering another magician in magic is not something you'll ever have to worry about."

"Huh. Interesting. Fascinating!"

"You don't sound as bewildered as I would have expected."

"I might need more knowledge before I can be properly confused."

"Oh, mercy on. Please try to contain your curiosity, if you can. Bear in mind that, beyond Fading, magic is not really a practical study."

"Of course, of course. And practically speaking, the goal of all of this is to 'lend ourselves' strength?"

"Yes, but that's not the only effect of Fading. It is from this lent strength that magicians also gain our other advantages, such as our speed."

"That's 'lent' as well, yes?"

"Don't be absurd, you can't 'lend speed.' The speed derives from the strength, although somewhat indirectly. Our minds can think much faster than our bodies can act. You can think through an entire fight in the time it takes you to swing one sword stroke. You can dream an entire week's events in a half-hour nap. But we aren't accustomed to thinking like that, at least not when we are calm and wakeful, because our minds have learned that it serves no purpose: we can only act out our thoughts at a certain speed, so why should we think faster than that?"

"Klanjad, I can think of several reasons why thinking faster might be useful."

"As can I; but this habit of slow thinking is developed very young, and it's so ingrained in us that non-magicians rarely even recognize the inhibition. But with the additional strength that magic provides, we can force our bodies to move faster—to a certain extent, of course. We can put more power into running, for instance, which transforms running into an almost leaping motion that lets us run much quicker than we normally could. As we practice living in a magically-accelerated manner, our minds naturally learn to think correspondingly faster, at least in certain circumstances. It's difficult to directly *teach* that aspect of magic because it begins as a reaction; but in the end, almost every magician gains enhanced reflexes to match their magical ability."

"Multiplied strength, increased speed of motion, and enhanced reflexes; I can see how this would be useful on a battlefield."

"More than you can possibly realize, Kenlin. A powerful magician is very difficult to kill and is a devastating morale-breaker for opponents."

"Is that everything, then? This is magic as I will learn it?"

"For the most part, yes, though there are a few more details you should know, such as the sense. Have you begun to sense magic yet?"

"Perhaps a bit, back in Likrásk. A wary, prickly sort of sensation, like the feeling of being watched, or of someone being uncomfortably close."

"Well said. It's actually very much like the feeling of being watched because the two sensations are closely related. People have some ability to sense when they are not alone, or when someone is around them, or when others are standing too close. In essence, people can sense *presence*. In day-to-day life, presence is so common that the sensation becomes numbed, and we're only aware of it in very extreme circumstances. But for magicians, the sensation spans multiple Strata, not just Jranjana, and the sensation in the other Strata is not so blunted as it is in Jranjana. Thus, when someone near a magician Fades or otherwise uses magic, we can sense the magic as an intrusion on our latent sense of presence. We magicians can make use of that to find when other magicians are near us. It's easiest for us to sense another magician if he or she uses magic, but there's always some residual sense of magical presence around a magician; in time, and with practice, you will learn to recognize even that subtle a presence."

"That residual presence, is that how you can tell whether someone was born a magician or not?"

"Yes. For instance, the moment I came near enough to recognize the presence about you, I knew you were a magician. Ranja, on the other hand, is not a magician and has no such presence."

"Interesting. So she cannot be sensed by magic at all, yes? Consequently, she can hide from magicians in a way you or I can never do."

"Yes, that is true, although that is small recompense for lacking the ability to Fade. Speaking of which, I think that concludes the basics of Fading and magic. I hardly need to ask, but do you have any questions?"

"About Fading? Surprisingly, I don't think so, at least not for now. However, there were a few other things you mentioned earlier. To start, how does Vanishing, the Misk magic, work?"

"Well, you already know the simplistic version: disappear here, reappear there. But if you want detail, I'll have to begin with an explanation of *creatures of magic*. Recall that, when you or I relax, we return to Jranjana alone, and so this is our native world. Creatures of magic, however, do not have a single native world; instead, they are naturally partisan to more than one Stratum and, when relaxed, it is as though they were Faded already. Misks naturally exist on five Strata—though they seem to pay little attention to the four apart from Jranjana except to capitalize on the strength they gain from them, so it's likely that the other Strata are fairly barren. Faeries naturally exist on three. Those are the only two creatures of magic of which I know, and certainly the only two of the Five Species who are creatures of magic."

"That is simple enough."

"Perhaps, but this is less so. Faeries, in addition to their native three Strata, can Fade to more at will, much as we can, though they seem to be vastly more adept. Misks, however cannot Fade to *more* than their native five, and they cannot Fade to any Stratum they are not native to. However, they have the unique ability to momentarily withdraw from one of their native Strata—the pertinent one being Jranjana—and reappear elsewhere; as I understand it, the technique is very much the inverse of Fading. That is the magic that we call *Vanishing*. You've actually seen Skralade Vanish once or twice, haven't you?"

"Four or five times, by my count. That's how he wounded Ranja, yes? He tossed his sword to himself, then Vanished behind her to catch it."

"Did he really toss it to himself? I was still fighting and didn't see, but that sounds like the sort of trick he might be able to do. Few Misks can Vanish as precisely or as often as Skralade."

"Why is that? You've mentioned that, for humans, the focus of Fading can be a strain on the mind; does something similar affect Misks?"

"In short, you ask what makes Vanishing difficult? I can't be sure as most of my knowledge of Vanishing's technicalities is some combination of rumor and guesswork. But if we're indulging wild conjecture, then sure! Why not? It seems reasonable that Vanishing would require focus similar to Fading, so it follows that a similar mechanism might make such magic mentally strenuous."

"Sounds plausible. Back in the mountains, you'd mentioned that human magicians—like my father—can become deranged if they overexert their minds with too much magic. Can the same thing happen to Misks?"

"I've never heard of such a Misk. As to whether it's theoretically possible, we can only speculate."

"But if we're indulging wild conjecture—"

"We're not. This is meant to be a practical conversation, Kenlin. You will never Vanish, and so you will never craze yourself by Vanishing too much; and even if you did, you wouldn't care anymore! So. Do you have any other *practical* questions about Vanishing?"

"I do. Every time I've seen Skralade Vanish, his weapons and clothes seem to get left behind. That's part of how Vanishing works, yes?"

"Yes, that's actually very important. When Misks Vanish, they can take nothing with them, and that is *incredibly* significant from a tactical perspective. Misks who Vanish will reappear naked and unarmed, which severely restricts the utility of Vanishing during combat. For example, they cannot appear suddenly behind you with a knife, slit your throat, and then Vanish away to safety. They can, however, appear suddenly behind you, grab *your own* knife and kill you with it, then Vanish away."

"Sounds rather unsporting."

"Ha! So it is, but it's also not the sort of thing they're likely to try. To even attempt it, a Misk would have to know exactly where you were and where your knife was, and then they'd need the skill to Vanish so precisely and on such short notice. Skralade *might* could do it, and I'm certain he would try if I were ever stupid enough to wear so much as a kirsk on my belt. But in general, it's something to be ready for, but not to be worried about."

"So, if Skralade is so unusual, how do typical Misks use magic?"

"In practice, most Vanishing is used for travel—moving quickly from city to city, for example. When possible, Misks prefer to Vanish to destinations where they can acquire clothing and weapons immediately after arrival. Vanishing into a combat situation is comparatively difficult and dangerous, and consequently very rare. Again, Skralade and his elites are an exception, but most Misks won't Vanish into a fight without a careful plan and a very compelling reason."

"I see. And what about Droál, and that…Necromancy, I think you said it was called?"

"Yes, Necromancy is the term for the unique magics of the Droál. But you've seen their magic in action, haven't you?

During the ambush near Natzut, it was Droálic Necromancy that smashed that cliff and killed your friends."

"I assure you, Klanjad, I remember. But how does that work? Neither Fading nor Vanishing would enable them to do what they did."

"That's correct. Necromancy is fundamentally unlike Fading or Vanishing. All other magics directly affect only the magician—making you stronger or quicker, moving you about, etc.—but Necromancy can affect anything in the world, magicians and non-magicians and even inanimate objects. Essentially, Necromancy allows for an imprecise form of telekinesis, which was previously thought to be impossible. How exactly it works is still a mystery."

"Still a mystery? It has been decades since the Droál invasion began, yes? Surely someone has—"

"Many have tried, Kenlin. *I* have tried. But the question is not so easy to answer: the Droál are hardly forthcoming with their secrets, and even 'cooperative' Necromancers have not been able to provide a cogent explanation. Their own understanding is so mired in ritual and religiosity that their form of reasoning makes sense only to themselves."

"Yes? And what do they say of themselves?"

"Oh, little of value. Drakzaad, the death god that they worship, apparently maintains a spirit army of the dead; and in answer to his worshippers' prayers, his spirit army will manifest in Jranjana, charge forward, and blunder into things with extraordinary force. I'm being flippant when I shouldn't be; whatever I think of the Droál's gods and superstitions, the effects of Necromancy are very real and very dangerous, as you've witnessed."

"If you hold the Droál's explanation in such disdain, you must have your own notion of how Necromancy really works."

"Must I? I can recognize a silly idea even if I don't have a better one. In this case, while we don't have an *explanation* for Necromancy, we do have some information about it. In particular, we know that the notorious Droálic chanting isn't just empty ritual; not the sound itself, but the meaning of the chant seems to be an essential part of the magic. With that in mind, we theorize that what they're actually doing is 'inviting' magicians from other Strata to come into Jranjana, do something specified in the chant, then depart."

"Who is 'we?'"

"What do you mean?"

"Whenever you speak of Necromancy, you always say, 'we know this,' or 'we theorize that.' Who is this 'we' you're referencing?"

"Myself and the few others who study such things. No further information on this topic is useful—or available—to you."

"Well! My thanks for being unambiguous about it."

"The pleasure's all mine. Are we done? I feel like we've strayed *very* far from practicality."

"Wait, one more question!"

"About?"

"Faery magic."

"No."

"Why not?"

"It's as useless as it is unfathomable. Nobody knows what the Faeries are capable of, Kenlin, and even history only provides us glimpses of what they can do. They are creatures of magic, like Misks; and they can Fade, like humans; but there are *things* that Faeries can do which are beyond my ability to explain or even understand. I didn't really believe the stories, not until I'd actually *seen...*"

"Really? You've *seen* Faery magic?"

"I've seen everything, Kenlin. I've seen Wisps in the marshes and Wildlings in the hills, the silver pits of Jísjani and the drydocks of Zirgrad. But nothing in the world is half so strange, nor so haunting, as the Nameless Forest of the Faeries. They can create apparitions, manifest as phantoms to magicians who Fade, split along their magic and walk away from themselves, and surely do more beyond what I can even imagine."

"This sounds like a story worth hearing."

"Yes, well... It's actually quite dull, mostly uncomprehending wonderings, not worth discussing today."

"Ha! Well dismissed, Klanjad; I never knew you possessed such subtlety."

"*Subtlety.* That's a laugh and a half coming from you, boy. Although you have managed to trick me into telling you about Faery magic, so well done there. Now, unless you have *practical* questions about magic, we should return to check on Ranja."

"Alright. That concludes our day of talking, I suppose. And tomorrow, the magic begins, yes?"

"... Something to that effect."

CHAPTER XVI:

There is *nothing* charming about a swamp.

Previously, Ranja had never spent much time in swamps. She had known them mostly by reputation, and that reputation was such that, when their flight from Likrásk took them to the marshes southeast of Ralua Lake, she had flatly refused to spend her convalescence there and had insisted that the cold wet of a wintery fen would be the death of her. Under normal conditions, of course, she would never have allowed herself to complain so shamelessly. But license to complain is one of the very few upsides of being a gravely-wounded invalid, and such liberties should not be forborne.

Yet Klanjad had been adamant—"Only a swamp can deter Unnatilz trackers for long, Ranja; they won't follow us into a wetland."—and Ranja had ultimately been forced to accept that she would be spending the entirety of the winter, and probably some of the spring, hiding deep in a swamp with her father and cousin. And they truly were *deep* in the swamp: Klanjad had not allowed them to stop until, from a hilltop on a clear day, he could not see the smoke from the nearest settlement. So it was there, three leagues beyond the borders of nowhere, on a dry little hillock in the heart of a bog, that they built their camp. And it was there, not three days after their arrival, that Ranja learned another truth:

There is *nothing* comfortable about a swamp.

In fairness, much of her discomfort wasn't really the swamp's fault. The early weeks during which her wound began to heal were agony: she was in pain, she was itchy, she was stiff and cramped and bored and angry. She was only allowed to move a little bit every day, and never without help from Klanjad and Kenlin; and the only thing to do during the endless hours while they were away was to lie still and curse this boredom, this pain, this misery, this humiliating helplessness, and this thrice-damned swamp.

But when they returned it was no better, for she knew what they had been doing: Kenlin was learning magic, and Klanjad would not teach him in front of Ranja because... Well, in truth, he had never told her why, and so she was left to draw her own conclusions. On good days, it was obvious that he just didn't want to tease her, or that that too much excitement might hinder her recovery, or that Kenlin's clumsy magic might hurt her or destroy the camp. But on bad days and in darker parts of her mind, she was sure that knowledge of magic simply wasn't *for* her.

Yet she could not let herself become resentful—she *would* not—and toward that end, Kenlin helped her by his obvious discomfort with the situation. He tried several times to give her an account of the training processes during the evenings while he tended to her wound. However, hearing what she'd missed was often worse than missing it entirely; and after she snapped at him in a moment of bitterness, he became less forward with his reports.

But he never shut her out, never denied her information if he had it; and it was for that, beyond even what he had done for her shoulders, that she was most grateful. Though she didn't always want to hear what he could tell her, she knew that all she had to do was ask; and somehow, that made not knowing easier. So at last, she began to make peace with her invalidity, and her days became less angry and less miserable...but no less long.

For there is *nothing* exciting about a swamp.

Weeks—*weeks*—passed during which she could not safely move on her own. She would try, of course, when no one was nearby to stop her, but pain and the fear of prolonging her recovery invariably reduced her to stillness. Incapable of anything else, she would sometimes rhythmically knock her head on the ground, over and over and over, just to remember how it felt to *do* something.

After most of a moon had passed, Kenlin contrived a sort of yoke-like splint that allowed her to sit upright and move a little on her own. She had immediately asked to come observe Kenlin's instruction in magic, and she had been immediately disappointed. "Don't be so crestfallen, Ranja," Klanjad had admonished. "There is much for Kenlin to learn about magic; and given his progress so far, I'm sure there will still be much for a very long time to come." But she couldn't even summon the spirit to join in the teasing.

However, though she was still trapped in the camp, she began to find small ways that she could help: stoking the fire, cutting and curing meat, and similar chores. Soon, Kenlin started bringing back sticks and saplings that she would carve, very gingerly, into skewers and staves. Then he started bringing in armfuls of grasses, which he showed her how to twist and pull into rope. When she had made more rope than they could ever possibly use, he brought chunks of flint and taught her how to strike rocks together to knap blades and arrowheads. The things she made were useful, and making them helped keep the boredom at bay. But though neither of them mentioned it, she had figured out quite early what he was really doing: with every new activity, she used her shoulders a little differently, and a little more.

There was a brief transition period when Kenlin felt that Ranja should still be wearing her splint, but she felt otherwise. He would, with great severity, ensure it was on before he left, and she would take it off again as soon as he was out of sight. This continued until, one day, Kenlin returned to find her with the splint on her back and a cheeky expression on her face. It didn't take him long to decide what had really happened, but he concluded that, if she was well enough to put it back on by herself, then she was well enough to not wear it at all.

At last, she was finally free of all the outward trappings of injury, and with no reason remaining for her to be confined to the camp, she demanded to be allowed to observe Kenlin's magical training the following day. Klanjad received this demand with a sort of philosophical ambivalence, neither encouraging nor forbidding her attendance. Kenlin was more enthusiastic (although his approval didn't really count for anything), but he did feel compelled to warn her that, during the weapon-wielding portion of the morrow's exercises, she should probably stand behind something.

Within a day's observation, however, Ranja was convinced that both Klanjad and Kenlin himself had dramatically undersold his abilities. Magicians in training, once they had mastered the basic technique of Fading, spent a great deal of time learning to use their magically-empowered bodies safely and efficiently; by most accounts, this usually resulted in spectacular displays of acrobatic clumsiness reminiscent of nothing so much as the flailings of happy weasels. But Kenlin was not half as clumsy as Ranja had been led to believe. On the contrary, most of his tumbles seemed to occur when trying unfamiliar movements, or when moving with unusually strong magic; and though his antics frequently left him scratched and bruised, he never caused himself any serious injury. When he did tumble, he was able to maintain his magic even as he lost his balance—an impressive display of focus—and as often as not, he would use his magically-enhanced abilities to recover his footing and keep going. She did notice that he seemed to struggle more with finer movements like footwork and swordplay, but she suspected that was more for want of interest than of capability. Kenlin liked big, grand, powerful movements; and judging by his expression, he found no end of joy in leaping high, sprinting madly about, and barreling into things.

Though she could not join in the training—no amount of wishing would make her a magician, and Kenlin was far too much of a hazard to spar against anyway—Ranja began exercising with her glaive as Klanjad trained Kenlin in magic. Moons on end of injury and convalescence had left her weak and stiff, but also antsy and sick of resting. It was painful at first, but soon her agility began to return, and her spirits with it. For the next two moons, she thrived in the freedom and returning strength of her body, which made her final realization all the more dissonant.

There is *nothing* to be missed about a swamp.

Of course there wasn't. To think otherwise was absurd. How could she possibly miss this dank, cold, smelly bog far beyond the edge of anywhere? Ridiculous; she would forget it within days. But still... No, once she was gone she would not miss this place, she had decided that. But for now, while they still lingered in the shadow of imminent departure, there was time enough for a little sentimentality.

And so she was in a sentimental mood, sitting outside the firelight contemplating the moon, when Kenlin came and sat beside her. Following her gaze, he commented, "It's a red moon tonight. Back in Irnaji, we called that a blood moon."

She nodded, barely attending. "How creative. It's red, therefore 'blood.'" But he cast her a look and, rather than stifle the conversation, she relented. "Yes, I've heard that term before too. 'Blood moon.' Lots of old superstitions feature them as various omens of evil."

Kenlin bobbed his head. "That's common, then? We heard such things from elders, but I'd always thought it was suspicious that blood moons appeared late in the summer, and usually when the wind smelled of smoke."

She continued nodding absently. "Yes. Smoke, not death, is what turns the moon red. Although fire and death frequently go hand in hand, especially these days."

He glanced at her face, but her eyes didn't leave the red moon. "You're quite familiar with these moons, then," he said. "Why does it draw your gaze so?"

She shrugged. "It's pretty." Then, after a long pause, "And...I think it means we'll be leaving soon."

"Klanjad said that?" Kenlin asked, surprised. Ranja shook her head. "Then how do you know?"

She shrugged again with a needless air of mystery. "Because of the moon."

"Ha!" Abruptly, Kenlin laughed, which irked Ranja somewhat: he was spoiling her gravitas. "Such a divination, especially from you. Don't mistake me," he continued, holding up his hands in a pacifying gesture as she shot him a dirty look, "I also think we'll be probably leaving soon, but—"

"What do you mean, 'such a divination, especially from me?'" Ranja demanded, pretending to be more irritated than she was. "You doubt my powers of divination? You don't know what I'm thinking."

"I don't think you're thinking about the moon, at least not directly."

"Oh? And yet you've come to the same conclusion I have. So what, then? If not because of the moon, what makes *you* think we'll leave soon?"

Kenlin waved his hands vaguely. "Well, we can only stay here for so long, yes? We've already been here many—"

"Many moons?"

"Ha ha, Ranja, well played. But yes, we've been here a long time, you've healed quite enough to travel, and by now our most recent knowledge of the war is more than a season old. All that doesn't sit well with Klanjad. Every day now I expect him to tell us to start preparing to depart. You know him better than I do; surely you've seen how it chafes him whenever either of us wonders what might be happening in the north."

She had seen that, of course; and even if she hadn't seen it, she would have known. "He's put far too much of himself into the fight against the Droál for it to ever be far from him," she said. Then, looking again at the red moon, she added, "And anyway, there's only so far that any of us can get from it."

"Such truth," Kenlin agreed obliviously. "This is the most remote place I've ever been to—even Irnaji was at least close to something at some point in history—so if Klanjad can't escape the war here, then he never will." Kenlin stretched, grunting at the slight, strangely enjoyable pain of muscles sore from training. "I think it's time, though," he said, nodding to himself. "I'm glad we're leaving soon. Assuming we are, of course."

She had no doubt. "We are."

"Good."

Good? Ranja bit her lip, hesitating. So far, Kenlin has missed every clue she had given him, which was fine—she was being cryptic and oblique just for fun, after all—but even so... "I don't know that I would call the situation *good*. We do need to leave, and so we will. But the circumstances..."

That, evidently, was finally clue enough. "Circumstances such as whatever you've divined from the moon that you're not telling me?"

"Oh, put it together, Kenlin. Blood moons come from fires, the moon is in the west, so something to the west has been burned. What is to the west?" He knew perfectly well that Likrásk, on the opposite side of Ralua Lake, was west of them; but judging by his uncertain frown, he still didn't understand. "What do the Droál do?"

"They...burn people and cities, I guess, among other things," he answered hesitantly. "But they're not..." He trailed off before he could say, "here in the southeast," which was fortunate; if he'd said that after having grown up near the ruins of Natzut, she'd have been *required* to mock him for it. Shaking his head as though clearing a mental logjam, he said, "Wait, you mean *that's* what burned?" Ranja nodded gravely, and Kenlin's uncertain frown deepened. "Small fires don't turn the moon red, Ranja. They'd have to burn...the whole city?"

She was still nodding. Kenlin fell quiet, frowning deeply, and for several minutes there was silence. Why? Eventually, Ranja couldn't help herself: "Does this really surprise you, Kenlin? How? You know they do this, you lived most of your life near such ashes. After failing to kill us in the city and failing to find us since, did you think they would just give up and go away?"

"No," Kenlin said, still frowning. "I assumed they were still looking. But Klanjad said even Unnatilz couldn't track us into this swamp, so..."

"So they would just continue looking and waiting indefinitely? Well, apparently not. Evidently they have things to do elsewhere and got tired of waiting for us to just come out and die." She caught herself; her quips and tone were getting a little sharper than she wanted.

But Kenlin seemingly hadn't noticed. "But... But then...why...?"

Ranja tossed her head. "Why burn the city? You ask as though there could be *any* answer that you or I would understand. Strategically, maybe they thought we still had allies there, or were trying to get Likrásk to join the war; or maybe they'd already been planning to attack the city and this was just a convenient time to use the extra force they brought to the region to search for us." She took a deep breath, catching herself again. She hated even thinking about this, though not nearly as much as her father did. More quietly, she said, "In the end, how much reason do they need? This is what they do; they've done it ever since they arrived."

Kenlin was watching her expression now—he'd looked up as soon as she'd interrupted—and he nodded. "No, I understand all that. What I was asking was, why didn't we intervene?"

"Oh." Ranja took a moment to consider her reply. "*Um...* Intervene how?"

Kenlin clicked his tongue thoughtfully, then shook his head. "You're right, that's a silly question."

"I didn't say—"

"You don't have to say it, Ranja," he broke in with a light chuckle, "it's fine, I know. And you're right; I just wasn't thinking."

That was a mean trick: he'd somehow made her feel bad for a callous comment she hadn't even made. "Kenlin... Well, in a sense we are intervening, eventually. That's where we'll go once we leave here soon; that's why we have to rejoin the Commune and continue the war. But there's nothing we can do to help the unprepared against armies that can sack and raze cities. It does no one any good for the Jazeiz to die."

"Nor to hide, it seems."

That caught Ranja's attention: something was troubling him. There was a peculiar note in his voice, as there often was when he was thinking more than he was saying. When he didn't elaborate after a moment, she said, "Well, we had to hide for a little while; we didn't have a choice. You think we've been in hiding too long?"

Kenlin shook his head. "No. Long enough, though. I want us to leave; it's time."

Again Ranja gave Kenlin time to elaborate, and again he said nothing. "It's time...for what?" Kenlin chewed his lip, frowning. "Is this because you've trained now? You...want to fight?"

He shook his head again. "I don't think so, at least not in those words. The fight in Likrásk... I don't *want* that again, as such. But I know that once we leave we will fight again, sooner or later, and I am stronger now, and I'm... *Hmm.* In some ways I guess I do want to fight, but I don't know if I want to want that. I... I want to understand what it's *for.*"

"... For?"

He clicked his tongue thoughtfully again, trying to choose words. "Remember back in the mountains, when I asked to learn magic?" She remembered that well. Asked to learn, had he? That wasn't how she would have described that conversation. She didn't comment, however, and Kenlin noticed her diligently not commenting; a sheepish grin flashed across his face, but he continued, "At that time, I talked about what would happen if we were attacked again, and how I would need to be stronger. But now we've been *here,* for moons and on, and no one has attacked us; and even if someone did, I could probably defend myself at least well enough to help us get away. So I'm strong enough, then, at least for a reasonable defense. Yes?"

Ranja's eyes narrowed, but he'd diluted his statement's overconfidence with enough qualifiers that she couldn't really object. "Well, here in the swamp, I suppose."

He nodded. "To defend, though. Not to intervene. Not even Klanjad is that strong; otherwise we'd already be in Likrásk, and the moon would not be red."

It was hard to guess where he might be going with this. She knew him well enough to see that something very clearly was at the center of these circling thoughts, but she had no idea what. "Well... I'm not sure I know what you mean by, 'strong enough to intervene.' That's not something you can do with magic; no one man can fight an army."

"Of course not, but... That intervention, that aggressive... That's the sort of thing it's *for*, yes? That's *why* we Jazeiz must be strong." Ranja clicked her tongue. He kept using that term: *strong*. She didn't like it. Skill, cleverness, preparation, power... There were so many distinct facets to the things she expected from herself. For Kenlin, however, there was no such nuance; it was all just *strength*. "We could stay here and defend and already be strong enough, but we're not doing that. We want to intervene; we want to attack."

She squinted, trying to see past that unreadable frown of his. "In a certain sense, yes. And that...bothers you?"

"No," Kenlin answered, shaking his head, "not at all. I like the idea. I like it very much. I just don't know...how much I like how much I like it."

Once again, Ranja waited for him to elaborate, but he didn't. "I'm not sure I understand," she said at length.

Kenlin looked very pensive. After a long moment, he began, "I ripped the limbs off a tree the other day..." Then, abruptly, he changed both his tone and his topic. "You know, for all the training and all the time since Natzut, I've only actually seen Klanjad in two real fights. Even in those, he only killed once: he killed that Misk in Likrásk, the one that wasn't Skralade. It was dark; I didn't really see it happen." He paused. "I didn't really hear it, either."

"*Hear* it?" Ranja asked, caught off-guard.

But he looked at her in surprise. "Of course," he said matter-of-factly, "you always hear your kills. Don't you? When you hunt, first you shoot, then you follow blood and tracks until you find it collapsed, panting, dying. It makes little dying sounds."

For all her training and martial skill, Ranja had grown up largely at court and had never hunted anything the way Kenlin described, even in their recent travels. She found what he'd just said a little chilling, and she had to force her face to not show it.

She must have succeeded, for Kenlin continued without pause, "People don't make little dying sounds, though. They make some, I suppose, but they also *say* things. I heard them. I didn't listen—I didn't even notice them at the time—but thinking back now, I remember that I could hear them pleading."

Ranja was both lost and slightly horrified; this conversation had taken a turn for which she had not been prepared at all. "What people? When was this?"

"At the gate," Kenlin said, exasperated as though she hadn't been paying attention. "The gate guards on the ground, the 'dead' ones. Nothing dies the moment you kill it; they fell down, but they were still *there*, still talking, still crying. Not like the sentry you killed earlier, the one with the dog. Remember? You stabbed him twice, so he was dead. That was a good kill."

"A 'good kill'…by *hunting* standards?"

"Yes, exactly. Clean, quiet, quick… It was a very good kill, better than most I've ever done. Sometimes deer run for ages. For that man, though, it only lasted seconds. I congratulated you at the time. Was that strange?" Ranja didn't have an answer, but Kenlin nodded as though she had given one. "It probably was. I thought it would be different with people, but it turns out that good kills are good kills. And those near the gate, those were *not* good kills."

At last, Ranja thought she saw a glimpse of what Kenlin was talking around. "Because they suffered?" she guessed gently.

Kenlin met her eye, but he didn't answer directly; behind his difficult-to-read expression, she thought she caught a glimpse of real unease. "Violence, I've heard, is one of those things that's supposed to 'affect' you in some strangely ineffable way. That's the word Irnaji's elders used when they talked about the sacking of Natzut: they said it 'affected' them, and that if I'd been older then it would have 'affected' me too." He paused and looked down, frowning pensively again.

Ranja understood, or thought she did. "Suffering," she said, "can be hard to...grasp. More so than violence, more so than death. And those gate guards were probably just hired swords, not really Droál at all. If now you can remember hearing them... I can see how that might disturb you more than the sentry did."

Kenlin looked at her again. "It doesn't, though," he said flatly. "I told you, I didn't even notice them at the time once they were on the ground; I didn't hear them. Now, in my mind, I can hear them pleading—pleading for death, I suppose, I can't hear the words, just the voices. But even so...it doesn't bother me." Yet he sounded more troubled than ever. "I would have thought it would bother me, with people, but it doesn't. And *that's* what bothers me."

Once again, Ranja wasn't sure what to make of this. Objectively, what he'd described, though jarring to hear, was very practical: dwelling on horrors was a mistake that tormented far too many, including her father. Cautiously, she said, "That...might not be worth all the bother, Kenlin. People who have fought and killed feel all sorts of different ways about it, and they use all sorts of different words to describe those feelings. Just because what you felt doesn't match the words you expected doesn't mean what you felt was wrong."

He cocked his head. "But what if what you didn't feel unnerved you?"

"Kenlin, what is this about?" Ranja asked abruptly. "What are you really concerned about, and why now? Our fight in Likrásk was moons ago. Has this been weighing on you ever since?"

"No," Kenlin said slowly, "not ever since. I didn't really think about it at all for the longest time. But now we'll be leaving soon, and I'm stronger, and I've never actually seen Klanjad kill someone, nor seen how they died after he killed them." He paused, but Ranja didn't prompt him, giving him time to choose his words. Taking a deep breath, he continued, "I think… I think I'm being prepared to do violence in ways and degrees that are…new to me. I ripped the limbs off a tree the other day, and later I wondered what it would have been like if that tree had been a man. 'Easier' was the answer I came up with: it would have been easier."

"Easier for you to tear apart a man than a tree?"

"Yes. Because the man isn't made of wood." The absurd simplicity would have been funny if the topic hadn't been so grim. Ranja didn't laugh, and neither did Kenlin. "Is that an unnerving thought? I feel like it is. And yet that's what all the training is for, yes? To become strong, to intervene, to be aggressive, to tear apart…" He paused again. "The gate guards I killed are dead—*we* killed are dead. But after we leave and join the war, we'll meet others like them. If I fought the ones from Likrásk again today, I could do such *horrible* things to them. Is that what I *should* do? Is that what Klanjad does? And if I do things like that…shouldn't it matter to me?"

At long last, Ranja understood what Kenlin had been talking around. "You're asking about appropriate force," she said with a comprehending nod. Kenlin neither agreed nor disagreed, but simply met her gaze. "You're asking if the kind of violence you can do with magic, the violence you've been training for, is…excessive. Right? Well, if that's your concern, Kenlin, then you should take another look at the moon and let that put your mind at ease."

His eyes flicked cursorily toward the blood moon. "That isn't real to me, Ranja. You've told me what it means, but…" He didn't finish that sentence; Ranja had chastised him too many times for saying things along the lines of, "not my disaster."

But now she wasn't chastising: "Then as someone to whom it *is* real, as someone who has seen the ashes fresh in dead hamlets in Kilgáire, let me give you my perspective. I hate pain. I *hate* it. Anyone or anything that creates needless pain is my enemy. You might imagine that would make me reluctant to cause pain to the Droál, but that's not true: any pain they feel is infinitesimal and irrelevant compared to the pain they cause. I celebrate anything—*anything*—that we can do to oppose them."

She'd felt the emotion building in her voice as she said this, and she took a few breaths to calm herself. Hearing her vehemence, however, Kenlin seemed intrigued, though still unsure. "Anything? That's…a lot. I'm not sure how I feel about that. Or rather, I'm not sure how I feel about how I feel about that."

"Don't go cultivating feelings about your feelings," Ranja retorted a little brusquely. "That's not helpful to anyone."

"Restraint—knowing where to stop—is an important part of magic."

"Restraint is an important part of everything, but it should only go so far. Once a fight has started, you don't want restraint and balance; you want victory, decisively, in as little time as possible and with as much violence as is necessary. *Anything*, Kenlin; don't let yourself overthink it. There is no violence you can do that would not be completely justified against the Droál."

Kenlin shrugged. "If you say so."

"I do say so," said Ranja a little grumpily; it had taken them a long time to get to the bottom of what was troubling Kenlin, and the fact that he still seemed uncertain was getting annoying. "And once you've seen the fresh ashes for yourself, you'll say so too."

Kenlin cocked his head at this, thinking for a moment. Then, nodding toward the red moon to the west, he said, "Fresh ashes like those?"

"Well…" Ranja sighed and shook her head. "Those ashes are fresh, yes, but we won't be going to see them. There's nothing for us there, and worse than nothing for Father. If I'm right (and I am), he'll have us skirt Ralua Lake on the north side, then rejoin the highway a few leagues from the city and continue north from there. We won't go back to Likrásk. Don't worry, though," she said with a wry, dark laugh as Kenlin frowned. "There are ashes like that all over the northeast. Once we reach the Commune and you join the war, you'll see. A little patience will provide you with all of the horrors you could ever want."

"Ha! I'll look forward to that," he said with a wry, dark chuckle of his own. Then they both fell silent. For her, the conversation was over.

CHAPTER XVII:

She had been right, of course, both about Klanjad's interpretation of the blood moon and about his response to it. He had announced their impending departure the following morning, and after a full day of preparing and gathering supplies, they set out the morning after. They journeyed north and west (as she'd known they would) through the wetlands around Ralua Lake, avoiding settlements and favoring caution over speed. All throughout the region were the unmistakable signs: a restive population, depletion and famine, and the occasional burnt-out homestead. At long last, war had come to the southeast.

Though they all saw the signs, no one commented on them beyond a passing observation. Kenlin in particular seemed a bit more contemplative than usual, Ranja thought, and his questions mostly focused on the surrounding region and their intended route through it. Perhaps he was still mulling over their conversation, or perhaps she had managed to impress upon him that scorched ruins were not a good topic to broach with Klanjad. Whatever the case, she gave the matter little thought.

At their brisk-but-cautious pace, it took nearly four days of trekking before they finally rejoined the highway a few leagues north of Likrásk. Knowing what lay to the south, Ranja had expected Klanjad to immediately turn them north, traveling as fast and far from the ruins as possible. But to her surprise, even though they reached the highway with a little daylight to spare, Klanjad said, "Let's find an out-of-sight place to camp, shall we? From now on, the days will be long and the pace will be quick, so we should all enjoy the rest while we can get it."

"I can do that," said Kenlin with a grin. "So in that spirit, I claim the first watch, and the best night's sleep afterward."

Ranja snorted. "Mind you don't accidentally watch the whole night through again. Or *do*, if you like; I won't complain."

But it had been a long time since Kenlin had overextended his watch, and he dutifully awakened her for the second watch when the moon was nearing its zenith. Rubbing the dreams from her eyes, she sought out the lumpiest patch of ground she could find and sat on it: it's harder to nod off when your seat is uncomfortable.

But it was difficult to be sure that she was actually managing to stay awake, for the nighttime prairie was vast and empty and unchanging. She blinked, and when she opened her eyes there was no way of knowing how much time had passed. There was the moon, and the stars around it, all in mostly the same places they had been before. And there were the last embers of the fire; had they been brighter a moment ago, or had she imagined it? And the windswept grasses still waved and hissed, and Klanjad still slept tensely where he'd been all night, and Kenlin... Kenlin was gone.

Ranja's first absurd reaction was that someone had kidnapped Kenlin from right within their camp, but her brain discarded that notion as soon as it was awake. Of course he hadn't been taken, he must have gone somewhere. He had gone...

"Father!" she yell-whispered in alarm, springing to her feet. "Father, Kenlin's not here, he's left the camp! I think he's gone to Likrásk!"

Klanjad had jolted awake at her first startled cry, staring about wildly for a threat; but as sleep gave way to thinking, he let out a deep, irritated breath. "Ranja, don't *do* that. You shouldn't scare someone awake unless you're trying to kill them; and even then, it's still rude."

"Did you not hear me? I said Kenlin's gone—"

"Yes, I heard you. So he's gone to Likrásk. Why would he would do that?"

"I don't know!" But her mind was now fully awake and racing, and the pieces weren't too hard to put together. "Well... I think he wants to see the ashes. We talked, he and I, and I told him—sort of—that he would understand the war, and our role in it, better if he could see... But I told him we weren't going there, and why, and that there would be other ashes later..."

Klanjad said dryly, "Yes, I can see why you'd think that would satisfy him, considering his well-known patience and lackadaisical curiosity."

"You're not helping, Father," she snapped, still flustered. But then she squinted through the darkness; it was hard to discern, but it looked as though Klanjad's expression was almost...pleased. "But then, perhaps you don't think this is a problem. You don't look as concerned as I would have expected. Or as surprised."

Klanjad merely shrugged. "I knew you'd talked, and I had some idea of what about. You told him he would understand once he saw? Perhaps you were right."

"And perhaps the Droál left sentries to watch the ruins, or guards on the road! Perhaps there are Unnatilz wandering the area who would love nothing better than to find a lone Jazei to hunt!" Vexation stopped her voice for a moment, and she shook herself. "I'm going after him."

"Through the sentries and the guards and the Unnatilz?" Klanjad asked, raising an eyebrow.

But there was no concern in his voice, nor—from what Ranja could see—in his face. She said suspiciously, "You really don't think there's any danger, do you?"

"There's always danger, Ranja. But the Droál have left this area; that's why we're leaving now, too. Something forced them, after five moons, to abandon the waiting game and move decisively against Likrásk. That tells me they have bigger plans in other places; that's not a signal we can afford to ignore. As for dangers here, they may still have left some dregs, of course. But there was no one watching the lakeside, no one watching the highway, no one using magic anywhere I could sense them; and if there are Unnatilz, the fact that they haven't found us yet suggests they aren't hunting in this area. So yes, it's always dangerous for any of us to venture out alone. But in this case, if it helps him understand…"

Ranja said exasperatedly, "Then why didn't you just take us all to Likrásk in the first place?"

But she knew the answer even before Klanjad began it, just as she knew to expect the darkness in his voice. "I could say that it's better for Kenlin to have chosen on his own. I could say I wasn't certain that he *would* choose it. But you know better."

"I know. And you won't come with me."

"Go if you must. I will follow at a distance, just for safety. But I won't approach the ashes. Meet me back here when you and Kenlin are ready, and we'll strike camp and be on our way."

There was nothing else to say. Hefting her glaive, Ranja turned to follow the highway south.

. . .

By the time Ranja arrived at Likrásk, the eastern sky had turned a gentle orange. The predawn light was wan, but it was enough that she could clearly see the wreckage.

And the wreckage was *everywhere*. The least damage had been done to the slums outside the walls, through the midst of which the highway passed. Here and there, small piles of rubble indicated where a shanty had been torn down and set ablaze, but for the most part the area was untouched by fire. A sparse few corpses, now half-decayed, littered the ground. It seemed as though the Droál had merely charged through this area, slaughtering and destroying as they went, but not lingering; their real business was beyond.

Ahead of Ranja, the half-light fell on the ruins of Likrásk's fortifications. When last she had seen them, these walls had been a patchwork of decrepit masonry and wooden palisades. But now the wooden sections had all been torched or hacked apart, and significant portions of the stonework had been pulled down. The gates looked to have been blasted open with a force that could only have come from Necromancy. Beyond the broken gates and ruined walls, all the ground was jagged darkness.

Ranja was gripped by a sudden hesitancy, somewhere between reluctance and fear: she did not want to go through those gates. She knew what lay beyond them, of course—she had seen it before—but she hated the idea of seeing it again. She knew these thoughts were a folly and a weakness, but she wasn't ashamed: some weaknesses are worth having.

She called out once; Kenlin didn't answer. She called again, louder this time, and still he did not answer. Perhaps something could have befallen him, but she doubted it. He was simply out of earshot; he was *in there.*

After a moment, Ranja decided to make her way to the west gate, the one that they had actually escaped by; perhaps then Kenlin would be closer, and she could call him without having to enter the city itself. As the light grew stronger, she picked her way around the city's edge through what remained of the slums, hardly glancing at the corpses she stepped over. There was nothing new for her there; in her short life, even without having traveled much outside Commune lands, she had seen death in so many forms already that she'd lost count. When preparing to fight, she would summon these dead into her mind to awaken a righteous fury and spur her into battle. But there was no battle today, and these were not the furious dead; these had died frightened and helpless, and the only thing their bodies evoked in Ranja was despair.

The sun had nearly broached the horizon when Ranja finally reached the city's western gate. Peering through, she found she could see the charred wreckage in far more detail, silhouetted as it was against the dawn. Foundations and the bottoms of a few stone walls, all blacked with fire, were all that remained of the structures that once stood in Likrásk. The rest was ash and fragmented, half-burned chunks of refuse. Here and there, Ranja could identify distinct shapes: a wrought-iron hinge, chipped and cracked crockery, a scorched bearskin rug, a shattered mirror. Nothing was left unharmed. The strongest buildings had been battered with Necromancy, the weaker ones left momentarily standing, and ultimately everything had been put to the torch. Out in the middle of the wider streets, away from the ruins of the buildings, heaps of smaller debris lay in dense, regularly-sized groups. Weird, twisted, knotted spires reached upward from these heaps like hellish reeds, with long, thick stalks that terminated in a few short, spindly appendages. But Ranja hated those; they were the worst of what she hadn't wanted to see, what her father couldn't stand to see.

A crunch of gravel startled Ranja badly. She spun about, her heart pounding in her ears but her hands steady on her glaive, but she found herself facing only Kenlin. He had come from somewhere to the west, away from the city; he didn't wait for her to ask where.

"They burned the old woman in her house and left her there," he said. He seemed strangely calm: his voice was mild and his stance relatively relaxed, as though he had run out of emotions—not drained, but somehow vacant and void. But the rising sun reflected in his eyes, speckling the emerald with fire, and his right hand trembled slightly. She could not be sure, but she thought she understood.

"I'm sorry," she said after a moment, "about the old woman. She was good to us when we needed her."

Kenlin didn't answer. What could he have said? They stood in silence, Ranja watching Kenlin and Kenlin staring at nothing. Then after a moment, he stepped past her, taking hold of her arm and beginning to guide her into the city. When she resisted, he let go and kept walking. Ranja sighed;

he could tell she didn't want to go into the city, but he also knew she would follow him in if he asked. She followed.

He didn't deviate from the main road, but walked straight toward one of the heaps from which the burnt, gnarled things reached up. As they got closer, shapes in the heap became more distinguishable: bumps and lumps amidst the remnants of a burned wooden cage. Ranja felt herself pulling back even as she walked forward. She hated this so; why did Kenlin want her here?

He kept walking mechanically until he was right at the edge of the charred heap. Then he crouched down until his eyes were level with the things that reached up. "It was difficult to make out details earlier, in the dark," he said in a flat tone. "These... These aren't just ashes. But these are what I should see, yes?"

Ranja was standing a few steps behind Kenlin, her eyes on the ground. He wanted her to say it. She knew what they were, but saying it made it too real. She took a deep breath. "Hands," she said. "They're burned hands, reaching up. Yes, this is what you should see."

"I see them," he said quietly.

"Do you understand now?"

"No. But I see."

It was several minutes before Kenlin stood. For a moment, he seemed to hesitate; the trembling in his hands was more violent than ever. Gently, Ranja stepped forward and took hold of Kenlin's arm just above the elbow. "Come, Kenlin; our war is not here anymore." For a moment, he didn't move. Then he turned and, with Ranja, walked away from the twisted, reaching hands.

. . .

Liberation... That's what I feel. The ashes have brought me...liberation.

No, that's wrong. This is horrific; this is unconscionable. The ashes have brought me shock, revulsion, nausea, indignation... What monsters could do this? What could be more horrid than this? How could anything—anything—be excessive or extreme against something so evil?

Anything. Anything. Against them, I can do anything. How wonderfully simple! With such a conclusion, how could I not feel liberated?

So why, at the same time, am I also frightened?

Chapter XVIII:

Kenlin and Ranja didn't make it back to the camp until shortly before midday. They found Klanjad waiting for them there. Kenlin had half expected his uncle to be angry, to berate him for going off on his own and to lecture him about the dangers of recklessness. But Klanjad said nothing. In fact, nobody said anything; apart from practical exchanges of information, the Jazeiz hardly spoke to each other for the rest of that day.

Given how little rest Kenlin and Ranja had gotten the night before, they hardly made any progress that day before making camp again on the increasingly open and barren prairie. The next day was better; they made excellent progress following the highway, and at the end of the day they had enough energy for a cursory bit of weapons training. However, Klanjad specifically forbid Kenlin from using magic. Kenlin hadn't been planning to anyway. He was still sifting his thoughts about what he'd seen at Likrásk, and it was difficult for him to focus his mind on anything else, nor did he have the curiosity to ask Klanjad what he was worried about.

But Klanjad's worries only became more pronounced as they continued north for two more days without incident. Ranja, stirring briefly from the silence that had darkened her mood since Likrásk, asked him about it—Kenlin was only half paying attention—and Klanjad muttered something vague about how, "There must be something happening," with the Commune and the war. *I should probably care more about what's bothering him. I will, I'm sure I will, once it's nearer. For the moment, though, I just want to think; traveling is an excellent time to think.*

The next significant town along the highway was Slionte, about four or five days north of Likrásk on foot, and as the

Jazeiz began their fourth full day of traveling toward it Klanjad seemed more agitated than ever. Ranja didn't comment, preferring to maintain her own brooding quiet; but Kenlin, to his own surprise, also felt a little oddly...off. *Is this just second-hand agitation from Klanjad?* He felt more alert today, less preoccupied with thoughts and memories and more attentive to the world around; and yet, for almost the entire day, the world around him was nothing more than empty prairie.

Except to the left. There's something... No, even there, there's nothing, it's just empty grassland. Why does the left feel so weird?

As the sun was setting and the time drew near for them to camp for the night, an odd, almost innocuous discomfort began to bother Kenlin's neck and left ear. He shrugged his shoulder and shook himself, but the feeling was still there. He turned toward it, frowning; the discomfort moved into his face and teeth.

Klanjad, whose agitation had now matured into tense readiness, was watching him. "You feel it?" he said, nodding grimly. "Your sense is keen. Even I wasn't sure until recently."

My sense? And you sense it too? "So...I'm sensing magic, then, yes. It feels weird; it feels different from before, when I sensed the Misks."

Klanjad nodded again. "Yes, Misks have a strong presence, and the ones you've encountered have all been very close. This presence is far away to the west, and it's residual— like mine would feel, if you weren't already accustomed to being near me."

The mention of sensing magic had woken Ranja from her reverie. She was listening, and at the mention of residual presence a hint of alarm had appeared in her face. "Unnatilz?" she asked.

"That's my guess," Klanjad replied, looking very grave. Then he shrugged suddenly, "Well! I can't rule out that it's an ordinary human magician who has enlisted with the Droál for some inconceivable reason. Or that it's a farm hand, or perhaps a milkmaid, who has enough natural magical talent to be sensed at such a great distance. With so many possibilities, I think we should stay on the highway and wait blithely to find out which is true. Thoughts?"

"I agree," said Ranja seriously. "Kenlin?"

"Definitely. Let's." And with that, they all turned from the highway and strode quickly eastward, away from the unknown presence.

But either the presence was following them or Kenlin's sense of magic was growing stronger with every step. After several minutes of brisk walking, he said, "Klanjad, I don't think I can disprove your milkmaid theory yet, but I'd like to bet against it."

"No bet," Klanjad answered, and all trace of humor was gone from his voice. "It's coming closer. We need to get out of the open—and, if possible, into water. If it is Unnatilz, there might be more than one, and if they aren't all magicians then they could be anywhere. Stay close to me, and be wary of any movement you see."

As the three of them broke into a jog, Kenlin said, "Remind me: why do Unnatilz fear water?"

Klanjad was now far too tense to bother with Kenlin's curiosity, so Ranja answered, "They don't exactly *fear* it, but they try to avoid it and they won't go into it. Unnatilz don't see colors like we do, they see some combination of heat and motion; so they can't see water very well, I think because water moves a lot and has its own heat patterns. Thus, if their prey goes into—"

"Enough," Klanjad ordered. "Save your breath, and keep your eyes watchful. Look for trees or taller bushes, anything that might grow along a waterway."

But even as their search became more urgent and the presence-sense grew stronger and stronger on the back of Kenlin's neck, the sun fell below the horizon and darkness swiftly overpowered the twilight. At this point, Klanjad was

glancing worriedly over his shoulder; Kenlin heard him
mutter, "The wind's in the east; and this is their hour, too.
Their terrain, their weather, their light... This is *all* for them."
Kenlin knew very little of Unnatilz, but he suddenly imagined
a fight in the dark against a creature that didn't need light to
see. He swallowed nervously and jogged a little faster.

"There!" Ranja stopped suddenly, and both men skidded
to a halt to see what she was pointing at. Perhaps a quarter of
a league to the north, she had spied a dark line of vegetation
that almost certainly indicated a stream.

Klanjad stared for a moment toward the faraway stream,
then glanced back toward the west; the unknown presence was
now unmistakably nearer. "Ittarshil," he cursed under his
breath, then turned to the north and broke into a run.

Kenlin had to run too in order to keep up; and Ranja,
who was shorter than the men, was nearly sprinting. Puffing
and gasping, they arrived at the stream within minutes only to
find that it was little more than a brook. As Kenlin and Ranja
caught a few deep breaths, Klanjad ran to the brook and
stepped in; it hardly reached his ankle. He cursed again and
kicked the water, sending a spray of droplets across the
opposite bank.

Ranja was badly winded from the run, but she managed
to gasp, "It's a herding region...downstream...must be...pond
or water hole..."

"I know," said Klanjad angrily, bounding back up the
bank. "We'll have to run for it and hope it's closer than our
pursuer."

"Pursuers," Kenlin corrected automatically. Klanjad gave
him a quizzical look, so he explained in short breaths, "I sense
two. Two magicians, anyway. Why, you sense more?"

Klanjad did not answer, but his face was still perplexed
as he turned and resumed running, this time eastward
alongside the stream. He did not push the pace quite as hard
as before, perhaps trying to conserve his strength. But the
presences continued to gain on them until Kenlin found

himself involuntarily glancing over his shoulder, staring fruitlessly into the darkness behind.

After several minutes of running they crested a slight roll in the land, and all three of them gave a cry of relief. There, a few hundred yards away, was a small farmstead of some kind; and on the near side of the settlement, the little stream emptied into what appeared to be a small but adequate pool.

By unspoken consent, they all shrugged off their packs and began to sprint. Kenlin started slower and followed a ways behind while Klanjad drove the pace in the front, practically carrying Ranja along now with a hand on the small of her back. They were perhaps three hundred yards from the pool when the pursuing presences suddenly loomed large in Kenlin's mind, and his head turned instinctively to look back.

As he looked back he stumbled and fell, and only that chance saved his life. He had been running as fast as he could go without using magic, but the thing that passed him was an indistinct blur. All that he could discern as he toppled was a knife flashing through the air where a less clumsy runner's throat would have been.

As Kenlin picked himself up off the ground, he saw that the Unnatilz had not turned aside after failing to kill Kenlin; he had been an opportune kill, not the real target. The creature streaked onward at unbelievable speed, charging down on Klanjad and Ranja.

At the last possible instant, Klanjad shoved Ranja out of harm's way and spun on his heel, ripping his sword from its sheath. At the same moment, the Unnatilz Faded and leapt into the air in a kind of pounce, holding a knife before it, putting its entire body weight and the full power of its jump behind the weapon. That blow would land with enough force kill through a shield and plate armor.

If Klanjad had been slower, or even slightly less powerful a magician, he could not have survived. As the Unnatilz flew toward him, Klanjad Faded to the limits of his magic and flung himself into an impossible twist, whirling toward his attacker and whipping his sword in a swipe from left to right. The sword struck the Unnatilz's outstretched forearms, severing one completely and cutting through the bone on the other. As the weapons and limbs tangled, the Unnatilz's knife was swatted away from Klanjad's chest; but the force of the Unnatilz's pounce could not be stopped, and the two of them collided and fell. The Unnatilz tumbled away, roaring in pain and trying in turn to grip each severed arm with the other one. Klanjad was bowled over backward; his ankle gave a loud *crack* and his head hit the ground hard. He did not cry out or get up.

But the Unnatilz was still conscious and, for all Kenlin knew, still dangerous. Ranja had pulled her glaive from her back and was approaching the wounded Unnatilz. Thrusting himself to his feet, Kenlin Faded and began to run to help.

But as soon has he Faded, he sensed the second presence behind him, and he looked back. Out of the darkness sped a second Unnatilz, and this one Kenlin saw clearly. The creature was half a head taller than Kenlin, with burnt-orange skin, wild reddish hair and glaring crimson eyes. It was bare-chested, clad only in a rough but light kilt, the sides of which were adorned with several knives, and it wore no shoes. Kenlin was now Faded and, he knew, running impossibly fast for a human; the Unnatilz was not Faded, yet it was catching Kenlin as though he were standing still. A deep, primal fear such as he had never experienced, neither as a hunter nor as a fighter, drove his heart into his throat: he had been chased by predators many times, but never before had he felt like prey.

Kenlin didn't even try to draw his sword, turn, and fight. As the Unnatilz gathered itself and pounced, its knife before it, Kenlin threw himself flat on the ground, guarding his neck with his hands and hoping the Unnatilz had jumped high enough to pass over him.

As Kenlin hit the ground, he saw from the corner of his eye that the Unnatilz had twisted in midair, amending its posture mid-flight, and for an instant Kenlin was sure he was about to die. But his tactic just barely worked, for the Unnatilz couldn't quite reach him as it flew over; the knife it held out to slice him barely caught at his shirt, failing even to draw blood. The creature's midair gymnastics upset its landing, and it stumbled as it hit the ground, giving Kenlin time to scramble to his feet and press the attack.

As he rushed the Unnatilz, Kenlin fumbled for his sword, but even as he drew it he passed its effective range. Leaving the sword half in and half out of its sheath, he Faded to his fullest and tackled the Unnatilz.

The creature was undoubtedly surprised by this tactic, and Kenlin took the opportunity while it adjusted to knock its knife from its hand. But an instant later the Unnatilz was in control, flipping their positions so that Kenlin was on his back with the Unnatilz astride him. Kenlin struck at the creature with his fists, but it seemed not to be injured even by the magically strengthened blows. Sitting back, it reached toward its kilt to draw another knife; desperately, Kenlin swung his arms, locked his hands behind the Unnatilz's back, and flared his elbows, obstructing the creature's range of motion. The Unnatilz elbowed Kenlin's left bicep, breaking his grip, then wrenched the arm around until Kenlin's own arm was across his throat. Fading, the Unnatilz pressed down violently. Kenlin struggled, yet even with his own magic he was not strong enough to break the choke.

But with the Unnatilz's hands busy pinning Kenlin's left arm, his right arm was free, and because his sword was still half drawn, he was just able to reach the grip. As Kenlin's vision turned into a tunnel, he pulled the sword out of its sheath and across the Unnatilz's back; the creature cried out in pain, and the pressure on Kenlin's arm momentarily diminished. Dangerously Fading further still—beyond any magic he had ever used—Kenlin threw his strength against the Unnatilz and knocked it up and off of him. Immediately, the creature reached for its knives, and such was its speed that it actually managed to draw them and get to its feet; but Kenlin stabbed from his position on the ground, penetrating a few inches into the Unnatilz's stomach. As the creature cried out, Kenlin rolled up into a crouch and stabbed again, running it through.

As the creature fell to the ground, relief flooded Kenlin's heart while a cackling roar of laughter flared in his mind, but there was no time to consider either. No longer under attack, Kenlin finally looked back to where Klanjad had fallen; he was still there, lying a few feet from the writhing Unnatilz he had wounded. Ranja was several yards north of them, fighting for her life against yet another Unnatilz.

The laughter in his head redoubled at the sight of this last Unnatilz, and his feet rushed forward of their own accord. But the narrowness of his survival so far had shaken Kenlin, and he wrested control of his body away from its laughing onslaught. *There could be even more; we need to get to the water!* Hesitating for a moment, he looked from Klanjad's unconscious form to Ranja's desperate fight and back again, then ran to his uncle. Still Faded, Kenlin lifted Klanjad and sprinted to the pool's edge, where he paused to look back at Ranja. She was skipping back and forth, slowly retreating toward the pool but barely fending off her attacker. Kenlin could not sense this Unnatilz, which must mean it was not a magician, but that was small comfort. Ranja was surviving by keeping it at glaive range, but it was only a matter of time before the creature's speed overwhelmed her.

Finally, as she was forced to hop back off-balance to maintain range, Kenlin tossed his unconscious uncle into the pool to protect him and ran back toward Ranja. She did not hear him coming and did not turn, but she shrieked out loud when he grabbed her about the waist from behind and began hauling her back to the pool at full sprint, pausing only to fling his sword at the startled Unnatilz. As the two Jazeiz neared the pool, Ranja screamed some warning just before Kenlin felt a sharp pain in his left shank—the Unnatilz had thrown a small knife to trip him. He toppled forward, but by that time they were too close to the pool to be stopped. They tumbled into the shallows, and Ranja pulled him into the deeper water and out of the Unnatilz's reach.

Kenlin waited several seconds before surfacing as cautiously as he could, already Faded to retreat back under the water should the Unnatilz throw another knife. The creature was standing on the bank, but it wasn't looking at him. Following its gaze, Kenlin saw that lights had been lit in one of the buildings nearby; the sound of the fight had alerted the settlement. Kenlin looked back at the Unnatilz just as it seemed to make up its mind. It turned away from the pool and dashed to its companion with the severed arms. The two of them spoke for a moment in some undulating, guttural language Kenlin had never heard. Then the uninjured Unnatilz thrust a long knife up through its companion's chin; the wounded Unnatilz went limp. The last Unnatilz then stood up and sprinted away into the night.

CHAPTER XIX:

"Kenlin, help me!" Shaking off the flurry of emotions that had swarmed him during the fight, Kenlin turned. Ranja had found her unconscious father and fished him from the bottom of the pool, but she was struggling to hold her grip on his limp body. "Get him out of the water, he's not breathing," she said urgently.

Kenlin waded over and slung Klanjad over his shoulder like a sack. *She's right, he's not breathing; there must be water in his lungs.* The pool was only waist deep here, so he stood up, secured Klanjad on his shoulder, and began to bounce up and down on his feet.

"What *are* you doing?" Ranja hissed incredulously.

Still bouncing, Kenlin answered, "This is what you do for drowning people; it shakes the water out of them." Ranja clearly had some choice invective for this practice, but before she could deliver it, Klanjad started awake and began to cough and splutter. "There, see?" said Kenlin, setting his uncle down in the shallows.

She was not convinced but contented herself with a skeptical frown. Klanjad, meanwhile, was spluttering out the last of the water in his lungs. "Are they gone?" he gasped. "I don't remember reaching the water."

"They're gone," said Kenlin. "The last one fled just a moment ago."

"There were more than two, then?"

"There were three," Kenlin answered, "but only two were magicians. Both the magicians are dead."

"I see," Klanjad nodded pensively, his breath returning. "There really were two magicians, then. That's...interesting."

Kenlin was about to why that was interesting when a sudden pain shot through his leg. "*Atch!* Ranja, what...?" She held up a small knife, the blade of which was bloodied; it took a moment for Kenlin to realize it was the knife the Unnatilz had thrown to trip him.

Glancing at the weapon, Klanjad asked, "Were you hurt?"

"Not really," Kenlin said distractedly. He took the knife in his hand, then reached back to probe the wound to his left calf muscle. The wound was small and clean and didn't seem to be very deep. When he tried to flex his foot, the pain made him wince, but he could do it. "It's only a flesh wound, it won't be a problem. And what about you?" he asked, turning back to Klanjad. "You took quite a fall, and I heard your ankle crack. Are you alright?"

Klanjad chuckled, but mirth was laced with more than a hint of stoicism. "As for the fall, I really don't remember it," he said dismissively. "And as for my ankle, why don't you look at it yourself and tell me how it is."

"I won't be able to tell you much in the dark," Kenlin pointed out. "You've sprained it at least, I feel sure of that. If we're lucky, that will be the worst of it, but I won't be able to tell more without light."

"Ligh'," mumbled a new voice. All three of the Jazeiz whirled—Klanjad sat bolt upright, Ranja snatched her glaive, and Kenlin clawed at his empty scabbard—but there was no threat. A wiry and very sleepy young man in a long nightgown stood near the edge of the pond, blinking at them. If he found anything odd about their appearance or behavior, he gave no sign, but continued drowsily, "I have ligh' on in the house— which is jus' all wrong, as this's the time for sleep. Whyn't ya come to the house, sleep on the floor fer now. We c'n talk in the mornin'."

Kenlin had no idea what to make of this; and from the alarmed looks on their faces, neither did Klanjad or Ranja. Klanjad said warily, "That's an abruptly generous offer, friend."

"Yes indeed," mumbled the sleepy man, " 'bruptly gen'rous. Nothin' else for it at the moment. Ye'r a miss-tree is what ya are, and I'm better fer miss-trees when I'm awake, s' I reckon I'll solve ya in the mornin', an' ya migh' as well be inside 'til then."

Kenlin struggled to follow the man's logic through his rural, low-Jazeskri dialect. "We're a mystery, and you don't know what to think of us...so you're inviting us into your house until you're awake enough to figure it out?" The man tapped his head repeatedly with one finger, which Kenlin could only assume was a confirmation of sorts.

Ranja told him baldly, "You're very trusting for no obvious reason."

"Hey," said the sleepy man with a dramatic, resigned shrug, "I mayn't be awake, but I mayn't be a fool. I heard the ruckus, an' I see a carcass yonder." He waved his arm in the general direction of the Unnatilz Klanjad had dismembered. "So y'all know yer way roun' a figh', an' I don', an' my brothers is all afield, an' the dogs with 'em, so hey," he repeated, and shrugged again. "All tha' said, wha's mine is yers; I couldn' stop ya from takin' it anyway."

Apparently he felt that the conversation was concluded, because he turned and trudged back to the nearest building, where a light shone through a window. There was a brief murmur of voices—the sleepy man's and a much less sleepy, much more alarmed woman's—and then there was silence: silence from the house, and for several minutes silence from the bewildered Jazeiz.

"I like him!" Ranja declared suddenly and brightly. "Honest, direct, practical... He's a real philosopher, this one."

Kenlin looked at her askance. "Honest, direct, and practical...philosophy."

"Well, what do you want, 'sagacity of the commons?' You understand what I mean, though."

"I'm not sure I understand anything that just happened," Kenlin retorted, shaking his head. "We killed two Unnatilz outside his house at night, rousing him as he was trying to go to sleep, and therefore he invites us into his home? Klanjad, is this a real offer?"

"I cannot begin to fathom why you might think I could answer that," Klanjad said flatly. He might have said more, but at that moment one of the house's windows opened and the sleepy man's head reappeared.

"Also," continued the man, "even if ya won' come in, would ya mind gettin' out o' the pool? Come mornin', I'll be wantin' to drink that water, so mind you don' muddy it, or...bleed in it, or otherwise." Then the window closed, and he was gone again.

"Kenlin," said Ranja with a sudden air of reproach, "stop bleeding in the man's drinking water. After all the hospitality he's offered us!"

"I do not know how genuine you're being right now," Kenlin declared. "Are you truly suggesting we take up his offer, enter a completely unknown home, and go to sleep there?"

She shrugged and said loftily, "Perhaps you should take a moment to think through our other options."

Alright. We could continue along and pitch our own camp, as we always do; but the third Unnatilz, which neither Klanjad nor I can sense with magic, is still out there and would surely catch us unawares. We might try to make it all the way to Slionte, which Klanjad said is close; but if it's not very, very close, Klanjad might not be able to walk there on that ankle. Alternatively, we could... But he couldn't think of more alternatives, and Ranja's irritating smirk was growing more smug with every passing moment. Ignoring her, he asked Klanjad, "Is your ankle too badly hurt, or do you think you can walk?"

Klanjad didn't bother with this question. "Give up. She's right. I don't like it even a little, but we have no better option. Ranja, help me to the house. Kenlin, go collect...everything.

And *be careful!* That third Unnatilz may still be nearby; do not hesitate to use magic if you think you need it."

Kenlin was on the very edge of his nerves as he ventured away from the water, ready to Fade and bolt at the slightest provocation. But nothing happened, and he was able to safely retrieve their dropped weapons and packs. When he rejoined his companions, he found them settling into the house's front room, which was separated from the rest of the dwelling by a closed door. Ranja had laid immediate claim to the room's only sheepskin rug and was already nestling happily upon it; her father sat propped up against a wall from which he could see both doors. "You're taking the first watch, then?" Kenlin asked as he handed Klanjad his sword.

Klanjad shook his head. "I'm taking *all* the watches tonight. Don't argue! I'm useless on one foot, so I won't need energy tomorrow while you two will need more than usual."

"Can you stay awake the whole night? I'm still not sure about..." He nodded warily toward the closed door, beyond which their abruptly generous host slept.

Klanjad was at least as uncomfortable with the arrangement as Kenlin was, but he said, "It is what it is, Kenlin. I can handle the watchfulness, so the only thing for you to do is to sleep and enjoy the shelter while we have it. And who knows? Maybe our host really is exactly what he claims to be. Maybe this house really isn't a trap."

Trap. They had all been thinking it, but Kenlin still wished the word hadn't been said. It echoed in his mind, made it difficult to fall asleep, and troubled and corrupted his dreams.

. . .

Kenlin came awake slowly, and that was strange. His head felt heavy, ponderous, and sluggish; that, too, was strange. He shifted his position, trying to get comfortable enough to go back to sleep, and only then did he understand what he was feeling. *I am warm. I am dry—or at least, drying. And it's not too bright in here, and the wind isn't blowing, and everything's quiet, and Klanjad's keeping watch. I am comfortable, and I am safe. I don't want to wake up because, for the first time in half a year, I don't need to.* And that, ironically, was the thought that awakened him.

He sat up, blinked owlishly, and looked around. The lamp, which had been lit when Kenlin fell asleep, was now extinguished, but the sky outside was bluing and cast enough light for him to see that this house was far more comfortable than any he had ever slept in. No wattle and daub here: these walls were of fresh logs trimmed so carefully that they hardly required caulking. The floor was of split wood sanded down and painstakingly polished. Overhead, the roof was thatched; but even the thatch was clean and orderly as though it had been done, or redone, very recently. Kenlin could not remember ever seeing a home like this; even Jlak's house in Likrásk had not been this beautiful. That house had been nice, and perhaps more luxurious than this one; but the niceness was impersonal, and the luxury was probably obligatory in that neighborhood. This house, though, was nice because it was loved.

The care and pride in the dwelling extended even to the furnishings, which Kenlin hadn't noticed the evening before. Klanjad had seated himself on the floor, but he hadn't needed to; several finely-crafted chairs were placed in corners or against walls throughout the room. An elegant wooden table was pushed against a wall, presumably to be pulled out for dining with guests. And in the table's absence, the center of the room was occupied by Ranja's bleached-white sheepskin rug. Kenlin had done little in the way of woodworking or decorating, but he tried to imagine: *How many days of work does it take to make a home this comfortable and lovely? How much care does this one room contain?*

"D'ya like it?"

Kenlin turned sharply. The door to the rest of the house, which had been closed a moment before, had opened silently (probably well-greased and meticulously balanced, in keeping with the rest of the house), and through the gap now peered the grinning face of their host. With a peculiar sort of prance, he swept the door fully open and bounced lightly through, beaming about as though nothing pleased him more than to have guests admiring his home.

Ranja, apparently already awake, obliged him: "It's a *wonderful* house. Thank you for allowing us into it." Both Jazei men concurred inarticulately.

The young man, smiling broadly, made a grand gesture that was somewhere between a nod and a bow. " 'Twas my pleasure, m'lady. 's not every day ya get the chance t' host Jazeiz." The blooming atmosphere of pleasantry wilted instantly as all three Jazeiz tensed, but their cheery host didn't seem to notice. He prattled on, "I'd heard there was Jazeiz near Likrásk, yon a season or two. But..." A sudden cloud seemed to flit across his countenance; and just as suddenly, it was gone. "...then I lef' there, an' came here. An' seemin'ly, so did you!"

Klanjad raised an eyebrow. "I think that about sums it up. You are correct, I am Jazei; might I know who you are?"

The wiry young man clapped his hand to his forehead dramatically. "M' manners! Knew I was forgettin' somethin'!" Then he spun on his heel and darted out of sight through the doorway behind him.

The Jazeiz all exchanged glances: Ranja's amused, Kenlin's blank, and Klanjad's perplexed. Meeting his uncle's gaze, Kenlin suggested helpfully, "I think he might be eccentric."

While Ranja dissolved into a fit of poorly-suppressed giggles, their host returned as abruptly as he'd departed. Evidently he'd gone to fetch his kirsk dagger, which he now proffered inexpertly to everyone in the room, waving it about in a wide-sweeping gesture outside of arm's reach for any of them.

I suppose it's more surprising that he has a kirsk than that he doesn't know what to do with one; farmers and craftsmen don't typically carry them. But this one almost looks like... Possessed by a sudden insight, Kenlin rose and stepped forward to touch—and examine—the offered dagger pommel. *Just as I thought: it's made of wood.* "Well met. Are you, perchance, a carpenter?"

The young man looked delighted. "Yes indeed! Jrizkil the carver, a' yer service! Wha' made ya think it?"

Returning his host's smile, Kenlin gestured at the room around them. "Quite a lot of very fine woodworking, all in one place."

"Isn' it?" Jrizkil agreed happily. " 's my pride and joy, it is. Well, 's my pride," he corrected himself with a laugh. Pointing toward the door to the rest of the house, he said, "My joy's back yonder, bu' she'll be ou' jus' soon. Her name's Laianna; 'sn' that a beau'iful name? An' I'm sorry, I migh've been babblin': wha'd ya say for yer names?"

Kenlin opened his mouth, but Klanjad beat him to it. "I am Gealvind," he said unhesitatingly. "This is my daughter Relshine, and my nephew Ranton." Kenlin shot his uncle a quick look of surprise, but Klanjad did not meet his eye.

Jrizkil took the names in his stride, declaring grandly, "Lovely to mee' ya, an' welcome to all! Now," he said, sitting in a chair with an air of getting down to business, "if I may be so bold, wha' brings a trio o' bedraggled Jazeiz to our humble home on o' las' nigh'?"

Kenlin and Ranja, following the host's lead, also found chairs to sit in, but they looked to Klanjad to answer the question. He said calmly, "We're travelling north. We had been planning to pass through Slionte today, in fact; but many these days would prefer that we Jazeiz never reach our destinations."

"Droál?" Jrizkil asked quietly; and in that one word there was no mirth, no joke, none of the vivacity that had characterized his every movement for the entire morning.

Klanjad hesitated at the question, but to Kenlin's surprise he decided to answer it. "Not directly Droál. What we fought yesterday were Unnatilz; but they were likely put to task by Droál."

Jrizkil nodded silently.

Before anything else could be said, a movement drew the Jazeiz's attention. A new pair of eyes—large, wide, medium brown doe-eyes—were now peering through the doorway from the rest of the house. Following Klanjad's gaze, Jrizkil also looked toward the door and, springing once more into exuberant action, bounded to his feet and half-dragged the reluctant woman into the room. "An' here's m' joy herself, my lovely Laianna! Laianna, here's our gues's: Gealvind, Relshine, and Ran'on."

She gave a fleeting little smile and a hurried curtsey, but she couldn't seem to bring herself to speak to them. Nervously, she turned to her husband and whispered, "You didn' tell me they's Jazeiz."

He seemed genuinely surprised. "Didn' I? Well, I s'pose I didn' see las' nigh', an' this mornin'... Well, ya did jus' get here." She shot him a reproachful glance, but seemed too bashful to pursue the matter in front of their guests.

Ranja said kindly, "You and your husband have our sincerest thanks for your hospitality." Looking up, Laianna met her eye and seemed on the verge of speech, but her courage failed her almost immediately, and she flushed and turned away.

Jrizkil appeared a little perplexed by his wife's behavior, but he shrugged and turned back to his guests. "So, y'said you were hopin' to pass through Slionte today? Isn' far, jus' up the road from here."

"How far?" Klanjad asked.

Jrizkil scratched his chin. "Two hours by ox cart, or half tha' walkin'. Can ya be doin' much walkin'? I see you've go' yer foot laid ou' there..."

Klanjad's reaction was hardly more than a slight narrowing of the eyes, but it told Kenlin that his uncle had by no means abandoned his suspicions, and this Jrizkil fellow was, among other peculiarities, *suspiciously* observant. But Klanjad's voice was mild as he said, "Yes, the foot is a consideration. I doubt I'll make it beyond the city today, but I don't think we can safely stay here. You mentioned an ox cart?"

"I did, 'cause I have one. Bu' ya know yer welcome to hid ou' here a day or two, if yer foot needs." At these words, Laianna noticeably stiffened, though she did not turn or make a sound.

But Klanjad had noticed her discomfort, and he said wryly to Jrizkil, "I think our staying here would be unwise for several reasons. Most importantly, our enemies in the area probably already know we're here, as one of last night's attackers survived. Could we hire your cart to take me into town?"

"*Pssh*, hire! I'll take ya, sure, bu' I can' take yer money for that! I take that cart into town ev'ry few days anyhow, t' sell my little woodworkin's, so you can jus' ride alongside them, all unsuspicious-like. We'll make a day of it!"

"Sounds festive," said Klanjad, deadpan. "But it *is* probably best that you come to the city, and you should consider staying there a few days. You as well, Laianna; anyone who remains here may be in danger should the Droál decide to investigate. And with that in mind... Jrizkil, you mentioned you have brothers who live here?"

"I do? Oh! *Her* brothers—which *are* my brothers, I jus' don' have the word connection. This's her fam'ly's homestead, ya see, her late father's 'n' all. I married into the fam'ly jus'... Has it really only been two moons, love?" His wife was now so agitated that she could barely manage a nod, but it had been a rhetorical question anyway. Jrizkil chattered on, "But they's afield with the flock anyway, an' they won' be back for the nex' six or seven days."

Klanjad looked inquiringly at Kenlin. *Why is he looking at me? What does he— Ah, a prognosis.* "If you're not well enough to travel within six days," Kenlin said drily, "then we'll have other, far worse problems."

Klanjad nodded. "Very well, then. Both of you should accompany us to the city, then quietly lodge somewhere until we're gone."

"If there's room on the cart, bring your valuables with you," Ranja added, "and leave your house open and unsecured. The Droál will almost certainly come to investigate; but if you make it easy for them, they'll be much less likely to become impatient and damage anything."

Another sudden darkness passed over their host's sunny disposition: "I'll bury the lamp oil, jus' so's they don' ge' any ideas." Then he immediately brightened and continued, "Speakin' o' buryin', is there a dead 'natilz outside from the figh'? I'll have to take care o' that 'fore we go, elsewise things'll come to eat it. Mind joinin' me on that, Ran'on? Gravediggin's much cheerier with two."

CHAPTER XX:

There were two Unnatilz corpses that needed burying, not just one; but the homestead was equipped with several good spades, and Kenlin and Jrizkil completed the task long before the sun was high and hot. When they were finished they all breakfasted on eggs and buttermilk. Kenlin and Ranja then helped Jrizkil and Laianna to load their ox cart with an eclectic assortment of woodcrafts, from furniture to flatware to tiny, hand-carved idols. Finally, the blond Jazeiz donned their cloth hats, Klanjad found a seat on the cart, and the five of them began their journey to Slionte.

This was not the first time Kenlin had seen an ox cart, for they had passed by many on their journeys; however, he had always assumed that the animals were tired, or were overburdened, or were going uphill, or had some other legitimate reason for walking so *incredibly* slowly. But evidently that was not the case, for the cart was lightly loaded and the ox was well-rested, yet the beast still trundled along at an excruciating plod, staring idiotically ahead and swaying like a drunk. "Does it always move like this?" Kenlin asked Jrizkil in amazement.

"Indeed he doesn'," Jrizkil answered brightly, mistaking the question. "I reckon he's feelin' good t'day—go' some bold new life in those ol' legs."

I've seen more lively vegetation. But Kenlin kept his opinions private and simply congratulated himself on neither owning nor planning to own such a dull, stupid, onerous, and odorous animal.

Jrizkil's "two hours by ox cart" estimate had been optimistic; despite a reasonably early start, it was past noon by the time the group reached the south gate of Slionte. Even before they entered the city, Kenlin began to note differences from Likrásk. That city had been surrounded by a dense and squalid slum which had added human stench to the city's fishy odor. Slionte, by contrast, smelled much less unpleasant; and, at least at this gate, there was no slum at all. *Do they have no desperate outcasts here? Or is there room enough in the city for everyone? Or perhaps they are simply stricter in their governance of land, driving the squatters away?* As they neared the walls, this last seemed more and more likely; here and there, small piles of rubble and refuse indicated where an unwelcome shanty had been torn down and set ablaze. *Ironic.*

The walls themselves showed an even starker contrast. Unlike the patchwork of palisades and crumbling masonry that had surrounded Likrásk, Slionte was encircled by an unbroken bulwark of high, thick, well-maintained stone. No fewer than eight liveried soldiers stood just outside the open gate. These guards, though not alarmed, were also not at dice; they cast their eyes over everyone and everything that approached the city, occasionally stopping someone to ask a question or inspect an item. As Jrizkil brought the cart near, the captain hailed him: "Jrizkil! Back again so soon? Carvin' anything?"

"Carvin' everything! Look here, see?" Jrizkil laughed, pointing to the myriad doodles scratched on the side of his cart.

The captain shook his head and chuckled, then nodded toward Laianna. "I see you've a whole crowd with you, the missus included. Who's all these?"

"Gealvind, Relshine, Ran'on," Jrizkil answered, waving his hand nonspecifically toward the Jazeiz. "Trav'lers from the south, go' pursued by some waylayers 'n' happened on the house. They're bound fer the Misplaced Mansion."

The captain nodded understandingly. "These waylayers why you brough' the missus? Well, well, I suppose tha's the prairie these days. Drive on!"

For someone whose manner is so gushy, he's remarkably adept at saying enough and no more. I suppose that's fortunate for us...as far as we know. As they passed through the gates, Kenlin tried to exchange a glance with his companions to see if they, like him, remained uneasy about their host and benefactor. But Klanjad's face was unreadable, and Ranja's only showed the polite passivity she wanted others to see. *Perhaps they truly aren't concerned. And why should they— why should any of us be concerned? Jrizkil has been nothing but helpful and generous towards us. But no one is generous for no reason, and that is why...*

He stopped mid-thought and physically shook himself. *Have I really become so jaded? Can I no longer even imagine simple, honest generosity?* Disturbed, he forced such thoughts from his mind and continued walking alongside the cart.

But the doubt and discomfort lingered, even as Jrizkil merrily chattered them along toward the heart of the city. Slionte was not as large as Likrásk had been, so it was not very long before the cart trundled to a halt before a large and old but well-kept timber inn. "The Misplaced Mansion!" Jrizkil declared grandly. "Not the only tav'rn in town, but the mos' central, and o' my mind the nices'. This'll be yer spot, less'n ya fancy accomp'nyin' Laianna an' me to market."

"This will do," said Klanjad shortly. The strain in his voice caused both Kenlin and Ranja to turn toward him in concern; from his drawn face and stiff posture, they knew his ankle must be very painful.

As the Jazeiz worked together to get Klanjad off the cart, Laianna said to her husband, "You can tend the stall fer a little without me, right? I've got some people I need t' see, won't be an hour."

"Alrigh', as ya please, love. Jus' come by whenever...yer..." But she, nodding vigorously, was already striding away down the street at a brisk walk. Looking bemused, Jrizkil continued to himself. "No worry at all, I c'n unload, an' set up, an' tend, an' sell... Adventure it'll be, then!"

"Have you lost your help?" Ranja asked.

Jrizkil shrugged and answered, "Oh, she'll be by soon's she's seen her frien's, or wha'ever. Can be nothin' slows me down too much, don' ya worry."

"If you need extra hands for the unloading and setup, I'll be happy to help," Kenlin offered, to the obvious astonishment of both Klanjad and Ranja. "It's the least I can do, after everything you've done for us."

Jrizkil looked delighted. "Well, tha's righ' friendly of ya, Ran'on. I wouldn' want ya put out at all, o' course, but... Tell ya wha', why don' ya help yer uncle there inta the Mansion, an' all set up. Then, if yer still up to help, jus' come find me in the market yonder. So?"

Kenlin nodded, trying not to laugh at the increasingly puzzled looks he was receiving from his fellow Jazeiz. "Very well. I'll join you in the market soon. Thank you again!"

As Jrizkil and his cart rolled out of earshot, Ranja looked Kenlin full in the face. "Do tell."

Kenlin shook his head uncertainly. "I'm not sure why, but I'm wary. I want to keep an eye on them, at least for a while longer. I want to see who all knows them and who comes by to talk to them."

Ranja looked skeptical, but she turned to her father to get his opinion. "Not unreasonable," said Klanjad between breaths. "They know who we are. And where we are. And that...I'm unlikely to be able to go somewhere else today."

Kenlin winced at the thought of what pain might elicit such a reaction from Klanjad. "It hurts that much?"

Klanjad shrugged stoically. "Cramped carts and bumpy roads... Come, Ranja, help me into a room where I can set this down properly. Kenlin, go to Jrizkil. Never take off your hat and keep your eyes lowered, but listen to everything and watch everyone. At the slightest hint of danger or betrayal, come find us immediately."

...

It took considerably longer to unload Jrizkil's cart than it had taken to load it. Jrizkil had the notion that the arrangement and relative positions of his wares would dramatically impact his sales, so every time Kenlin unpacked something, he would *hem* and *haw* and rearrange everything to accommodate the new article. None of this seemed to impair Jrizkil's ability to engage with passersby. Person after person—some customers, some conversationalists—stopped to strike up lively discussions on any number of topics. Many knew Jrizkil by name, and the conversations frequently devolved into happy banter and running jokes.

He is, then, what he seems to be. As Kenlin's suspicions became assuaged, his observations began to focus less on Jrizkil and more on the city that surrounded them. At a glance, it seemed very similar to Likrásk, though less odorous and better maintained; but on closer inspection, a thousand subtle cues marked the cultural difference between the two cities. A weariness had dominated the atmosphere of Likrásk: toil and poverty and the decline of trade in a time of war had taken their toll. By contrast, the people of Slionte were tired, but they refused to become weary. They contended with the same shortages that had afflicted their southern neighbor: the most vicious conversations Kenlin witnessed in the market involved haggling for food and other necessities. But even the haggling, once finished, gave way to a stalwart friendliness that Kenlin could only attribute to camaraderie. *Yes, the city faces the same hardship Likrásk faced; but Sliontens face it down together.*

Kenlin lingered until he was fully satisfied that Jrizkil really was the gregarious, abruptly generous carpenter he seemed to be; and then he lingered a little longer, just observing the market. At last, as the sun was beginning to lower, Kenlin bade Jrizkil farewell, asking him to pass on their thanks to Laianna when she returned; then he went back to Klanjad and Ranja at the Misplaced Mansion. Upon inquiry, the innkeeper guided him to the correct room, and once Ranja had removed the barricades from the door, he was able to join them within.

They had rented a second-storey room with two beds: Klanjad lay on one bed, Ranja sat on the other, and Kenlin's bedroll and possessions had been thoughtfully set down for him in the middle of the floor. Kenlin cut his eyes at Ranja (she returned the look completely unabashed) before turning to Klanjad. "How is the ankle?"

"Better." But the curtness of the response belied its intended fortitude. Kenlin was about to offer to make poppy tea, but Klanjad cut him off: "What news from the market? Need we fear exposure or betrayal?"

Kenlin shrugged. "Jrizkil continues to seem exactly as he always has. He apparently knows, and is known by, about half the people who frequent the market. And before you ask, I was mindful of the other people in the market, but none of them seemed suspicious either. The children playing in the area were completely heedless, not like they were in Likrásk. And when anyone did ask who I was, Jrizkil just told them I was his idiot cousin, and no one inquired further."

The phrase *idiot cousin* was, of course, too amusing for Ranja to let pass without comment. But before she could employ whatever witticism she had in mind, they were interrupted by an unexpected, urgent knocking at the door.

All trace of levity instantly vanished from the room. Kenlin's hand went to his sword, Ranja quickly slid from the bed and reached for her glaive, and even Klanjad readied himself to move. The knocking came again, more urgent then before, but this time it was accompanied by a voice: "Ran'on? Sorry, ya in there? Karik said this's yer room…"

Jrizkil? Why would he come here? Unsure, Kenlin looked to Klanjad for guidance, but the older Jazei simply shrugged and nodded toward the door. Kenlin said, "Jrizkil, is that you?"

"Yep, 's me. Can ya open?"

It is Jrizkil's voice, to be sure. But something is wrong, he sounds very hasty and stressed. Without opening the door, Kenlin asked, "Are you alright? Has something happened?"

"No, no, we're alrigh'; bu' yes, somethin's happened. Can ya jus'..." At last, Kenlin opened the door to reveal the tense and uncharacteristically worried Jrizkil. He managed a fleeting smile—"Much obliged."—before continuing hurriedly, "So, Laianna's jus' back, she's had bad news. Tha' third 'natilz, the one ya didn' kill? 'parently it attacked her brothers this mornin'."

Kenlin's heart sank. *After all they've done... Will this sort of danger trail behind us wherever we go?* Aloud, he asked, "How many were hurt? Is anyone dead?"

Jrizkil shook his head. "None dead, thank the bones; bu' one's hurt, apparently pretty bad. She's already sen' the healer along, bu' she's fran'ic fer gettin' back as soon as may be, an' I'm comin' with her. Can ya take care o' my wares an' cart? The two of ya should be able to manage, no trouble, won' take ya two hours. I can prob'ly come back for 'em in a day or two, bu' righ' now..."

Seeing Jrizkil so obviously stressed and overwhelmed made the request hard to refuse; but while Kenlin forced himself not to immediately agree to help, Ranja asked from within the room, "Take care of them how? We certainly won't be able to watch over them in the marketplace."

"Oh, 'course not, 'course not. Laianna's go' a friend in the north city who said she'll keep on an eye. If ya can jus' load up the cart an' take it there, that'd jus' be no end o' help."

"The north of the city?" Ranja pressed. "That's a bit general. How would we find your friend and be sure we'd left the cart with the right person?"

Though she'd said nothing to commit them, Jrizkil's face brightened. "Ya'll do it, then? Wonderful! When ya get near the north gate, jus' ask for Svorline, she's known roun' there."

Kenlin said hesitantly, "I don't fancy knocking on doors..."

Jrizkil waved away that objection. "No need fer tha', anybody on the stree'— Or ask a' the gatehouse, if ya'd rather, someone there'll know her. An' if they don', jus' turn the car' over to the gate guards. They'll watch it like they seized it, an' I'll jus' square it with them soon's I can get back. How's all that, make sense?" He was clearly still in haste. Though he was waiting for real commitment from Kenlin, his impatient shuffling was already inching him down the hallway, back toward his wife and the road to their home.

Every moment of silence from the Jazeiz was deafening. A look of alarm was frozen on Klanjad's face while Kenlin still struggled to keep himself from agreeing to help unreservedly. Ranja seemed torn and uncertain; but as the indecisive silence became painful, she said to Jrizkil, "Just go. We'll find a way to take care of it; go see to your family."

An obvious wave of heartfelt relief washed over Jrizkil's expression. "A thousand thanks, m'lady! A thousand thanks, all!" Then he dashed away down the hall.

Kenlin closed the door. *It's good that we'll help, but I should have said what she said long before. I am becoming too jaded; that was much harder than it should have been.*

As though to contrast Kenlin's thoughts, Klanjad announced flatly, "I don't like it."

Of course you don't. "Well, Klanjad, I doubt it's how Jrizkil was hoping to spend the evening either," he retorted a little more sharply than he'd intended.

Ranja still looked undecided. "You can't deny, Kenlin, that it *is* all very sudden. I don't think any of us like suddenness."

"Was our arrival last night in Jrizkil's pool—our fight outside his home, which is what brought the Unnatilz to his family in the first place—was that not 'sudden?' Yet he reacted pretty graciously, I think."

"Don't get snippy with me," Ranja reproved hotly. "I'm the one who said we would help him, remember? I'm simply pointing out that Jrizkil—consistently, throughout everything he does—is an extremely sudden person, and that's not how we like to operate."

Kenlin took a deep breath and, reluctantly, nodded. "You're right. I can't deny that those things are true."

Klanjad shook his head. "I still don't like it," he repeated. "I don't like it at all. The whole thing is too...too..."

"Sudden?" Ranja offered innocently.

Klanjad shot her a reproachful look before formulating his thoughts clearly. "I don't like putting any of us in the open, certainly not if there's nothing worth gaining by the risk. There is nothing for us to gain here at all; we would be helping him purely for the sake of it."

Is that not enough? But aloud, Kenlin asked, "Alright, so much for the gain. But really, what are the risks?"

Spotting risk, however, was Klanjad's forte. "You'll be out in the open in an unfamiliar city, separated from me, doing singularly suspicious things like loading somebody else's wares onto a cart you don't own. That's bound to draw attention; and since we already know that the Droál have agents active in the area, attention is the very last thing we want."

Ranja said, "If your main concern, Father, is that we would be in the open during the loading and transit process, is there a way we can still help while avoiding the open? For example, could we wait until after nightfall, when there would be fewer people to see and to ask questions?" Kenlin and Klanjad both had reservations about that idea, but she cut them off before they could object. "Yes, I *know* that's not the perfect idea; but shouldn't we at least spend a little energy looking for a better one? Since we can't increase the gain from helping, can we minimize the risk?"

CHAPTER XXI:

They ultimately settled on the idea of hiring townsfolk to load and move the cart while Kenlin supervised from an inconspicuous distance. Ranja was able to secure the assistance of two local louts in exchange for a night of bottomless pitchers, which in turn was procured from the innkeeper for one dinel upfront. Ranja then returned to Klanjad while Kenlin oversaw the packing and delivery of Jrizkil's possessions.

The ox, Kenlin thought, was a perfect counterpart for the two aspiring inebriates they had hired. It was evening now, and the ox seemed weary after its long day of standing about in a bovine stupor. By contrast, the helpers (who hadn't had a drink since slightly earlier in the day) were at risk of losing their stupor, and the fear of sobriety lent urgency, though perhaps not efficiency, to their packing efforts. But it was only once the cart was laden and moving that the ox and the drunks truly came together as a team. One shambling, semi-sober human stood on each side of the shambling, semi-sentient work beast; and each placed a hand on the ox's shoulders, ostensibly for guidance but more likely for mutual support, both emotional and structural. Thus linked, they all swayed together and lurched in harmony up the main road to the north.

Kenlin followed at just enough distance that they probably couldn't hear him snickering into his hand like a child. And the comedy didn't end there: every minor obstacle on the road presented new opportunities to bungle the basics of locomotion. At one point, they encountered a similarly-guided ox cart going in the opposite direction, and all parties involved just stared at each other stupidly while the evening sky grew visibly darker.

At last, after full minutes of stillness had passed and Kenlin was beginning to suspect that his helpers had forgotten that they were going somewhere, a soldier arrived from the north to investigate. At first he only seemed interested in the delay, which he quickly resolved by guiding the southbound ox around Jrizkil's stopped cart. Halfway through that process, however, he noticed the disorderly heap of woodworking and furniture. He asked one of the drunks a question that Kenlin could not hear; then, apparently dissatisfied with the answer, he craned his neck and looked around in the crowd.

Kenlin sighed. *He doesn't believe it's theirs, and he's concerned that they've stolen it. In fairness, that's not an unreasonable theory, but I suppose I should go explain the situation before he apprehends my helpers.*

As Kenlin began to make his way toward the cart, the soldier gave a loud whistle and waved; in response, two other soldiers stepped out of an alley a little way to the north. *Odd; what were they doing in there?* The two other soldiers quickly joined the first, and the three of them placed themselves in front of the ox cart so that it couldn't move forward. *Why are they all wearing their helmets? Aren't those uncomfortable, and unnecessary unless there's danger at hand?* As Kenlin came closer, he at last could hear what the soldier was saying: "Don't lie to me, this is *not* your cart. Did someone, perhaps, charge you to move this for them?" *"Charge you."* That's an odd turn of phrase; and in high Jazeskri, not the dialectic stuff I've heard elsewhere today.* The drunk's muttered answer was too low for Kenlin to hear, even though he had nearly reached the cart by now, but the soldiers were clearly not pleased. They exchanged dark looks among themselves—and with a fourth person, a man in a nondescript black cloak and hood who was standing off to one side. *Did he just come out of the same alley as those two soldiers?*

There was no breakthrough idea, no moment of realization. He took a step, and he was walking to resolve a misunderstanding; and when he took the next step, he was rushing in to reverse a trap. Instinct moved his hand, pulling a wooden chair from the pile atop Jrizkil's cart. The sudden movement caught the eye of the black-cloaked man who tensed, pointed, began to shout—and crumpled as the chair, thrown with the strength of Kenlin's magic, splintered against his head. *Hahahahahahahaha!* Then Kenlin was among the 'soldiers,' his sword drawn and alive even as they scrambled for their weapons in panic. The first two fell from brutal hacks into their collarbones, one nearly decapitated; the last, impaled through the throat, slid from Kenlin's sword to gurgle his life away on the ground.

Enough, slow down! And stop laughing! As Kenlin's mind caught up to his body, he wrestled himself back under control, shaking his head as the mad laughter suddenly crescendoed, then just as suddenly faded to a lurking chuckle. Back in command, he quickly looked about for more threats, but there were none: everyone he could see was running, screaming in fear of *him*.

"Please… Mercy!" Kenlin's mind-laughter made a quick resurgence as he whirled toward the voice; but it was merely one of the drunks, cowering in stupefied terror at his feet. "P-please don' kill me!"

Don't kill him? Why ever would I kill him? Did he not see that this was an ambush? But… How could there have been an ambush? How did they know… "They were looking for the cart?" he said aloud, phrasing it as a question even though he already knew the answer.

The man nodded, quaking. "Th-they said they knewed whose cart it were, an' that it weren't ours. B-but we didn' tell 'em that, they kn-knewed it already!"

Of course they knew, that's the only reason they'd be here. But how? Unless Jrizkil somehow— Oh, One above! As the realization drove the breath from his lungs, the depth of their peril drained the color from his face. *I have to get back to Klanjad and Ranja right now! We have to get out of Slionte!*

But as he turned back toward the center of the city, his eye fell on the body in the black cloak. *Was he really even part of it?* On impulse, Kenlin paused to look inside the nondescript black cloak. *A sword and a jack of plate. He was definitely one of them. Or rather, he is one of them: he's still breathing.*

Still breathing, even after such a blow to the head? Impressive. Perhaps I'll rip his throat out, see if he can still breathe when—

Kenlin's hand had actually moved to the unconscious man's neck, but he suddenly jerked away as though he had been burned. *No! What am I thinking? "Perhaps I'll rip..." I can't do that, he isn't even conscious! How can I kill him like that?*

But...I can't leave him here alive, he could be dangerous! Perhaps I could tie him with all the rope I don't have; too slow, I'll have to just break his wrists. But what if he's Droál, what if he's a Necromancer? I suppose I could gag him, but that's nowhere near secure. Perhaps I should cut out his tongue...and break his wrists, and leave him lying in agony in the street to await captivity, where the best he could hope for would be execution to end the suffering. That's kindness, yes?

It could not have been more than half a minute that Kenlin stood over the unconscious man, struggling against both the reluctance which he knew was irrational and the eagerness which he never thought he'd feel—which frightened him. But every moment he delayed was a threat to Klanjad and Ranja. He gnashed his teeth, he cursed his own qualms, he even put his hand back on the unconscious man's throat. But the frightening eagerness did not return, and without that, Kenlin simply could not bring himself to do it. At last, the strain became too much to bear—*And dammit, I've delayed too long already!*—so he reached down, picked up the man, and began to run back southward with his unconscious foe on his shoulder.

Every step, slowed as it was by this useless deadweight, was an indictment of Kenlin's weakness. Every slap of the man's limp arms against Kenlin's side was a mockery. *Damn myself, damn my own stupid indecision! The right course is obvious, so why is it not easy? But it is easy: just a little stab, or a little choke, or crush, all so much easier than carrying a limp villain halfway through the city. Pathetic! But perhaps good will come of it, yes? Perhaps we'll be able to use him for some sort of leverage; or maybe Klanjad will be able to get information from him. Yes, that can be the purpose I've "spared" you for; when we reach the Misplaced Mansion, Klanjad will—* But as he rounded a corner and came at last within sight of the inn, his worst fears were proved far too mild.

The Misplaced Mansion was burning. Flames raced quickly across the building's thatched roof, and smoke poured thickly from the second storey windows. The fire did not seem to have engulfed the main structure yet, but it soon would; and to help the process along, someone in the crowd was throwing torches in through broken windows.

As Kenlin crept closer, still carrying the unconscious man on his shoulder, a sudden gust of wind blew the fire high, brightly illuminating the entire scene. A dozen armed men, clad in cloaks of darkest blue, were prowling the streets before and around the burning building. *Droálic Necromancers, like the ones that attacked us near Natzut!* Two of the Droál were lighting and throwing torches into the Misplaced Mansion, and three others were menacing the growing crowd of Sliontens, herding them back across the street. The rest were spread out in the street and adjoining alleys, their eyes on the building's exits, ready for whoever might come out.

In the very center of the scene, directly in front of the door, stood one more figure, whose cloak had a violet hue and appeared to be of a finer quality. *A Misk! But no, I sense nothing; none of these are magicians, at least not conventional ones. Yet this one is clearly different.* As his comrades threw fire, or cowed the crowd, or watched anxiously for anyone to try to flee the inn, the violet Droál stood like a statue with his empty hands at his sides. Perhaps it was a trick of the firelight, but it looked as though the man's head was rhythmically bobbing and swaying, ever so slightly, as though under his hood he maintained a constant, silent chant.

Kenlin froze and ducked down, still distant enough to escape notice. *Too many! A dozen Necromancers, maybe more! Perhaps I could distract them... But what could I hope, that I might divert two? Three? If I could get close enough, perhaps I'd have a chance; but if they spot me, if they use their Necromancy, they'll crush me before I can even pose a threat!* Suddenly, the unconscious man on his back stirred and groaned. Kenlin pulled him down and covered his mouth roughly. *Don't you dare cry out and make this worse!*

As the building filled with smoke, its occupants began to stagger through the door into the street, choking and coughing. Every time a figure appeared in the doorway, the Droál would tense; but a moment later, they would relax again as one of them stepped forward to drag the choking victim out of the way. *They know he's still in there—that they're both still in there—and they're watching the back and sides as well. But perhaps they won't have to come out, maybe they can hide and survive the smoke until...*

But there was no *until,* for an ambush like this would not have neglected to delay or divert Slionte's response to the fire and violence. No help would come, and Klanjad and Ranja knew it as well as Kenlin did. They were cornered at last; and with Klanjad's injured ankle, there was not even a chance that they could run. *And, of course, the Droál know that too. They know we have no choice but to fight; they know Klanjad will have to come out.*

The Droál in the street tensed again as the unmistakable silhouette of Klanjad appeared in the doorway. He stood tall despite the smoke, and he carried his unsheathed sword in his right hand; but as frightful a figure as he struck, he still moved with a slow, painful limp.

The blue-clad Droál raised their swords to a ready posture, but the violet one still did not so much as flinch. They all stared at one another for a moment, Klanjad answering their looks of fear or impassivity with a menacing glare. Then he threw back his head and screeched a loud, high, horrible sound Kenlin had never heard him make. *Yet I know that scream; I've screamed that scream! When Ranja was hurt in Likrásk, this was the sound that came to me.* Hearing it now awakened a chorus of echoes in Kenlin's head, which melded and morphed into that same implacable, insatiable cackling laughter. His body physically jolted, his fingers dug into the face of the man whose mouth he covered, and his arms uncontrollably clenched and trembled.

The Droál in the street blanched noticeably at Klanjad's scream, and several Sliontens in the crowd covered their ears—Kenlin's captive groaned—but the violet Droál still did not move. As the scream finished, Klanjad suddenly Faded and sprang forward. Perhaps if his ankle had been healthy he would have been able to close range quickly enough to dominate the fight, but his injury slowed him down as the violet Droál finally reacted. With astounding speed for a non-magician, he swept his right arm around and down, as though he were throwing something at Klanjad's knees, and instantly the overwhelming *presence* of Necromancy manifested, surged forward, and swept Klanjad's feet from beneath him. Then, even as the first Necromancy's presence dissipated, the man swung his left arm overhead and down. Again, the Necromancy manifested instantly and crashed down onto Klanjad, but this time it did not dissipate. In under a second, it was all over: Klanjad, the mighty Jazei, lay helpless in the street, pinned to the ground by the terrifyingly swift power of the violet Necromancer. *What is that man?!*

As soon as Klanjad was pinned, the rest of the Droál had rushed forward, probably intending to bind him as he lay helpless. Their leader in violet seemed to relax; his left hand remained extended toward Klanjad, but with his other hand he brushed back his hood. As the firelight fell on his face, Kenlin could see that even now the man was still chanting silently, almost absent-mindedly. His lips and tongue formed the words of his profane prayer, but the corners of his mouth were drawn back into a wide leer of victory.

Leer while you can, bastard! I've got to get over there; but how can I fight that? If I can interrupt his chant, that might free Klanjad. But where is Ranja? And why is Klanjad just lying there, not struggling? Even if it would do no good, surely he would struggle, unless... There's more to the plan.

Sheer fortune saved the violet Droál. As he leered and chanted, his head lolled back arrogantly and his eyes drifted slightly upward; and if not for that, he would never have seen Ranja leap silently from the second storey window. From a running start within, she vaulted off the sill, flew over the heads of the Droál who had gathered around Klanjad, and fell like a falcon toward her prey, whose face turned to terror as she descended. Only by the barest margin did he save himself, toppling backward as Ranja thrust her glaive close enough to cut his violet cloak.

But although he had survived, his chant was disrupted, and his Necromancy vanished as suddenly as it had appeared. Four blue-clad Droál had come near to Klanjad when he was pinned; their blood sprayed the street as the Jazei thrust himself to his feet in a whirl of magic and steel that even Kenlin struggled to comprehend. The rest of the Droál scattered away in terror. Klanjad lunged after them, but crippled as he was by his ankle, they were able to outpace him.

Meanwhile, Ranja and the violet Droál were locked in intense hand-to-hand combat. They had both recovered from their tumbles well, but the Droál had immediately closed in past the glaive's effective range, forcing Ranja to abandon the weapon and fight with her hands. She was skilled, but so was her opponent, and for a moment they seemed evenly matched. But she needed to overpower him outright, whereas he merely needed a chance to resume his chant.

He extended his arm, holding it out like a lever to be grabbed, and whether on reflex or simply because she had no better option, she took the bait. As she pulled him into a throw, Kenlin saw him go limp, his limbs and face relaxing as his lips began again to move in silence. Ranja completed her throw, and the Droál hit the ground hard; but even as she moved to pin him down, his eyes flew open and his hand surged forward. The Necromancy returned in a rush, and Ranja was blasted backward, spinning through the air to land in a heap on the ground.

Klanjad, who had been rushing to his daughter's aid, was now mere steps from the violet Droál, and another piercing scream tore from his throat as he lunged. Still on the ground, the Droál threw his other hand out frantically, unleashing another rush of Necromancy. The presence seemed frayed this time, panicky and imprecise, but it was enough to buffet Klanjad to the side and buy the Droál enough time to scramble to his feet and, once again, swing his hand over and down, pinning Klanjad to the ground with Necromancy that did not dissipate.

And it's over again! I tried, I couldn't get there to help, not with... The pent-up energy in Kenlin's body from fear and fury and frenzy was nearly too much to contain. Though he was not intending it, he could feel from the tension in his own body—and from the way that the man writhed—that he was crushing his captive painfully. *Quiet, you! It's your fault, you're holding me back, why can't I— But I couldn't have gotten there that fast, even if— Damnation!*

He had been trying to advance stealthily to a range from which he could rush in. But as the chaos of the fight subsided, he was forced to stop once more, for the Droál were once again in control and alert. The violet Droál, no longer leering arrogantly, still held Klanjad pinned with the Necromancy that he seemed to guide, or at least to signal, with his left hand; his right hand was directing two very unwilling blue-clad Droál to approach Klanjad again. Several yards away, Ranja was on her feet; but she had been knocked far from her glaive, and two blue-clad Droál were slowly advancing on her with swords drawn. The remaining four Droál were alert, watching their defeated foes, the empty streets around them, the burning inn beside them—and then the crowd.

So far, the crowd had done nothing more than watch in frightened fascination. The various displays of power had sent about half the Sliontens fleeing in fear, and the remainder had been cowed into a sort of terror-struck trance. But suddenly a voice, rough with age but loud and clear, cried out, "Oi! Them's Droál!" As one, the Droál turned their heads, and the crowd shrank back from the source: a little old man, bent with years and balancing precariously on a cane, was pointing accusingly at the violet Droál. "Them's Droál, an' t'other's Jazeiz!"

Unconcerned but irritated, the violet Droál returned his attention to Klanjad and gestured to one of his comrades to deal with the old man. The nearest blue-clad Droál stepped forward, but the old man's defiance seemed to have roused his countrymen. The advancing Droál balked as an angry murmur built among the people; but the old man, encouraged, wobbled forward. "Oi! We don' take Droál 'round here! You let 'em go now, see?" And he raised his cane and swung it with all his strength against the violet Droál's back.

The old man's boldness was echoed in the growing anger of the crowd, but the violet Droál was neither intimidated nor impressed. The cane's blow had not even been enough to break his concentration, but the defiance had caught his attention. Reaching back with his right hand, he grabbed the old man by the shirt, pulled him around, and shoved him toward the burning building. As he pushed, a rush of Necromancy caught the old man in the gut, lifting him up and hurling him, alive and screaming, through the weakened building's walls and into the inferno within.

An instant hush; then an instant, furious roar. The crowd, momentarily enraged beyond their fear, surged forward as one, dozens of angry hands reaching vengefully for the violet Droál. However, though he was certainly surprised by this reaction, he was not unduly concerned. While his blue-clad comrades readied themselves to fight a mob, he dispassionately swept his right hand toward the advancing crowd, batting them away with Necromancy as though they were but swarming gnats. They toppled backward, shaken and in disarray, having failed to do more than momentarily distract the violet Droál; but that distraction was enough for Kenlin.

You idiot! You monster! Look what you have done! He didn't know to whom these thoughts were addressed, nor did he care. The murder—the blatant, needless murder!—had finally broken through his doubt. His worried indecision vanished, and the vacant space was filled with roiling, seething, cackling, *living* rage and elation. The world flashed red in the firelight—or perhaps just red in his eyes—and without a second thought, he wrenched the head of his captive, breaking his neck. Even before the body hit the ground Kenlin was sprinting headlong toward the man whose death filled his mind. As he ran he Faded, and as he Faded he screamed the same scream Klanjad had screamed, the same scream that had torn from his throat in Likrásk, the scream that echoed and laughed in his head, and it felt *good*. The violet-clad Droál heard his scream and turned, but Kenlin was much too fast and much too powerful. The death blow clove from neck to sternum, cutting so deep that the blade became stuck in the bone and, as Kenlin's momentum carried him onward, dragged the mangled man along like a split and spitted puppet. Kenlin dislodged his weapon in time to impale one of Ranja's attackers, and then he crushed the throat of the other with his bare hands. Ranja, who had flung herself out of the way of his charge, shouted something to which he paid no heed. He looked back north, saw the remaining Droál fleeing in panic, and his feet began to move. The cackling and screaming echoed and swelled in his head until he thought his mind would break.

CHAPTER XXII:

A smoldering calm, a placid fury, settled on Kenlin as the last of the Droál crumpled to the ground, slashed through the stomach. The others had not made it far, for he had chased them down in the wide street and slaughtered them as they ran. But this one had turned aside and fled into an alleyway; he even managed to cross two streets before he was caught and eviscerated. Now as he lay in the dirt, his agonized groans and sobs bounced tonelessly off Kenlin's ears. For a moment, the dying man's face brightened with hope as Kenlin knelt beside him and placed the flat of his sword against him; but Kenlin merely cleaned his blade on the man's cloak, then walked away.

He'd only been gone for a minute or two, but the scene at the Misplaced Mansion had markedly changed already. Ranja and Klanjad seemed to have rallied the crowd from their terror, and Ranja was now exhorting them to begin a firefighting effort. Klanjad, leaning on a local for support, had limped away from the fire and chaos to a bench at the edge of the market square.

At Kenlin's approach, Klanjad looked at him with a peculiar mixture of wariness and respect. "There you are. You have a flair for dramatic, well-timed rescues, it seems."

That should have gotten a quiet laugh from Kenlin, he knew; but despite the echoes of mad cackling in his mind, he was in no laughing mood. "I won't argue that it was dramatic," he said, shaking his head. "But as for my timing, it almost could not have been worse. I should never have put you two through that."

Klanjad frowned uncertainly. "It sounds like I'm missing some context."

Shall I explain? Well, why not; he cannot possibly think less of this than I already do. Struggling to phrase his feelings, he began, "This...has not been a good day for us, Klanjad."

After a moment, when Kenlin didn't continue this thought, Klanjad said mildly, "What gives you that impression?"

Not now! "Don't make light of it. You two almost died just now, all because I'm an idiot."

"Alright," Klanjad answered seriously, "it seems I certainly need more context." But Kenlin was still struggling to formulate his thoughts as anything less than a furious, self-lambasting tirade, so he said nothing. Klanjad seemed to understand. Perhaps trying to offer an indirect approach, he pointed to something several yards away. "Can you start with an explanation of that?"

Kenlin looked; it was the corpse of the black-cloaked Droál that he had carried all the way from his own ambush in the northern part of Slionte. "It's dead," he said shortly.

"Right, that is the only relevant information of which I was already certain," Klanjad answered drily, but not angrily. "A Droál that attacked you, I assume?"

Kenlin nodded, staring at the ground. "That one and three others were on the road to the north gate. They were waiting for the cart."

Klanjad scratched his chin. "You must have hit him *very* hard to knock him all the way from the north gate to here."

Kenlin met his uncle's eyes abruptly. "I killed the others at the ambush, but this one survived. So I carried him, on my shoulders, all the way here. And I crouched with him here, in the shadows, keeping him alive as you two nearly died. And then I killed him here."

The silence that followed lasted nearly a minute until Ranja jogged up to join them. She looked from her father to Kenlin and back again, then ventured, "You two seem cheery. Did one of us die?"

"Well, the day's not over yet," Klanjad replied, too distracted to really think that comment through. Recovering himself, he asked, "Will they be able to deal with the fire?"

Ranja shrugged. "They have a well nearby, and city officials are beginning to arrive and coordinate the efforts. They might be able to contain the blaze to just a few buildings, I think. But the inn itself is beyond saving, along with anything still inside, including the rest of our possessions."

Klanjad tallied lightly, "Well, I keep the dinels on me, so we have our money, our clothes, our weapons... All in all, it could have been far worse."

What, is he trying to mollify me? Kenlin said darkly, "Once again, let's not make light of it. This was a disaster, and the fact that we barely survived is hardly a cause for celebration."

Ranja cocked her head. "What's put you in such a fine mood? I thought we did rather well, all things considered. Obviously, it would have been better if we hadn't almost died, but against such an attack..."

Watching Kenlin's face, Klanjad said, "I think Kenlin wishes he could have gotten here more quickly."

If only. "More than that," said Kenlin, shaking his head, "I should have foreseen the attack. I had all the information I needed."

"You had the same information Father and I had," Ranja countered dismissively. "But we all agreed on a way to minimize the risks, and that's probably why we're alive."

Kenlin was only half listening. "A good man helped us, and I really wanted to help him. And that was all the bait they needed."

"Hey!" Ranja snapped, commanding Kenlin's attention again. "I won't let you put the blame for this on yourself. I wanted to help him too, remember? I thought as you thought, that Jrizkil was a good man who had put himself at risk just to help us Jazeiz; and, like you, I really believed the story he told when he came to us in the inn. Perhaps we should have known, but it seems he's a much better liar than I had ever imagined he could be."

Ha! Jrizkil. "Well, our most convincing lies are the ones we genuinely believe, yes?"

That comment gave her pause. "I see... You suspect Laianna, then?"

"I don't suspect; I know it was her." An intense bitterness welled up in Kenlin's mouth, and his hitherto placid fury began to seethe. "None of us trusted her—I didn't, so I'm sure you two were even more wary—and if she had come to us herself, or if we'd even suspected her involvement, we would never have taken the bait. She must have known that. So she sent her husband, who we *would* trust, to relay her cockamamie story about the third Unnatilz attacking her family, probably hoping to play on our guilt and responsibility for putting them in harm's way. And I fell for it." By this time, the spite and anger in Kenlin's voice were so intense that his voice had lowered to a harsh, self-castigating snarl.

Ranja was still considering all this, reexamining everything she had noticed in the past day. "But even so," she said slowly, "it wasn't just you. We all thought—"

"Of course, we all fell for it, not just me. But I had additional information, information about what *didn't* happen, which it never occurred to me to share with you. I was with Jrizkil for hours—*hours*—in the marketplace; so I knew that, in all that time, Laianna never joined us." At this, Klanjad groaned quietly and shook his head, while Ranja's lips mouthed a tiny, unvoiced *oh* of understanding. Kenlin felt a sarcastic smile twist his face. "Now you see, yes? She said she'd be back within an hour, but she was gone for the whole afternoon. Then, mere minutes after I left the market, she returned with urgent news of her family? She didn't want to talk to me directly, she wanted Jrizkil to do it for her. The timing should have made it so obvious. *You* couldn't have known, and *you* couldn't have known, but *I* should have known. And instead, I pushed us headlong into the trap, risks be damned but for you two. If everything had been up to me, we would *all* be dead."

There was a long, dark, unbroken silence.

After nearly a minute, Ranja said in a small voice, "Sometimes, it seems like we—Father and I—live in a world of suspicions and ambushes. It can be hard to discern—"

Enough! "Don't, Ranja! I— I'm sorry. Thank you, but don't. This isn't the sort of thing that can be talked through or reasoned away. It's not that kind of problem. Everything that's happened tonight happened because *I failed,* and the only thing to be done is for me to never fail like that again."

Ranja's expression had become unreadable after he'd cut her off; she gave no response now, but simply looked at him impenetrably. Klanjad, however, nodded seriously: "Good." Then, abruptly changing topics, he said, "Well, as eager as I am to move on from here, I doubt there's much more we'll be able to accomplish tonight. My ankle was displeased by the fight back there."

"I don't think there's any reason to rush," Ranja commented. "Unlike in Likrásk, we don't need to flee into the night: we won this fight."

Kenlin grunted dubiously, "*Hmm.* Aren't there always more of them?"

"In the *world*, there are, but I very much doubt they have reserves in Slionte. If they'd had more forces here, they certainly would have deployed them against us in the ambush, all at once."

"It was a rather minimal crew that attacked us, wasn't it?" Klanjad mused. "One Dragluz, one Drendu, a dozen or so Necromancers, and *no Misks.*"

Kenlin had never heard some of those terms before. "The purple one was called a 'Dragluz,' then?"

Klanjad nodded. "They're an elite order of Droálic Necromancers; they can perform Necromancy individually, and as you saw they're very dangerous. They're almost never seen on land this far from Droál holdings, but there's no mistaking them: they wear violet cloaks of office and perform fast, powerful Necromancy that no other order can match."

"And Drendu?"

"Well, several orders of Droál have been known to wear black cloaks, but the Drendu are perhaps the most dangerous. They're nearly as fast as the Dragluz, but they use their Necromancy for hand-to-hand combat, not telekinesis. I'm actually rather impressed that you were able to kill one so easily."

Kenlin shrugged. "I saw him before he saw me."

Ranja interjected, "Circling back to your observation that there were no Misks here, Father, is that surprising? You and Kenlin can sense Misks, making them a risky addition to any plan for an ambush."

"Sensing the Misks didn't help us very much in Likrásk," Klanjad pointed out. "But I think your second point is more intriguing: I don't think this ambush was planned in advance. The ambush they had prepared for us in Likrásk was much larger, and we only survived because we escaped before the main force could catch up to us. Compared to that, this ambush—even if you include the Unnatilz who attacked us yesterday—seems almost vestigial. I think these were the Droál's resident garrison (for lack of a better word) for Slionte, and they simply hatched a plan with whatever resources they had when Laianna betrayed us to them."

"So if Skralade isn't here," said Ranja, deducing her Father's thoughts, "you want to know what could be important enough to call him—and all his brethren—away from another chance at killing you."

"Exactly. I had assumed that, if we were ever caught in another ambush, he would swarm us with as many Misks as he possibly could. But there are no Misks *at all* here, not even a watchman to Vanish away with news of us and return with reinforcements. Something is happening, something important enough to wholly occupy the attention of Clan Eyjazinka, and I want to know what it is."

Kenlin looked sharply at his uncle as the mad voice in his head began a low, drawling chuckle. *Is he suggesting what I think—what I hope he's suggesting?* Slowly, he said, "I think I know of someone with contacts among the Droál."

"She won't know anything," Ranja countered immediately. "If she actually *is* Droál, then she'll have disappeared long before you can reach her. And if she was merely working for them, then she was just a tool, probably threatened and frightened into spying for them."

"But she knows where we can find the Khardalesh," said Klanjad quietly. "As you said, there are probably no more Necromancers in Slionte; but the Droál would not have brought their spies to the ambush, and Laianna clearly knows how to find them."

"This is not a good idea," said Ranja, a growing note of alarm in her voice. "Even without obvious impending danger, we shouldn't be splitting up, not tonight. Do you really expect her to tell you something important enough to justify that sort of risk?"

Kenlin asked quietly, "Is that an unreasonable expectation?"

"I don't think *reason* has much at all to do with this proposal," Ranja retorted. "What, are we going to catch and interrogate Laianna, then catch and interrogate whomever she betrays to us, then continue into a full counter-espionage effort before we leave town tomorrow morning?"

Klanjad said, "If the Droál are launching a major operation, I can't waste opportunities to learn about it. This is what I do, Ranja."

"But is this *why* you're doing it?" she said, still with a worried note in her voice. "Because it sounds to me like a thinly-veiled excuse for retribution."

Klanjad paused briefly before replying. "That, too, is something I have been known to do."

To this, Ranja had no answer.

After a silence, Kenlin said, "If she hasn't fled entirely, she'll be with Jrizkil at their homestead. Should I question her there, or bring her back here to you?"

"Bring her to me. But fear alone might be enough to loosen her tongue, so she may panic and reveal important information as soon as she sees you. Try to remember everything she says, but the most important task is to bring her back to me."

"Use magic to run through the open prairie quickly," Ranja added, her discomfort still evident in her voice. When Kenlin and Klanjad looked at her quizzically, she shrugged. "We think there are no magicians around to sense you, but the third Unnatilz is still afield. If you stay Faded whenever you're far from buildings, then..."

"That's good advice," said Klanjad, nodding as her voice trailed off. He turned back to Kenlin. "Go, and bring Laianna back to me alive."

A dark, thick, heavy sense of satisfaction filled Kenlin. *Yes. I will find her.* The placid fury and the low chuckling in his mind had combined into a deep, simmering *purr.*

...

Kenlin did not allow the dark mood of his mind to cloud his judgement. He approached Jrizkil's house from the southwest, swinging far from the road and advancing cautiously through the vegetation around the stream. But the homestead was quiet; a light shining through the window of the front room was the only indication that anyone was inside.

Warily, Kenlin approached the house from the rear and peered in the window. *What happened here?* Though the crude glass made the scene difficult to discern in the candlelight, the room appeared to be in disarray, and he thought he saw a corpse lying on the table. He crept around the house and carefully approached the front door. It was ajar; he pushed it open.

As he entered, his eyes and his memories each tried to show him a completely different sight. His memory showed him the beautiful, comfortable, lovingly-furnished room in which he had breakfasted only this morning with Jrizkil and Laianna. But that room was gone, replaced by the new room before his eyes.

The corpse on the table was of a man in a mottled grey cloak, his flesh and clothes torn apart by multiple ragged gashes. *His cloak is in the Droálic style; this must be a Khardalesh spy, one of Laianna's contacts.* The man's eyes and mouth were open, as though his last scream of pain had been cut off at the throat and still remained trapped in his lungs. A gore-covered saw lay discarded on the table beside the corpse. Fresh blood steadily *drip, drip, dripped* into a pool on the floor.

The rest of the room was littered with the wreckage of the house's once-beautiful furnishings. The chairs had been thrown about, the crockery had been smashed, and even the sheepskin rug had been flung aside into the pool of blood beneath the table. In the far corner of the room, where the faint light came from, something lay huddled as though in fear or pain. Kenlin approached.

The huddled form was Laianna, dead, curled up in the corner as if she had been trying to shelter herself. Her clothes were torn, her skin deeply scratched, and massive bruises blotched her entire body. One of her arms dangled brokenly like a snapped tree branch. Her face and ribs had been pummeled and smashed unmistakably: she had been beaten to death.

Beside her, a single candle burned in a bowl just beneath the curtains by the window. A closer look revealed that, beneath the candle, the bowl was filled with lamp oil. This building, and all its occupants, were condemned; and when the candle had burned low enough, fire would take them all.

Kenlin turned away, leaving the corpses and the candle as they were.

When he stepped outside, he glanced about as he had not done before. He started as he saw, no more than twenty yards away, Jrizkil sitting comfortably in a shallow, freshly-dug hole in the ground. He motioned Kenlin to come nearer, his movement curiously feeble and uncoordinated. As Kenlin approached, Jrizkil greeted him with a weak chuckle. "So ya know, eh? C'm over, sit; 's cheerier with two."

The freshly-dug hole in which he sat was a shallow trench, about two yards long and one wide. Jrizkil was sitting at one end of the trench, looking relaxed, his arms resting casually on the ground beside him. At his invitation, Kenlin slowly climbed in and seated himself at the opposite end, facing Jrizkil.

"Fancy seein' you here," said Jrizkil lightly, but with a strange weakness, or chill, compared to his customary conviviality. "I though' she'd done fer y'all fer sure."

Inexplicably, Kenlin chuckled aloud and smiled a genuine smile, but not of happiness. "Well, she tried. Some friends of hers made their introductions."

Jrizkil threw back his head and laughed to the sky—a wild, merry, hollow sound. There was nothing to echo off in the prairie, but Kenlin could hear echoes of the laugh, ever so faintly, in dark hollows in his mind. "Friends o' hers, indeed! Well, I only hope ya gave 'em the Jazei welcome they deserved."

Kenlin nodded, and Jrizkil laughed again. Then, gesturing toward the house, Kenlin said, "It seems that you also, *uh*. . .welcomed a visitor."

As suddenly as it had come, the laughter vanished from Jrizkil's face; when he nodded, his manner was almost somber. "Maybe, maybe. Or maybe I's the one payin' *him* a visit. I been startin' to think he an' his were here before I ever was."

"What makes you think that?"

Jrizkil gave a mirthless *huff* of laughter. "I never sawed him here before, him nor his ilk. An' she couldn'a met 'em in town, at leas' not on the regular; we were insep'rable, she never wanders off alone like she did t'day."

"Perhaps they met her here, but in disguise, without the cloaks."

Jrizkil smiled knowingly. "No. I would'a known, jus' as soon as I sawed 'em. An' then I...well, I would'a sawed 'em."

There in the darkness, sitting at opposite ends of the shallow trench, they shared a quiet, morbid chuckle.

When the moment had passed, Kenlin said, "So you recognized him today, and hence...the scene in there? Was he here when you returned?"

"Not jus' when," said Jrizkil, shaking his head, "but then nor was her brother, what she said was wounded. Then *he* showed up, an' suddenly everythin' made a lot more sense."

"So then you sawed him, as it were. And her?"

Before answering, Jrizkil took a moment to examine his left arm; after a brief inspection, he brought his right hand over and ran a finger along the underside of his arm from the wrist half way to the elbow. Then he looked up and said briskly, "Soldiers an' saws destroy things sharp an' fas'. Spies an' fists hur' all as much, jus' slower. Seemed fittin'."

"That's rather dark of you," Kenlin commented.

Jrizkil threw back his head into another wild, empty laugh. "Hahahahaha! Mayhap it is, Ran'on! But then I suppose ya came back to scold her calmly fer her evil ways, p'raps ask her a few polite ques'ions?"

"Actually, you're not far off," Kenlin answered. "Klan—Gealvind wanted to know..."

But at Kenlin's clumsy attempt to remember the pseudonym, Jrizkil smiled. "He's Klanjad, in'e? Oh, don' worry; 's few enough Jazeiz lef' in the world to get too confused, Ran'on."

"Kenlin."

Jrizkil's smile broadened. "An' a pleasure it is t'meet ya, Kenlin. I thank ya fer tellin' me yer name, an' I promise I'll take it...well, no further pas' here, methinks."

There was another pause as Jrizkil looked again at his arms, this time focusing on his right forearm. Kenlin remarked, "You'll make but slow progress that way, so I think we have some time. How do you know so much about Droál?"

"Seen 'em," said Jrizkil evasively, still examining his arm. "You ought'a know; guess where."

Kenlin considered carefully before answering, "Likrásk was put to fire less than a moon ago, but you said you've been married to Laianna for two."

At Laianna's name, Jrizkil paused noticeably. He rested his arms back on the ground and looked at Kenlin straight-on, nodding slowly. "Yer close, jus' off. I hail from Véle, 'bout half a day's walk into the fores' southwes' of Likrásk. Lo's o' trees fer lovely carvin's there. Lovely carvin's, lovely trees...an' my lovely Arijye, an' our bubbly baby boy. T'was win'er comin' on when strange folk—strange clothes, strange ways, strange gold, strange disinteres' in buyin' anythin' but words—came to town. I got an eye fer people, an' I never forget a face nor a mannerism. I knew righ' off that they were at more'n they said, but I didn' know..."

As Jrizkil fell silent, Kenlin prompted, "I take it they targeted the more remote villages before turning their attention to the city?"

Jrizkil looked up suddenly; and when he spoke again, his voice had become a drawn-out, strained, wretched moan. "I was *in* the city," he said, "sellin' carvin's on the day when. I sawed the smoke from afar, but I never imag'ned..." Anguish overcame him, and he covered his face with his hands. When his hands came away, his face was stained dark and glistening.

After several minutes of silence, Kenlin said quietly, "So then you came north?"

"So I did indeed," Jrizkil answered, abruptly recovering his earlier hollow flippancy. "Had my cart, had my tools... I sold carvin's at every village from there t' here, 'til a fella told me he was lookin' for a carver to do up his fam'ly's homestead all pretty."

"And that brought you here," Kenlin completed, the rest of the story now clear in his mind. "You came to the homestead, met Laianna, fell in love…"

"Love," repeated Jrizkil, over-pronouncing the word as though he could taste each sound. "Yes, I though' it was that, an' I tol' myself as much. But if I did fall…I guess it didn' work, did it?"

"Work?"

He nodded toward the empty house nearby. A sudden brightening of the light in the windows indicated that the candle had finally burned too low. Jrizkil said, "How much love d'ya think's in there righ' now?"

Kenlin watched as the light within the building became brighter and brighter, and the thatched roof began to smoke. "I suppose it didn't work."

"All my love," said Jrizkil quietly. The growing firelight revealed a half-peaceful, crooked grin on the man's face. "She gave me a presen', ya know? Jus' after I met her. A blank o' black rowan heartwood from the northeas'—righ' fine an' very dark. I made this from it," he said, holding up the wooden kirsk dagger Kenlin had first seen this morning. But Jrizkil could not hold up his arms for long now, and he chuckled quietly as they flopped back to the ground. "Arijye used t'give me presen's like that. Maybe tha's why I firs' thought…why I 'loved' Laianna, too. But Arijye burned, an' Laianna burned her, an' now Laianna's burnin'… A whole cycle o' love, isn' it? Everybody burns."

They watched the growing inferno together for a while. At length, Kenlin said, "I don't think I can comment, Jrizkil. I don't think I've ever loved, truly."

Jrizkil threw back his head for another wild, empty cackle to the night skies. The fire was now bright enough to reveal the bloody streaks that lacerated his forearms, and the razor-sharp carving knife with which he continued to cut himself. "Loved truly!" he laughed in spite of his dwindling strength. "Wha's *truly*? Did I love her? Or *her?* Did anybody love me? Maybe even she'd'a betrayed me, given time!" He cackled again, and the burning house hissed and cracked in chorus with his joyless jollity.

"No, I'll tell ya *truly*," he resumed at last, his breaths now irregular gasps of weakness and mirth. "*Truly* is *shortly*. Not short an' broke off or false; short an' *dead*. The mos' importan' piece of any carvin' is the varnish, finishes it, seals it up, preserves it so's it can' be touched, *done*. The mos' importan' piece o' any story is the stop, takin' leave of the characters a'fore everythin' falls apart again. The mos' importan' piece o' love...is death."

Kenlin looked back to the once-lovely homestead, now consumed by the roaring inferno. "In that case... You love them both?"

One more hollow laugh into the sky, but this one quickly devolved into a fit of feeble coughing. Jrizkil did not care; he laughed and choked until his eyes watered and his legs began to spasm. Kenlin did not move. At last, Jrizkil's throat cleared enough for him to catch a few wheezing, rasping breaths. "Yes indeed," he whispered. His eyes closed, and the crooked smile once again twisted his face. "I love 'em both. I love 'em all!"

They sat together only a few minutes longer before Jrizkil's breathing ceased, but Kenlin sat for some time afterward, contemplating the corpse opposite him. At last he stood, climbed out of the grave, and laid Jrizkil's body flat. Just before he began shoveling dirt in, he reached down and took the kirsk from the corpse's belt, putting it in his own. Then he filled the grave and, leaving it unmarked, turned back toward Slionte.

CHAPTER XXIII:

Before he had left to find Laianna, Kenlin had told Klanjad and Ranja about the disemboweled Droál dying in an alley. When he returned, he was not surprised to find Ranja waiting for him in that same alley, though Klanjad and the Droál were nowhere to be seen. At Kenlin's approach, she stood up and eyed him questioningly. "How was your expedition?"

He shook his head. "Unsuccessful: she was dead when I arrived."

He half-expected that she wouldn't believe this, but if she had doubts, she kept them to herself. Instead, in the same level interrogative, she asked, "And how are you?"

He considered for several moments before answering. "Better. I am better."

Without changing her expression, she nodded slowly, understanding all his meanings. Then she led him through a short maze of alleyways toward one of the city's western gates. When they were within sight of the walls, they found Klanjad sitting in the courtyard of a stable. He nodded in greeting at their approach, but did not rise; his leg was stretched out before him with his injured ankle resting gingerly on the ground.

Perhaps noting the absence of the hostler, Ranja asked, "Were you able to get horses, then, Father?"

"Three bedraggled nags," Klanjad answered, nodding, "but not at unreasonable cost. They're no chargers, but they'll get us to Janísla."

Kenlin asked in some surprise, "We have a destination, then? So that last Droál actually had something informative to say?"

"We have a tentative destination, and that Droál knew but little, though more than nothing. I had hoped... But I see you haven't brought Laianna with you. Do you happen to remember if she said anything before—"

"I didn't kill her, Klanjad. Jrizkil realized what she was and killed her before I arrived, along with a grey-cloaked man that I assume was one of her Khardalesh contacts. So, no: by the time I arrived, she had nothing to say."

Klanjad seemed unsatisfied, but he merely shrugged. "Well, so it is. And Jrizkil is dead too, I suppose?"

Kenlin nodded, "By his own hand." From the corner of his eye, he saw Ranja glance at the wooden kirsk in his belt, but she did not comment.

Klanjad noted drily, "Well, I think that makes corpses of almost everyone I've seen or spoken to since I returned to the southeast. If nothing else, I'm thorough. Anyway, as I said, the Droál I interrogated had little information to give, but it was enough that I think we should hurry, as quickly as we can, north to Janísla."

"Why? What did he say?"

Klanjad hesitated. "Well, what he said directly was that the Commune would soon fall, and that the march of the Droál could not be stopped, and that the fires of Drakzaad would cleanse this world, and other classic Droálic insights. But he spoke of specifics, not the generic grandiosities that most Droál favor: the Commune is going to fall *soon*, the Droál are marching unstoppably *right now*, and so on. Extrapolating a bit, I think it's safe to assume that the stalemate in the north is no longer in effect, and that the Droál have fielded an army to attack one of our cities."

"But he didn't say which city?"

"He... He spoke of the 'pillar of the Commune,' which would typically suggest Ñaj-Gadan," answered Klanjad doubtfully, "but it's hard to imagine that they might really hope to take it. Skaradarn would be a more sensible target; but any siege of Skaradarn would have to be able to resist relief efforts from Viarlin."

Ranja scoffed aloud. "Relief efforts! And when has Viarlin ever acted for any reason beyond shortsighted self-interest? Do you really think they would deploy to lift a siege on Skaradarn?"

To Kenlin and Ranja's surprise, Klanjad did not seem to have a ready answer for this. "You're not wrong," he said with an uneasy frown. "It would be odd for Skralade to risk a march on Skaradarn unless he were sure that Viarlin wouldn't intervene, but...it's not unthinkable that they might reach such a result through diplomacy."

"Diplomacy?" Kenlin repeated, incredulous. "I had never even considered that the Droál might be open to diplomacy. Is it possible to negotiate with them?"

Klanjad chuckled darkly. "Of course it is—in the short term. Throughout the war, various truces, ceasefires, and conditional surrenders have been attempted. When such arrangements inevitably fall apart, the Droál always aggressively promote the story that *they* weren't the ones who violated the agreement."

"Surely only fools would believe that, yes?"

Quirking an eyebrow, Ranja remarked, "Yes, but only fools hold power in Viarlin."

Kenlin expected Klanjad to step in and clarify what must be an exaggeration; but to his surprise, the elder Jazei just nodded grimly. "It can't be that simplistic," Kenlin said, looking from Klanjad to Ranja and back again. "The news you heard was that the stalemate was broken and that Ñaj-Gadan was under attack, yes? How did we go from that to the assumption that Viarlin made a deal with the Droál to sacrifice Skaradarn?"

When Klanjad did not answer, Ranja said, "Well, for my part, I struggle to think of anything else that could plausibly end the stalemate, unless the Commune did something stupid." Klanjad made a face indicating that that was always a possibility, but he said nothing. Ranja continued, "The crux of the stalemate was that both sides held secure positions opposed across the Kilgáire Wastes, and marching a campaign across that desert would be an extraordinarily risky endeavor."

"Why?"

"To start with, both sides have multiple strongholds along the front, which can all move to support each other if any one of them is attacked. Furthermore, there's nothing to pillage or live on in Kilgáire, and the defenders would of course torch their own fields if invaded; so any army that crosses the Wastes must be fed entirely via supply lines—long, arduous, dangerous supply lines through open and hostile terrain. A siege of Ñaj-Gadan could theoretically be supplied by sea, I suppose. But Ñaj-Gadan can be supported by Skaj-Kraskedir and Janísla as well as by Viarlin and Skaradarn; and even without support, Ñaj-Gadan's defenses make it uniquely difficult to besiege."

"That was a lot of information, Ranja."

"Well I'm sure you, of all people, aren't going to complain that your questions are being answered."

Kenlin laughed at this. *The quip wasn't even that funny, but...it feels good to laugh.* "You're right, I can't complain! So how does Viarlin's passivity break the stalemate?"

"Because it would leave Skaradarn unsupported and vulnerable," Ranja answered immediately, clearly ready for this question. "The road from Ñaj-Gadan to Skaradarn leads through Viarlin, so Viarlin has the power to withhold or impede virtually all support. And if the Droál take Skaradarn, that will give them a foothold across the wasteland from which they can supply further campaigns."

"It sounds like supplies are a major consideration."

"Well, food is important, Kenlin."

"But if that's such a central issue, then why are you so sure that they wouldn't attack Ñaj-Gadan? You said they could supply that assault by sea."

"Yes, that's—" Ranja began, but Klanjad cut her off.

"Attacking Ñaj-Gadan would be suicide," he said dismissively. "The city is the seat of the Commune's power, within a week's march of every other major garrison except Iskena, and it's defended by the strongest walls in Jranjana. It's also a city in two halves separated by a bridged chasm called the Karkéde Channel; both halves of the city must be besieged at the same time, and both can be supplied by land, by sea, or from Gadan Lake. The city controls the only mechanisms to move ships from the sea to the lake, so the Droál would either have to either haul ships overland or build new ones to cut off the lake-side resupply route. In sum, an effective siege of Ñaj-Gadan would require two separate land forces and two separate littoral forces—and those would be arrayed against the strongest fortifications in Jranjana, in the very heart of Commune territory."

I can't even begin to grasp the scale of what he's describing, and yet...he's concerned? "It sounds like an impossible undertaking."

Klanjad looked up sharply. "Yes. It should be." Then he stood and, bracing himself against a wall with his hand, limped wordlessly around a corner and out of sight.

When they could no longer hear the sound of Klanjad's feet, Kenlin commented, "He hasn't done that in quite some time. Did I do that?"

Ranja shook her head. "I did. I shouldn't have dwelt on Viarlin so, not when we're all already tired."

"He hates them that much?"

"He does, with good reason. Viarlin has always championed the Commune's most inept policies, and they've blocked more than a few of Father's attempts to counterattack the Droál."

"So it really isn't unreasonable, then, to imagine that they might negotiate some sort of neutrality with the Droál?"

Ranja shrugged. "As I said, I can't think of anything else that would break the stalemate. But then, we don't really *know* that the stalemate actually has been broken; we're just speculating based on the words of one suffering, dying Droál Necromancer."

Now it was Kenlin's turn to shrug. "Well, speculating is fun, and we've nothing better to do until it's light enough to depart. So, do you think the Droál was lying and that none of the cities in the north are under attack?"

Ranja chewed her lip for a moment before replying. "You left that Droál in…quite a state, Kenlin. People dying like that, if they're offered peace, usually have little gumption for lies and little patience for loyalties. I don't think he was lying. He might have been *wrong:* Commune-held cities probably seem all alike to most Droál. Perhaps he just mixed up Ñaj-Gadan and Skaradarn in his mind."

"Klanjad wasn't exaggerating, then, when he described Ñaj-Gadan's defenses?"

"No, that was no exaggeration. I think calling such a siege *impossible* is probably going too far, but the resources they would need to even attempt it make the whole thing hard to envision."

"Yes? What all would they need?"

"For an army? You want me to just make up a number? Alright… Fifty thousand, at minimum."

Kenlin physically started. "Fifty thousand…*people? Are* there fifty thousand people?" At this, Ranja burst into unrestrained laughter. As she struggled to regain control of herself, Kenlin shrugged, grinning sheepishly. *I suppose the question must have been naïve. Still, fifty thousand seems…*

As though in answer to his thoughts, Ranja nodded and said through her subsiding giggles, "It's hard to fathom, but there are *many* more than fifty thousand people in the world. In fact, there are more than fifty thousand soldiers in the combined armies of the Commune: I think the last estimate I heard was that around eighty thousand fought for the Commune, and just over a hundred thousand are believed to fight for the Droál. But those numbers are totals. A single deployment of fifty thousand would be *staggering*."

Kenlin shook his head in bafflement. "Eighty thousand and a hundred thousand... I have no idea what to make of numbers like that. If that many people can be soldiers, how many people are there in the world?"

"Fewer every day that the Droál remain in Jranjana," Klanjad interrupted abruptly, returning from around the corner. "Come," he said, "the stars are fading. Ranja, please teach Kenlin how to not fall off a horse, at least no more than once per hour. I want us to be on our way as soon as it's light enough to see the road."

Ranja stepped quickly after her father, and Kenlin followed. But he asked quietly, "I'm still curious, though; do you know the number?"

Ranja chuckled. "Millions, Kenlin, but there are no good estimates for how many millions. Soldiers are recruited and armed in specific numbers, but it's much more difficult to try to tally everyone everywhere."

Millions! He whistled low. "I can't even imagine—"

"You needn't imagine that which is real," Klanjad called back shortly. "Get accustomed to massive numbers, Kenlin, for you'll only hear more as we journey north. You'll see armies the size of a town and cities the size of a mountain. You'll see the lives and labors of countless people channeled together to fuel a war. And when we finally reach that war, you'll see death at a scale beyond what you ever imagined for life."

CHAPTER XXIV:

Klanjad's dark mood, and Kenlin and Ranja's resilience in the face of it, only deteriorated as the day progressed and they all began to dwindle for lack of sleep. But they camped early and slept well that night, and the next morning found them all refreshed and ready to inflict another long day's travel on their horses. *It's undeniable, but nonetheless peculiar, that a horse is not an ox. Jrizkil's ox immediately filled me with an intense disdain that I had only ever felt for chickens and choosy eaters, but this horse... There's a resigned world-weariness in it that I can't help but respect. I think it's aware that it's substantially bigger than me, and yet it has decided to do as I tell it, if only so that I'll stop bothering it. I can't say that I truly understand or empathize with its motives; but the stoicism of its worldview strikes me as honorable, and somehow inherently worthy. One above, I am so bored.*

More than fifty leagues of road lay between Slionte and Janísla: fifty leagues of flat, featureless grassland stretching from horizon to horizon. Tiny, destitute villages lurked in the clefts between little hills and clung to the tepid trickles that passed for rivers in these parts. *And they're all the same! League after league, village after village, nothing ever changes. Or is it simply my eyes that see them so?* He looked closer, trying to spot something familiar, perhaps something that recalled Irnaji; but to his surprise, even his own memories of Irnaji had grown indistinct and foreign.

At long last, near the end of the fifth day from Slionte, the featureless prairie began to wrinkle into a rolling, sparsely-forested hillscape. They didn't travel far into these hills before camping early that evening, for Klanjad told them, "This is the last lonely stretch of road before we reach Janísla."

He was not wrong. Within two hours of setting out the following morning, they were trotting through their fifth village that day. Soon, the villages were so close that the entire region seemed to be one massive, bustling settlement without divide or boundary. Then, abruptly, they reached the defenses of the city of Janísla.

The first line of defense was a palisade wall, three yards high and built from logs so thick and sturdy that they must have been imported from a more forested region. A dense clutter of refugee hovels crowded up against the palisade, but none dared to venture beyond it. *And I think I know why: that palisade is just within bowshot of the walls.*

Between the palisade and the city walls, a wide, flat artificial wetland offered archers a clear view of anyone foolish enough to try to stray past the pickets. *Ugh, and it's some vile combination of moat and mass-scale cesspool. It reeks!* He tried to imagine an army attempting to cross it; they would have to wade through that muck under a constant hail of arrows, carrying their grapnels and ladders, the fortunate slogging onward toward the walls while the wounded toppled headlong into… "That is *foul*," Kenlin declared aloud.

"Such truth," said Klanjad and Ranja together, both with equally disgusted looks on their faces. Klanjad added, "It's even worse than you think it is, Kenlin, and that's all I'll say. Come, let's get upwind of this…"

Thankfully, the fortifications, as imposing and disgusting as they were, parted to let the road through: a gap had been left in the palisades, a causeway led over the cess-moat, and the gate itself was open, though heavily guarded. Soldiers with halberds stood across the gap in the palisades, keeping the refugees from the slums from entering the city. Kenlin was hesitant to approach the guards—every recent experience had taught him to be constantly wary—but for once Klanjad's instinct seemed to be less cautious than Kenlin's, for the elder Jazei steered his horse directly toward the guards without the least concern. As soon as the guards noticed their approach, they passed through a quick series of reactions: concern at the approach of riders; astonishment as they saw that the riders were Jazeiz, perhaps even recognizing Klanjad; nervous pride as they snapped to attention at the Jazeiz's approach; brief consternation as the Jazeiz did not slow down; followed by haphazard scampering out of the way as Klanjad rode right through their line without so much as a sideways glance or change of expression.

When they were about twenty yards beyond the scattered line of guards, Ranja said reproachfully, "That's not funny, Father."

Straight-faced, Klanjad replied, "It's a little funny."

But once they were inside the city, Klanjad took a more constructive approach to his interactions with the local militia. Inquiring at the gatehouse, they learned the name of the commander of the city's southmost garrison. "Erkajin? Erkajin of Guardél?" Klanjad inquired with genuine surprise—and a warmer note—in his voice.

The captain at the gate nodded vigorously, eager to please. "I think he does hail from Guardél, sir, yes I do, sir! Shall I announce your—?"

"No. At which garrison can I find him?"

"Yes, sir! I mean... The barracks are near the walls, sir, toward the south-east of—"

"Good. Back to your duties."

"Yes, sir!" the captain declared as Klanjad was already spurring his horse onward. Kenlin peered about curiously, but he quickly had to give up gawking at the city to focus on navigating it; the streets soon became so crowded that the Jazeiz were forced to dismount and lead their horses. Fortunately, Klanjad's ankle had healed swiftly since Slionte, and their destination was not far into the city anyway. The sun had only just reached midday when they arrived at the city's south-eastern garrison. Klanjad seemed to have some prior knowledge of the location and, without asking for guidance, escort, or announcement, strode unhesitatingly to a large building near the back of the complex and barged right in. Ranja and Kenlin followed just behind. The grandness of their entrance was somewhat undermined by the fact that it was a very sunny day outside, so none of the Jazeiz could see in the indoor dimness; it took several moments of blinking for them to perceive that they were in an empty front room and that no one had been present to witness their dramatic ingress. Undeterred, Klanjad pressed forward as soon as he could see the next door, and this time he successfully interrupted a meeting.

Half a dozen men in varying military paraphernalia had been conferring around a table. At the Jazeiz's entrance they all stood abruptly. All were surprised, and a few looked concerned, but the one seated at the head of the table broke into a wide, warm smile. "Well, fancy! The Jazei lord himself, back from the dead yet again!"

Without replying, Klanjad strode quickly across the room. With an air of fast friends long separated, the two men clasped hands; then, finding that to be insufficient, they embraced. "Never believe it, Erkajin! You've died under my command too many times to be that credulous."

Kenlin looked questioningly to Ranja: *Who is this man?* Ranja, her eyes wide with surprise and interest, shrugged and kept her focus on her father.

Still smiling broadly, Erkajin turned to the others in the room, who were still standing about looking confused. "Leave us. Gada, see that this messenger is fed and looked after. And fetch a scribe, take a copy of the message, then send the original on to the court. But remain nearby, all of you; we will continue this discussion in the afternoon—perhaps with the attendance of our newest arrivals."

The room's occupants agreed with stereotypical military enthusiasm and marched smartly out of the room as though intending to impress Klanjad with their formality. *Ha!*

As Kenlin closed the door behind the last of the exiting soldiers, Klanjad feigned innocence: "Am I interrupting?"

"You're always interrupting, Lord Klanjad," quipped Erkajin easily, sitting down again and inviting the Jazeiz to do the same. "But in this case, I'd actually rather say you're late. Had I known you were coming, I would have delayed this meeting to wait for you."

"Would you? But didn't you just say I was dead again?"

"Yes, but you're always dead, Lord Klanjad." Klanjad laughed, and Erkajin continued cheekily, "You should be wary of that: one of these days it might prove fatal. But before we go into specifics, won't you be so kind as to make the introductions?"

Klanjad was predictably concise. "Ranja, Kenlin, Erkajin," he said, indicating each in turn. "My daughter, my nephew, my fellow perennially dead soldier. Or at least he used to be, before he gained the authority to condemn others to valor."

Erkajin chuckled, but would not allow the introductions to be quite so cursory. Turning to Ranja, he drew a kirsk dagger and presented her the pommel. "I've heard much of you, my lady, from your father and from others. It's an honor."

"And a pleasure," she answered warmly, touching the pommel. "Many of my father's friends are dead, but I've met few who have sustained it so hardily."

I think that joke has outliv— has gone on quite long enough. As Erkajin turned towards him, Kenlin said preemptively, "I have no macabre witticisms for the occasion, but as Ranja says, it's always a pleasure to meet a friend of my uncle's."

Erkajin nodded thoughtfully. "Your uncle... Am I right, then, that you are the son of King Ranton, and so the rightful king of Natzut?"

First Jlak, now this man. Does it really matter to these people? "You are right, yes, but that city is razed and abandoned. In fact," he continued, deadpan, "I really only have two subjects, and they're both in this room."

It took just one moment for Klanjad and Ranja to parse that comment, whereupon Ranja's jaw dropped with indignant hilarity—"How *dare* you!"—while Klanjad slapped the table and howled with laughter.

Erkajin, chuckling as well, looked from Klanjad to Ranja to Klanjad again, then back to Kenlin. Shaking his head, he managed, "Well, good luck, your highness!" before he and Kenlin, too, were overcome with laughter.

When they at last managed to regain a modicum of gravity, Klanjad said, "Well... Now that we're all acquainted, tell me how I died this time. Were there witnesses?"

"No, it was even less official than usual," Erkajin replied, shaking his head. "No direct witnesses. I wasn't privy to all the details, but from what I understand there were reports that the Droál—and Skralade in particular—were aware of your journey and had resolved to hunt you down. Then, when winter came and you didn't return, certain parties took that as a sign that Skralade must have succeeded."

Darkly, Klanjad asked, "And did these certain parties happen to hail from Viarlin?"

"Oddly, no," answered Erkajin to Klanjad and Ranja's obvious surprise. "Again, I wasn't there, I haven't been to Ñaj-Gadan in more than a year; but the loudest voices speaking of your demise apparently came from Iskena. Viarlin, for once, seemed to be supplying a voice of reason, reminding the Commune how many times you've been declared dead before and advising that we should take no rash action until you returned. They even promised to substantially fund an expedition to reoccupy Natzut, should your report recommend it."

A tiny catch-breath from Ranja told Kenlin that she had deduced something, but neither of the older men heard her.

Klanjad commented drily, "Viarlin's opposition is always frustrating, but their support is terrifying. Have they revealed their ulterior motives yet, or do we remain in suspense?"

Erkajin took a deep breath, hesitating. After a moment, Ranja said, "So it's true, then? The Droál have marched on Ñaj-Gadan itself, and Viarlin has negotiated to allow it?"

Very slowly, Erkajin shook his head. "To allow it? Not quite, my lady. If recent reports, including the one I've received today, are accurate, the Droál have launched simultaneous assaults on both Skaradarn and Ñaj-Gadan...and Viarlin has marched on Skaj-Kraskedir."

Blank, empty silence greeted this revelation. As unfiltered shock covered Klanjad's and Ranja's faces, Kenlin asked sharply, "To be clear, Skaj-Kraskedir is a Commune city, yes? So if they've marched against it..."

Erkajin nodded gravely. "According to our latest reports, Viarlin has allied with the Droál and openly declared war on the Commune. We have been betrayed."

The shock had faded quickly from Ranja's countenance to be replaced by a deep, thoughtful frown, her eyes flicking back and forth as she reexamined all her assumptions. Klanjad, still with the dazed expression of a man who has been slapped, waved his hands slowly as though to bat away his confusion. "That's... That is... Well, that's just not plausible. Even with treachery in mind, *three major cities* at once, one of which is Ñaj-Gadan? Is this... How many men?"

"This has all happened within the last twenty days, Lord Klanjad, so I don't think we can put too much faith in our current estimates."

"How many?"

"Well... Skaj-Kraskedir reports fifteen thousand, which presumably includes as many as ten thousand from Viarlin. The first reports from Skaradarn also said fifteen thousand, and no second reports have come. And the most reasonable estimates we have from Ñaj-Gadan say twenty thousand on either side of the city, without considering their navy."

"Absolutely not," Klanjad declared flatly. "Someone is lying about the armies facing them, and lying monstrously. *Seventy thousand?* They would have to halve every garrison north of Guardél, and *empty* every garrison south of it. What if the Commune had attacked while they were mustering? No, Skralade would never allow them to take such a risk."

Ranja shook her head slowly. "I disagree, Father: Viarlin mitigated the risk. They could almost guarantee that the Commune would remain passive, and that the Droál would be well warned of any action that might be taken. Did you not just say, Erkajin, that they were the ones urging inaction? Not aggression, not negotiation, but *inaction?*"

Erkajin nodded gravely. "And inaction—or *recovery*, to be more precise—would have been a wise course, if not for their treachery. Yes, my lady, I think they did help the Droál to manage risk, stalling our politics and clouding our espionage to give them time to amass this force. But even that would not have been enough, I think, and so... So the Droál brought, by sea, an entirely new army from their homeland."

Now Klanjad was alarmed. "How many from that?"

"... Again, I can't completely trust our current reports, but... As many as two hundred ships. Thirty thousand fighting men."

Silence.

Long silence.

When Klanjad spoke at last, it was in the smallest voice Kenlin had ever heard from him. "We don't have an answer for this. Skralade is moving to end the Commune in a single massive campaign. This is not a push; it's a death blow."

Silence again, this time for so long that every other sound—the drafts through the walls, the creaking of their chairs, even the tense whispers of their breathing—seemed magnified in Kenlin's ears. *Ranja's eyes flicker and her fingers twitch; I can almost see the busyness in her mind. But Klanjad... Have I ever seen him look so lost?* After several long minutes, Kenlin asked, "So what is being done? How are we responding?"

Erkajin seemed a reluctant to answer; after a few deep breaths, he said, "To my knowledge, there is no coherent plan yet. The information I have just told you has been arriving piecemeal over the past several days, and the leaders of the eastern cities have not yet had time to coordinate."

"Well, Skaj-Kraskedir is neither fortified nor supplied to withstand a siege," Klanjad said, stirring from his shock, "so the obvious course is for Janísla and Iskena to converge at Skaj-Kraskedir, then see about breaking the eastern siege on Ñaj-Gadan. There's no new animosity between Iaile and Merejor, I hope?"

"No, my lord," Erkajin answered hesitantly, "so far as I know. But Queen Iaile is far away in Iskena—"

"And she'll not hear the news you've heard today for another day at least," Klanjad completed, clicking his tongue frustratedly. "And allowing time on top of that for couriers and mustering... No sooner than eight days to Skaj-Kraskedir, even if Merejor can convince her to march immediately."

"I think that's quite optimistic, Lord Klanjad, considering that King Merejor, too, is far from Janísla."

Klanjad seemed baffled for a moment, then groaned aloud. "Tell me he's not..." but Erkajin was already nodding, and Klanjad's sentence ended in another groan: "...in Ñaj-Gadan. Called to council, I assume, by our erstwhile loyal compatriots? Worse and worse. So then who— Not the *prince?*"

Erkajin was still nodding, though now he was bent over the table with his head in his hands, incredulous at his own news. "The king expected to be gone no longer than half a moon and appointed no military regent for his absence. Thus, by default, the authority to command falls to his heir."

"Who is *twelve years old.*"

"And to whom the fate of the Commune, it seems, is beholden."

Klanjad cursed under his breath, "*Ittarshil!* Well, then. Will the boy march?"

"He will not," Erkajin answered with certainty that clearly both surprised and concerned Klanjad. "When I returned to Janísla, my experience under your command brought me recognition—and to some degree, influence—beyond my rank. But of late, I have seen my official window into the court and high command diminished. Now, after days and *days* of catastrophic reports from the west, every morning I expect to receive orders to at least begin making ready to deploy. Every morning, I am disappointed. And most recently, I hear that the debate in court—in the prince's ear—centers not on how we can most effectively resist the Droál, but on whether we should follow Viarlin's example and stop trying."

Klanjad's eyes narrowed. Slowly, he said, "Merejor would never stand for such treason. Even speaking of such things would see an advisor's influence, and perhaps his life, destroyed—should the king ever return to learn of it." Erkajin nodded gravely; he had no other reply. Klanjad pressed, "How did this happen? How did we *allow* this to happen? Haven't we friends of our own to protect us from being so easily outmaneuvered?"

Erkajin gave a twisted, rueful smile. "The king's most trusted advisors are part of the royal entourage; even now, they are with him in Ñaj-Gadan. And the prince, in their absence, must make do with *alternative* advisement. As for the rest... If we knew what had happened, my lord, we would have prevented it. I am sorry. We have failed. I have failed." All hint of a smile, rueful or otherwise, had vanished from Erkajin's face. *Such is the face of failure.*

Klanjad's head now rested on his palms, his fingers rhythmically drumming his brow in a sort of pensive self-flagellation. He muttered, "And so the world burns, but before we can put it out we must argue the urgency with a child. Skaj-Kraskedir may well crumble whilst we argue. And yet...we must argue, mustn't we?" A subtle, sharp note in her father's voice caused Ranja to raise her head in alarm.

Erkajin said carefully, "I think a more direct approach—at least, a *much* more direct approach—risks winning the battle at the cost of the war. The effect on Merejor alone—"

"Of course I know that, put that from your mind," said Klanjad, flapping a hand dismissively. "But might the army march without orders? How many are loyal to you? How many do you suppose *I* could rally?"

This suggestion had a remarkable effect on Erkajin: his eyes brightened, and he sat suddenly straight and spoke crisply. "My reputation exceeds my command, Lord Klanjad. On my influence alone, we could likely march with, *um*...by tomorrow, two regiments and a cavalry column. Given another day or two, and with your influence, we might double that."

"Five thousand, optimistically," Klanjad muttered, calculating. "Five thousand to march, while ten thousand or so remain in Janísla awaiting leadership from an ill-advised baby. Five thousand...against *seventy* thousand..." There was a long silence as Klanjad pondered deeply, kneading his forehead as though to make a solution rise in his mind. But after several endless minutes of kneading and pondering, he began to chuckle humorlessly. "Alright, then. We'll immediately send word to Iaile, who will gladly leave a mere five thousand in her restive homeland and march with ten thousand to our aid. We ourselves will march with five thousand two mornings from now, arriving just in time to coordinate with Iaile and liberate Skaj-Kraskedir without a single casualty. We will then absorb the willing and able-bodied garrison and turn our attention toward Ñaj-Gadan. The Droál will inevitably redeploy to combine their besieging forces, whereupon we will fight and rout a defending army roughly twice the size of our own. All clear?"

Kenlin said, "I have questions."

"Inevitably."

"You're as humorous as ever, Lord Klanjad," said Erkajin, who didn't look remotely amused. "But joking aside, what is to be done?"

Klanjad threw up his hands. "What *can* be done? If Janísla does not march in force but absolutely everything else goes swimmingly, then *at best* we could hope to liberate Skaj-Kraskedir and Ñaj-Gadan with a far-too-costly victory over the besiegers—as you said, losing the war to win the battle. No, I won't lead another death march against such odds. Our only chance lies in full deployment and careful coordination with Iskena. So to that end... I suppose we must send a courier to Iskena and wait for a reply; and while we wait, we will sit in Janísla and argue with a child."

"But Skaj-Kraskedir is away from the front, it's not provisioned... Do you really expect them to resist siege for that long?"

Klanjad shook his head grimly. "Skaj-Kraskedir will fall. And Skaradarn will fall. But perhaps," he continued bitterly, "if we argue *very* well, we might can act soon enough to save Ñaj-Gadan and avenge whatever is left of Skaj-Kraskedir. Maybe."

Erkajin fell back in his seat, crushed. A long, empty silence filled the room. Then, at last, Ranja spoke: "There is another option."

Kenlin looked at her curiously. Erkajin kept his dejected gaze focused on nothing. Klanjad, after a moment, glanced up sharply and said, "Well?"

She had sat in pensive silence for so long that she had sunk back and low into her chair; but now she sat up straight and spoke quickly to Klanjad. "We need the full strength of Janísla, but it won't deploy without King Merejor. Might the five thousand we *can* deploy be enough to buy time while we—the three of us—break into Ñaj-Gadan and bring him back?" A look of deep skepticism took over Klanjad's and Erkajin's faces, but Ranja pressed on. "Listen. Five thousand may not be enough to break the siege on Skaj-Kraskedir, but they should be enough to delay it: the besiegers will be reluctant to commit to an assault while threatened from behind, even by a smaller army. If Skaj-Kraskedir can survive for even half a moon, that should be enough time; our friends here can coordinate with Iskena while we three retrieve King Merejor from Ñaj-Gadan, bring him back here, then march with the full might of Janísla and Iskena."

Klanjad clicked his tongue thoughtfully. "Five thousand deployed immediately—but to harass, not to fight. Meanwhile, we and a picked few... There and back in ten days... It's risky, Ranja, very risky."

"No more so than your plan of waiting and coordinating," Ranja retorted to general surprise. "In fact, the proposals are very similar. We both think we should not seek battle until we have all the strength we can muster. But by merely *threatening* battle, we can—"

"Yes, I see, I see," Klanjad cut her off, waving his hand. "You could be right, perhaps it's not much more of a risk."

"It certainly *sounds* risky," Erkajin said with a look of concern, "especially to yourselves. Did you not say, just moments ago, that you wouldn't lead a death march?"

"I did say that, but sometimes... Old habits, you know. And if our options are either to venture forth and gamble for victory or to stay here and wait for defeat... Better a death march than a death sit, don't you think?" Erkajin did not find that funny at all, but he had no reply.

Kenlin, however, still had questions. "Is there really no simple way for us to convince this prince to deploy now? Should we not at least try?"

"We will certainly try," Klanjad said doubtfully, looking to Erkajin, "but what success can we hope for?"

Reluctantly, Erkajin admitted, "Little. We've already been out-maneuvered in this court, and with so many poisoned tongues in the prince's ear... And even if we did manage to gain his cooperation, such highly placed foes will continue to delay and disrupt and—"

"Yes," Klanjad interrupted darkly. "Guardél. I remember."

"Then it sounds like you have made your decision."

"I have. Immediately, we must dispatch a messenger to Iskena to get the coordination process started. Then, in what time we have left today, I will go to the prince and do what I can to convince him. After that fails, you will take me to meet whomever you think I might be able to influence. I will make it clear that you, Erkajin, have the honor of commanding this heroic mass-desertion and that your command has my full endorsement. But I will not stay for the muster; I will be off by tomorrow morning at the latest."

Kenlin remarked, "I notice you keep using the word *I*."

Klanjad gave him a sidelong look. "Well, for the first time in many moons, Kenlin, you have a real choice. You're here now; welcome to the war. If you wish to continue accompanying me, I think there's still much you can learn. But, if you like, you can also choose to remain in Janísla and argue strategy with a twelve-year-old."

"Ha! Need I even answer?"

Klanjad grinned; "I think I can guess your mind." Then, affecting a somewhat more severe expression, he turned to his daughter. "Ranja—"

"No."

"For your safety—"

"No."

"As your father—"

"No."

"I insist—"

"No!"

There was a brief pause during which Klanjad tried to maintain his deadpan in the face of Ranja's unruffled aloofness. Then Kenlin snorted, and the stalemate was broken; they all three dissolved into laughter.

Erkajin laughed along, though unwillingly. "You are like your father, my lady. Admirable, but I do wish you would have a bit more care for your own safety."

"We are Jazeiz," Ranja replied lightly. "Safety is the luxury of the unambitious. And considering how active our foes have been within Janísla itself of late—how much they've risked, and how much they depend on our failure—I don't think we can reasonably expect this city to stay 'safe' for long."

"Truth," Klanjad agreed, the mirth quickly fading from his face. "And if we aren't careful, it may become a very, very worrying truth. Mind the shadows, my friend; they grow long in Janísla of late."

Erkajin nodded soberly. "These days, my lord, they grow long the world over. Mind the shadows."

Chapter XXV:

The prince, unfortunately, was afflicted by the sort of illness that develops suddenly in the afternoon with no warning, and has troublingly nondescript symptoms, and is certainly not deadly but will tragically prevent his majesty from granting any audiences today, so you might try again tomorrow but the healer warns that the malady may be of uncertain duration, however the court thanks you most sincerely on behalf of his majesty and wishes you a lovely evening. As the frilly-looking courtier flounced back into the palace leaving Ranja irritated and Klanjad livid, Kenlin reflected that he'd never before heard such delicately derisive pleasantries. The experience left him feeling disgusted and yet oddly refreshed, as though he'd been sneezed on on a hot day.

Their meeting with Erkajin's fellow officers was much more productive. Of the men in attendance, well more than half pledged to march under Erkajin's command without orders, or even against them. Others doubted the obedience of their soldiers, but they pledged to do everything in their power to ensure that Janísla was ready to march when the time came. A pair of cavalry captains expressed tentative willingness, but requested time to propose the idea to their subordinates directly. At the end of the day, just over four thousand soldiers were committed to march—fewer than Erkajin had hoped for, but still enough (according to Klanjad) to threaten the siege at Skaj-Kraskedir.

The Jazeiz departed the city the following morning with an escort of a dozen mounted infantry, spare horses, and more supplies than Kenlin thought they could ever need. Ranja, laughing at him, assured him that this was the correct quantity of supplies for such a company on such a journey, and that they would travel more quickly because they wouldn't need to resupply as they went. That was all probably true, but it didn't stop Kenlin from feeling like a provisions trader.

But the provisions dwindled swiftly—the long days and aggressive pace wore heavily on both mounts and riders—and their once-stuffed bags had become limp and light by the evening of the fourth day. They were now less than a day's ride from Ñaj-Gadan. The current plan was to approach the siege the following day, scout their options, and find a way to infiltrate the city after nightfall. But with every story he heard from passing refugees, Klanjad became more anxious. "They's Droál tents for *leagues* ou'sside the city, like they built a whole 'nuther city right around it." "Never see'd so many ships, so many men, nowhere!"

"Perhaps," Ranja had suggested, "they are exaggerating? Out of fear, or out of some misguided storytelling—"

"They are exaggerating," Klanjad had interrupted curtly. "They always do. But *such* tales as these..." He did not elaborate further, but a broody agitation settled on him and persisted through the rest of the day. When at last, near sunset, they dismounted and began to camp, Klanjad bade Kenlin and Ranja sup without him. "There was an inn at that last village, not half a league back. I'm going to see what news I can gather. I want to know more about what we'll find tomorrow."

"If I didn't know you better—" Kenlin began innocently, but Klanjad cut him off.

"Yes, I will drink, not to stupidity but to good rest. You two should rest as well. Tomorrow will be the longest day of your lives."

Dutifully, after camp was set and dinner was eaten, Kenlin tried to go immediately to sleep; but though his body was tired from the day's ride, his mind was restless. *Oh, it's useless, I won't get to sleep until I can at least quiet my thoughts. I should have gone for a drink with Klanjad if that was an option, which it probably wasn't. Well, at least he'll get some good rest when he comes back. If he comes back.*

Giving up on sleep for now, Kenlin sat up and began to stoke the dying fire. Ranja glanced up dispassionately. She was not even trying to sleep, but lay on her stomach, propped up on her elbows, drawing idly in the dirt. As Kenlin leaned over to see what she was drawing, she cast him an offish look. "Do you mind?"

"Seldom, and very poorly," said Kenlin, unabashed. "And yet still too much, such that it interferes with sleeping. What are you drawing there?"

She eyed him unfavorably, then shrugged. "Shapes. The eastern walls of Ñaj-Gadan, that sort of thing. The shapes that we might see tomorrow."

Might see? Perhaps she, too, thinks... Watching her face closely, Kenlin asked, "Do you suppose he has gone?"

"Gone?"

"Gone on ahead, gone to Ñaj-Gadan without us."

To Kenlin's surprise, she chuckled quietly and shook her head. "You still don't know him at all, do you?"

"I know how he loves you," Kenlin answered quietly. "And I wonder... If the siege is really as bad as we've heard, I wonder if he might choose to leave us—you—out of it."

"Then you don't know me," Ranja answered just a little sharply. "'Leaving me out of it' is not an option. If he were to not return, I would know where he had gone, and then I would follow."

Kenlin shook his head. "You wouldn't waste your life on a suicidal effort like that, Ranja. I think you're more rational than that; and moreover, I think *Klanjad* thinks you're more rational than that."

Ranja scoffed, "Then you don't know either of us. But Father knows better. He knows I don't make idle claims, and he knows I won't let him leave me."

Ah, it seems she's being unsubtly subtle again. "I see. He knows that...from experience?"

She quirked an eyebrow. "How do you suppose I came to be on *this* journey? Do you imagine that was his idea?"

Kenlin had never thought much about it, but suddenly an image formed in his mind of Ranja on horseback galloping across the countryside in mad pursuit of her fleeing father, and he had to force himself not to laugh aloud. "That sounds *quite* absurd. Details?"

She shrugged. "Whatever you're picturing is probably not far off. It *was* absurd." But she didn't look as though she thought it was funny. After a moment, she concluded quietly, "I *will* follow him. And that's why he will never leave me."

After perhaps a minute, Kenlin ventured, "I guess I had always assumed that the whole expedition was Klanjad's idea, and that your participation was just a part of the plan."

"You know better than that," Ranja chided. "You know perfectly well that I'm nearly as ignorant as you are of Father's travels, so you know he wasn't in the habit of bringing me along."

"Years ago, yes, when you were very young and he was operating beyond the front. But Natzut is far from the front, and you were older, so..."

She half-smiled. "Yes, those factors made a difference. But only to me, not to him. Not until I *made* them matter."

"He actually tried to go alone, then? You followed and tracked him down?"

"That's the gist of it," she replied, even the half-smile fading as she returned her attention to the dirt. "But I don't want to talk about this anymore."

Kenlin, of course, did want exactly that. However, he had no desire to drive Ranja into an even more somber mood, so he cast about for a related, but perhaps less sensitive, topic. "So... It seemed that Erkajin and Klanjad are quite good friends, but had not seen each other for some time. You had never met him before?"

Ranja shook her head. "I might have heard Father mention the name, but I'd certainly never met the man. Now *there's* someone who could tell you about Father's doings; he actually participated."

"They kept mentioning Guardél. But if that's the Guardél campaign I've heard about, wasn't that more than ten years ago? And didn't they lose?"

"True and true. That was before Father's doings became the stuff of rumor and myth, back when he fought in the open. Alongside Jendraski, he marched with the army of the Commune into one of the greatest strategic disasters in history."

"We've discussed this briefly before, I think. Didn't they lose *two* armies in that campaign?"

"The *Commune* lost two armies. More specifically, Jendraski 'the Bold' of Ñaj-Gadan lost one army, and Gavalan 'the Wise' of Guardél lost another. Father was present in both cases, but not in command."

Kenlin frowned. "I thought he co-commanded the Jiánse army with Jendraski, yes? Or am I misremembering that?"

"You're remembering a lot more than you originally implied," Ranja commented, suppressing a grin. "Yes, allegedly Father did 'co-command' that campaign. But I think he was really more of a second-in-command; Jendraski is older and, at least at the time, was more experienced and far better known than Father was. And, in fairness to Jendraski, the loss at Jiánse wasn't half so unreasonable as at Guardél."

"Oh? What was the difference?"

"Well, for one thing, Jiánse was the Commune's first real encounter with Skralade, and—"

"Really? I didn't know—"

"Hush! Father may cut me off as he likes, but not you! As I was saying, the Commune knew nothing of Skralade at the time, and nobody anticipated that the Droál would have such a commander. Furthermore, though the Commune was routed at Jiánse, many of the soldiers survived, regrouped, and eventually returned with the new army Jendraski and Gavalan brought south the next year. And that's the army that was massacred, almost to a man, at Guardél. There, you may now give reign to your impetuousness."

"Thank you. I had no idea that Skralade commanded at Jiánse. Did he and Klanjad meet each other there?"

Ranja snorted. "What, on the battlefield? I suppose I don't really know, but it seems unlikely since they're both still alive. But after the battle, while Jendraski returned north to raise another army, Father (according to what few accounts exist) stayed. It was during that time, I think, that he and Skralade learned to hate one another."

"I see." A small inner voice of responsibility observed that this conversation was not helping Kenlin get to sleep. *No, but this is vastly more interesting.* "I don't suppose we know what Klanjad and Skralade did in Jiánse to foster such mutual animosity?"

"Not specifically, no," she said with a shrug. "As the story goes, Jiánse resisted occupation so violently during that period that, when Jendraski and Gavalan returned to liberate it, the Droál simply retreated rather than trying to hold the rebellious city. If that's true, then I'm guessing Father's residency there wasn't what you'd call *passive*. The Droál recaptured it, of course, later that same year, but the city's been a challenge for them to control ever since. That, I imagine, does nothing to recommend Father to Skralade. And as for Father... Well, if he didn't hate Skralade after Jiánse, he certainly hated him after Guardél."

"Theirs is a weird sort of hatred," Kenlin mused, "at least on Klanjad's side. They clearly despise one another; and yet, just as clearly, Klanjad has quite a bit of respect for Skralade."

"It is odd," Ranja agreed. "It's very reasonable, though. He's a Misk, and a monster, but also an *extraordinarily* successful warrior, tactician, and strategist. As heinous as Guardél was, even Father has told me it was a masterpiece of maneuvering."

"Yes? What exactly happened?"

"*Exactly*, all sorts of things happened. The short version, however, is that a staggering number of people were massacred, including the Commune's entire army. It was the first time since Natzut and Flunjat that the Droál had razed a city and butchered and burned its populace like that, and Guardél was larger than Natzut and Flunjat combined. The dead from that disaster numbered many tens of thousands; the survivors number in the hundreds. No one is sure how Father and Jendraski—and, apparently, Erkajin—escaped that death trap alive."

Ranja looked down and resumed drawing in the dirt as Kenlin sat back, trying to organize all this information in his mind. Something about this talk of Guardél reminded him of a story he had heard long ago, and that in turn reminded him of something Klanjad had told him about Faery magic. "I might have the geography wrong, but I think I have a theory about how Klanjad survived."

"The Nameless Forest?" Ranja said without looking up.

"That's...where the Faeries live, yes?"

"That's right. And yes, it's very close to Guardél."

"I begin to suspect I'm not the first person to suggest this theory."

She laughed. "It's a popular story, but it's just a story, nothing more. The Faeries don't interfere in the affairs of the other Races, and there's no real evidence that Father ever went to the Nameless Forest in the first place."

Really? But when he was telling me of Faery magic, I think he actually said outright that he'd been to the Nameless Forest. But if he hasn't told her, should I say? Or would it rankle to know...?

Surprised by his silence, Ranja had looked up and, apparently, read some hint of his thoughts in his face. "Kenlin," she said suspiciously, "are you keeping secrets from me?"

Nope. "Not I," said Kenlin innocently, "and that's why I was just about to tell you that Klanjad mentioned the Nameless Forest when we were discussing Faery magic. I think he stated fairly clearly that he'd been there."

"He told you that?"

Don't take it that way, Ranja. "It came up in conversation. This was around the time when we first arrived in the swamp, when you were still gravely wounded and I was just beginning to learn of magic."

There had been a note, just the slightest quaver, of hurt in her voice; but with a quick shake of her head, she recovered herself. "That's extraordinary!" she said with a growing smile. "I had always hoped that was what happened—it makes for *such* a better story—but it just seemed like wishful thinking. The Faeries hardly ever intervene, even when people seek them out, the March excepted."

"The March?"

"You've forgotten the *Faery March?* At the end of the War of Men and Misks, after the Infanticide, Zadarj sought out the Faeries, and everybody fought Clan Eyjazinka..."

Ah, I do remember this. "It's been a *very* long time since we discussed that, Ranja. Didn't you promise me a detailed telling of Zadarj and the war sometime? Maybe even the *Lay?*"

"Sometime, but not tonight. That's quite a long story, and even I don't have a clear memory of all the details—and obviously I haven't memorized the whole *Lay*. The Faery March, though, is easy to remember. In the final campaign of the War of Men and Misks, the Faeries fought alongside Zadarj the Djinn-Slayer to overthrow Clan Eyjazinka's domination of Jranjana."

"Right, I remember now. That was the only time when Faeries really influenced history at scale, yes?"

Ranja made a face as though she didn't like that wording. "Faeries have certainly influenced history, Kenlin. But yes, there's never been another event quite like the Faery March."

"Why not?" As Ranja gave an exasperated sigh, Kenlin pressed, "Consider it, Ranja. In the War of Men and Misks, the Faeries played a crucial role in the rise of humans—a role that helped determine the course of Jranjana for the past millennium. If just one campaign by the Faeries can have such an impact, why don't they intervene more often?"

Ranja raised an eyebrow. "In other words, why haven't the Faeries helped us in our fight against the Droál? You're making a very common mistake in thinking of Faeries as allies—in any literal sense of the word—of humans in general. Faeries are not like any of the other Species: they do not form tribes, build cities, establish governments... It's almost unheard of for them to even travel in groups. The Faery March was unique in history, and it probably couldn't have happened without both Zadarj's friendship with Nandaad and the outrage caused by the Infanticide. Also, keep in mind that the March led to more Faery deaths than any other event in recorded history, and many Faeries are probably old enough to remember it."

Kenlin opened his mouth to reply, but she preempted him. "That's not to say, however, that we haven't *tried* to secure their support. I had always suspected that Father spent at least part of his unknown years trying, and now that I know he's been to the Forest, I'm more sure than ever that he has attempted it. But it doesn't surprise me that he failed, for Faeries are not like humans. While many humans strive to influence history, often together, few Faeries have ever done so, and the ones who do almost exclusively act individually: Iuleard with his *Grimoire*, Evikasta with her maps and discoveries, and the Wanderer with his memories."

Kenlin nodded, for he knew all three of these names. Iuleard was an almost mythical figure who had written the *Grimoire*, the quintessential and yet legendarily incomprehensible treatise on the Faery conception of magic and the nature of reality. Evikasta had been an explorer and mapmaker who had laid the groundwork for cartography ever since. And the Wanderer, of course, was Jranjana's greatest storyteller as well as a character in many of his own tales, assuming... "You've told me before that you believe the Wanderer exists, even though you've never met him, yes?"

Ranja rolled her eyes. "Of course the Wanderer exists. There's *far* too much evidence to believe otherwise."

"Alright!" said Kenlin, grinning and putting up his hands in surrender. "Although, to be fair, there are quite a lot of stories of Leiver and Kaeno too."

"That's different, Kenlin. Kaeno actually was an historical figure, although his name was Kaene and his real life wasn't particularly interesting. And Leiver's a folk hero; his name gets attached to any story at all so long as there's some excuse to mention rings."

"And how is that different from the Wanderer? If you have a character who's introduced halfway through your story, just give him some serpentine daggers and mention the necklace, and there! Your story suddenly has credibility, all thanks to the wholly unverifiable presence of the Wanderer."

Ranja opened her mouth to tell Kenlin exactly why he was mistaken, if only she'd had an argument to that effect. "You're not...entirely wrong," she admitted reluctantly. "But it's absolutely certain that the Wanderer is real, and the fact that he's used to lend credibility to otherwise implausible stories is just further evidence of that. Nobody adds Leiver to a story in order to make it *more* believable."

As Kenlin laughed at this, from his memory he heard the echoes of their voices—Vaai, Kahand, Jranzak, Dzan, Ijki, Graddij, and Adanedi—as they had bantered about this very topic so long ago. But the echoes, though unexpected, were not bitter, and they and Kenlin, and another, all laughed merrily together until Ranja gave him a quizzical look. "Such truth," Kenlin said to her, finally recovering himself, "Leiver certainly doesn't add credibility like the Wanderer does. On the other hand, they're used very differently, yes? Leiver is almost always the main character of his stories, whereas the Wanderer pops up, sometimes for only a moment or two, in stories about other people."

"Exactly!" she rejoined. "That's a characteristic of the Wanderer's stories. He appears in many of his own tales because he knows what happened because *he was there*, but the stories themselves are about others. That's who he is: he is the storyteller of Jranjana, not the story itself."

"So then, he is only attested in stories that are allegedly 'his own?' Are there no stories that feature the Wanderer as a main character?"

She shrugged. "There are some; I know one. But whether or not such tales are credible, they're much rarer. Most stories that include the Wanderer feature him more tangentially, either because they're one of the Wanderer's own stories or because they're trying to masquerade as one."

Kenlin cocked his head. "Interesting. Just how rare are these stories centered on the Wanderer? I don't think I've heard any."

"As I said, I only know one," Ranja answered with another shrug. "And even that one is hardly credible: it's rife with anachronisms and misapplied cultural norms."

"Those sound like the sorts of problems that won't bother me at all. Can I hear this story?" This request prompted them both to reevaluate how they were spending the evening. *Well, I couldn't sleep before, and now I'm more awake than ever. I suppose if Klanjad returns and finds us both still awake, he'll be angry. But then again, he very well might be angry regardless, so I may as well make the most of it.* Seeing that Ranja was thinking along similar lines, Kenlin prompted slyly, "You know you want to."

Ranja narrowed her eyes and gave Kenlin a long look. "You're lucky I can't sleep either." Then she began the tale.

Hidden away in the mountains, hiding from the world, the Misk clan Varayan dwelt in peace, a small but ancient and proud tribe. The chieftains of Varayan had long sought only solitude for the clan, but alas for such simplicity, for gentleness is quickly washed away in the rushing waters of life.

At the high tide of Varayan, the chieftain had a daughter whose beauty and spirit were admired by all. Tatia was her name, and none who met her could speak ill of her. Sweet was her manner, clear her gaze; her hair was the sleek black of a night breeze, her eyes shone like polished jet, and her skin was like ivory. She was loyal to her clan and would defend the little villages in times of war; but in peacetime she was wont to be found seated on a rock by a stream overlooking the road, watching the travelers pass.

It happened in the summer that the Wanderer passed by the place where she sat. In these days, the Wanderer was yet in his youth, golden of hair and eyes, and he loved to sing; and as he passed by the place where Tatia sat, he sang a song that the flowers turned their heads to hear. Tatia, too, listened to the song, and when the Wanderer was quite near she called to him.

He, turning, found her exceedingly fair, and he approached her with sweet words and smiles. She returned both, and they sat merrily in the mountains until the sun had set.

And she would return to the stream, day by day, and the Wanderer lingered to see her; and they became first friends, then lovers, until the summer's leaves were all but gone and winter's snows waited to rush down from the mountaintops.

As the cold crept into the dales and passes, there came a messenger from a nearby clan, a powerful clan: their chieftain, one Kevle, had heard legend of Tatia's beauty and charm, and he wanted her for his bride. And Clan Varayan held council in concern, and the chieftain of Varayan said to Tatia, "Daughter, unless it is too repulsive a task, you must give yourself to these foreigners; for though we may fight them and live for a while, they are far more powerful than we. If you will, you may save our clan." And Tatia answered, "Chieftain, Father, for the sake of our clan, I will do this thing."

And no more did Tatia go to the rock at the stream by the road, though her heart cried out to go; and the Wanderer was sorely pained and knew not what to think until heard the news of the approaching wedding. Then he wept bitterly, and tore at his golden hair, and he sought comfort in lonely places.

But through the land was hunting an Unnatilz called Ogner, a friend to the Wanderer who knew of his love for Tatia; and when this Unnatilz heard of her betrothal to Kevle, he said to himself, "This cannot be; it is ill fate and fortune to steal the love of another. I will be ill fate and fortune to this Kevle. I will hunt the thief of my friend's love."

And so Ogner lay in wait for Kevle as he passed on his way to marry Tatia. But ill fate sought Ogner that day, for as he leapt to slay Kevle, his prey spotted him too early, drew his sword, and slew the Unnatilz. Then he took the Unnatilz's head and, going to Clan Varayan, he asked, "Whose head have I here?" And they told him that it was Ogner, friend of the Wanderer. "This Ogner was my enemy, and friends of his friends are my enemies. Are you, then, my enemies?"

And Tatia stepped forward. "It is through no act of ours that Ogner became your enemy, nor is it our wish to be your enemies as well."

"Then," said Kevle, "as you are my bride, prove to me your loyalty and good will; send forth this Wanderer from your lands, never to return, or else bring me his head."

And Tatia wept in her heart, but for her clan she kept her face still. "My husband has spoken," she said for all to hear. "Let the Wanderer wander no longer among the Misks of Varayan." Then she retired alone to her chambers and wept the night through.

And the Wanderer heard naught of these things for years on end, until at last he emerged from his refuge in lonely places. Then did he approach the gate of Varayan and asked to see Tatia; but he was turned away, for Tatia had decreed that he might never walk among her clan. It was then as though the last of the Wanderer's heart had burst, and he—

Kenlin and Ranja both turned abruptly at the sound of a hasty approach. A moment later, Klanjad strode swiftly into the firelight and, without a word of greeting, gestured commandingly for them to rise. Exchanging an uncertain glance with Ranja, Kenlin hazarded an attempt at humor: "Good news?"

The flat, frozen look with which Klanjad responded immediately crushed all levity in the conversation. "No," he said, "not good news. We must set out now. Ñaj-Gadan will be overrun by nightfall tomorrow."

Overrun? Does he mean...? He cannot possibly mean that.

Ranja seemed to share Kenlin's incredulity. "When you say *overrun*, you mean—"

Klanjad turned his flat, frozen stare on her, and she fell silent beneath it. After a moment, he said in a hollow voice, "The inn held bad news, nothing but bad news, and from a reliable source. The Droál army here is substantially larger than anticipated, containing thirty thousand soldiers on this side of the city alone." Ranja's eyes widened and her jaw dropped in blank astonishment. Klanjad continued grimly, "And worse. A short while ago, a panicked rider arrived from one of the closer towns: at sundown, the Droál breached the city's main eastern gate, and Ñaj-Gadan is already aflame."

CHAPTER XXVI:

The east wind blew cold and dusty that night, but the Jazeiz soon outpaced it. They had sent back their escort with news for Erkajin: "Tell him to be wary," Klanjad had said, "for the Droál have committed more might to this assault than I ever would have imagined. Save Skaj-Kraskedir if you can, but stay agile and be watchful: the host at Ñaj-Gadan will not remain preoccupied for long." Then they were off, driving their tired horses at a canter and trusting the road not to trip them in the dark. Kenlin, who had first mounted a horse less than half a moon ago, struggled just to stay in the saddle, but the horse was clever enough to follow Klanjad's on its own. They proceeded without incident until, ahead in the west, the horizon began to glow red.

A red glow in the west? But the sun set hours ago; this is the wrong dawn. Moments later, they crested a hill and reigned in their horses as they saw, at last, an unobstructed view of the scale of Droálic fire.

A league or more yet lay between their vantage point and the gates of Ñaj-Gadan, and yet even from this distance it was clear that the city was larger by far than every human settlement Kenlin had ever seen. But it was night, and strictly speaking the city itself could not be seen; Kenlin could only estimate its magnitude by the brightness with which it burned. "There must be a thousand fires! How big is Ñaj-Gadan?"

Klanjad's back was to Kenlin, so his expression was hidden; but there was a tone in his voice that Kenlin had never heard from him before: *dread.* "That's not Ñaj-Gadan," Klanjad uttered blankly, almost uncomprehendingly. "See there, where those furthest fires form a broken line? That is Ñaj-Gadan, only just beginning to burn. The rest of what you see are the torches and campfires of the Droálic army."

"One above!" Ranja gasped.

They remained still atop the hill for several minutes, gazing in horror and awe at the scene before them. Kenlin could not begin to comprehend the scope of the disaster. Ranja, drawn up tensely in the saddle, stared at the fires with fascination and dismay. Klanjad kept his back to them, and his shoulders were very, very still. Then he whipped his reins to the side and turned his horse shoulder-to-shoulder with Ranja's so that he and she faced one another.

Abruptly, Klanjad reached out and took hold of her by both shoulders, staring very intently into her face. She seemed startled, and perhaps even unnerved, but she returned his gaze steadily. Then, as something was wordlessly communicated between them, she slowly began to shake her head.

In spite of himself, Klanjad smiled a bittersweet smile, and his eyes fell fleetingly on the black aster pendant she wore. So quietly that Kenlin felt sure he wasn't supposed to hear, Klanjad whispered, "So much like your mother." A moment's silence passed as Klanjad struggled with himself. "Very well. Then do not stray from my path, not for an instant. When we reach the city, I do not know what will happen; but even with the utmost caution, this may be the very last night for the Jazeiz."

Ranja nodded, and Klanjad released her shoulders. But before he could turn away, she dropped her reins suddenly and caught his hand in both of her own. "Father!" she breathed; and Kenlin, not wishing to intrude, turned his head away, though he could still hear. "Father, I'm afraid..."

"I know."

"When he cut me, Father, back in Likrásk... It hurt *so much*... Promise me, Father: if they cut me again, and I can't stay with you, and... *Please* don't let it hurt."

A moment passed in which they said nothing. After, Klanjad whispered, "Be strong, Ranja. I fear too, you know I do. I fear...the fire..."

"I know, Father. I won't let them, not to you. I promise."

Another moment's silence caused Kenlin to look up. Ranja had turned away, hiding her face in her hands. Klanjad, however, looked Kenlin in the eye. "Flee."

Flee. The very idea triggered a soft, high, mocking chuckle from somewhere in the depths of Kenlin's mind. The chuckle grew a little louder and arced into a cackle as a crooked smile came over Kenlin's face: "Never."

Klanjad answered with a single wordless, approving nod.

Then, speaking quickly to both of them, he said, "Within the next few hours, the Commune will be driven back through the eastern city. They may slow the Droál's advance at the canals for a time, but numbers and Necromancy will carry this fight. Instead, Jendraski will put up only enough resistance to cover his withdrawal to the Tower."

"Thus, we also must make for the Tower," Ranja deduced.

Klanjad nodded, "Yes, and quickly. Our first task is to get inside the walls, but we have no time for subtlety or scouting. Until we are in the city proper, this is what must pass for a plan: we will stay together, stay mounted, and do what we can to outrun the alarm we cause."

Kenlin resisted a sudden impulse to laugh aloud at this. *Restrain yourself!* "Klanjad, near the gates there will be more and more Droál crowded together, trying to get in, yes? How are we to 'outrun the alarm' by running *toward* our enemies?"

Klanjad answered evenly, "The chaos will work in our favor: all available Misks are likely to be busy at the front, and the Droál present will be focused on marching. Nonetheless, it's almost inevitable that we will eventually be identified and attacked; and when that happens, we must *keep moving anyway.* We can lose any pursuers in the lower city once we reach it." Kenlin opened his mouth to comment, but Klanjad cut him off coldly. "I never claimed it was a good plan, Kenlin, but we have no time. If you have a better idea, this is your last chance to bring it forward." Kenlin closed his mouth with a snap. Without another word, Klanjad whipped his reins, wheeled his horse, and led them again toward the burning city.

The darkness of the night reduced the passing scenery to mere glimpses and silhouettes; even so, it was clear that many thousands of people had inhabited this area before... But though the road led them through town after town, there were no lights in the windows, no songs in the taverns, and the smoke on the air carried no smells of cooking. These were ghost towns, and the few who hadn't already fled now cowered and shivered within their homes, waiting to die.

The Jazeiz rode on. As they neared Ñaj-Gadan, the air became thick with smoke. The scent momentarily threw Kenlin's mind back to Jrizkil's homestead, to Likrásk, to a half-remembered inferno from before he could truly understand—*Not now!* The memories faded, but the crackling energy in his mind merely retreated a little, thrumming.

The transition from town to camp was so abrupt that Kenlin was almost as surprised as the Droál. He had seen the torches in the distance several minutes before, but just as they reached the light, Klanjad slapped his horse's flank, leading all three Jazeiz into a gallop right through the unprepared Droál checkpoint. Catching a glimpse of the startled guards, Kenlin gasped: here at last were the Bronze Invaders, the shining gilded horde that had razed Natzut so long ago! They were far behind before he could see them properly; Klanjad did not stop to attack, presumably hoping to leave the Droál more confused than alarmed. Nevertheless, Kenlin was left with the fleeting yet absurd impression that an army of these soldiers, with their bronze helmets and bronze-plated coats, must appear glorious in sunlight.

Now the dice were cast, and the Jazeiz's hope of reaching the city lay, as Klanjad had said, in outrunning their alarm. The idea was ridiculous in theory, but in practice, it was surprisingly easy to simply ride through the Droál camp, at least for a while. They were in full gallop now, and Kenlin's attention was primarily focused on staying mounted and keeping up with Klanjad. Glimpses of new sights—bonfires, marshalings, musterings, thousands upon thousands of tents—vied for attention in the corner of Kenlin's eye, but he did not have time to mark them.

They had turned off the main road soon after entering the camp, favoring secondary routes; and, had he had leisure to think about it, Kenlin would have found that odd. But after a long while of weaving through the Droál camp, the reason for the indirection became clear when the Jazeiz returned, at last, to the main thoroughfare: an army marched here. Even in the smoke-choked starlight, the many thousands of Bronze Invaders shimmered as they *tramp, tramp, tramped* toward the ruined gates of Ñaj-Gadan.

As soon as they returned to the main thoroughfare, Klanjad reigned his horse to a quick trot. Ranja and Kenlin followed suit, and for a moment they advanced alongside the Droál unharried, as though they were but a few more member of the Droálic host. *How many thousands!* They were only a few hundred yards from the city's main gate, and the wide road was filled edge-to-edge with rank upon rank of bronze-clad Droálic soldiers. *Tramp, tramp, tramp.* There were so many that, for lack of space on the roadway, the Jazeiz were forced to ride their horses several yards to the left of the advancing column. Though they pressed forward, the horses whinnied and complained, for the ground here was uneven. *No, not the ground; the dead pave this pathway.*

Dragging his attention from the vast host marching into Ñaj-Gadan, Kenlin at last took note of their surroundings. As it neared the gate, the road here was forced to pass between two outstretched arms of Ñaj-Gadan's imposing walls; any attackers would be forced to approach the gate through a hail of arrows not just from the front, but from both flanks. The impact of this was clear: the dimly-lit ground over which the horses stumbled was thickly littered with countless arrows and arrow-stuck corpses. But the defense, it seemed, had fared no better; the battlements atop the walls were cracked and crumbling, showing evidence of Necromantic pounding sustained over several days. Though Kenlin could not see the dead on the wall tops, their efforts had obviously been inadequate and their deaths had been in vain. Ahead in the darkness, several large spherical boulders lay near the wrecked ruins of the city's gates, and the endless army of the Droál marched on. *Tramp, tramp, tramp, tramp.*

A commotion was building behind them, and though Kenlin could not understand the words he was sure of the meaning: *The alarm has caught up to us at last.* Klanjad spurred his horse to go faster, and Kenlin and Ranja followed suit. But though the animals tried to comply, the ground was too littered and uneven; it was only a matter of time before one of them stumbled.

Kenlin's horse fell first and, inexperienced as he was, he did not know how to free himself from the saddle before horse and rider both hit the ground. The horse tripped to its knees, then twisted and fell onto its side, pinning Kenlin's leg—*Get off!*—even as, from the corner of his eye, he could see the bronze-clad soldiers turning toward him. As the horse flailed, Kenlin felt a powerful pressure on his leg—*I said, get off!*—before the animal managed to regain its feet and rise, painfully twisting Kenlin's foot that was still caught in the stirrup.

Atch! Damn you! It was not a red flash, but a sudden wave of heat and energy, accompanied by a mental cry of furious exhilaration, coursed through Kenlin's body. Fading, he kicked viciously at the horse; the animal cried out and stumbled sideways, but Kenlin's foot was freed. With the speed and reflexes of a magician, he scrambled to his feet and looked about. The Droálic soldiers on the road were turning toward him, and a few had raised their shields and weapons. *Is that a challenge?* His sword was in his hand; he didn't remember drawing it.

And suddenly it seemed as though he had stepped away, separated from himself, and he watched in cackling rapture as he launched an attack on the Droálic column. He was a spectator of his own body, cheering as it slashed its way through the first few soldiers, booing as his enemies reformed and cowered behind their shields, applauding as their shields were beaten and dented and ripped away, laughing uproariously—

"Kenlin! Here!"

Ranja's shout was barely audible over the din of fighting, but it was enough to make him pause, turn his head—and suddenly he saw through his own eyes again. *What am I doing?* He glanced quickly about at the soldiers surrounding; they quailed as he looked at them, bumping into one another as they stumbled backward, trying to disappear behind their shields. A weird, wide smile crossed his face as the cackling voice in his mind burst into a gale of laughter. *Hahaha! Though not just now, perhaps another time.* But he couldn't resist a parting feint, starting suddenly toward the cowering soldiers as though he would attack them again; they shouted with fright, falling over each other in their haste to get away. Now he laughed along with the voice— "Hahahahahahaha!"—as he Faded and sprang, faster than any of them could prevent, back to the more open space beside the column.

Ranja and Klanjad had not waited. A hundred yards or so ahead, he saw Ranja spring lightly from the saddle next to Klanjad's wounded, dying horse. *There's a commotion there; they're fighting through the gate without me!* Still Faded, Kenlin sped across the distance in an instant, dashing right past Ranja, and threw himself toward the fracas in the gateway.

Kenlin had trained with Klanjad for many moons now, but only rarely had he seen his uncle unleash his full power. Even to Kenlin's enhanced perceptions, Klanjad was a blur; he struck, moved, and struck again with such speed that the blood of each kill would mingle in the air with the blood of the next three. *In half the time, he's torn a far larger rift in the Droál column than I did. Well then, perhaps I need to—*

But even as Kenlin leapt toward the Droál, Klanjad whirled, caught him by the arm, and stopped him in his tracks with irresistible force. They were both strongly Faded, and strong magic distorts perception, so Klanjad kept his words curt and clear: "Pointless!" Then, gesticulating to the right, he barked, "Alley. Go!"

The sheer shock of Klanjad's magic—the speed with which he'd turned and the power with which he'd grabbed Kenlin's arm—had shaken Kenlin back to himself again. He nodded, turned, then darted to the indicated alley. Ranja was already moving toward the same alley, appearing slow for lack of magic. Kenlin wondered for a moment whether he should try to help her along somehow, though he felt sure she would not appreciate it. But before he could consider further, Klanjad darted in behind, caught his daughter about the waist, and hauled her into the alley alongside him. She shrieked in surprise, but Klanjad did not stop. Still strongly Faded, he sped down the alley and took a few seemingly random turns before wrenching open a door and shoving both Kenlin and Ranja inside.

As Klanjad shut the door, both Jazei magicians released their magic. Ranja, rubbing her neck, moaned, "Don't *do* that, Father, that wasn't necessary!"

"Quietly!" Klanjad snapped in a coarse whisper before rounding on Kenlin. "What in the *Depths* was that?"

Silence now? Where have you gone, laughter? "I honestly don't know, Klanjad," he answered, shaking his head. "It's... Before, when I've—"

Klanjad cut him off with a wave of his hand. "Does your mind only function at extremes? If you're not overthinking, then you're not thinking at all!"

"He knows, Father," Ranja interjected sharply. "Now is not the time for this."

Klanjad paused for a moment to collect himself. After a few deep breaths, he said quietly, "We *stay together*. Control yourself. Act only when I say. There may come a time to turn loose your energy and power; but for now, *restrain yourself.*"

Kenlin nodded earnestly: "Yes, Klanjad." But in the back of his mind, the laughing voice again began, unbidden, to chuckle.

Ranja, returning to pragmatic concerns, said, "We haven't much time. What next, Father?"

Klanjad clicked his tongue. "Well, we're inside the walls, and it looks like the Droál here are savvy enough not to set the entire city ablaze before they try to march through it. How many hours since sundown?"

Ranja shrugged. "Four or five, perhaps six."

"Between two and twelve," Kenlin offered, which earned him a slap on the arm from Ranja.

"All very helpful," Klanjad commented humorlessly. "But even four hours would be more than enough for the Droál to reach the canal. If they've had longer, then they'll probably have had time to build new bridges and start marching on the Tower itself. If so, then that column at the gate will advance straight through the city, all the way up."

"We'll follow the wall, then?" Ranja surmised.

Klanjad nodded. "To the wall. That should avoid the main contested areas, take us around to the canal, then upward to the Leaping Bridge."

Kenlin was on the point of asking for clarification—his knowledge of Ñaj-Gadan was insufficient to understand what was being proposed—when a sudden noise caused all three Jazeiz to whirl. From the impenetrable shadows deeper in the building, something had shifted its footing; and now, as they allowed silence to fall again, they could the rustling of clothing and the sound of frightened breaths. Small breaths. *A child?*

Klanjad, perhaps, thought something similar, for he relaxed ever so slightly. Nevertheless, he called into the darkness, "I don't like surprises. Show yourself!"

A few seconds of silence followed this demand before a woman's voice, hushed with dread and desperation, whispered, "Please. *Please* don't 'urt us." There was a sound of shuffling footsteps, and a small huddle of figures emerged from the deeper gloom: a young mother, with a child cowering behind each leg and a baby asleep in her arms. *I hadn't even considered it, but this must be her house. Everywhere... Most of these buildings are homes, aren't they?*

Klanjad and Ranja moved almost immediately, turning toward the door as though there were something here that they did not wish to see. Over her shoulder, Ranja said quietly, *"We* won't hurt you."

However, as she opened the door to leave, enough light entered the room for the woman to glimpse Klanjad's and Kenlin's hair. She gasped, "Jazeiz? Jazeiz! Oh, One above! Are you...?" But Klanjad and Ranja had already stepped outside, so the woman turned toward Kenlin. Her voice was breathless from long despair mixed with abrupt, unexpected, inconceivable hope. She begged, *"Please,* m'lord... Are you 'ere to save us?"

Save you? We could try to hide you, but they would surely find you, catch you, burn you. You could try to run, try to find a way out of the city; but you would not get far, not even if you abandoned the little ones. And as for following us, even we will be hard-pressed to survive our road. Save you? You cannot fight, but you are in a battle. You cannot run, for you have been caught. You cannot be saved:

"You are—" But he stopped himself. Turning on his heel, he followed Klanjad and Ranja out the door without finishing his sentence: *already dead.*

...

Ñaj-Gadan was built on a cleft tor that straddled the narrowest stretch of land separating the Inner Sea from Gadan Lake. The city was split into eastern and western halves, and each half was divided into "upper" and "lower" quarters separated by the famous canals of Guivarja. The lower quarters were built mostly on flat land. The upper quarters, however, rose with the tor, following the narrowing slopes upward until they almost met at the summit. But, with only a hundred or so yards separating the east and west cities, the ground suddenly fell away in a great chasm that cleft the city, and the entire hill upon which it was built, in two. This was the Karkéde Channel, the primary outlet of Gadan Lake and perhaps the most famous waterway in Jranjana. At high tide, the Channel flowed like a quick river, energetic yet orderly. But at low tide, when the sea beyond the Channel fell far lower than the lake, then the waters roared and surged with the chaotic violence of an avalanche.

From the midst of this Channel rose the colossal Gadan Tower, by far the largest, tallest, and grandest structure in Jranjana. From its layered foundations and buttresses in the lower half of the chasm, the Tower stood several hundred yards high, rising above the Channel, the chasm, the city, and the entire countryside for leagues upon leagues in any direction. The Tower, in turn, served as the central and sole support for the Leaping Bridge. This bridge was really two bridges, each connecting one half of Ñaj-Gadan to the Tower by means of a single unbroken span of stonework. The Leaping Bridge, and the Tower through which it passed, provided the only direct land route from the eastern half of Ñaj-Gadan to the western.

"So it's to this Tower that we think the Commune will retreat, yes?" Kenlin asked Ranja, panting slightly as they jogged behind Klanjad along the tops of Ñaj-Gadan's walls.

"That's my best guess," Ranja replied. "Assuming the western city hasn't been breached as well, Jendraski will want to fall back through the Tower, regroup, and then either continue to endure siege or try to break out to the west."

"Will that work?"

"How should I know, Kenlin?" she answered irritably. "The Tower could theoretically be held indefinitely; it's well-fortified, and the Droál will be reluctant to use Necromancy near it for fear of destroying the bridge. The western city gate, however, is nearly identical to the one on this side, so whatever tactic they used to breach the east may work just as well in the west."

Kenlin nodded, but did not pester her with further questions. They were now atop Ñaj-Gadan southern walls, following the arc of the fortifications around the city's perimeter toward the upper city. This route was slightly longer than a direct path, but it would prevent them from having to improvise a crossing of the canal. Furthermore, as Klanjad had anticipated, they faced no opposition on this path because every available soldier was busy in the city.

And the noise emanating from the city—the shouting, the screaming, the distant roar of fire, and the inexorable *tramp, tramp, tramp*—became harder to ignore the further they pressed on. When they passed over the canal, the wind was blowing from the southeast, and the sea-sounds it carried lent the entire night an incongruous air of tranquility. But as they began to ascend toward the upper city the wind changed to the northeast, and this wind carried with it the smoke, the screams, and the *tramp, tramp, tramp, tramp.*

Ñaj-Gadan was a vast city, but without opposition or obstruction the Jazeiz made quick progress until they began to near the summit. Then, when the noise and the haze were almost unbearable, they at last encountered their first foes since the skirmish at the gate. Kenlin snatched for his sword as a rush of energy coursed through him, but he paused as Klanjad shouted, "No magic!" *What? Why? Without magic, how can I...?* He shot Klanjad a questioning glance, which Klanjad returned with frigid sternness. *Very well.* Forcing his unruly spirits into compliance, he allowed Ranja to rush past him (she was still a far more dangerous fighter than he was without magic) and tried to support them as best he could.

It was slow, exhausting, and terrifying. The Droálic soldiers on the wall were surprised and frightened by the Jazeiz's arrival, but they were heavily armored and there were many of them. *This would be so much easier with magic! Surely we could— Ah, that's why: there are Misks very near. I hadn't noticed before. Be more alert! We mustn't attract their attention until we're ready to fight them.*

And who isn't ready? Ha! Let them come!

"No!" Kenlin snapped aloud, halting abruptly and looking about as though his own impetuousness were a companion that he could rebuke. *No... Restraint. Patience! There will come a time, very soon; Klanjad will tell me when.*

Nobody answered, so Kenlin rejoined the fray.

The wall top clash could not have lasted more than a few minutes nor involved more than a dozen soldiers, but it seemed many times as long and dangerous. At last, however, Klanjad threw his final opponent over the battlements as the remaining soldiers fled down a flight of stairs and into the city. The Jazeiz rushed ahead. Finally, they rounded one last corner and suddenly found themselves on the edge of the summit plaza of eastern Ñaj-Gadan.

This was the heart of the battle, the destination for every *tramp, tramp, tramping* Droál in the eastern city. The spacious, open plaza was packed with Droálic soldiers from the access roads to the low wall before the precipice. Though the Jazeiz stopped dead in their tracks at the sight, no one noticed them. The entire throng was focused only on pressing forward, crowding together to join the fight on the bridge.

The Leaping Bridge itself leapt from the clifftop in a single magnificent arch to the looming Tower, barely visible in the haze. The battle, however, was not in the Tower but on the bridge itself. From what Kenlin could see, it appeared that the Tower's armored door had been damaged somehow, so its occupants had formed a desperate defense on the bridge while craftsmen tried frantically to repair the door.

But even as the Jazeiz watched, the defense was wavering. Kenlin sensed a storm of magic; Misks, Fading, and even small amounts of Necromancy were all part of the intense combat on the bridge. Against overwhelming odds, the defenders held their line and fought bitterly; but the magic, the Misks, and the endless mass of advancing Droálic soldiers could not be resisted for much longer.

"Father!" Ranja shouted. "If that line breaks, the door is *wide open.*"

"I know. *Ittarshil!*" Klanjad cursed, staring about quickly for an idea. His eyes settled on the threshold of the bridge, where the Droálic soldiers were crowding together as an entire plaza of soldiery tried to squeeze onto the bridge. "Run there!" he ordered suddenly, pointing. "They're packed too tight, we can panic them. Move fast, kill everything, and scream as you have never screamed before!"

Klanjad and Ranja immediately charged down the steps and into the massed soldiers below, both screeching the high, raw war cry of the Jazeiz. Kenlin had expected to do the same, and he braced himself for the cackling voice and its attendant wildness to return in a rush. But perhaps because he was ready for it, this time the passions did not overwhelm him. Instead, the wild energy and the mad laughter took a moment to compound, echoing and building in his mind until the cackling laugh could not be contained. It burst forth from him aloud, and each cackle grew louder and harsher and higher until the very last one transformed into that *decadent* Jazei scream.

He did not follow his uncle and cousin down into the plaza. With glee and abandon he instead launched himself into a Faded leap, soaring over the heads of the Droál to land recklessly on the parapet overlooking the precipice. *Hahahahaha!* He danced unobstructed along the top of the low wall, screaming and laughing and raining blows down on the terrified Droál as he passed. A few swung their weapons at him, but his magic was too powerful; he dodged or parried their attacks with ease, *and woe to the fool who catches my eye!*

Yet despite the rapture and the frenzy, he never let himself lose control. Following Klanjad's instructions, he moved swiftly to the threshold of the bridge and, a few sword-strokes later, had cleared a small space for himself as the bleeding, crying, dying Droál cowered away behind their shields. *Hahahahahaha!* His unobstructed path along the parapet had been quick, but Klanjad and Ranja soon caught up and took positions beside him. Then the three Jazeiz planted their feet and slew, screaming and slaying until the eyes of their enemies rolled in terror. The empty space around them became blood-soaked and broad—no soldier would dare approach them—and they turned their fury on their foes still crowded together on the bridge.

On the other end of the bridge, the Commune soldiers defending the Tower had heard the Jazei war cries; and with heartened shouts of their own, they pressed suddenly forward. Forced back on the front and ambushed from the rear, the Droál on the bridge began to panic. Another chorus of Jazei screams, another splash of their comrades' blood, and what little morale they still held was utterly shattered.

Had Klanjad not pulled Kenlin to the side of the bridge, he would have kept screaming and slaying until his body gave out from exhaustion. But as Klanjad pulled him out of the way of the growing rout, he shook himself and saw with amazement what they had done to their opponents. *They're running like rabbits, they're attacking each other, they're milling about wildly, some are even jumping from the bridge. Ha! Such fear! They plunge willingly to their deaths rather than face the Jazeiz! And those who run will collide with their own reinforcements and spread panic amongst their allies... In their fear, they fight for us!*

A few panicking Droál aimed glancing blows at the Jazeiz, but they defended themselves with ease and simply allowed the fearful to pass, to spread dissent and terror through their own ranks. The wild energy was again receding from Kenlin's mind, but it didn't go far, and he was glad. Gone were the qualms that had cursed him in Slionte, gone were the doubts and inhibitions that had held him back for too long. *Oh yes, this is what it was for. This is what I can be!* His mind and he shared a hearty, deeply contented chuckle.

Within minutes, the Droál had fled, and the bridge and courtyard were nearly empty of living foes. Ranja watched the last of them flee with an odd, uncertain little frown, as though there were something she was missing, but Klanjad seemed satisfied. "They will regroup," he said with a pragmatic air but a contented grin. "We trapped and panicked something like a cohort and may have routed as much as a regiment, but they will send in another regiment within a few minutes."

"Yet that is a few minutes that we have when we thought ourselves out of time." The Jazeiz turned; a tall, brown-haired, thickly bearded man came toward them across the bridge. The Commune soldiery followed him, giving Kenlin a clue who this must be. "Would that you had arrived six hours ago, Klanjad: this is the fourth line I've tried to hold since night fell, and your absence has been noted and felt." But though there was weariness in his voice, the bearded man was smiling.

Klanjad seemed to be on the brink of saying something quippy, but as he looked at the bearded man's face, he changed his mind. "Would that I had come sooner, Jendraski. I don't know if I could have held your lines. But would that I had tried."

Jendraski shook his head, still smiling. "Don't steal my melancholy from me, Jazei," he said with a chuckle. "I'm short on bravado today, and those are the only two sentiments I'm permitted. But all that aside, it's good to see you again, old friend."

"And you." Though both were dusty and bruised and splattered with blood, they embraced with the warmth that Klanjad showed only for companions of many campaigns.

Turning from Klanjad, Jendraski looked to Ranja to offer her a formal greeting, but she cut him off. "I saw Misks," she said urgently, "fighting you on the bridge. Where did the Misks go?"

"Patience, my lady!" Jendraski replied laughingly. "The Misks Vanished away when they heard Jazei war cries. No doubt they will—"

"Back to the Tower!" Ranja screamed, sudden fright in her voice, and she seized Klanjad's arm and began shoving him further onto the bridge. "We have to get to the Tower!"

There was the briefest of moments in which everyone simply stared at her; Klanjad was stumbling along as Ranja pushed him, but the Commune soldiers were standing in the way, baffled, questioning. Even Kenlin was confused. *What...?* But as she cast him a wide-eyed, terrified look, he took action. "Move!" he bellowed at the soldiers. "Do as she—"

In that instant, Kenlin's magic sense flared wildly, and the magnitude of their peril became terribly clear. *The Misks Vanished, they were not panicked or routed. Theirs was not flight, it was a tactical retreat, and the bridge is filled with abandoned weapons...* He looked ahead and behind to confirm what he knew he would see: Misks, dozens of Misks, had appeared in the middle of the Leaping Bridge and in the plaza behind them. Just as the Jazeiz and the Commune had trapped the Droál on the bridge, so had Clan Eyjazinka trapped the Jazeiz between two full-strength platoons of Misks. And as Kenlin turned back toward the plaza, he saw a look of triumph on a face he could never forget: *Skralade!*

Suddenly everyone was shouting, but the chance to run for the Tower was gone. The Misks, picking up weapons from the ground, advanced smoothly with the practiced and methodical step of veteran killers. Kenlin called upon the frenzy in his mind—*Come to me then, you bastards!*—but though energy and determination came at once, the words in his head were not joined or echoed by the cackling voice. *You flee?*

You fear?

But the Misks, if they were at all fearful, did not show it. There was neither haste nor frenzy in their steps as they closed in, herding the humans into an ever-tighter knot. Skralade, however, seemed neither as tense nor as militant as his brethren. He stood tall, his eyes fixed on Klanjad across the space between them; Klanjad returned his gaze murderously. For a short moment, the two of them simply looked at each other; hatred saw hatred, fury saw exhilaration, indomitable resolve saw raw, superlative triumph.

We cannot let them trap us here, we have to get to the Tower! Jendraski, evidently thinking along the same lines, commanded, "Jazeiz to the rear; cut through them, get us out of here!" For just a moment, no one moved; then, as one, all three Jazeiz whirled to press the attack against the Misks blocking their escape.

That moment, when the Jazeiz were in motion and the shield wall was still adjusting, was exactly what the Misks were waiting for. With a chorus of shouts they darted toward the line of humans, and the speed and precision of their attack took an immediate toll as eight soldiers fell, slain before they could even properly raise their shields. The humans leapt forward to counterattack, and all was melee.

The fighting was so quick and intense that everything else faded to a peripheral blur. Skralade remained on the landward side of the fight, perhaps dueling with Jendraski, but the Misks on this side were every bit as fearless and deadly. In the close-quarters of the bridge, Kenlin found himself hacking fruitlessly at an every-cycling army of Misks, each ducking back or Vanishing away from danger even as another Misk stepped in to attack from another side.

Enough! There was no cackling, but a blast of frustrated, furious energy flung Kenlin into a reckless charge right through the middle of his enemies. They were taken completely by surprise, and two or three were bowled over before they could alter their tactics to compensate. They would then have surrounded Kenlin had not Klanjad and Ranja reacted immediately, pushing into the void behind him and turning his suicidal one-man charge into a Jazei spike driven through the Misk line.

Klanjad's presence quickly drew the focus of multiple Misks, and for a moment Kenlin found himself paired off against a single opponent, a smallish Misk with straight, unkempt hair. Kenlin pressed his attack, slashing viciously. The Misk gave way to avoid being overwhelmed, then suddenly dashed forward, trying to dart in under Kenlin's guard. *Poor decision, Misk!* Still Faded, Kenlin kicked powerfully at his enemy's knee, but the Misk was gone. *Vanished!* As the creature's sword clattered to the ground, Kenlin felt hands grasp his head from behind, ready to break his neck. *Ha! Try it.* The Misk tensed, twisted...and was utterly unable to overcome the strength of Kenlin's magic. With a growing grin on his face and chuckle in his mind, Kenlin tore the Misk from his back and slammed it onto the bridge below. *Now die!* He thrust furiously, and any other opponent in any other location would have died there, pinned to the dirt by the impaling sword. But the Misk was gone— *He Vanished again!*—and the sword stabbed into stone, not dirt. The blade stuck, bent, then snapped under the force of Kenlin's thrust.

But the Misk had not gone far and gave Kenlin no opportunity to recover himself. Rolling to its feet and charging in again, the Misk's left hand swept up another dropped weapon from the bridge and swung it toward Kenlin's face. Though still stunned, Kenlin's magic was just fast enough to catch the approaching sword-arm with both his hands. But the attack had been a feint; the Misk had previously grabbed another weapon—a broken war axe—in its right hand, and that axe was now swinging in a high arc to chop through Kenlin's spine.

Yet the Misk's left arm was still caught in Kenlin's hands, and he wrenched it down toward the bridge even as the axe descended toward his back. Though the arm did not break, the Misk cried out in pain and was dragged down, unbalancing his strike and causing the axe to swing awry. Instead of burying the axe head in Kenlin's back, the haft instead broke against his hip, the axe head snapping off and flying into the fray behind them. *Too close! You've fought well, Misk, but now——*

The sensation was unmistakable, and its sudden presence cut through the focus of every human and Misk on the Leaping Bridge: *Necromancy!* There was no time for Kenlin to cover his head or brace himself; the Necromancy came crashing down upon him, slamming him and everyone else in the fight to the ground. As he tried to raise himself, he could hear Klanjad cursing, but by far the quickest to his feet was Skralade, still on the landward side of the bridge, looking frantically about. His eyes settled on a knot of four of the violet-clad Droál—Dragluz, evidently having run into the plaza during the fight—who had their hands raised to conjure another wave of Necromancy.

Skralade bellowed something at the Dragluz, but Necromancy gathered regardless and crushed everyone against the bridge once more; the bridge creaked and rumbled beneath them. Again Skralade was the first to his feet, yelling furiously at the Droál. They ignored him, caring only to destroy their foes and heedless of the cost. Kenlin, however, suddenly understood Skralade's wrath. *The Misks still hold the advantage in this fight, and their position is far from dire. The Dragluz attack indiscriminately. Their Necromancy might help or hinder the Misks—or it might do something no other force present would be strong enough to do: it might destroy the bridge.*

Once again the Dragluz brought their hands up in preparation for their Necromancy. Obviously desperate, Skralade Vanished and appeared again among the Droálic comrades. He killed two with his bare hands before they could react, and a third was distracted from his Necromancy, but the fourth could not be forestalled. Down came the Necromancy, only striking a portion of the bridge near the south railing where Klanjad had been fighting.

The impact was far smaller than before, but the effect was everything Skralade could have feared. A piece of the bridge gave way—not much, but just enough that the ground beneath Klanjad and the Misks around him began to crumble. Klanjad was ready; he gathered his feet to leap from the falling bridge. Similarly the Misks in the affected area all Vanished as one, reappearing on firm ground. *But they are scattered, disordered, and unarmed; they will have to scrounge for weaponry while Klanjad will land with sword in hand!*

But as suddenly as it had come, the triumph in Kenlin's mind died. Skralade, his face full of furious refusal, took drastic action. He Vanished once more, reappearing immediately on the disintegrating bridge behind Klanjad. As the Jazei began to leap, the Misk flung himself forward, tackling his archenemy to the collapsing ground beneath them. Klanjad, caught by surprise, threw out his hands to grasp at the bridge; his sword flew out of his fingers and skittered toward Kenlin, but he was not so lucky. *No!* Kenlin lunged forward, and he saw Ranja and Jendraski do the same, all for naught, for Skralade was victorious at last. The bridge beneath the pair fell away completely, and Misk and Jazei tumbled together into the abyss.

CHAPTER XXVII:

Animals! Savages! AaaaaarrrrraaaAAAAAAEAA!

The Jazei scream burst from Kenlin so powerfully that it rattled in his throat and ripped at his voice, yet it was but a faint echo of the furious cacophony that filled his mind. He Faded by instinct, sweeping up Klanjad's sword before hurling himself into a furious assault on every Misk he could see. He smashed bloodily through one's guard—*Where is your strength now?*—before whirling to eviscerate another—*Be quick, worm!* A Misk Vanished from the corner of his eye, and Kenlin spun in place, catching it by the throat even as it tried to ambush him from behind. *Die now! Die in terror, die in pain, die, die!* As the creature's eyes bulged and its windpipe cracked and collapsed, Kenlin shook it like a ragdoll and screamed in its face like a madman.

"Mazlecoi! Lecoi, lecoi!"

That voice... You! Turning, Kenlin saw Skralade picking himself up from the ground nearby, bellowing orders at his comrades. The Misk had evidently Vanished again immediately after falling, reappearing above the stable bridge for a painful but safe landing. *Skralade!* Kenlin immediately dropped the dying Misk in his hand to charge forward wildly, but he scarcely had time to see the alarmed expression on Skralade's face before— *Again! He's Vanished again! Damn you!* "Damn you, you animaaaaAAAEAEAA—" and the last word devolved into another high, tearing screech at the sky.

For there was nothing else to scream at. Skralade was gone; they were all gone! *Cowards! Vermin! Come back here!* For half a minute, Kenlin dashed madly about the bridge, still Faded, hunting wildly in every direction for anyone or anything on which he could unleash his fury.

"Kenlin!" A hand caught his arm, and he spun to face his assailant, but the hand was Ranja's. There was a strange light in her eye, a kind of frozen frenzy that mirrored and yet contrasted the chaos in Kenlin's mind. "Focus now, Kenlin!" she commanded. "I need you here. Get in the Tower. Get them all in the Tower."

Strangely, the sharp urgency in her demands cut through to Kenlin's consciousness. *Enough! She's right, our foes are gone, now is the time for...* But he had no idea what now was the time for, and he was in no state to think about it clearly. Instead, he looked around at the surviving Commune soldiers on the bridge, all of whom were staring at him with mixed wariness and awe. He swung his arm violently at them— "Inside!"—before turning and striding briskly into the Tower.

When they were all inside and the now-repaired door was shut, Kenlin remained far too agitated to stand still; he prowled back and forth glancing at everything and nothing, his hands trembling with ill-contained, directionless energy. Ranja, by contrast, was hyper-focused, and she aggressively turned her attention on Jendraski. "What are the conditions in the Channel?"

Jendraski was distracted, eying Kenlin with some concern. "Is he alright?"

Ha! What a stupid question. "Never better!" *Idiot.*

"The Channel?" Ranja insisted. "Is there anyone down there? What's the tide?"

Jendraski, still peering uncertainly at Kenlin, answered slowly, "No, my lady, I don't think anyone is down there. The Tower has been mostly evacuated, and the tide is now ebbing; the Channel is far too dangerous right now for anyone to venture into it."

For anyone, you say? Kenlin, afire, opened his mouth to ask for directions, but Ranja cast him a quelling glance. *Alright, Ranja; your way, then.*

Turning back to Jendraski, she said, "Thank you, but we must go nonetheless. I'm sure you understand." Jendraski opened his mouth to say something polite that Ranja had no time for. "We came from Janísla in search of Merejor; does he still live?"

Jendraski nodded. "He was alive and well this afternoon, at least. He is commanding a regiment in the western city, which has not yet been breached. Does Janísla march to our relief?"

"How costly has the loss of the eastern city been to both armies?" Ranja asked, ignoring the question. "Do you have an estimate of remaining strengths?"

"I can guess at those things," Jendraski replied coolly, "but you have not answered. Is Janísla on the march?"

"Yes and no. What have you heard of the other cities being attacked?"

"You are not making this easy, my lady," Jendraski remarked without favor. "You ask many questions in exchange for no answers. I understand if your heart is racing, but you must calm yourself—"

She interrupted, "We do not have time for this, general, none of us do. I need information in order to understand how to proceed: whether or not you can hold this Tower until flow tide, whether the strength you have left is enough to break out or even enough to be worth salvaging, where in all of that I should send Merejor..."

"Respectfully, my lady, these sound like decisions that you should not be taking upon yourself."

This reprimand, mild as it was, silenced Ranja for several moments. Though her demeanor remained almost expressionless, Kenlin could see her warring emotions in the set of her jaw, the tension in her neck, the twitches of her fingers, and the carefully controlled breaths she allowed herself. "You are right, of course," she said at last, mastering herself. "Forgive me. Janísla does not march, nor will it without direct intervention from King Merejor himself. A few thousand march, under my father's orders, to harass the siege of Skaj-Kraskedir; but without additional support, they can do little more than buy time."

Jendraski looked grave. "I had not yet heard that Skaj-Kraskedir was besieged. We... I fear we were unprepared for such a campaign as this."

"True," Ranja replied more frankly than politely. "And perhaps you won't be able to respond effectively. But even now, there may be ways to minimize the loss—depending on what losses you have already suffered in Ñaj-Gadan today."

Jendraski shook his head sadly. "Too many, my lady. We've struck better than we've suffered, I think—we slew many before they even brought those accursed boulders against the gates—but they still hold a vast numeric advantage, and our walls have not been sufficient to even the odds. At a guess, I'd say we have a few more than fifteen thousand left in the city, a few regiments of which are emergency conscripts."

"Tolerable," Ranja remarked, biting her lip as she considered the possibilities. "But with the eastern city lost, it would be almost impossible to return Merejor to Janísla directly. Have you boats with which one might escape through the canal?"

"Certainly not out to sea; the Droálic fleet here is unlike anything I have seen before," Jendraski said, shaking his head. "As for the lake, we were sending messages that way at first, but the Droál began patrolling with small barges full of Necromancers to smash our boats. Under cover of night and with no magicians aboard, a small boat *might* could—"

"Right, too risky, and there's nothing we could do to make it less so," Ranja interrupted impatiently. "How goes the siege in the west, then? Do you think there's a chance you could break out?"

Jendraski frowned. "I don't think there's any hope in 'breaking out,' my lady. If we must do battle with a larger force that wields Necromancy, best to do it from behind as many fortifications as possible. No, we will hold the western city as long as we can and await relief. The Tower and bridge are easily as defensible as the walls."

"Which walls? The walls you lost at sundown?" Ranja retorted; her tact was declining as her temper was rising. "Forgive me if that strategy doesn't flood me with confidence. And as for waiting for relief, general, I'll say it again: no one is coming. Skaj-Kraskedir is besieged, Iskena is distant and restive, and Janísla is ruled by a child with poison in his ears. Ñaj-Gadan is a death trap, and if you—"

She could not sense it, but the reaction from Kenlin and Jendraski caused her to start and turn as well. There, near the barricaded door—inside the Tower—was a Misk! Kenlin's wild energy leapt at the sight, but the Misk Vanished away before there was any chance to attack it. *Damnation! But how did it get here? And why did it come?*

He glanced quickly at Ranja, but she looked as bewildered as he was. Jendraski, however, looked grim. "A scout," he muttered darkly. "Our time is shorter than even I had imagined."

"Was that a Misk?" Ranja asked, confused and alarmed. "How did he get in?"

"Paintings," Jendraski answered shortly. "We are betrayed." Evidently that meant something to Ranja, for she paled and asked no more questions. Jendraski turned to a captain nearby. "Be honest, good man: have we enough stalwart soldiers on-hand to resist a fast Misk onslaught within the next...minute or so?"

The captain was caught by surprise. "Minute or so! Well, m'lord... We might could... Maybe if we..."

With a sympathetic smile, Jendraski said to the man, "Fear not, I understand. Get your men out of the Tower and form them up on the western bridge, and quickly. On your way out, spill every lamp and oil bucket you see. Then stand your ground and wait for us to join you."

As the baffled captain hastened to obey, Ranja asked incredulously, "You're burning out the Tower?"

"As I said, we are betrayed, my lady. Misks will overrun it in a matter of minutes; consider it, and you will understand. But for now, come with me. We must light the fire and be off."

But as he turned to leave, beckoning the Jazeiz to follow, Ranja shook her head. "I told you before, general, that I'm going down, not out. Father is in the Channel, and I'm going to find him."

There was haste in his stance and in his body, but as Jendraski looked at Ranja, there was nothing but compassion in his face. "My lady, your father... I am sorry. But the chasm is deep and jagged, and even the water at the bottom is no less deadly than the rocks through which it rushes."

Bizarrely, this brought a cold smile to Ranja's face, and she even laughed aloud. "You people never learn, do you? Father *does not die!* He is down there, and I will find him, and Kenlin will help me."

At this, Jendraski looked to Kenlin as though expecting him to either second or subvert Ranja's claim. Though his wild energy was calming and he had stopped prowling back and forth, his merry recklessness remained. *We can hardly hope that he's wrong, but she knows that as well as I. And as for the danger— Ha!* "Go," he said to Jendraski, nodding toward the room's western exit. "Go to your soldiers. We will light your fire here."

Jendraski frowned thoughtfully at both of them for a moment. "Strange children of a strange family," he muttered.

Ranja answered simply, "We are Jazeiz."

I sense... There, gathering on the periphery of my awareness... "They're coming, Ranja," Kenlin told her quietly.

Jendraski said warningly, "Are you sure of your course, Jazeiz? I cannot protect either your departure or your return;

and without the Tower, we may not be able to hold the western bridge for long."

"Don't try," Ranja replied, speaking urgently. "Listen to me, general: *you must break out of Ñaj-Gadan.* This city will fall, and Skaradarn will fall, but there may still be a chance for Skaj-Kraskedir. If you can get Merejor back to Janísla, then just maybe—"

She still could not sense the Misks, but this time she did not need to, for the room was suddenly *full* of them. As Kenlin half-involuntarily shrieked a war-scream and sprinted toward the Misks, Jendraski shouted to Ranja, "My lady, the fire!" By the western door of the room stood several casks of oil, perhaps intended to have been ignited and poured from the battlements. Jendraski, Fading, hurled two of the casks to smash against the floor. The contents spread over the wooden floor in the middle of the room, and Ranja snatched a lamp from the wall and flung it into the center.

Kenlin was hard-pressed. Though the Misks were unarmed and unarmored, there were many of them and they had been prepared for his reckless charge. Misk after Misk leapt onto him and simply held on, trying to drag him to the ground or wrest Klanjad's sword from his grasp. But the fire surprised everyone. The Misks howled, writhed, and let go as their legs were dragged through the flaming grease. Even Kenlin, startled from his frenzy, yelped and leapt away from the growing inferno, slapping at the flames on his boots.

Fire! Why would they...? Ah, but the Misks and Droál cannot occupy the Tower if it's aflame. As long as it burns, it buys time for us and for Jendraski. He looked about for Jendraski, but with the fire now raging and smoke rapidly filling the room, the general was already gone. *And so should we be.* "Ranja," Kenlin shouted over the din, "let's go! Which way?"

She was already at the room's western door, beckoning him to follow. "Over here! In the next room there's a staircase that— Kenlin, the door!" Suddenly she was pointing through the flames to the Tower's armored eastern door, which led back to the Droál-occupied eastern city. The oil had seeped through the floorboards and failed to spread all the way to the room's edge, leaving a narrow strip of fire-free floor beside the threshold. Three Misks had squeezed precariously into this space and were now carefully trying to work the door's heavy bolts without stumbling into the blaze behind them.

Unbidden and unwelcome, the cackling voice suddenly loomed loud in Kenlin's mind. *Ha! Let them open it, I want—*

No, not now! If they get that door open, they'll get weapons—and perhaps even reinforcements—and pursue us all the way down the Tower and into the chasm. And if they extinguish the fire, not only the chasm but also the entire western city will be—

"Kenlin, wake up! Help me!"

Kenlin slapped his own face hard, silencing the discord at least for a moment. Ranja had grabbed the last of the oil casks, but she was not strong enough to throw it all the way across the room. Fading once more, Kenlin grabbed the cask from her hands and flung it toward the door.

But by now, the Misks had recovered from the surprise of the fire, and they too saw what the Jazeiz were attempting. As Kenlin swung the cask to throw it, one brave Misk sprinted desperately toward the center of the room; then, too late for Kenlin to adjust, it leapt into the path of the throw. The cask struck the creature in the stomach with such force that both toppled backward into the flames. The Misk landed on his back, and he screamed in agony as fire coated his bare flesh. The cask landed on the Misk, then rolled away, and though fire eagerly climbed over it as it rolled through the oil, the vessel did not break.

My turn!

Kenlin's feet leapt forward before he could restrain them, and it was all he could do to steer himself toward the cask, lying intact near the edge of the oil fire. But the remaining Misks saw his aim and, abandoning all caution, dived forward to stop him. As before, they darted in with almost suicidal abandon, and Misk after Misk was able to grapple him before he could wound or strike them. Another Jazei scream tore from his throat, but the wild energy in his mind was suddenly chilled by an unprecedented thought: *What if I am, at last, overmatched?*

The fight was desperate on both sides, Kenlin fighting to reach the cask and the Misks fighting to stop him. But as the Misks focused their energies against Kenlin, they left only one to oppose Ranja—the same young Misk that had faced Kenlin on the bridge. For a time, it seemed the creature would be able to keep her at bay, even though he had no weapon. Then, from the corner of his eye, Kenlin saw her press forward suddenly, closing range—a bizarre technique with a glaive, but the Misk did not know enough to be wary of Ranja's tricks. Deftly, he slipped past the glaive's blade and snatched at the haft with both hands, immobilizing the weapon but leaving his face exposed. Even before he had finished moving, Ranja released the glaive and bounded forward, clawing at the Misk's eyes and leaving long, bleeding scratches across his face and forehead.

The young Misk gave a cry and staggered back, startled and momentarily blinded by his own blood. Ranja ducked past, sprinted to the fire's edge, and reached without hesitation into the inferno to grab the last oil cask. Flames coated the sides of the cask—they licked at her hands, scorched her ear, and singed her hair as she hoisted it onto her shoulder—but she ignored them. She took a few steps around the edge of the fire to bring her close enough to the Misks at the door. Then, gathering all her strength, she hurled the burning cask into the air.

Her throw was true. The cask smashed against the fortified door itself, drenching the door, the floor, and all surrounding Misks in a flash flood of flaming oil. The Misks at the door howled in agony, the Misks throughout the room shouted in anger and dismay, and Ranja shrieked her shrill, piercing, victorious Jazei war cry. Then, *thwack!* She collapsed mid-scream; the young Misk had dashed the blood from his eyes and struck her on the head with the haft of her own glaive.

There was a horrific Jazei scream—*I'm screaming?*—and the grappling Misks, previously tightly-locked in combat, were flung about like leaves in a gale. *What—?*

Hahahahahahahaha! Kenlin saw his attack from many perspectives—from his own eyes, from aside as an observer, from a strange view that was around and through and *in* a red-running cacophony in his mind, his ears, his eyes, threatening to overwhelm his senses all at once. He saw himself as many, all converging viciously on the Misk who had felled Ranja. Some corner of Kenlin's mind noticed that the creature had not struck her again, but now stood looking at her collapsed form with an expression of…wonder? *Die, die beast!* Kenlin was mere steps away when the Misk woke from his reverie, saw Kenlin's charge, and Vanished away to avoid certain death. Ranja's glaive clattered to the ground beside her.

Kenlin slid to his knees beside Ranja, and as he lifted her to his shoulder, a modicum of clarity returned to his mind. *We've got to get out of here! She said there were stairs; could we…* But the remaining Misks, picking themselves up after Kenlin's burst of fury, were now encircling the Jazeiz. There was no longer a chance that they might be able to unbar the door before the room was consumed by fire, but they might at least prevent the Jazeiz from escaping. *I can't fight them with her on my shoulder; I can barely fight them without. And yet, just a moment ago… But how? Was I stronger?* In the lull as Kenlin failed to spot an opening, the Misks were beginning to arm themselves with debris—some of it aflame—from around the room.

Too late! If we must go down, then down we go! The idea was neither wholly conclusion nor wholly instinct, but appeared fully-formed from the mixing maelstrom of Kenlin's thoughts. Fading to his fullest, he began furiously pounding his hands and heels against the floor below him. The floorboards began to groan and splinter from the beating. When a gap appeared between two boards, Kenlin thrust his hand into it and began tearing the wood away. A few Misks started forward, but Kenlin rounded on them, screeching, and flung a ripped-up floorboard that forced them to jump back. Turning once more to the splintering floor, Kenlin desperately leapt into the air and slammed both heels against an exposed support beam. Softened by fire and weakened by Kenlin's assault, the beam gave way with an earsplitting *crack*. The surrounding boards followed suit, and Kenlin and Ranja plunged through the floor into the darker room below.

Kenlin landed unsteadily, yet he managed to not drop either Ranja or their weapons. His eyes struggled to see after the conflagration above, but there was no time to let them adjust. He lurched hastily toward the faint silhouette of a doorway, then through that into the room beyond. *She said there were stairs; where are the stairs?* He could only glimpse one more doorway in this room, so he dashed through it, immediately lost his balance, and careened down the staircase beyond. By magic and luck he managed to keep his feet, banging against the walls until he crashed headlong into a door. *Damnation!* Too impatient to feel in the dark for the latch, Kenlin Faded and smashed the door open with a kick. But it was no help; whichever room was beyond this door, it was windowless, fireless, and utterly dark.

"Damnation!" Kenlin cursed aloud, stepping through the door and instantly banging his shin against something. Ranja moaned on Kenlin's shoulder. *Is she alright? Does she know this place?* "Ranja, wake up! We're somewhere in the Tower, but there are no windows here, I can't see. Ranja?"

"Hey, hey! You're in the jails!"

It was not Ranja's voice, and it emanated from somewhere further into the room. Kenlin started badly, whirling toward the voice and swinging both weapons blindly. The sword struck into something wooden; the glaive hit nothing. "Who's there! Who are you?"

"I... Ataland. I don't think we've met."

"Friend or foe?"

The voice paused for a moment as Kenlin tugged Klanjad's sword free of whatever it had hit; the blade rang softly in the darkness. "I'm going to go with friend, I think," said the voice matter-of-factly. "And as your new friend, d'you mind if I ask you a favor?"

"What?!"

"Great! If you could help me—"

"Silence! Who are you?"

"... I feel like we're starting to go in circles, friend. I'm—"

What fresh lunacy is this? "Enough! Sorry. I don't care. How do I get out of here?"

The voice took on a note of exasperation now. "There's a door over there. Now, do you see the problem?"

"I *can't* see," Kenlin shouted back angrily.

"Exactly! But I can! If you'll just let me out—"

Enough! "Stop! Stop. Let me think." Despite the urgency of the situation, Kenlin forced himself to slow down and try to comprehend... *Is this some new trick of my mind? But no, I'm hearing sounds, not thoughts. And he said we were among the jails...* "You're a prisoner here?"

"Yes, yes! That's why I need you—"

The voice fell silent as a series of loud *thumps* reverberated through the floor above. *The Misks have decided to pursue us, they're leaping through the hole to come down here. I haven't time for...whatever this is.* Holding Ranja's glaive out in front of him like a staff, Kenlin began to make his way through the room. *And then what? I'll blindly find the stairs by chance, yes? Or will I have to try to tear through the floor again?*

"The Tower's falling, isn't it?" the voice asked from the darkness, now in a hushed tone of concern. "I mean, not falling *over*, I mean there's Droál inside it, right?"

"Why would a prisoner know that?" Kenlin asked absently, his attention still focused on trying to navigate the room in the dark.

"They said the walls were breached when they came to conscript everybody. But if they're already *here*, if they're *in* the Tower... Shit... Listen, you *have* to let me out."

I said enough! "Unless you can help me, be silent!"

"I can help! But you have to let me out first."

"*Why?!* Assuming you're even *real*, of which I'm not convinced, why in the Depths would I trust you? You claim you don't need light to *see*, also you're in *jail*, and you say the Commune came to conscript everyone, but *you're still here*—"

"Yes, but that's just because they...didn't...trust me."

Kenlin threw up his hands—*This can only be madness!*—and took another step into the darkened room. His foot banged painfully against some unseen piece of furniture, and he cursed aloud.

But the voice had not given up. "Okay, yes, they didn't trust me. They didn't trust me for the same reason I can help you, the same reason I can see in the dark: I'm half-Unnatilz."

Unnatilz...like the creatures whose reputation alone drove us into the swamps near Likrásk, the creatures that hunted us and almost killed us all near Slionte. Half-Unnatilz...like Uzkrendid. Uzkrendid the Bastard. Uzkrendid, traitor to his own kind.

From the darkness, the voice spoke with a note of reproach laced with the faintest hint of anger: "Don't be that fool."

Do not press me! And yet... "You really can see?"

"I can see everything. I see you, the girl, the sword, the spear thing, the key to my cell over there, and the door that will get us all out of here. Free me, and I swear to you that I will lead you wherever you want to go."

Through the open door behind him, Kenlin heard the hushed voices of Misks coming carefully down the stairs. *Out of time.* His decision made at last, Kenlin turned and began blundering blindly toward the source of the voice, banging painfully into everything in his way. The voice said, "Is that a yes? Great! So, the key's over— Yes, this is my cell here, but it's locked and—"

"There's no time." Reaching out in the darkness, Kenlin found the metal bars of a jail cell, Faded, and wrenched them out of their holdings. As the voice gave a shout of surprise and alarm, Kenlin barked, "Now get us out of here!"

"Grúnlib! That's… Okay, this way." A rough hand closed on Kenlin's wrist and began leading him through the darkness, moving quickly and surely without ever making a sound. "Stairs now," he warned, and Kenlin prepared himself so that he staggered only a little on the first step. They descended ever deeper into the windowless depths of Gadan Tower. The darkness was impenetrable, but the half-Unnatilz never faltered and the voices of the pursing Misks soon fell far behind.

Kenlin counted at least seven more staircases before he began to hear the roar of rushing water. "Is that the Channel?"

"Yes."

"We're near the bottom then, yes?"

"Not quite. The Channel is…loud."

He was correct on both points. They continued to descend and the roar of the Channel continued to grow louder and louder until, at last, they reached the docks built into the base of Gadan Tower. The space resembled a natural cove; the mid-high ceiling arched over a pool containing a few tiny skiffs moored to wooden docks. A small archway in the southern wall, covered by a portcullis, opened directly onto the Channel; through this archway came the dim red glow of the firelit night, as well as the relentless, deafening roar of the Channel.

After the darkness and relative quiet of the Tower, the light and noise nearly overwhelmed Kenlin's senses, and he paused for a moment to collect his wits. The half-Unnatilz looked at him and crowed delightedly, "You *are* Jazei! I couldn't see for sure in the dark, but from the screams and the magic... That's *excellent!*"

Kenlin returned the look, finally getting his first real view of the creature. He was both like and unlike the Unnatilz Kenlin had seen near Slionte. Like them, he had wild reddish hair and a ruddy-orange complexion; but his build was more lanky than muscled, and the features of his face and expression were less bestial and striking. He was nearly as tall as Kenlin, but so spindly as to almost appear weak. And yet he stood and moved with the poise of a gazelle, as though his very gangliness had become a strength. The overall effect cast this creature as the quintessential odd man out, the unwanted yet incorrigible runt of an otherwise proud litter.

As Kenlin stared at him, the creature laughed and fluffed his wild hair with his hands as though preening. "Feast your eyes, Jazei! You're not the first, and you won't be the last!"

Kenlin blinked and shook himself. "Sorry. I've never seen a half-Unnatilz."

"Hya! And I've never seen a Jazei! There's people still coming down the Tower, though; d'you mind if I gawk at you later?"

On Kenlin's shoulder, Ranja suddenly stirred. "Kenlin?" said she blearily. "Kenlin, what's happening? Put me down."

"Hey, she's awake," the half-Unnatilz noted needlessly.

She was unsteady as Kenlin set her on her feet, but the glare she sent at their guide was firm and fierce. "Kenlin, who is this?"

"Not an immediate threat," Kenlin said, cutting off the creature's attempt to reply. "Are you alright? You were struck—"

"On the head, I can feel it, thank you." She still seemed dizzy. "Why am I alive? That Misk had my glaive..."

"Thoughts for later, Ranja. We're at the base of the Tower, but Misks are pursuing us and there's a portcullis over the way out. What do we do?"

"There's a portcullis..." she repeated, still shaking her head dazedly. "Can you lift it?"

"Can I what? How? Where's the wheel?"

"The wheel's higher in the Tower. But can you just...pick it up? With magic?"

"I can't stand on water, Ranja; and I'd certainly sink the boat if—"

"Right... Right." She pressed the heels of her palms against her temples as though she could physically hold her thoughts together. "And you can't go up again?"

Kenlin shook his head. "They'll be here in moments."

She clicked her tongue, allowing herself just a few more seconds to try to think of other options, but there were none. "In that case... The portcullis doesn't go far below the surface. We'll have to swim under."

"You're going to *swim* into the Karkéde Chanel at ebb tide?" the half-Unnatilz asked incredulously.

Ranja shot the creature an icy glare, then stepped defiantly toward the docks before them. However, her gait was still unsteady from the blow to the head. Kenlin caught her by the elbow as she stumbled. "Hold onto me, and hold this," he said, handing her the glaive. "I'll do the swimming."

As she climbed onto Kenlin's back, the half-Unnatilz remarked amiably, "From a lousy starting point, this plan is getting worse by the *moment.*"

Annoyed, Kenlin snapped, "Do you have a better idea?"

The creature laughed aloud and threw his arms wide dramatically. "What would I do with a better idea? Bad ideas are *so* much more interesting!" And with that, he took two quick steps onto the docks, leapt high, and dived gracefully into the water.

"Who *is* that?" Ranja asked in bewilderment, but she cut off the answer before Kenlin could give it. "Never mind, tell me later. Try to grab the portcullis as we go under it. If the current gets hold of us..." She did not want to finish that sentence, and Kenlin did not want to hear it. Tucking

Klanjad's sword into his belt and taking a last deep breath, he gathered his strength and jumped into the water.

In the artificial cove among the docks, the current was deceptively calm. Kenlin could not see well in the dim light, but by swimming forward he soon found the bottom of the portcullis. He gripped it tightly, then carefully pulled himself underneath and out into the open Channel.

Not Misks nor magic nor Necromancy nor any river he had known—nothing had ever seized Kenlin with the terrifying ferocity of the Karkéde Channel. *One above!* He Faded reflexively, and only the strength of his magic prevented him from losing his grip and being ripped away from the portcullis. Instead, he dangled horizontally a yard below the water's surface, clutching with his fingers as the rampaging torrent snatched at his feet. But Ranja had no magic to strengthen her grip; Kenlin thought he could hear her bubble-choked scream as the Channel tore her away and dragged her into the rapids downstream.

No! Not her too! It wasn't the cackling voice; no fit of fury or elation came to Kenlin's aid. *No, no, no!* There was no other option: he released his grip on the portcullis. There was no magic in Jranjana powerful enough to fight this current, but his additional strength and speed were sufficient to allow him to scramble to the surface and direct his trajectory just a little—just enough.

By a miraculous feat of tenacity, Ranja had managed to catch the haft of her glaive across two underwater rocks, momentarily stopping her deadly tumble through the rapids. But the Channel was vastly too mighty to battle for long; in a moment or two, either she or her weapon would break from the water's fury. However, the delay was enough for Kenlin to catch up. He grabbed her about the waist as he passed; and she, anticipating him, dislodged her glaive and grabbed him about the neck again. They were now in a place where the water was only a yard or so deep, but it flowed so relentlessly that standing their ground was impossible. Instead, Kenlin waited for his feet to strike a relatively flat rock; then, Fading further than he had ever managed before, he leapt from the water in a random direction, hoping that wherever they landed might at least have something to grab.

He was almost lucky: his leap took them westward toward the cliff wall of the Channel. Had there been flat land at the base of the cliff, he would have landed on it. Instead, he crashed painfully into the sheer rock face, failed to find a handhold, and slid immediately back into the Channel below.

No! No! This cannot be, I cannot die here, I cannot let her die here, not this way, not after so much! Where! Where is the cackling strength? Is it not of me, am I not it, will I just let myself die—

It was panic—genuine, mind-numbing panic—that drowned Kenlin's thoughts as he scrabbled frantically, blinded by fear and spray, for a handhold while he and Ranja were washed alongside the cliff face. Then suddenly his hand was caught, and he instinctively Faded and grabbed the arm that had caught him. "Ow, ow! Not so tight!"

The half-Unnatilz! Somehow, the creature had managed to escape the deadly waters and climb onto a ledge above the surface. From there, he had followed Kenlin and Ranja downstream, scrambling alongside the Channel until at last he managed to catch hold of Kenlin's wrist. "Pull me up!" Kenlin screamed.

"I can't," the half-Unnatilz screamed back, its face contorting in pain from the strain on its shoulder. "It's too much, I'm not magic!"

He can't... But he can't just hold us here, either... The panic receding somewhat from his mind, Kenlin shouted, "Ranja, can you grab his arm?"

She tried, but she was tired, dizzy from being struck, and now half-drowned. She could not pull herself high enough out of the water to catch the half-Unnatilz's wrist. However, she was just barely able to raise her glaive such that, if the creature could free his hand, he could grab it.

He understood, for he shot Kenlin a quizzical look. Kenlin shouted, "Do it!" Nodding, the half-Unnatilz quickly released Kenlin's arm and snatched at the glaive, catching it by the haft just below the blade. The current immediately began to haul Kenlin away downstream, but he had finally had a moment to examine the cliff nearby. Fading once again, he thrashed furiously as though he were trying to swim upward—and by the strength of his magic and his desperation, he succeeded. One-handed, he caught hold of a ledge nearly two yards above the water's surface, then quickly pulled himself up with magic. Turning back upriver, he saw that the half-Unnatilz still lay face-down on a lower ledge, clutching Ranja's glaive even as the ravenous current threatened to drag them in and swallow them both. Kenlin ran to them and threw himself down beside the half-Unnatilz. By sheer force of will, Ranja managed to keep her grip on the glaive as Kenlin began to pull it. Then they were close enough that he caught her by the wrist, and moments later, both Jazeiz and the half-Unnatilz collapsed gasping on the ledge, safe for now from the lethal grasp of the Karkéde Channel.

CHAPTER XXVIII:

The half-Unnatilz recovered quickly and sat, rubbing his shoulder and wincing, as the Jazeiz coughed and gasped. Magic had enabled Kenlin at least to mitigate his tumble through the Channel; it was only a few minutes before he too had caught his breath. Ranja had been treated far worse by the rapids, but the dimness of the light from the fire-reddened haze hid many details. Not until Kenlin watched her struggle to her hands and knees, choking up throatfuls of water, did he see just how punishing her night's ordeal had been.

Her palms were burned and blistered from having thrown the flaming keg during the fight in the Tower. When she touched the back of her head, her fingertips came away red; the blow which had knocked her unconscious had left a horrible, bleeding welt. Her boots and breeches had been partly shredded when the Channel had dragged her over rocks. And, judging by the way she favored her left arm, it had nearly been torn from her shoulder when Kenlin had pulled her up onto the ledge.

Despite all this, she recovered her breath not long after Kenlin had; yet for another minute she remained hunched over with her eyes closed, breathing slow and deep. "Ranja?" Kenlin ventured. "Are you alright?"

She nodded without looking up. "I am alive," she declared with an air of finality and a curious note of vindication. "I survived it. We survived it. It can be survived." Kenlin did not reply.

The half-Unnatilz, however, was less reserved. "'Can be survived' is, I think, a pretty low standard for experiences," he said conversationally. "Don't get me wrong, I do agree that we're alive. I just feel that, if 'not dead' constitutes a positive development in your life, that may say more about you than about the experience in question."

Kenlin was far too overwhelmed to parse that train of thought, and Ranja clearly didn't care to. Fixing the creature in a piercing stare, she said, "Who are you?"

"I'm Ataland," he replied cheerfully, slapping his chest once for reasons Kenlin assumed were cultural. "By the look on your face, the pleasure's all mine. But regard—"

"Where did you come from?"

"Originally? Or today?"

"He was a prisoner in the Tower," Kenlin said to Ranja.

Her eyes narrowed. "You found him as a prisoner," she repeated incredulously, "whereupon you decided to free him, then let him accompany us from the Tower?"

"It was too dark for me to see, so he actually *guided* us from the Tower," Kenlin corrected. "After which he jumped into the Channel with us and, just now, pulled us both onto this ledge."

She did not answer, but her expression remained deeply suspicious. Turning back to Ataland, she asked, "For what crime were you imprisoned?"

"Bender," Ataland answered easily. "Don't remember it myself, but me and my mates got sloshed on the upper west, then apparently got into a brawl with some constables. From what I heard later, I kicked one, yelled that they'd never catch me, then drunkenly ran *into* the Tower—"

"And where are your 'mates' now?"

At this, Ataland paused, and a little of his levity seemed to ebb. "Probably dead. Everybody in the Tower was conscripted a few hours ago, me excepted. For obvious reasons," he concluded, indicating his face and hair.

Ranja was nodding her head almost imperceptibly, her suspicions solidifying into a theory. "You're half-Unnatilz," she said. "Half-Unnatilz come from Garna."

"True, for the most part," Ataland answered. His flippancy had cooled into a relaxed blankness.

"You have a very human accent."

"Thank you. As do you."

"How long ago did you leave Garna?"

Ataland shrugged. "About ten seasons, more or less. Is there something specific you're looking to learn about me?"

Ranja hesitated, then decided to speak bluntly. "I don't trust you."

"I get that a lot," he said with another shrug, the aspect of his cheeriness returning. "My kind have that reputation. I don't take it personally."

Being a bit harsh, aren't you, Ranja? "Keep in mind that we've only known him for a quarter of an hour, and he's already pulled us out of harm's way twice."

She was clearly not mollified. "That may be true, Kenlin, but we have no way of validating this charmingly quaint narrative: no witnesses, few details, no facts. The Tower has very limited space; people aren't typically jailed there for mere drunken capers."

Ataland snorted and quipped, "Hya! Try kicking an upside constable in the saddlebag, see where *you* end up."

Kenlin bit back a grin, but Ranja's expression did not change. *Does she think he's a spy? It's hard to imagine what a Droálic agent would gain by helping us. But if that's what she thinks...* Meeting Ranja's eye, Kenlin said with a shrug, "If you really want me to, I can." Ataland shifted his weight ever so slightly, but did not otherwise react.

Ranja was clearly taken aback. She opened her mouth, then closed it again without saying anything. After a long pause, she said hesitantly, "Father would. Wouldn't he?"

"I don't know."

Neither did she.

When the uncertain silence had lasted several seconds, Ataland spoke again. "I'd heard that Klanjad the Jazei has a daughter," he said to Ranja as though this were nothing but a polite and friendly chat. "That's you, I'm guessing?" She answered only with a flat and unfavorable glare, which

Ataland took as confirmation. "Excellent! And you...probably aren't her father."

Ha! "That does seem unlikely."

"Her brother?"

"Cousin." Ranja now shot Kenlin a reproachful look, but he shrugged unapologetically. "He already knows who we are, Ranja." She did not reply, but turned her gaze away disapprovingly.

"Interesting. *Really* interesting," Ataland said, peering eagerly at each of the Jazeiz in turn. "So if his daughter's here, and his nephew's here, then am I right to conclude that Klanjad himself is here in Ñaj-Gadan?" Neither Kenlin nor Ranja answered this question, but something in their expressions, some subtly grave pallor, must have alarmed him. "Okay... I'm not sure I want to hear the answer to this, but... He's not dead, is he?"

"*No,*" Ranja declared forcefully.

Ataland looked to her to elaborate, but when she made no move to do so, he turned to Kenlin. *Should I tell him?* Kenlin glanced at Ranja, but she did not respond, so Kenlin made his own decision. "Klanjad fell from the Leaping Bridge," he said, pointing upward toward the clifftops hidden in the haze above. "That's why we came down the Tower: we're looking for him."

"Oh." All ease and levity were gone; Ataland seemed, at last, lost for words. "Well... Shit."

"We have to go, Kenlin," Ranja said abruptly, the sharpness of her tone indicating that she had lost patience with this conversation. "We have to go back to the Tower."

"You what?" said Ataland.

"Father could be anywhere from there to the Channel's mouth. We have to start at the Tower and continue downstream until we find him."

Kenlin shook his head doubtfully. "I don't think he's there, Ranja. I would have been able to sense him from inside the Tower, and I didn't. And furthermore, if he didn't land in the water and wash downstream, then he would have landed on stone. After such a fall to such a landing, would you really want to see..." That image—the body broken over unbreaking rock—was burned indelibly into Kenlin's memory. Ranja had seen that body too, but the face had been of someone she did not know, and so the sight had been gruesome yet unremarkable. But now, in her mind, Kenlin had given that body a new face, and only too late did he realize how cruel such a vision might be.

As she blinked and swallowed hard, Kenlin opened his mouth to apologize, but she shook her head to silence him. "It's...not a matter of what I want to see," she said, her voice a study in self-control. "We have to find Father. That is all."

Ataland remarked, "Even if you do want to go back to the Tower, are you sure you can?"

I can't decide he's brave, or stupid, or selfless, or simply rude to keep inserting himself in this conversation.

Ranja growled frigidly, "Your input is not welcome on this, creature."

"Oh, it never is," he returned with a smile. "But honestly, look at the Channel. Look at the cliffs. Southwards, it's a bit more broken and navigable, but north? Unless you can climb like a squirrel, you'll be back in the water before you're halfway to the Tower."

He's not wrong. Ranja looked to Kenlin, and he knew immediately what she would ask. "My magic helps with many things, Ranja, but dexterous climbing is not among them."

"So how about this," Ataland interposed before anyone could preempt him. "Why don't I go back to the Tower while you two start making your way south toward the Channel's mouth? I can, in fact, climb like a squirrel. I'll go north, look around, and come back to you with news of whatever I find." As both Jazeiz hesitated, he added cheekily, "It's a lot like telling me to go away, except you also stand to learn something."

Where's the trap? He could tell our enemies that we're down here, but they already know that. He might find Klanjad and attempt to harm him; but if Klanjad's beneath the Tower and somehow still alive, then he's beyond our reach and within Clan Eyjazinka's anyway. Is there anything else? Kenlin exchanged a look with Ranja, and he knew she was thinking similarly. *If this is a trap, I can't identify it, and that's what I find unsettling.*

Finally, Ranja turned back to Ataland and asked bluntly, "Why are you trying to help us?"

Instantly, a wide grin broke over Ataland's face, and he bobbed his head back and forth merrily. "Well, you know… Would you believe me if I said I genuinely admire your father? Would you believe me if I said I'm terribly bored after being stuck in a cell for days and on? Would you believe that I'm a part of a bogglingly convoluted conspiracy to save your lives so I can gain your trust so I can use your trust to take your lives later?" Neither of the Jazeiz had a clue how to answer that. Ataland threw back his head and crowed, "Hya! See you soon!" So quickly that even Kenlin would have struggled to catch him, the half-Unnatilz sprang straight from his seat to a clinging grip on the cliff above. His fingers deftly sought out tiny cracks and crevices, and he indeed scrambled like a squirrel over the sheer rock face more swiftly than Kenlin would ever have dared. Within a minute, he was hard to see in the hazy dimness of the ravine; and a minute later, he was out of sight.

Staring into the haze where Ataland had disappeared, Ranja said sullenly, "I don't like helpful people." In spite of himself—in spite of stress, exhaustion, and the desperation of their current situation—Kenlin laughed aloud at this. Ranja could not quite manage a laugh, but neither could she suppress a somewhat sheepish grin. "You understand what I mean," she said as Kenlin's laughter abated. "It's a lot to consider. I collapsed in a room full of fire, certain that I was going to die; but then I awoke on your shoulder, having escaped that inescapable situation under the guidance of some half-Unnatilz you found in a cell in the Tower. How did you even get us out of that burning room?"

"I fought my way out, more or less." *What sort of question is that?*

"That was an entire room full of Misks, Kenlin."

And? "Alright, then: they stood aside politely and allowed us to leave."

She cut her eyes reproachfully at him but did not pursue the topic. "Then, as you were fleeing, you took up with that fellow."

"I stand by that decision. We're outside the Tower, and we're still alive, yes? I credit Ataland for both of those."

She didn't answer for several moments, her expression contemplative but unreadable. At length, she said, "Slionte was a hard lesson to learn. Perhaps it's even harder to apply."

Kenlin answered gravely, "I can't argue with that. On the other hand, everything he's done so far has been to our benefit, and I can't think of anything he could do to make things much worse." She made no answer, but continued to look inscrutable. "But if you saw such a possibility, you should have told me. I would have killed him."

Her glance became very piercing: "Would you?"

Would I? "... Yes."

"I believe you," she said slowly. "I believe you really did give me that choice. I didn't know what to do with it. That's not much like either of us, is it?"

They both fell silent for nearly a minute, thinking about this night. *How long has it been since the sun went down? So few hours ago. We pitched our camp with the soldiers and talked about Faeries as Klanjad went to the inn for news. He told us to rest well, for tomorrow would be the longest day of our lives. One above. And the sun has not yet risen again.*

But as endless as the night seemed, it still was passing. The haze above, loweringly lit by the fires of Ñaj-Gadan, choked the sky with smoke and held back the half-light. But the haze in the ravine had begun to mix with an early morning mist from the sea to the south. It tasted different: less of heat and ash, and more of water with the faintest touch of salt.

Ranja's thoughts, too, had turned to the passing time. She said, "Come, Kenlin. I don't trust this Ataland as you seem to, but in this at least he's right: Father must be further down the Channel. Let's go."

As Kenlin looked up and met her eyes, such a swirl of emotions rose in him that he would have struggled to name them: pity, hope, sympathy, reluctance, fear. Sentiment and sense were at war in his mind. He wanted to prepare her somehow, to say things that would make her loss, if it happened, just a little less painful. *But I have no special wisdom here; there is nothing I can say that you don't already know twice over. I, too, hope to find him, but to speak of it as certain is too far even for me. And yet, you are nobody's fool but your own, so if you choose to fool yourself...* "Alright. Let's go."

The crags that formed the ravine's side were, as Ataland had said, less sheer to the south than to the north. Nevertheless, the Jazeiz made painfully slow progress as they scrambled amongst the rocks, walking where they could and clambering where they must, dogged by the omnipresent roar of the Channel below. Gadan Tower and the Leaping Bridge that passed through it were built at the narrowest, highest, and sheerest part of the chasm. Southward, though still insurmountably steep and high, the clifftops seemed to lean back a little, allowing a bit more light in and a bit more sound out. The ravine became less deafening, less menacing, and less oppressive. Further along, the Channel itself began to widen, too, allowing the current to disperse its fury more broadly. It still hissed and sprayed violently below them, but contrasted with the vicious torrent beneath the Tower, these rapids appeared almost placid.

Though it seemed an eternity, they had probably been moving for no more than half an hour when they heard

Ataland hailing them. "Not bad, Jazeiz! I suppose you're not mountain folk, and you'd never outpace an Unnatilz, but on the whole you're making great progress!"

Well, so much for your assessment. Being careful not to slip off the narrow ledge on which he stood, Kenlin looked toward the voice. Bizarrely, Ataland was actually *in* the Channel below them, standing casually atop a rock that just barely breached the water's surface. "Why are you over there?" Kenlin asked.

"Oh, don't worry, the water's much less dangerous here," Ataland replied, waving a hand dismissively. "I stayed on the cliffs for the scary parts, but once you get out of the narrows, there's plenty of rocks and things to hop on."

"Did you find my father?" Ranja's voice was controlled and even, but Kenlin could hear the tension in it.

Ataland took a deep breath. "Right, that's the other reason I'm down here and not up there. I didn't find your father. I did find a fresh blood splatter on the edge of a rock: somebody fell from a great height and smashed something there—probably a hand or arm, I didn't find brains. But as for who it was... Well, I've never smelled your father, so I just don't know."

Kenlin looked to see how Ranja would react, but she had completely mastered herself since their earlier discussion. She said, "So you have no news of his condition, but you claim he's not upstream of us. I...appreciate you having looked, Ataland. And you came back. In your place, I don't know that I would have come back."

"And that makes you suspicious all over again, doesn't it?" said Ataland with a shrewd grin. "'Why would he come back? What's he hoping to gain? He keeps acting all helpful and friendly, so it has to be a trick, right?'"

Ranja was unabashed. "I won't apologize for being guarded, nor will I stop: preparedness runs in my blood. But you *have* helped us so far, and for that I am appreciative."

"Well, don't thank me yet, I haven't gotten to the troubling part," Ataland answered grimly, causing Kenlin to turn around sharply. "Recall that I found blood, but I didn't recognize the smell? Well, I smell it again now, and much stronger than before. Whoever smashed their arm on that rock, they were near here very recently, and they were bleeding a *lot*."

"Where?" Kenlin and Ranja demanded in unison.

Ataland pointed southward. "Over there somewhere. I can't see what's there, the haze is too thick. But you'll get there soon enough, your route over the cliffs gets easier in a moment."

"Can you not get closer?" Kenlin asked urgently. "Go look, tell us what's there."

Slowly, Ataland began shaking his head. "I don't think so, Kenlin," he said with a wary smile. "I think it's better that I stay out of the way until you've found...whatever you'll find over there. Like I said, you won't have to wait long; we are very close."

"Kenlin, go," Ranja urged. "Go fast, use your magic. I will catch up to you."

Magic was more of a hazard than an asset while climbing, but the cliffs here had leaned back enough that it was possible for Kenlin to bound from ledge to ledge. Within fifty yards, it became clear that they had nearly reached the Channel's mouth, for the unending *hiss* of the now-gentler rapids began to blend with the distant, rhythmic *crash* of surf. The mix of smoky haze and morning mist was now so thick that Kenlin could hardly see a dozen yards ahead, and since he did not know what to look for, he started to worry that he might miss it.

But as soon as he saw it, he knew. A small beach of coarse sand lay nestled in a fold of the cliffs. Even from the cliff in the hazy dark, Kenlin could see the blood: a large dark patch near the top of the beach split into two smaller tracks that ran down toward the waterline. Kenlin Faded and clumsily leapt the remaining distance. He landed in the water, trying to not disturb the marks on the sand until he could examine them. *Fingers, elbows, little flecks of blood. Someone came out of the water here; they were bleeding a bit, but not horrifically. But further up... They crawled here, and then the crawl marks stop, but there are prints. They got up? No, these prints are of bare feet... Misks came. They picked him up, dragged him a bit higher, and... They cut off his hands.*

Kenlin had formed no conscious expectation of what he might find at the pool of blood, but he would never have expected this. *They cut off his hands.* As though in a trance, he reached down and picked them up. The left hand was smashed and bloodied, presumably from having struck the rock that Ataland had found, but the right hand was unharmed save for the single clean cut that had cleft it from its arm. *I know this hand; I cannot mistake it.* No voices, no cackling, no reply of any kind: the recesses of Kenlin's mind were deserted. *They cut off his hands.*

He did not hear Ranja arrive, nor did he realize she was there for several minutes. When at last he noticed her standing beside where he knelt, he started to his feet and dropped Klanjad's severed hands. She remained perfectly still, staring down at them as they lay in the pool of her father's blood. A wan and hazy light filtered in from the open Channel, but she was turned away from it; her face was hidden in shadow. *Ranja, I... What can I say, Ranja?*

Instead, she spoke. "If you cut the hands from a dead man, you leave behind the body, not the hands." Her voice was whisper-thin and taut; she was like a sharp blade bent to the brink of breaking. "He is alive. Look there."

She pointed without taking her eyes off the blood and hands. Kenlin looked where she indicated. "Yes, I see. There, where the blood trails end, someone had beached a boat. They came here for him. They did this. Then they put him in their boat and rowed away."

In that same taut tone, she commanded, "Focus, Kenlin. Focus your magic. Do you sense them?"

He looked at her again, but her face was still obscured in shadow. He closed his eyes to focus on his magic. "Yes, I sense...them." *I sense Klanjad, ever so faintly, far to the southwest. And I sense the one who is with him.*

"Skralade?"

"Yes. I am certain of it. He came here personally. He did this himself." At the moment Kenlin had recognized Skralade's presence, the place in his mind from which the cackling voice came seemed to awaken. But there were still no words, no cackling laughs, no sounds of any kind. Instead, Kenlin's head began to fill with a dense and palpable silence. No, it was more than mere silence, more than a simple absence; this was a void, a vacuous null which, by its very emptiness, foreshadowed the violence with which it must be filled.

"Skralade has Father." At Ranja's voice, Kenlin turned mechanically toward her. She had moved at last, for she now stared straight ahead, unseeing, at the cliff wall before her. "And he knows we went to the Channel, and he knows why." A little light fell on her face: her jaw was set, her lips pressed thin, every muscle was half-tensed against itself, and she trembled slightly. "They'll guess we came here, if they haven't already sensed it. Then they'll return...so we must go...he has Father...there is no time, I cannot stop now, I cannot..." But even as she fought herself, the ice in her expression began to crack. Suddenly it splintered, and she fell to her knees, covered her face with her hands, and cried.

Chapter XXIX:

The emptiness in Kenlin's mind was vast, but Ranja's cries did not echo there. He could hear the sounds of her sobs, but they passed through his thoughts like a wind in the desert. There was nothing to obstruct their flight.

Mechanically, he knelt beside her and put a hand on her shoulder in...solidarity? Understanding? Comfort? She tensed at his touch as though she might shake off the gesture, but she did not push him away. After a moment, she began angrily dashing away the tears. "I cannot cry now! This is foolishness, I have to stop, I...I..." But even as she struck the tears from her cheeks, fresh ones flowed anew, and she buried her face in her hands again.

Kenlin said nothing for several minutes while Ranja tried in vain to cry herself calm. *You ask too much of yourself, Ranja! All day we marched, and all night we rode and fought and survived, and you without even magic to ease to ease your trials. You cannot continue like this.* "You need to rest," Kenlin told her at last. "You're exhausted. We haven't much time, but is there a chance you can get at least a little sleep?"

"S-sleep?" Though sobs still caught at her voice, she instantly sat up straight and rounded on him. Her eyes were wreathed in tears and brighter than he had ever seen them; they glittered like the edge of an over-sharp razor. "What do you m-mean, sleep?"

"You're spent, Ranja; I've had magic to help me through this night, and I'm nearly spent. We cannot stay for long, but you *must* rest."

Her catch-breaths began to subside as despair gave way to other emotions. Her tear-stained eyes never left Kenlin's, but behind them a tension was building as her mind began to analyze. In a thin, hoarse tone scarcely above a whisper, she said, "You intend to leave me."

Kenlin was caught completely off-guard. "What? No, Ranja, I—"

"If I go to sleep," she continued, her voice rising, "you will leave me. You will use your magic to go back up the Channel, or to try to scale the cliffs, or something else that will bring the Misks to you and take you away from me. You want to leave me alone!"

Ranja, no! "Truly, Ranja, that thought had never crossed my mind."

"Don't lie to me!" Tears were again starting in her eyes, but her face was now twisted by a frantic fury unlike anything Kenlin had seen from her before. "What do you mean, *sleep?* We can't sleep here, that's idiocy and you know it! You'd *never* tell me to sleep, you wouldn't dare—unless you wanted to leave me here anyway!"

"Ranja, look at yourself! Listen to what you're saying! You're in hysterics, you're not your own master right now. This is exactly why you—"

Had he been prepared, his magician's reflexes would have allowed him to evade her hand. But she moved with no warning at all, and her wild backhanded slap caught him right across the eyes. As he reeled backward in surprise, she pounced and slammed him to the bloody sand, her fists furiously gripping his shirt as she shouted, "You *are* planning to leave me! I'm not my own master? How dare you, *how dare you* plot to abandon me here while you run off to, what, play at heroics? Die in blood and glory? *Save me?*"

Alright, then! He snapped back at her, "You're ahead of yourself, Ranja, and I honestly hadn't thought about any of that. But since you mention it, why not! You can hide and hope to sneak through, but the Misks can sense me, however faintly, even if I don't use magic. Alone, you stand a chance of evading capture; and especially if I draw them away, that chance might well be your only opportunity to survive."

He tried to rise to his elbows, but she, wilder than ever with hateful tears streaming down her cheeks, threw her entire weight on top of him and slammed him back to the sand. "Coward!" she screamed in his face. "Coward! You *can't* leave me all alone just because *you* still have the arrogance to think that your pointless death will mean something! Or do you fancy yourself so strong that they won't rip you apart like a lamb in a wolf den? Idiot! Coward! *You will stand with me*, and we *will* press through this together. I won't let you give up, *I won't let you* choose the easy way!"

"What in any of this strikes you as 'the easy way?'" Kenlin retorted hotly. "I leave, I fight, I die. I stay, everybody dies, and I might not even get to fight! You want that we should die without even taking some of those bastards with us?"

"Are you too stupid to even *want* to think?" she screamed back. "You just want to act, to act, to get your pathetic violence and glory in your strength, and never a thought beyond! *Father is alive!* How dare you even *think* to throw your life away when Father needs our help!"

"Well, help him, then!" Kenlin rejoined, shouting back at last. "Come now, tell me your clever plan! How do we help Klanjad, how do we even get off this beach? Shall we go up the cliff? Certain death, even for me. Perhaps we could swim up the Channel, or out into the sea? Or shall we simply wait? Perhaps a boat will spontaneously appear!"

Hysterical fury still contorted her face, but her tear-soaked eyes flickered with active thought and energy. "They know we're here; they'll send someone to kill us. When they come, we'll take their boat."

You're better than that, Ranja! "Oh, yes, surely they'll just send *one* boat carrying weak and inadequate soldiery. How lucky for us that they don't have overwhelming force available, with archers and Misks and Necromancers to spare!"

Undeterred, she tried again immediately. "At the lowest tide, it's possible to wade from the Channel's mouth all the way to the western shallows. If we start now—"

"Then instead of dying on this beach, we'll have the chance to die on a different, slightly more westerly beach, yes? They can sense my magic, Ranja! I cannot hide! I'm now more convinced than ever: the only hope for either of us to survive is for me to lead the Misks away from you."

Fury, frenzy, sorrow, fear, hysteria, perhaps every emotion she had ever felt roiled together in her tortured demand: "*Don't you leave me.*"

"Get off, Ranja," Kenlin snapped angrily.

She did not move, so he grabbed her by the shoulders and shoved her. She resisted, but he was larger and stronger and threw her easily to the side. As he sat up and brushed sand from himself, she demanded again, her voice still on the brink of breaking, "Don't you leave me, Kenlin!"

The heat of the altercation was fading from Kenlin's mind, and he took a few deep breaths to calm himself. *You're your own worst foe, Ranja. I wasn't thinking that far ahead. But now that I am...* As he slowly brought his temper back under control, he did not let himself look at Ranja's face; there was torment there that he didn't want to see. Instead, his eyes fell on Ataland, who had followed them and now sat on a rock a few yards out into the water. "What about you? What do you say to all of this?"

Ataland gave a gentle *pah* of humorless laughter. "Why would you ever imagine that I would want to be a part of *this* conversation? Believe you me, I'm quite content to have no opinions whatsoever on any topic right now. You and she clearly have some things that need agreeing on; I don't think my input would be anything more than unwelcome noise."

Such callous pessimism, not that I can contradict him. "Nevertheless, I would have your input, if you'll give it. This decision involves you too. If I were to draw away the Misks, then you also may have a better chance to survive."

This time, Ataland actually scoffed. "I'm not such a fool as to think you're actually concerned for me," he said. "And if you are, then *you're* a fool. You're Jazeiz. I'm nobody. Make the decision that's best for you, and don't you worry yourselves about me. Whatever you might think of them, I'm content with my odds."

No fear, no regret, not even bitterness. Is it maturity, or abandon, or fortitude, or impotence to accept such vicissitudes without complaint? But the half-Unnatilz seemed unlikely to yield, and Kenlin decided not to press further. Instead, he glanced again at Ranja; she still lay in the sand where he had pushed her. A few minutes of silence had allowed her to breathe herself to some semblance of composure, but her flashing emerald eyes were fixed on Kenlin with undiminished intensity. "Ranja, I don't know what you want me to say to you."

"Swear," she answered flatly. "Swear to me that you won't throw yourself into reckless, pointless dying. Swear to me that you won't leave."

He shook his head slowly. "I'm not going to swear that. And the only reason you're telling me not to leave is because you already know that I should."

"You want that to be true. You want the excuse to give up." Her reply was thick with disdain, though he couldn't tell to what extent she was affecting it.

But he refused to be baited. "The excuse to give up… How many excuses do I need? I'm tired, I'm sore, I have nothing but my choice of hardships before me, and not one of my choices can lead to anything good. No, I don't need more excuses to give up; rather, I think I need an excuse to not."

She answered darkly, "We are Jazeiz, Kenlin; and to us, everything you've just said is despicable. Our fathers would be ashamed."

"That won't work on me, Ranja," said Kenlin, shaking his head with a bitter smile. "You already know you can't tweak me that way. You already know why. And you're avoiding the question. Wherever I go, my presence will inevitably draw Misks to myself; so if you have an answer, tell me: what excuse do I have to draw Misks to you, too?"

By now, her spirits and rhetoric were largely back under control, and she changed her tack in an instant. "What is it you imagine I will do, Kenlin? You leave, I escape this place, and then what? Do you suppose that you'd be giving me some great gift, the 'chance to survive' without context or qualification? Think *very* carefully about what sort of 'gift' you're trying to inflict upon me. Why do you get to give up and die, self-satisfied at the nobility with which you curse me to struggle on alone? And I will struggle on, Kenlin. Father is alive. You know how I will struggle. And where I will go. And how it will end."

Nothing she said had introduced anything new to the conversation, and yet Kenlin had no answer. He sat in silence for several moments, chewing his lip. At last, he said, "So what is it you want, Ranja? I cannot see a way for us to survive this, so... You don't want to struggle on, yes? You'd rather that we die together?"

She hesitated, choosing her response carefully. "I want to struggle on," she said at last, "but not alone. If you choose to die now, then you willingly abandon me, Father, and everything that makes us all Jazeiz. And for what? An easy death? A 'noble' death? Who would even witness it? Or do you seek to impress Skralade with your valor?" That comment hit a mark; as Kenlin scowled, Ranja pushed further. "Do you think he'll find your so-called sacrifices laudable? Perhaps you respect him so much that you'll willingly honor his triumph: 'Well fought, Misk, now let me ensure your victory is as clean and complete as possible.'"

"Don't press too far, Ranja," Kenlin warned angrily, but her comments had already had their intended effect. The long-silent sounds in Kenlin's mind had awakened, ever so quietly, at the mention of Skralade's name. *She is not wrong: to voluntarily reveal myself, especially by seeking out Misks when they are at their strongest, would all but give Skralade everything he could wish. She goads me the rest of that drivel about honor and nobility... No, she is certainly not right, but neither is she wrong.* Shaking his head, he said with a sigh, "This would all have been so much easier if you had just gone to sleep."

In spite of everything, a hint of a bitter smile appeared on her face. "I have never aspired to make your life easy."

Ha! Such truth. For several minutes they sat in tense and unresolved silence. Ranja's eyes never left Kenlin, and he could feel the impelling weight of her focus. He resisted and allowed the silence to stand, though he had no real reason to do so. He wasn't evaluating the options: there were too few options to fill the time, nor was there enough information to evaluate them. Rather, he simply sat in silence, hardly thinking at all, waiting for himself to accept the decision he had already reluctantly made. "Alright, Ranja," he said at last, "we'll do it your way." *For now.*

She did not sigh with relief, nor did any of the tension leave her manner. Nevertheless, there was genuine gratitude in her voice as she whispered, "Thank you."

"Please don't. So what is it you want to do, what is your plan? You said something about wading through the shallows?"

She nodded. "The southern cliffs of Ñaj-Gadan rise directly from the sea, and there are no beaches near the mouth of the Channel. However, at low tide, it is possible to wade along the base of the western cliff all the way to the shore, from which there's a dry route to the lands west of Ñaj-Gadan."

"That's the region where the western half of the Droálic army is encamped, yes?" Kenlin noted.

Ranja replied calmly, "Correct."

Ataland ventured, "I assume you know that wading along that route is—"

"Yes," she interrupted curtly, "I'm aware. This won't be easy, and it won't be safe, but it's what we're going to do."

"And what will we do about the inevitable army of Misks that will be waiting for us on the western beach?" Kenlin asked. "They *will* sense me, Ranja; and as soon as we reach an accessible place, they will come for us."

"*You* say that they'll come for us," she countered with more vehemence than reason. "*I* say that we should address that problem when we know it's real, and not before. Perhaps it will be as you say; or perhaps we'll be able to move quickly enough to elude them; or perhaps they will be too busy fighting Jendraski to notice you; or perhaps their senses aren't as acute as you imagine."

Oh, come now, that's a cheap excuse for rationale. But before Kenlin could further abuse Ranja's desperation, Ataland interrupted again. "How well can they sense you, really?" he asked. "Some of my half-brothers are magicians, so I know a little about how it works. But they couldn't really sense each other at much distance, especially when they weren't actively magicking."

Even Kenlin found this interruption unwelcome. He replied coldly, "If the Misks here today are as incompetent as your brothers sound, then perhaps we stand a chance after all."

"Well, that's something to hope for, then, isn't it?" said Ataland merrily. "But joking aside, the nearest Misks should be either back at the Tower or out beyond the western gates. Can they really sense you from so far away?"

Kenlin shrugged. "Perhaps they can't sense me yet, but I can sense them, which means it's only a matter of time. And they aren't..." Kenlin frowned suddenly, focusing on his sense of magic. *What...?*

Noting the change in his countenance, Ranja asked tentatively, "Kenlin? You sense something?"

I sense...something. "They aren't only far away, in the Tower and wherever. Some are near... Some are very near..."

"There are already Misks in the western city?" Ataland said in alarm, but Kenlin shook his head.

"No. Or yes, but also no. They're in the western city, but they're... I don't really know how to describe it. They're *flickering*, somehow."

"Flickering?" Ataland repeated warily.

"Are you saying they're Vanishing about?" Ranja asked.

"No. I've sensed Vanishing before. This is different. This is...very strange." He rose slowly to his feet, staring up at the cliffs above as though hoping to see something, anything, that could explain what he was sensing. "There are several of them, maybe many, but I can't count them because they're all the same. Or maybe there aren't many, just the one from many places, like echoes in a cavern. But it's not quite places, either, for they're not... I sense them, but I can't *find* them."

Ataland said concernedly to Ranja, "D'you have any water? The Channel water here's a little briny, but you two have had a long day..."

"Ha! It has been a long day, hasn't it?" Kenlin answered before Ranja could. "Perhaps I'm simply overdone. Or maybe I'm going mad. Or maybe...they really are there. And there, and there, and there."

Ranja said, "Kenlin, what are you talking about? Who are 'they?'"

"I don't know. They're not Misks, I'm nearly certain of that now. They seem almost residual, like Klanjad. But always with Klanjad, I would sense *where* he was; these, though... Even though I sense them, they don't seem to really have a *where*."

Ataland said bluntly, "I was confused. Now you've explained, and I am more confused."

"Then we're all of a mind," Kenlin rejoined absently, but his focus was still on the bizarre magic. After a moment, he said, "I want a better look. Or a better 'sense,' I should say. I'm going to Fade; Fading makes the sense of magic keener."

"You *wha*—?"

"That works both ways, Kenlin," Ranja reminded him, cutting off Ataland's incredulity. "If you Fade, you'll be able to sense them better, but they'll also more clearly sense you."

"True. But they already know we're down here, yes? Also, I used magic just minutes ago when traversing the cliff face. Fading again won't reveal anything they don't already know."

"Did you not sense these strange presences before, when you Faded on the cliff?"

Kenlin shook his head. "They weren't here then; I would have noticed them."

"And would they have noticed you? Will they?"

"I don't know. And I only know one way to find out."

She clicked her tongue, thinking. Kenlin had not explicitly asked for her recommendation, an omission that was certainly not lost on Ranja; nor was it clear, even to Kenlin, whether he would honor her request if she told him not to Fade. Nevertheless, he waited for her response even as the strange, flickering sensations became ever stronger and stranger. She, watching him closely, began nodding her head as though she could read his thoughts in his eyes. She glanced quickly at the water behind her, then back to Kenlin. "Our escape will be swallowed by the tide," she said. "If you must... Be swift."

He Faded.

Chapter XXX:

As Kenlin Faded, Ranja could not have cared less whether he would be able to learn anything about this strange magic. In her mind, this was surely the work of either Misks or Necromancers, both of which meant the same thing: time was running out for them to escape this thrice-damned Channel. But she had acquiesced and told him to Fade because telling him otherwise would have risked exhausting her influence altogether, and no matter the cost, she *would not* lose Kenlin now.

Kenlin was pacing about, tilting his head this way and that, bewildered by things that were beyond Ranja's perception. She took the opportunity to close her eyes and breathe, just for a minute, willing her scattered wits back under control. She felt the gentle wind from the sea, tasted the salt and smoke in the air, felt the cool sand beneath her fingers, soft, damp, blood-soaked, no! In her mind she reeled away, shocked and appalled and frantic; but her body did not move, and only her eyes flew open and stared down at the sand to see... Not bloody. No, the blood was higher up, but not here. This sand was damp with water. Just water.

In part to distract herself, she said to Kenlin, "Well? What do you sense now?"

He shook his head, baffled. When he replied, his words were queerly accelerated and slurred, as was common when the Faded spoke. "I sense... Well, they aren't Misks or Necromancers, that's certain. The way they flit about is like nothing I've ever sensed before; they focus and blur from place to place, almost as though they're dashing about an alley and occasionally peering through doors. I can sense that they're there, even when they aren't really; but then they'll peer through, and I'll suddenly catch a glimpse, and then they'll blur away again only to come back somewhere else."

As was often the case, Kenlin's woefully inadequate attempts to explain magic were more irritating than informative, but Ranja resisted the impulse to quip. Instead, she said mildly, "Peering through doors... They're searching, perhaps? Do you think that the Droál have found a way to use Necromancy for reconnaissance?"

Kenlin shook his head again. "No. This is very clean and orderly, nothing like the chaos of Necromancy that I've sensed before. And it isn't searching, exactly. I think *reconnaissance* might be a good word; it almost seems as though it's surveying."

"It?"

"Yes. I thought this before I Faded, and I'm certain now: there are many, but every one is the same. At any given time, two or three might be peering in, but it's—" Kenlin fell suddenly silent, and he turned to Ranja with a look of alertness bordering on alarm. "It's here, Ranja. It's blurred, but I can still sense it...*around* us."

In the silence that followed, Ranja could think of only two explanations: either her cousin was going mad right before her eyes, or what he was sensing could only be... "Faery magic?"

Kenlin opened his mouth to reply; but instead, he bellowed in alarm, leapt backward, and snatched at his sword. Ranja immediately dived for her glaive and scanned the cliffs around them for threats. Ataland, too, had risen to a ready crouch, staring about like a startled hare. But nothing happened, and nothing continued to happen for several long, tense moments. Then at last, Kenlin half-whispered in that peculiar magical slur, "I see someone, Ranja."

"Where?"

"Here. In the magic." She turned to face him, convinced he must be misspeaking. But Kenlin was pale as a corpse, staring wide-eyed at nothing at all. "I hear him talking to me, Ranja. And I think he can hear what I'm saying, too."

To this, Ranja had no reply at all except to stare at Kenlin in blank bewilderment.

"No," said Kenlin after a pause. Then, a moment later, "I don't care if you're certain. Who are you?"

From his perch on the rock in the water, Ataland uttered, "What in the *shit*...?"

"No," Kenlin declared again, and this time it was a decisive rejection. "No, I don't believe that. This is some trick of exhaustion, or maybe fever."

"Kenlin, what's happening?" Ranja asked urgently.

Looking at her, Kenlin hesitated; then, disconcertingly, he laughed with sudden abandon. "I'm having a conversation in magic with the Wanderer. Either that or I'm losing my mind. What do you suppose?"

Once again, she had no answer she was willing to say.

Kenlin, however, was now fully convinced that he was living out some kind of stress-induced hallucination, and strangely he seemed to find that conclusion relieving. His attention returned to the speaker that only he could see, and after a moment, he said with a chuckle, "The very idea that you could say something to convince me is ridiculous. Either you'll tell me something I don't know, which I obviously won't find convincing because I won't know it, or you'll tell me something I already know, which is rather a cheap trick for a dream."

"Well, he seems to be having a nice conversation," Ataland remarked to Ranja with a nervous chuckle. "Perhaps it'd be best for us leave him with his new friend and get the *hell* out of here."

"Go, then," Ranja answered scornfully, then turned back to her cousin. "Kenlin, stop Fading," she urged him. "We need to leave, we have to reach the beaches before the tide returns."

Still chuckling unsettlingly, Kenlin held up his hands and said, "Hold a moment, you're both speaking over each other and saying the same things. You'll be gratified to know, Ranja, that the 'Wanderer' here agrees that we should be off as quickly as possible, and that wading to the west is our best choice. He also says... What?" A moment passed as Kenlin gazed, with increasingly skeptical attention, into emptiness. "Sure, fine. He also says to tell you that the beauty of the Silvered Court is brightened, yet diminished, by the loss of its Raven Rose."

"He— You—" There were phrases in that message that Ranja had not heard for many, many moons, and to hear them suddenly from Kenlin was such a shock that, for a moment, she was completely incoherent. "You don't— I haven't— Kenlin, stop Fading. Stop it, right now!" Uncertainty came over Kenlin's face; but after one more glance at things she could not see, he complied and ceased his magic. She pressed him, "Why did you say that? What do those things mean?"

"I don't know," he answered warily. "That's just what he—it—the phantom said. I thought it must be nonsense, yes?"

"It's not..." It was absurd—it was almost too preposterous to consider—but she swallowed her incredulity for the moment. "Fade again. If the phantom is still there, ask it what that sentence means. Tell me what it says."

The uncertainty on Kenlin's face was quickly transforming into bewilderment, but again he complied and Faded. For a few moments he looked around, as though he could no longer see what he had seen before; then he started as something appeared suddenly before him. "One above! Alright. She wants me to ask you what your message means." Another moment passed as Kenlin seemed to listen. Then, turning to Ranja, he relayed, "Supposedly, 'Silvered Court' is some posh appellation for the gentry of Iskena; and 'Raven Rose' apparently refers to you. Is that true?"

He was correct on both accounts. She made no reply, but her astounded silence quickly gave Kenlin his answer. He turned once more to the emptiness before him, less skeptical now but more suspicious than ever. "It seems you are not what I thought you were. Then what are you?"

As Kenlin listened to the phantom's reply, Ataland said to Ranja, "So he got that *right?* He didn't know, then he did... So the magic voice is real?" Ranja was still reeling at the idea, so she simply shook her head in astonishment. Sounding amazed and yet oddly impressed, Ataland asked, "Is this usual for you Jazeiz? Is it like this everywhere you go?"

Before Ranja could award that question the derision it justly deserved, Kenlin exclaimed, "Enough! Enough. Quiet for a moment, please; let me hear only one conversation at a time." To the phantom, he said, "If you really are the Wanderer, then how is it that you're here? What strange magic is this?" Whatever answer the Wanderer gave was concise, but evidently unsatisfactory: "Convince me or leave me be."

"You people have a *unique* approach to diplomacy," Ataland commented under his breath. Ranja curtly waved him to silence.

But Kenlin's aggressiveness had evidently succeeded, for the Wanderer's next response was both longer and more compelling. After listening in attentive silence for nearly a minute, Kenlin said, "I see...and I think I understand. The 'Fading' conceptualization of place is just a simplification, yes? And if you broaden it... Are the *Strata* just a simplification too, then?"

Though she understood little of it, this sounded to Ranja like the start of a potentially long and extremely off-topic conversation. "Kenlin, the tide!"

Her interruption seemed to dislodge him from his train of thought, and he shook himself to collect his wits. "Right. The tide. ... Yes, I know there are Misks, and Droál, and whatnot, but we have to try something. ... Well, how long until the dawn? We can't wait for it, Wanderer, not unless the tide will wait as well. … Explain how. … So if I refrain from Fading, you think that will work? You think they'll be deceived?" Throughout this entire exchange, which lasted for several minutes, Ranja had hung on every word and expression of Kenlin's in an attempt to guess what he was hearing, but without much success. After this most recent pause, Kenlin snorted doubtfully. "*I* would be able to tell the difference. But if you think it might help, I can't and wouldn't stop you. … So you say. We shall see." And with that, Kenlin finally ceased his magic.

Ranja immediately demanded answers. "What happened, Kenlin? What did he say?"

Kenlin chewed his lip doubtingly for a moment before answering. "Well, he'd guessed before that we would try to wade to the west; and, like me, he's concerned that I'll be sensed and swarmed by Misks as soon as we come nearer to them. But he claims he wants to help, and that he thinks he knows how to 'hide' me from the Misks, at least for a while."

"How does one hide a magician?"

Kenlin shrugged. "In a confusing cloud of magic, perhaps. He says that Misks can sense his phantoms just as I can, but that they'll have difficulty distinguishing me from the phantoms so long as I avoid Fading and stay at a distance."

Ranja nodded as she began to understand the idea. "So the phantoms might be able to draw Misks away, preventing them from converging on us because they won't know which magical presence is really you."

"That's his hope," said Kenlin, still frowning dubiously. "I'm not sure I believe it will work, though."

"I don't know either," Ranja answered. But a new reservoir of determination was suddenly welling up within her: "Let's find out." For until now, she had fought on because it was all she knew how to do, and she had resisted despair purely on the strength of blind principle. But at last, reasonable or not, right or not, she saw the faintest glimmer of hope that she and Kenlin might both escape this place alive;

and so she swore to herself, on the yet-beating heart of her father, that she would stop at nothing to find him again and keep her final promise.

. . .

The roar of the sea against the cliffs beneath Ñaj-Gadan was legendary: songs and stories were wont to call it, "the Voice of Gadan." A rocky slope beneath the sea's surface forced the waves to rise, charge, and hurl themselves against the cliffs with a strength that would shame Necromancy. The cliffs yet defiantly stood high over the waves, but the sea was winning this war. Pebble by pebble, century after century, the sea raked at the rocks that faced it, dragging grit and boulders down to create a semblance of a shoreline along the base of the cliff. The shore did not trouble the waves—they surged across it without so much as stumbling—but at low tide, the gravelly sand was just near enough to the surface that the brave and foolish could wade, if they dared, from the mouth of the Karkéde Channel to the gentler beaches away to the west.

As Ranja slogged her way through the knee-deep brine at the base of the cliff, she could feel hysteria boiling in the pit of her stomach and she fought it with every dreg of her will. Each wave that washed over her brought a new flood of fear, but she *must not* lose control now. If she were to slip and miss her footing, the waves that now washed around her waist would snatch her up and smash her against the cliff face. Then the retreating wave would drag her back and hand her to its successor, which in turn would rise up and heave her against the rocks again. And again. And again.

She paused, shutting her eyes and grinding her teeth as she tried to flush the fear from her mind. She told herself she was being absurd: how silly to fear the sea! Roar as it might, she had faced more fearsome foes by far. But by now, she had little more control of her emotions than she had of the crashing waves around her. At the furthest edge of exhaustion, every feeling is an extreme: hope becomes giddiness and fear turns to paralyzing terror.

A hand fell on her shoulder; she jumped at the touch, but her eyes remained shut. "Ranja," Kenlin yelled over the roar of the waves, "we have to keep moving. If the tide rises soon, or if the wind swings south—"

"I know!" she snapped, her mood veering wildly from fear to fury before she could subdue it. She took a deep breath and, releasing it slowly, said more calmly, "I know, Kenlin. I'm coming. Keep going, don't wait for me."

"Ranja, I'm not..." He stopped himself from finishing that sentence. She opened her eyes and looked at him. She knew what he had been about to say—"I'm not going to leave you."—and the fact that he refused to say it was a reminder that her struggle today was by no means over.

The uncomfortable silence lasted for several moments as Ranja looked at Kenlin and he refused to meet her gaze. Finally, he put a helping hand about her waist; and, pride be damned, she steadied herself on his arm as they resumed their journey together with redoubled, if dogged, determination.

The most hazardous part of their path lasted no more than a quarter of a league, but to Ranja it felt like the longest journey she had ever endured. Even Kenlin, taller and stronger than she, began to stumble and founder as he fought through wave after wave without his magic to help him. Once, when Kenlin had lost his balance and Ranja was helping to pull him up, she glimpsed in his eyes the intensity of his frustration. "Don't do it, Kenlin," she warned. "I don't need magic here, and neither do you. We can do this."

He dutifully climbed to his feet, but the frustration remained in his face and voice. "It would be so much easier— for everyone—if I did. I could carry you to the sand, then leave and lead our foes away. I don't like having to rely on fortune and phantoms."

"I don't like being carried," Ranja retorted glibly. "And you would only make things easier for me for a few short hours. Likewise for you, as you would only *have* a few hours. But for Skralade, you would make his life easier for many years to come."

In spite of himself, Kenlin chuckled drily. "Alright, alright, I know. But be warned, Ranja: you won't be able to use that trick on me forever."

"Won't I? I'm starting to think I might." He chuckled again, but his spirits remained low. As they resumed their unending trudge through the waves, Ranja cast about for some other topic to distract them. "You mentioned the phantoms; do you still sense them?"

"I do. They are spread throughout the city to the north of us, flickering about. I'm still not convinced that they'll be mistaken for human magicians. However, the Wanderer seemed confident, and perhaps it will be enough to at least sew uncertainty."

"Can you sense any Misks yet? Can you tell how they're reacting?"

He hesitated. "I'm not sure. I *think* I can sense some Misks; and if I can, then they're spread out in a line parallel to the phantoms. But it's hard to be certain, as the phantoms make everything more confusing."

"That's actually much more encouraging than I had expected, Kenlin. It sounds like the Wanderer's idea might be working, at least more so than you seem to think."

He cast her a sidelong glance and gave her a nudge with his elbow. "That's odd. *My* cousin is a hardened and notorious skeptic. Who are you?"

She laughed aloud at this, and as petty as it was, it felt *so good* to laugh. Though Kenlin did not laugh along, he did smile; and together, they continued to press on.

Annoyingly, their companion Ataland was as unfazed by the waves as he was by seemingly everything else. He had neither weapons nor shoes, and he had discarded his shirt as soon as they had reached the water below Gadan Tower. Thus unburdened, the half-Unnatilz gleefully pranced through the water, almost heedless of the waves through which he so easily slipped. He had quickly outpaced the Jazeiz and only waited for them when they were quite far behind. By now, he was more than a hundred yards ahead and had climbed to a precarious perch on the cliff to allow them to catch up.

Ranja did not trust him, not one bit. Though Kenlin seemed unconcerned, far too many questions remained unanswered for her liking. Who was Ataland? What was he really imprisoned for? Why was he trying to help them? How was he so comfortable in water when most Unnatilz were well-known for their fear of it? This was certainly the wrong time to pursue these questions—there were far more important matters at hand—but the mere fact that these questions existed cast suspicion, in Ranja's eyes, over all his actions.

Neither could she ignore what Kenlin seemed blind to: ever since Kenlin had rather unsubtly offered to kill him, the half-Unnatilz had never come within combat range of either Jazei. He was discreet about it, for he drew near enough to converse easily and he always found a way to keep his distance without seeming rude. She thought that he might be underestimating her cousin; fully Faded, Kenlin might yet be able to kill Ataland before he could react. But perhaps he wasn't trying to make himself impossible to kill, but merely difficult enough to be not worth the effort. She could hardly blame him for taking such precautions; in fact, she rather admired his adroit balance of discretion and circumspection. Nevertheless, her unshakable feeling of suspicion drove her thoughts back to that moment in the Channel when Kenlin had given her the choice; and she wondered, over and over, whether she had made the right decision.

Their progress was slow, but at last the Jazeiz began to draw close to Ataland's perch. At their approach, the half-Unnatilz stood and waved an arm to get their attention. Exaggeratedly, he clapped a hand over his mouth, then tapped his nose twice and pointed away to the west. Kenlin nodded, and though she could neither sense them nor smell them, Ranja also understood: enemies were not far.

Ataland climbed down from the cliff, and the three of them continued for only a few minutes more before Ranja felt the texture of the sand beneath her feet begin to soften; and, a short time after that, the sand rose at last above the sea. After wading for so long, Kenlin and Ranja felt suddenly light and strangely unbalanced without the water around their legs. They staggered above the surf, tripped, and collapsed upon the sand, giggling like children as relief washed over them.

Ataland, though he still stayed beyond arm's reach, stood near enough to watch the Jazeiz curiously. "You two have had a right day of it," he said as quietly as possible, nodding in agreement with his own ineloquent observation. "We can't stop here though. I smell... Well, to be true, I'm not fully sure who all I smell. There's gobs of people over there, and you know how soldiers can be about rank. But I think a few at least are close. Not terribly close, but... Unless we go over the wall to the north, we're going to encounter them."

Kenlin was still lying in the sand, but the giddiness of his relief had passed. "Climbing the wall, as such, would not help," he said. "There is a Misk ahead of us; but there are also Misks in a line to the north, and perhaps even a few inside the city."

"To counter the Wanderer's phantoms?" Ranja asked.

Kenlin nodded. "That seems most reasonable. They can't tell which presence is me, but they also know there's only one of me. So they've spread out and surrounded the whole lot."

"And they'll investigate every presence that comes near their line," Ranja guessed, her heart sinking. "And whoever spots us first will simply Vanish away to tell the others where we really are."

"Where *I* really am," Kenlin corrected meaningfully. Ranja shot him a cold glance, but he met her gaze with an emotionless calm. "If I'm correct, they'll soon begin to close in—tighten the noose, so to speak. And that is how they'll find me."

"Not if we move fast," Ranja retorted immediately. Both of her companions looked at her skeptically, which was entirely fair because even she didn't know what she was going to say next. But there was no other choice—she could not allow Kenlin to convince himself to leave, for she would not be able to dissuade him this time—so she said on, and said at random, "The Misk on the beach, straight ahead of us, is the key. Every other Misk in the line will have two companions nearby, but the Misk on the end will only have one. If we can overpower that Misk before he Vanishes away, we'll have a brief opportunity to make our escape before his comrades sense something is amiss."

Ataland remarked, "It's not a great plan, as plans go."

Ranja was on the cusp of a *very* nasty response when Kenlin cut her off. "There's no opportunity there, Ranja. Even if we manage to kill him without magic, they'll sense his death as surely as they would sense his Vanishing."

"Then we won't kill him," Ranja countered, her voice strengthening as her improvised excuse for a plan gained momentum. "Misks can be knocked senseless, can't they? If Ataland or I can get close, we can knock him out and slip right through the line; his comrades won't even realize that anything happened until he wakes up."

"Sneak up on a Misk, don't kill him, just punch him in the face and run away," Ataland summarized, grinning broadly. "Now *this* sounds like a plan!"

Words could hardly express the loathing Ranja felt for Ataland in that moment. Kenlin, however, ignored the ill-timed jollity and regarded Ranja with a calm, calculating expression that she didn't like at all. "Let us make a deal," he said to her at last. "We will stay together for now, at least until we can see the Misk on the beach. But once we reach him, *I* will assess whether you or Ataland will be able to, as you say, knock him unconscious. If you can, then you try it, and we'll see what happens. But if you can't—and remember that I'm the one making that assessment—then I will leave, go to the north, and draw the Misks away; and you have to promise that you won't try to follow me, that you'll escape and live and make sure that I don't die for nothing. Yes?"

He had said it was a deal, but she had no power to negotiate. If she refused, he would leave now, and all her struggle and suffering would have been for naught. "Yes, Kenlin. I can do that."

"You promise? I know what promises mean to you."

She had opened her mouth to agree perfunctorily, but his allusion to more meaningful promises halted her. Had he heard that conversation, when she had spoken to Klanjad just a few hours—and a whole lifetime—ago? But she had no choice; there was nothing else for her to say. Nearly choking on the words as she spoke them, Ranja said, "I promise."

Meeting her eyes, Kenlin nodded slowly. "I believe you."

They advanced quickly now, trusting to the rolling sands, curving cliffs, and hazy air to keep them somewhat concealed. After only a few minutes, both Kenlin and Ataland became extremely cautious, indicating to Ranja that danger was very near. Then at last, as they peered carefully around the final shoulder of the lowering cliffs, they saw the Misk.

He was on horseback, prepared for a pursuit, and he had positioned himself in the very center of a broad, clear, flat stretch of sand: he was nearly unassailable by stealth. And if that were not enough, no fewer than six mounted Necromancers surrounded the Misk, supporting him and looking to him for leadership. The Necromancers looked slightly bored, insofar as their mood could be read through their homogenizing cloaks. The Misk, on the other hand, was alert and keenly aware. Ranja squeezed her eyes shut and, just for a moment, allowed herself the luxury of despair: it was *impossible* for them to even approach that Misk unseen.

But she dismissed the despair nearly as soon as she felt it, for as decadent as it was, it was useless to her. One last time, she reviewed the alternatives that she knew could not succeed: Kenlin's bow had been destroyed in Slionte; Ataland would never attempt such an assault just because she told him to; and if she did not act now, Kenlin would quickly make all her choices irrelevant. She bit her lip, steeled her nerves, and summoned up her last reserves of courage and gall.

Kenlin began in a whisper, "Ranja, I don't think you'll be able to— Ranja, no!" But he saw too late what she was doing. Not asking for permission, assistance, or wishes of luck, she crouched low and darted out from behind their concealment.

Her intention was not to be seen, but only to stop Kenlin from acting unilaterally. Once beyond Kenlin's reach, she quickly dived behind a small dune and began to throw sand onto her clothes and hair. She was still wet from the sea and the sand stuck to her in a thin coat. With the tiny protection of this little camouflage, she gripped her glaive tightly, ignored Kenlin's hissed demands from behind her, and began her impossible advance.

It was an arduous and almost suicidally dangerous approach. She scrambled from cover to cover, using anything and everything she could to hide herself from the watchful eyes of her foes. As she neared the half-way point, the Misk spurred his horse a few steps forward, squinting into the misty morning light toward the place where Kenlin and Ataland were concealed. Good, she thought, for he was separated from the Necromancers. There was no hope that she would be able to knock him unconscious; but in his isolation, he would be easier to kill.

She knew not how long she crawled and dived and crept forward through the sand, drawing ever closer to her target, arcing to the north in the hopes of approaching from outside his region of focus. And astonishingly, it seemed to work; after what felt like hours of crawling and clambering, she was at last a mere fifteen yards northeast of where the Misk sat on his horse. He was craning his neck, looking toward where Kenlin hid away to the east. Stealth was no longer useful at this range, but the Misk's preoccupation might just be enough… She clasped her shaking hands onto her glaive and prepared to charge.

She would never know what tipped him off to her presence and caused him to look about at precisely that moment, but even as she prepared to move, the Misk turned his head suddenly and looked directly into her eyes. Likewise, she would never know why she didn't jump up, rush him, throw her glaive, anything. She had been spotted now, she couldn't possibly hope for more than a fighting chance, and yet she did not fight. She simply looked at the Misk, and he looked back at her.

She thought he looked young; his face had a clean, unweathered look that distinguished it from Skralade's battle-scarred visage. His skin was pale, like that of most Misks, and his wispy black hair fell in a disorderly tangle about his ears and brow. The hair could not hide a series of scratches, not bleeding but fresh and unbandaged, across the Misk's forehead, and she took a quick breath of surprise: this was the same Misk she had fought in Gadan Tower, whom she had clawed and who had struck her with the haft, not the blade, of her own glaive. His eyes were as black as jet and his lips were pale and thin, but his eyes were not squinted in fury or fear and his mouth was not tensed for command. Ranja did not know what her eyes and face expressed, but despite every reason to do so, she did not move. They simply stared at each other, Jazei and Misk, for a single silent moment.

Then, abruptly, the Misk slid from the saddle. Ranja started, but he had dismounted on the opposite side of his horse and she no longer had a clear path to attack him. As she hesitated, the Misk called to the Necromancers. Though she had rarely heard the Misk language spoken aloud, she understood what he said. "Jazeiz traztekirsk! I sense them to the south. They are in the sea, they are trying to swim past us. Come with me, come! Leave your horses and your cloaks. We will surely kill them, but we have to get in the water!"

Upon hearing that there was a chance for the glory of killing a Jazei, the Droál asked no questions. They eagerly dismounted, cast their cloaks aside, and sprinted away toward the sea as the Misk urged them on. As they ran off, the Misk looked one last time toward the place where Ranja lay. He touched his left shoulder with the first two fingers of his right hand, a solemn expression on his face. Then he turned and followed his companions southward to the sea.

It was over before Ranja could begin to comprehend it. The path before them was suddenly clear; better, they now had horses to speed their flight and cloaks to disguise them. But it couldn't be so, it couldn't... It must be... But if there was division among the Misks, then...

As the intense energy that had driven her so far began to fade away, Ranja struggled in vain to understand what she had just witnessed. It was a fleeting glimpse, she knew, of machinations far from anything she had yet encountered; but as to the implications, she could not begin to guess. She no longer had the strength.

So she lay there in the sand, stunned and drained, for nearly a minute until she heard footsteps approaching from the east. In a coarse whisper, Ataland's voice crowed, "Well, that just about beats all, and no mistake! I won't even *pretend* to know how you managed to—"

"Get horses. Go." It was Kenlin's voice, as curt and crisp as she had ever heard it. Moments later, he grabbed her by the shoulders and flipped her onto her back so that she stared directly into his face. There was a maelstrom of sentiments there: concern, anger, fright, relief, betrayal. He said darkly, "Ranja. You promised me."

She meant to say something victorious, or justified, or at least glib; but when she opened her mouth, all she could say was, "I'm sorry." He did not reply. "I'm sorry," she repeated as tears of hurt, isolation, and overwhelming exhaustion started in her eyes. She grasped at his shirt, tried to pull him close; he held her at arm's length. "I had to, Kenlin. I'm sorry. I had to."

He gave no answer, but shut his eyes as he seemed to struggle with himself. Slowly the tension in his body relaxed, and his head bowed until his brow rested against her shoulder. She clutched at his head and fought the compulsion to cry. Never, in such a moment of triumph, had she ever felt so wretched.

There was no time to linger, but Ranja was at last utterly spent. She let Kenlin pull her to her feet, let him help her onto a horse, let the Necromancer's cloak be draped around her shoulders and head, and followed behind as Kenlin led their trotting retreat westward. She saw, with the glazed eyes of one half-dreaming, how they approached the Droálic camp and were allowed to pass without question, their cloaks buying them credibility in the preoccupied encampment. Then she saw them leave the Droálic camp: there was some sort of commotion to the north and people were marching and shouting, concerned by things far away and insensible of the Jazeiz trotting past right before their eyes. And still Kenlin led them on, out beyond the camp and into the half-abandoned villages that stretched for leagues to the west of Ñaj-Gadan. Through alleys, through gardens, over hills and across fens… Once, Ranja almost managed to summon the energy to ask Kenlin where he was taking them. Was he riding at random? Was he following a phantom? But a jostle in the road robbed her of all curiosity and reduced her, once again, to the brink of collapse. For nearly an hour more, she had no energy to question as the entire force of her will focused on simply staying in the saddle.

At last, Kenlin led them to a halt before an abandoned homestead. Ranja slumped from her mount and fell in a heap to the ground. At Ataland's encouragement, she picked herself up, though she hardly cared, and stumbled through the front door and into the building. A bed! This was a one-room cabin of sorts, and opposite the only fireplace was a single narrow, filthy, straw-covered cot. Ranja collapsed onto it without hesitation and fell immediately into an abyssal slumber.

When she awoke many hours later, the light in the windows was dim. Ataland was nowhere to be seen, but Kenlin was standing by the hearth, Faded, deeply absorbed in a conversation with the fire.

PART III

"Alas again," she cried afresh,
    "To see my Lord with madness violence meet!
        What desperation drove you, Lord,
        So viciously to swing thy sword
        That men and Misks together gored
And strew about the chunks of flesh?
    Did madness flow from whence you feared defeat?"

With stonish calm he said, "Not I;
    Defeat was never further from my thought.
        But all before my eye was red
        And saw I with my mind instead.
        And all I saw was weak and dead;
They lacked them but a touch to die
    When on that raving battlefield I fought.

"No, saw I not my grim demise
    Though Misks uncounted 'round me ever stayed.
        Saw I their bottled blood inside;
        I rent the flesh and split the hide
        And all that came before me died.
And thus! See on the field it lies:
    Each rended head too weak to flee my blade!"

—*The Song of Rage*, verses 22:24. Excerpted from
Canticles of Zadarj, a collection from the third century of
the Silvered Court, inspired by the memories of the
Wanderer.

CHAPTER XXXI:

He slept badly.

The first time he woke, he was falling backward, staring up at a smoke-choked sky lit red from below by a world on fire. "No!" he cried out in fear, but the bridge beneath him had crumbled to dust, and he fell down, down and away. In horror, he watched while his friends on the bridge raised their hands, hiding their faces as they desperately tried to fend away the rabid wolves. They failed; they fell; and, screaming still, they were devoured. "No!" he screamed again in hate and despair, but the fiery haze swallowed the scene above even as the narrowing walls of the chasm around him rushed up and smashed against his back. His fall was deflected, he spun wildly, he was flung further out in the abyss, and the pain and dizziness blurred the world into a whirling, hellish maelstrom. *Crash!* He hit the cliff again, and this time the jagged rocks ripped at his back, tearing flesh from his shoulders. Howling in pain and fury, he twisted like a falling cat, clawing at the air, and as the rushing cliff rose to strike him once more, he hurled out his fist to strike back. So vicious was his blow that his hand embedded itself in the stone, breaking his fall by slamming him violently against the cliff. He swung his other fist and smote the rock again, shattering it beneath his assault as he smashed and smashed. Above, there was a roar: the cliff itself was failing, disintegrating into a rockslide that would soon crash down upon his head. Ha! He did not care. Heedless of the collapse, heedless, heedless, he shut his eyes and struck and fought and smashed as though he would smite the very mountain down.

He woke again, and the chasm faded from memory into an indistinct, featureless echo. He was on his hands and knees; the floor beneath him was of sturdy, well-worn wooden planks, and he smashed at it like a child in tantrum, helpless against his punishment. All around him, the world was roaring. He looked up. Fire! Everywhere, fire! The tower was aflame, and the heat and smoke burned his eyes and choked his breath. Someone screamed; there, in the very heart of the inferno, was Klanjad! Kenlin lunged toward his uncle only to instantly recoil with a cry, scorched by the searing heat. Before him, Klanjad ignited and burned like an oil-soaked effigy; he collapsed to one knee as tongues of fire raced up his legs, enveloped his face, licked at his eyes. Reaching out with both hands, the burning figure screamed with Ranja's voice: "Kenlin! Help me, Kenlin!" Kenlin again lunged forward, turning his face away from the unbearable heat as he reached into the fire, caught his uncle's hands, pulled—and toppled backward as the hands broke off at the crumbling, ashen wrists. Severed, the hands continued to cling to him, continued to burn. "No!" Kenlin cried, terrified, trying to shake free of the shackling, immolating death-grip. "Help him, Kenlin!" Ranja's voice screamed again, and Kenlin saw with horror that Klanjad was being dragged backward, further into the fire, by a figure whose translucent visage shone unnaturally clear, as though even fire and smoke would not dare to obscure him: Skralade. "No! No!" But the dead, fiery hands would not let go; they dragged Kenlin back, jerked him to his knees; he could not move! He held the hands as they held him, anchored and anchoring, helpless. He opened his mouth to scream again, and hideous sound rushed forth: a howl of fear, a howl of frustration, a howl of refusal, then anger, then rage twisting into a vile cacophony of hateful laughter strained taut into a mind-shattering screech. But it came not from him; he was thrown aside as another charged past, this one unhampered, unhesitating, screeching, insane! Shocked, petrified, he watched as Kenlin leapt eagerly into the inferno, a flaming sword in his hand, and unflinchingly drove the blade straight through the heart—hearts. Harder he thrust, then up, until he hoisted high above his head, spitted on fire, the ashing corpse of Klanjad impaled together with the writhing, wailing figure of the accursed Misk. "Yes! *Yes!*" But the word was a leaf in a river of screams, for the screeching continued all the while without pause, sung high like a madman's anthem. But now they screamed together, looking on, looking up, seeing and holding and hoisting their tortured foe. They lost track of time; perhaps it ceased to pass. The fire failed to roar. The mad screech faded to an ineffable ringing. The scene slowly hardened as the ravenous fires began to thicken and freeze. When all was quiet and all was cold, he looked at them—one kneeling, one standing, one screaming from the outside at the other laughing madly within—but he did not speak. Silence had conquered this place, and none could know how long its reign would last.

He woke a third time, and the frozen tower likewise faded to a half-remembered echo. He was curled up on the floor, shivering in the silence. It was too cold, much too cold. Why? He opened his eyes and looked up blearily; judging by the light in the window, the sun had set at last. He closed his eyes, the dark and silence inviting him back; but no, it was too cold! He looked around; there had been a fireplace…there! And beside it, a pile of dry wood. Crafted instinct—a lifetime of waking up shivering, yet surviving—goaded him to move. He did his best, but he could only roll to his hands and knees and crawl. *Ah, I hurt! One above, how I hurt!*

Soreness, stiffness, cold, and the lingering heaviness of sleep made him clumsy at first, but these discomforts slowly dwindled as his blood began to flow. There was another sensation, however, that did not diminish; instead it grew clearer and clearer until it was undeniable and unignorable. *Not a dream, then. There's a phantom here, probably the same one from this morning. The Wanderer. He's waiting for me.*

It wasn't reluctance or boorishness that made Kenlin slow to respond to the phantom. It had come, he knew, for him, and it was not his intention to keep it waiting. But he needed to gather himself, needed to prepare… He needed this fire, and to be warm, in order for him to attend to whatever the Faery had to say. Yes, that was it. This first, and then he would Fade. The Wanderer had already waited, perhaps all day long; he could wait a little longer.

After several minutes more, the fire had been built and Kenlin's mind was beginning to thaw. *Well… Alright. No excuse for further delay.* After quickly checking that no other magicians were near enough to sense him, he Faded. He could still see the cabin, the wooden walls and the stone hearth and the firelight playing over all. His eyes worked as they always had. But in magic he saw with other eyes, too: strange landscapes, shifting shadows, wastelands and emptiness—and soon, as before, the hazy figure of a Faery. "Greetings, Wanderer."

The phantom had the form of a man, smaller and slighter than most humans but perhaps typical for a Faery. He wore no clothes that Kenlin could see in magic; his fingers, however, sometimes idly fiddled with something invisible about his neck, implying that his physical form, wherever it was, was likely clothed. His large eyes and wavy hair were of a golden hue so bright as to seem almost unnatural. Their brightness drew Kenlin's gaze, yet eluded him somehow: whenever he tried to focus, every attempt to coalesce the image seemed to render it even more unfixed and fluid. His eyes and mind, already set at odds by the magic, would contradict each other more and more insistently until, the longer and closer he looked, the less he could be sure what he saw. It was easier, he found, to not try to look directly. Instead, he kept his eyes glazed and vacant, staring at the fire while the Faery's apparition lingered in the rim of his perception, a gold-hued blur illuminated by strange lights from uncertain sources.

But though Kenlin could not easily see the expression on the Faery's face, there was obvious concern in his voice: "Greetings, Jazei. You seem… Are you not well?"

Ha! Of course he wasn't well. What a ludicrous question! *Yet physically, though in pain, I am not seriously injured. Is that what he's asking?* Being uncertain how to answer this question was absurd; it made him smile. *But I suppose any other response would lead to further questions, so...* "I'm splendid, Faery. How are you?"

The Wanderer surely heard the sardonicism in Kenlin's reply, but he did not press or take offense. "I am...sad, Jazei. This has been a sad day for all."

A tremor of mixed emotions stirred in Kenlin; he contained them. His only reply was to bow his head in silence.

"And yet," the Faery continued, "in spite of all, the Jazeiz survived. You are here; and Ranja, too, escaped alive? Good."

"And Klanjad?" Kenlin asked quietly.

The Wanderer hesitated. "He breathes. He sleeps and wakes. But living? I think he would not say so."

"You've met him?"

"Seldom; once in flesh, and twice or thrice in magic, as we meet now. I tried to contact him today, but he would not Fade for me. I think he may have been overcome, or perhaps in pain. What I sensed seemed...not as he once was."

I believe it. They cut off his hands. "They cut off his hands."

The Wanderer paused, but not in hesitancy; the silence was of grief and respect. "I am sorry. He was a great Jazei."

"*Is* a great Jazei," Kenlin corrected a little sharply. "You said he was still alive, yes?"

"I said he breathes, and sleeps, and wakes."

"And feels pain?" The Wanderer did not answer, and that was answer enough. Kenlin shook his head. "You really think the Jazeiz survived, Wanderer? I don't think so. Not really. All we earned is a little agency to choose how we die."

At this, the Faery cocked his head sharply. "Yes?" Kenlin did not elaborate, but the Wanderer's expression darkened as he began to make deductions. "No. No, you cannot be thinking of that. There is no hope in it. You will never reach him, Jazei; and you will *never* survive."

Ha! Such truth; but what of it? "To be honest," Kenlin admitted, "I'm still surprised to have survived that Tower. And the Channel, and the wading, and the beach… But regardless, I can't pretend to believe we'll last much longer. They've won, Wanderer. There is no true hiding for Jazeiz, and the fighting is all but finished. The Commune had no answer to this last campaign even before they lost their greatest city. Ñaj-Gadan is vanquished; who will stand against the Droál now?"

"Jranjana," said the Wanderer, and there was a darkness in his voice that hinted at deeper meanings. "No matter the cost, no matter the consequence, when there is nothing left to wait for, I fear Jranjana will fight. The Jazeiz, perhaps, might shepherd and aid them—except if they choose to not survive."

Kenlin shrugged. "'Choose.' If all choices are but different paths to the same end, what sort of choice is that? And if that's all there is…why choose the slow way?"

The Wanderer frowned, chastising, "How is it you speak like this, Jazei? Are you not kin to Klanjad, the scourge of Droál and indomitable tormentor of Misks? Are you not the heir of a lineage that has never, *never* been content to die? 'Why choose the slow way…' These are not the words of a Jazei."

In spite of himself, Kenlin smiled bitterly. "Ranja told me something like that. 'Our fathers would be ashamed,' she said. But really, I think she was just trying to manipulate me, saying whatever she needed to say. When that ploy didn't work, she immediately moved on to another. Her goal the entire time, all she really wanted, was for us to get to a place where we could try to go after Klanjad."

The Wanderer asked gently, "You resent her for this?"

Kenlin shrugged again. *I'll get over it.* "Her ways are her own, and she has reasons. She made a promise."

"To her father?"

"Yes. The details aren't important, but her decision, I think, is made. She'll do anything to keep her promise to him."

The Wanderer was quiet for several minutes. "This is sad to hear. I am sorry that Jazei ways, and traditions, have fallen so low as a rhetoric of convenience. They were not always."

This comment, though not quite fair to Ranja, called to Kenlin's mind the grandiose tales of Jazeiz he had heard as a boy: noble warriors, liberators, champions and kings. Contrasting these fantasies with the life he'd now lived for nearly a year, he was suddenly and perversely inclined to laugh. "Ha! I'm not sure I believe we've *fallen*, Wanderer. Our ways, as I know them, are rarely if ever convenient, but I somehow doubt we were ever what the stories speak of." A courteous impulse told him to apologize for his impertinence: who was he to tell the Wanderer which stories were true? But a different impulse intervened—*Apologize? Or call him out?*—and his words changed to a challenge even as they passed his tongue. "Am I wrong, Faery? If you truly are the Wanderer, then you have known Jazeiz for nearly as long as we've walked Jranjana. You knew the great Jazeiz of old, even the Djinn-Slayer himself. Tell me truly: if you had told Zadarj that he would never succeed, and that he would surely die, do you think that would have swayed him for even a moment?" Once again, the Wanderer did not answer, and thereby did. Kenlin chuckled quietly. "I don't mean to trivialize. But to claim that what I'm saying is somehow *un-Jazei*, and that Jazeiz would never choose a fast path of violence nor walk into a deathtrap... I simply don't believe it. I don't think Ranja believes it. In fact, I think she herself will have us do exactly that; she's just picky about which particular deathtrap."

The Wanderer, frowning deeply, merely replied, "As you say, I have known many Jazeiz. This... It saddens me to hear."

Kenlin did not reply; silence fell between them. Kenlin added more wood to the fire, which soon grew hot enough that he had to stand and step back. Several minutes more passed. At last, with a twang of frustration, the Wanderer said, "It concerns you not, then, that you will never succeed in recovering your uncle? I would tell you, if I thought you knew not, of the hatred borne for him by even the highest of Droál commanders."

"Skralade."

"Him, and others. Tales of the Jazei Klanjad's shadowed war should be sung from high stages; instead, they will die as secrets that none may ever know. But the *Droál* know, and in measure do they hate. And now that he is at last within their power, do you suppose they will allow *any* chance of his rescue?"

Kenlin was still sifting through these considerations in his own mind, and he didn't have all the answers. But as the Faery posed his question, a glimmer of comprehension occurred to Kenlin. *Ah, Ranja... I think I understand you at last.* To the Wanderer, he said, "Perhaps we don't really need a rescue, then. Perhaps we only need to get close."

"But this you cannot do," the Wanderer replied firmly. "Today, your uncle is held in the east, surrounded by more Misks than have been gathered outside an enclave in many a century. Tomorrow, where? Think you he will be taken to a place more accessible? I tell you, Jazei, never less than a brigade will stand between you and your uncle, and Misks and Necromancers besides."

A brigade, you say. "I don't know that term. How many in a brigade?"

The Wanderer seemed a little irritated—the specific number was clearly not the point—but nevertheless he gave an answer: "A thousand men."

"A thousand men," Kenlin repeated. *Ha! I wonder...* "That's probably too many, yes? Even the stories don't speak of Jazeiz killing a *thousand*, not even the stories of Zadarj. I suppose I wouldn't need to kill the full thousand, though. After the first few hundred...well, the rest would probably run for their lives, yes?"

Now the Wanderer was annoyed. "Jazei, you *cannot* be so foolish as this."

Kenlin laughed. *Of course not. And yet, why not?* "Perhaps not a thousand," he said lightly, "but surely more than ten. Twenty? How many of them, I wonder, in exchange for one of me?" The Wanderer regarded him uncertainly. With another quiet laugh, Kenlin continued, "How has this last moon been for you, Wanderer? Mine has been...shall we say *eventful?* Eschewing hollow modesty, I was strong in my magic when tonight's moon rose last. Since then—at a rate that's surprised even me—I have only become stronger. In Slionte, I killed as I never had before. I then surpassed myself before the gates of Ñaj-Gadan. Again in the plaza. Again on the bridge. In the Tower, I fought as though I were someone else entirely: someone *powerful.* If you'd asked me a moon ago—even if you'd asked me yesterday—I would have said I could never do those things. But now that I *have* done, it makes me wonder: what sorts of things can I do tomorrow?"

"You can die," the Wanderer answered coldly, "at the hands of a foe so insurmountably numerous that even the grossest hubris must be insufficient to conquer them."

Hahaha! "Oh, be at peace, Wanderer," Kenlin said dismissively. "I know I can't kill them all. In fact, that's exactly the knowledge that tells me every choice we have is the same. But if I can't kill all, is it so strange that I should wonder how many? Thirty days ago, I could count my kills on two fingers; a day ago, on two hands, or thereabouts. In Ñaj-Gadan I had more to worry about than counting; but I didn't have enough fingers anyway, and the count would have become muddled by the addition of a few Misk lives." *Ha! And yet, what a callous way to— No! I will not see it so, not this time.* "Does it shock you, Faery, to hear me speak this way? It shocks me; or, at least, it still disturbs me a little. That's silly, though, yes? For what has been required of me this past moon except to kill, and to live, and to keep living in order to kill again? This, it seems, is the role I play; this is me as Jazei. And what luck! Apparently I'm good at it, and getting better every day." *Hahahahaha!*

By this time, Kenlin was speaking to himself more than to the Wanderer, and so he was almost surprised when the Wanderer answered, "One hundred."

"Pardon?"

"One hundred, Jazei. Or half. Or twice. How much of their blood will you measure against yours? 'To kill, to kill, to kill...' Your arrogance speaks, but it is despair which presides. How many, you ask, in fair exchange for your life? None! There is no *fair* to be had. You wonder of Jazei ways? Your uncle would tell you, and so will your cousin: there is no sea of Droálic blood fit to be measured against a single drop from a Jazei."

Yes. Kenlin answered darkly, "So if I can't have a sea, then I will take what rivers I can get. Don't pretend to not know what I mean when I say that all choices lead to the same end, Faery. The Commune is crushed. The Droál have won; the world is theirs, and they may destroy it however they please. There is no place left in Jranjana for the Jazeiz. Our only prize, I think, is one last liberty to choose our end—not *if*, but *how*."

The Wanderer shook his head in disbelief, or in rejection. "This, then, is your resolution? Hopeless of overcoming your defeat, you instead would glory in it?"

At the open disapproval in the Faery's voice, a reflexive and belligerent *yes* rose to Kenlin's throat; but, with difficulty, he restrained himself. Taking a deep, calming breath, he said, "I wouldn't say *resolution*, Wanderer. *Conclusion* might be a better word, in more ways than one. It's inevitable now: the Jazeiz will end. If you're right and we cannot reach Klanjad, then that's how he will end. But even if we cannot succeed, Ranja must try, so that's how *she* will end. And as for me... Though I have a general idea of how I'll end, I find myself curious about the particulars. How long? How far? How many?" He paused, then added as an afterthought, "How would I be remembered if I had lived in the times of stories?"

"All times are the times of stories," the Wanderer answered. "Had you lived long ago—alongside Gealvind, or Karkéde, or Zadarj, or Mitakotta—how would you have been remembered even I cannot say. But if all this comes to pass, if the Jazeiz finally fall, how *will* you be remembered? This I can say: you will not."

Kenlin shrugged. *It matters less whether I am remembered, I think; I'm just curious to know how I would have been.* But this thought he kept for himself.

The Wanderer, however, had more to say. "Yet you are wrong, Jazei, to believe this unremembered end is fated. You are wrong to say the Droál have won."

Don't patronize me. "They broke the unbreakable city, Faery. Ñaj-Gadan was supposed to be nigh impregnable, and they conquered it in a matter of weeks, all while attacking— and presumably conquering—multiple other garrisoned cities *at the same time.* The Commune couldn't withstand them, and now it's gone. What else remains that's even worthy of being called their enemy?"

"Jranjana!" the Wanderer declared again with a fervency bordering on heat. "Yes, the Commune is broken, and the Droál remain. That war is all but over. It is the *next* war that I fear, that I prepare for, and so I have been doing for nearly a decade, ever since I saw it before me like a storm on the horizon. The *next* war will be fought against Jranjana itself, and against such a foe the Droál are hopelessly overmatched."

... What? Kenlin shook his head in bafflement. "I see." *I don't see.* "The next war...will be fought against Jranjana... You draw a distinction, then, between Jranjana and the Commune?"

The Wanderer nodded. "The Commune *of Kings* is a diplomatic collective representing the Order of the world that was. By *Jranjana*, I mean the land, and the people who live on it, and the ways in which they live, all as a unit."

Landmasses don't go to war. "And apart from the Commune, how many armies march for Jranjana?" Despite his best efforts, Kenlin's ebbing patience was evident in his voice.

The Wanderer, with a click of his tongue, retorted, "They are two archnemeses who bear the surname *wit*; one grasps without laughing, one laughs without grasping, and neither, it seems, is your ally tonight." *How very…esoteric.* But before Kenlin could figure out whether he was insulted or not, the Wanderer continued, "Remember you the Mad Summer of the Kirjane, when first the Jazeiz came to power? Know you how close came the world to ruin when Lakradaz commanded the Infanticide? Then scoff not at the threat of a war with Jranjana, Jazei. I remember fifteen centuries of conflict, from the fall of Imxada to the rise of the Droál, and I tell you there is *nothing* I fear more than if Jranjana goes to war."

"Peace! Peace." Though perhaps he'd been overly acerbic in his skepticism, Kenlin hadn't intended to provoke the Faery. To calm the conversation, he opened his mouth to apologize; but suddenly, as before, the apology morphed on his tongue into something else entirely. *Step back? No, challenge!* "If you're asking whether I know of events that illustrate whatever point you're trying to make, I clearly do not. I know little of the Infanticide except that, if I remember correctly, it began a chain of events that led to the end of the War of Men and Misks. And the other thing you mentioned… 'Mad Summer,' you said? I don't think I've heard of that at all."

"That is unsurprising," the Wanderer said evenly. "Few in these days have heard of that summer. Fewer still tell of it."

Then why would you expect…? Annoyed, Kenlin said, "In that case, of the two events you mentioned specifically, one was a direct precursor to victory, and the other was so historically unimpactful that it's all but forgotten. Yes? And yet these are the stories that frighten you? Help me, Wanderer, for I do not understand."

He'd let his impatience get away from him again, but this time the Faery did not bridle at the provocation. Instead, nodding his head slowly, he said as though to himself, "Yes. You are right. So long I have lived with what I know, sometimes I forget..." The Wanderer paused, but not for hesitation; within the pause, his entire manner changed. When he spoke again, his voice was dominated by a mild yet resonant tone, as though his words reverberated in the ears of the listener. There was a palpable melancholy in this voice, like a lonely echo in the mountains. This, the voice said, was no mere story. "I remember..."

Tomorrow in Kirjane begins the first festival of summer, and the lilac city is bedecked with early flowers. It has been a good spring for wine, and the countryside vineyards are glad with the hope of a song-worthy vintage. Slave after slave brings cask upon cast to the villas in town, for at sunset tomorrow these villas will open to welcome all Misk revelers. Three days of festivities, three nights of enjoyment, and music and wine and performance of stories, and artisans sharing the joys of their talents... Ariska is elegant, and Kigrei is mighty; but in beauty and culture, no city can stand beside lilac Kirjane, the hill city, laureled with flowers, incomparable jewel of the world.

I've come for the festival, and to hear music; a slave boy, they say, whose voice wounds like a dagger, yet soothes like a lover, and hurts and heals both in the span of a song. But by sunrise tomorrow, new topics are pressing, for word has arrived from the cities a'north. The Jazeiz, they say, are invading near Garna, and all Eyjazinka—and all Misks should fear.

But Kirjane is south, and no war has come near it for four hundred years since Jarliske's demise. The Jazeiz, they've heard, are some new kind of human: too warlike for slaves, too few to be soldiers. Too troublesome, that! Let them be, if they will. Leave the wars to the north, and the south will stay merry.

And merry we stay. Now the festival's ending; we've all but forgotten the troublesome tale. Then another word comes! And another! And more! And each message, for Misks, becomes ever more frightening. The north is afire! Mighty Kigrei has fallen! But how can it be? How could slaves cause such ruin? A shadow descends on the city of lilac as Misks, and their households, fear what they know not.

But the countryside slaves hear the same tales reversed: the Jazeiz are coming! O, liberty's heralds! Humanity rises! Misk news travels fast, but horse riders will follow. As midsummer's heat begins mounting to solstice, a human arrives on a horse from the north.

In the market I am, telling tales to the children; I see the man enter, still mounted, and grasping a flag with a spike. Without pausing he rides to the fair city's center. He springs from his horse as the silent crowd watches. He stops. He removes the bindings from the furled banner. Into a crack in the pavement he rams the spike on his flagpole, planting it. Then away he walks as a wind unfurls the bannered emblem of the Emerald Eye.

And silence rules the marketplace; as days go by, the silence gathers hate. That very dusk, the flag is gone; when sun returns, the flag is back. The second night, it's gone again; the second dawn, again it flies. Constabularies intervene; they burn the flag and post a guard. By morning, Emerald Eye's returned, its pole impaling through the guard-Misk's corpse.

Investigations. Executions. More attacks; now Misks stay home at night. For murder of a cruel master, all his slaves are damned and hanged. Constabularies come back home to empty houses; slaves have fled, hateful defiance scrawled upon walls in family's blood. In fright, some Misks dismiss their slaves. Nowhere to live, these humans roam the streets and take, and tear, and claim, and burn, and ever grow in numbers more uncountable, unquenchable, insatiable, unstoppable.

They burn the art. They kill the flowers. They ransack the villas for all that they please, fine wine drunk in gulps to lend mirth to monstrosity, or poured down the throat of an unwilling woman, or flung in the face of a death-beaten Misk lying broken and helpless. And day upon day! For an unending summer of madness they filthy themselves with their disinhibition. I hate them! I hate them! To think I once wished for this—hoped for this! Hoped they would one day be free. Such *freedom!* Such *pleasure!* What hedonist pig could be vicious enough to call this madness liberty?

I cannot endure it. I cannot remain here. So north do I go; I will see where more than the name of the Jazeiz has come. I will see what could possibly hope to redeem the atrocities brought by the Emerald-Eyed banner.

By this time, the Wanderer was visibly trembling with the intensity of his remembrances; when he stopped speaking, he bowed his head and breathed deep, calming breaths.

Kenlin waited until he was quite sure the Faery had finished speaking, then commented, "It is not easy for me to see the humans—the liberated slaves—as villains in your story."

The Wanderer shook his head, though he did not look up. "Not villains. There are few villains in memory, nor heroes. Only people."

Don't deflect with semantics. "As you please, Faery, yet you strongly disapproved of how the *people* acted in your story. In fact, I got the impression that you thought more highly of human enslavement than you did of human freedom, yes?"

The Wanderer looked up, and for a moment Kenlin saw him clearly through the magic as the golden eyes looked unblinkingly into the emerald. "Yes, I did. It was a memory, Jazei; and in that memory, I thought as you say. But it was not *freedom* that I saw, and hated, in Kirjane, though I mistook it so at the time. Not freedom; savagery.

"There is a base, bestial mindlessness that stands in disdain of everything idealistically called *humanity*. Until the

Mad Summer, I had never seen it before, for I had only ever seen Misks and humans in, at worst, hostilely civilized settings. Even after, though I have watched for it, I have only seen this madness exceedingly rarely. It appears in times and places where the bonds of civilization very abruptly cease to apply, whether due to liberation or unfettered despair or a sudden accession to tremendous power. In an individual, this madness is repugnant. But when many give into it all together, they become capable of barbarities that even the most disgusting man in civilization would call unconscionable. In fifteen centuries, I have never seen aught to compare with a lovely city, for a single summer, overrun with such abhorrent chaos; but ever since, I have terrified myself with the thought of a whole world gone thusly mad."

Ah. "So this is the 'ruin' you mentioned that the Infanticide almost brought upon the world? I suppose that, too, is something you remember?"

The Wanderer nodded very slowly, almost reluctantly. "Yes, Jazei. I do. If I must." Kenlin did not reply. The Wanderer took a deep breath and released it in a slow, bracing sigh. "I remember…"

Pain! Pain is an anchor. Pain is a prison. A foolish wisdom claims that Misks cannot be captured nor restrained; try, and see them Vanish. But this man knows the truth. Though tethers may fail and shackles fall away, a sudden, searing pain will bind them. Flood their minds with agony 'til naught remains for magic, and all but the greatest Vanishers are powerless to flee.

I cannot watch! I cannot look away! I hear the mother wailing from inside, pleading vainly; and I hear the baby cry, uncomprehending, frightened just to hear his mother's wails. But no! The babe is silenced! The mother's screams redouble, but the man outside is quiet, lurking by the door, his oil lamp lit in hand.

The door pulls in, a Misk steps out, and the oil lamp smashes on the killer's head! The man and Misk together soak with oil; they light; they burn, the man his hand and Misk his head. The other Misks come running out. The man strikes wildly with his burning hand; he falls back spilling guts upon the road. The Misks rush to their fallen kin, but a human crowd has gathered now. They know. They *all* know.

The Misks are overmatched, and so they Vanish, leave their burning kin to die. He tries to Vanish too, but no! The pain of burning keeps him here, and no one in the crowd would have it else. They gnash their teeth, and screech, and kick, and rip, and crush the ribs, and break the limbs, the mother comes, she takes his eyes!

He cannot leave; I cannot stay. I do not watch them tear the Misk apart.

Though the Wanderer seemed not quite so shaken by this memory, Kenlin had even more objections than before. "Once again, Wanderer," he said, this time not waiting for the Faery to calm himself, "I struggle with the sympathy you seem to feel for these Misks. This was a memory of the Infanticide, yes? So those Misks were there to *kill infants?* Perhaps you do not fully understand how unforgivable that is to us, Faery, but—"

"You are wrong!" the Wanderer declared so suddenly and forcefully that Kenlin drew back. "I understand well the minds of the humans who executed that Misk. Yes, executed, I say, for I deny not a bit that his death was earned. But the *manner* in which they killed him, Jazei, and the *satisfaction* with which they killed him, and *who* they were who killed him... Jazei, when ordinary folk turn 'righteously' to torture, it is a sign that the bonds of civilization are frayed indeed, thin and frayed. Two hundred years after the Mad Summer I saw these events, town after town, wherever the slaughter was being enforced; and in the viciousness of human vengeance I saw the ghastly specter of Kirjane."

"Good!" Kenlin retorted angrily. "Good for them, I say! Kill them all, make them suffer, and take as much satisfaction in it as you can! You speak of art, and music, and beauty, and whatnot, as though any of that could be weighed against so much as a day of Misk domination. So what if their so-called civilization was destroyed? Small price to pay; their 'civilization' was enslaving humans and massacring babies. To the Depths with it! Burn it all down! The Misks proved, beyond doubt, what monsters they were. Any fire is a good fire if it catches Misks in the flames!"

As Kenlin said this, his voice grew louder and stronger with every condemnation; it reverberated through the tiny cottage and echoed, and was answered, in the wastelands of his mind. But the Wanderer contrastingly became wide-eyed and urgent, as though in Kenlin's voice he heard the very thing he feared most. "This, Jazei! Don't you see? This, that you say, is precisely what we *must not do!* Yes, the dominion of Misks in those days was horrific, and their violent overthrow, even had it come through chaos, *might* have been the better of two worsts. But it *didn't have to* come through chaos, Jazei! Do you not see? It is only the impatience, the reckless fury of the vengeful, that damns the good of a flawed Order alongside its evil. Any fire, so you say? Kirjane was one fire. One city, one fire, but the price of its chaos—art, music, stories, lives as well—was such that none can ever fully remember it. Such is the nature of true loss. I feared, Jazei, I feared that *all* of Jranjana would succumb to such madness when Lakradaz ruled the Infanticide. *Imagine* such loss!"

"Again, Faery, the Misks were enslaving and murdering—"

"And think you that anarchy is preferable? Think you so highly of mayhem? *I remember!* Even now can I see the wreckage, the destruction, and death. With naught to hold them back, I saw *liberated* humans indulging depravities that even the cruelest master would scarce have dared to consider—and the victims Misks and fellow humans alike! Indeed, Jazei: set forth a choice between civilized oppression and anarchic barbarity, and no wise man could tell you which is worse."

Kenlin opened his mouth heatedly—*I know exactly which I would choose!*—but the Wanderer cut him off. "And so, when the Infanticide pushed Jranjana to the brink and that choice lay before us, we chose *neither.* Think! What would have happened in Kirjane if the Jazeiz had come in force, not just in name? Much the same as happened when they *did* come in force at the end of that Mad Summer: they would have brought a new Order, and with that they would have replaced the old Order of the Misks, leaving no space for a savage interregnum.

"And *that,* Jazei! That is the solution we sought when the Infanticide brought Jranjana to the precipice of anarchy. Before the world could fall to chaos—*before* the old Order could collapse with nothing to replace it—we destroyed it ourselves and installed something new. Do you see?"

Perhaps... Perhaps I'm beginning to. But who...? In a measured tone, Kenlin asked, "You keep saying *we.* 'We sought a solution.' 'We destroyed it.' But do you mean... I thought you didn't participate in the Faery March, Wanderer. Did you?"

The Wanderer hesitated. *Maybe he has said more than he intended.* At length, the Faery answered carefully, "That March, as has been often told, was led by Zadarj the Jazei and Nandaad of the Faeries. In those days, however, I was never far from my brother in magic and counsel." Kenlin was momentarily taken aback; he had forgotten that Nandaad the Djinn-Master and the Wanderer were brothers. The Faery continued, "No, I did not fight; I am no warrior. But the Faery March could only have happened at a very specific point in time, for many reasons. Had not Zadarj been alerted to the truth of the Infanticide, and had he not been persuaded to pursue the unprecedented aid of the Faeries, and had not the Faery March visibly broken the Misk dominion within a matter of moons... As I have said many times, Jranjana was on the brink. A few moons more, and the people would have made their own war—first with the Misks, then with themselves—and I tremble to think of the following darkness."

The Wanderer stopped, but Kenlin did not fill the silence; there was too much to think about in what the Wanderer had said. The details matched with what he already knew of the War of Men and Misks. Near the end of the war, in the aftermath of the Breach, the Misks had gained the upper hand because their chieftain, Lakradaz of Clan Eyjazinka, controlled the last of the known Djinn, or so the stories said. The Jazeiz, overmatched at last, had been driven into hiding, with Zadarj and many others retreating to the mountain fortress of Natzut in the southeast. Thinking himself victorious at last, Lakradaz had sought to cement the dominion of Misks forever by solving the so-called birthrate problem: human mothers bear children in shorter timeframes than she-Misks can, to the great disadvantage of Misks throughout the War. To address this, Lakradaz ordered the Infanticide, a secret mandate whereby a portion of all human newborns—some stories said as many as nineteen in twenty— were to be systematically murdered. It was outrage over this abominable mandate, the stories said, that drove the Faeries to finally renounce their neutrality, ally with the Jazeiz, and shatter the might of Misks in the legendary campaign known as the Faery March. And that was the narrative Kenlin had always heard: that the Misks, by their own monstrousness, had ultimately sealed their doom.

But the Wanderer hinted at a much more nuanced perspective than Kenlin had ever considered. For a moment, his mind's eye glimpsed the vastness of history not as a story—continuity, characters, beginnings, endings, and conviction about "the way it was." Instead, for the first time, he saw the past as a chronicle of worlds, every world a day, and every day riddled with uncertainties from the day before and consequences for the next. *But this is all the Wanderer sees, yes? This is why, instead of stories, he speaks of memories. That which he remembers didn't come to pass just because that's how the story goes. He remembers the doubts, the choices, the fears; he remembers how things that never happened still influenced things that did.* To his own surprise, Kenlin felt a new sense of understanding for the Faery. He had foreseen something, centuries and centuries ago, that haunted him; and so, unwilling or unable to forget, he had spent the past thousand years in a perpetual vigil, watching for signs of events he never remembered having happened, and never wanted to.

But now, nearly a millennium later, he sees the past in the present; and once again, he is afraid. Kenlin, making an effort to speak gently, said, "So this war with Jranjana, as you call it... This is what you fear will follow now that the Commune of Kings has been destroyed? You think the Droál, like the Misks long ago, will not be able to suppress those they have conquered?"

In the silence of their conversation, Kenlin's perception of the Wanderer's phantom had grown faint and unclear. Nevertheless, through the undulating haze of the magic, he thought he saw the Faery nod. "Yes, Jazei. This is my fear. What the Droál cannot understand is the same that the Misks could not understand, and that Lakradaz would never hear: by the time of their victory, they have already lost. The Misks, in their case, had lost the race for children. In the two hundred years of the War, so many humans had been born and so many Misks killed that there simply were not enough Misks to enforce the Infanticide, even had they all been willing to obey so heinous a mandate. At the very threshold of his triumph, Lakradaz *could not win*; he could only lose in battle or lose, as I have described, in chaos.

"For the Droál, it is similar: strong as they are, they are far too weak to enforce so unbearable a regime over so vast a land and people. Worse, while the Misks were few in number and required little food, the Droál field thousands upon thousands of soldiers who must be supplied overwhelmingly with crops grown on Jranjanan soil by Jranjanan farmers. The same is true for other craftsmen: Jranjanan weavers, Jranjanan metalworkers, Jranjanan horse breeders... Chaos does not support conquests, and so the Droál require, and thus far have enjoyed, the meek cooperation of Jranjanan common folk who imagine that, if they just keep their heads down for long enough, eventually *somebody* will save them. Thus, always, are stories told.

"But what, think you, will happen when they hear that the Commune lies dead on the battlefield? That no one is coming? Some will give up. A few may even embrace the Droál, telling themselves (as may be true) that any other course would be worse for them. But these who at first accept will be concentrated in the cities, where the Droál garrison their soldiers and where their power is plainest to see. Out in the countryside, the farmers are too many, too widespread, too self-sufficient; there simply are not enough Droál to successfully impose their will."

"You think there will be provincial rebellions?" Kenlin asked.

The Wanderer shook his head even as he seemed to agree, "There will be; there have been. Toward them, the Droál are merciless. As we have said, military might comes from Order, and Order belongs to the Droál. No, the true power of the farmers is not of action, but of inaction. Why, they will ask themselves, do we plow extra fields to put food in the bellies of invaders we hate? Why provide for our enemies? And so they will stop—not all, but some—and when the Droál come to tax their harvest, there will not be enough to collect.

"And so the supplies will begin to fail, and the Droál must respond with the only tools at their disposal: they will deploy soldiers from the cities to subdue the countryside. The more they retaliate, the more the farmers will hate them, and the Droál will be forced to take ever more soldiers from the cities—the restive, hungry cities—to secure the food supply. When winter comes, the cities will be starved. One city, none can guess which, will become *too* starved; hungry and angry, the people of this city will riot, destroy the Order, and the city will fall to anarchy. *And no one will come to repress them.* Who would? The dispersed soldiers in the countryside? The diminished garrisons of other angry, hungry cities? No one. But tales will travel—The Droál can be overthrown!—and city after city, Kirjane after Kirjane, will crumble to chaos."

Kenlin nodded slowly, contemplating. After several minutes, he said, "That's quite a story you tell, Wanderer. It's not a memory, though."

"It might be," the Wanderer answered darkly. "It is a dream of mine, a nightmare. I have had many. How is it you said? 'When all choices are but different paths...' My nightmares of late are all of either Droálic Order or anarchic chaos. I have not the wisdom to tell which is worse."

Ah, I see a rather belabored pattern emerging. No! No sarcasm; be direct. "And, as before, you would prefer a third option, yes? If you're hoping for another Faery March, I don't think I can be your Zadarj." *No?*

But at this idea, the Wanderer frowned a little and shook his head. "Would that— But no. As much a hope as that might be, I cannot wish it. I would not wish it. But it is moot in any case, for the idea is impossible. The Jazeiz have no Zadarj; the Faeries have no Nandaad; and no matter the tales of burning and death, my people will never be rallied as once they were. Victory was costly, and the Forest is slow to forget. No, Jazei, there will be no second Faery March.

"Nor is there another power left, I think, strong enough to overcome the Droál and champion a new Order. A thousand years ago, the war was won; but in this war, we have already lost. That is why I say it is the *next* war, the 'war' of Jranjanans against Order, for which we must prepare. It is too late to prevent the chaos; instead, we must hope to mitigate it."

"As you wish the Jazeiz had done in Kirjane?"

"As they *did*, at summer's end. The ruination of Kirjane was the work of only about three moons, at the end of which officials from the Jazeiz came from the north. As was Jazei practice at the time, the new Order they installed was designed to be familiar without being disappointing: the structures of Misk society were largely preserved, but with humans in power and slavery, as a codified concept of ownership, condemned and forbidden. By that time, nearly the entire Misk population of Kirjane had been driven out or murdered; and the humans, having tasted for a season of life without Order, were glad to welcome the Jazeiz.

"And I say again because it is important: all this the Jazeiz achieved without war. No soldiers marched, no battle was given. Do you see? Vicious anarchy alone, without need for soldiers, will topple a hated Order; then, after the Order is gone, the anarchy's viciousness will turn against itself. But! If a new Order—not hated, not already rejected—is brought before the people as an alternative preferable to chaos, they accept it—*without war*. Do you see?"

Kenlin frowned. *I think I'm beginning to see, but I'm not sure I agree.* "So you believe this…principle will also apply to the Droálic conquests, yes? The Droál have already won this war, and nobody has enough strength left to prevent the cities from becoming desperate, rebelling, and falling to chaos, as you say. But once chaos has weakened the Droál's hold on a city, you think the rebelling people will be open to guidance—your 'new Order.' So instead of trying to prevent these Mad Summers, you hope to abbreviate them?"

The Wanderer paused, as though his reply weighed heavily on him and he must brace himself to give it. "Yes, Jazei; I cannot prevent the chaos. And yes, as you are about to remark, I am well aware of how swiftly ruin came upon Kirjane. To mitigate it, we must be swift to respond when anarchy rises; but no matter how swift we are, I know… I know there will be loss. But the swifter we are, the more we can save, and the better we may be able to restore at least a portion of what was lost."

"Restore? How? You said much of what was lost in Kirjane was lost forever."

"So it was; and so will some of the loss for other cities be. But if we are swift, we can outpace the worst of the damage; and if we are prepared, we may be able to restore it.

"The destruction of physical artifacts in Kirjane was tragic enough—much beauty was lost in that way—but far more damaging was the loss of the artists who not only created the new, but remembered the old. Painters, sculptors, weavers, storytellers... Their bodies were desecrated in the streets, and when Order was finally restored, no one remained with the will and ability to recreate what had been ruined and forgotten. But this, at least, I can prevent because for this I have prepared. For nearly ten years, ever since I first became concerned that the Commune might truly lose their war, I have worked to gather arts and artists from all over Jranjana to one of the most remote and defensible cities in the world: Inajaz. Here I have brought the masters of many arts and encouraged the patronage that allows them to live and work. Here I have taught stories—not just told, but taught—more earnestly and broadly than ever before, until not a fire burns in the northwest that does not hear a tale told from my memories. Here, far from the malice of Droál and the menace of anarchy, I have hidden the seeds of the beauty and culture of Jranjana. Yes, much will be destroyed in the coming years, but so long as Inajaz stands, much will also be preserved. With the aid of the Jazeiz, we can defend this city; we can outlast them; and, when chaos throws their power into disarray, we can venture forth at last to offer a new Order and to bring back the stories, the arts, and the beauty that would else be lost forever."

Ah... Inajaz. I think I finally understand what he wants. "Inajaz is the mountain city in the extreme northwest, yes? That's where you've gathered all your arts and artists, that's where you yourself are…and that's where you would like the Jazeiz to come."

The Wanderer nodded vigorously. "Yes! Yes! Inajaz will be our refuge, our fortress, where we——"

"——can wait for the coming chaos, right." *Don't cut him off! Why not? He'll put up with it; he wants something from me, yes?* "So you will hide in the mountains, presumably hoping the Droál won't concentrate their force against so small a city, and wait for their empire to collapse in on itself. This will happen, you think, city by city; and as each city falls to anarchy, you will…do what? Dispatch some official delegation to march through the gates and declare to the rioting residents, 'Stop the chaos, we've brought a new Order!'" *Enough! Stop it!*

The sarcasm did not escape the Wanderer, yet he was undeterred. "Mock as you like, Jazei, but it may well be just so simple. If not, then we will adapt. But I have *been* in a city of chaos, and I have seen how churning and unstable are the wills of those caught in such a place. Chaos despises nothing more than itself, and its victims perpetually turn toward anything they hear that so much as resembles a plan, an Order. When there are many such plans, they all conflict, and the chaos remains; but if one voice is stronger, strong enough to gain prominence——"

"And your voice, you think, will be strongest? From what you describe, Wanderer, the people in question will have just thrown off the yoke of Droálic rule—something *Jranjana*, meaning the Commune and their 'Order,' failed to do—and will be engulfed in infighting over their own future. Why would they give heed to you, an outsider, and the 'Order' you bring? Why would they even hear out what you have to say?"

This, however, was the very question for which the Wanderer had been waiting, and he pounced on it like a cat. "Not what *I* have to say; what *you* have to say! What the *Jazeiz* say! Do you see? Long ago, when restive human slaves overthrew a city, it was Jazei authority that calmed the violence. Later, when they threatened to cast down Order throughout an entire empire, again it was Jazeiz that stilled them. Do you see? The oft-told stories of Jazeiz are all of violence and war, yes; but throughout history, their greatest power has been to soothe, not to inflame. Respect for Jazeiz, *faith* in Jazeiz, is so integral to Jranjanan humanity that you, the voice and image of their most cherished legends, have immeasurable power to make them listen. For that is the *true* role of the Jazeiz! Jazeiz make it that battles are fought on battlefields, not in streets and homes. Jazeiz make it that farmers can farm, and builders can build, and weavers can weave, for the war will be waged by *warriors*. And even in the darkness of chaos when people know not where to turn, Jazeiz can be—have been!—the guiding voice of authority, of leadership—of Order!"

Kenlin nodded slowly as the final pieces of the Faery's vision became clear. "This is why you don't want Ranja and I to go after Klanjad," he concluded quietly. "You're worried that we'll die, and you think you need us. Or, rather, you need a Jazei."

"I . . ." The Wanderer hesitated as though unsure whether he should even say what he planned to say. When Kenlin looked up inquiringly, the Faery gave a slight shrug and nodded. "It had been my hope for many years that your uncle Klanjad, should the war come to a hopeless end, would come to Inajaz and take up the task I have described. This, I fear, is impossible; Klanjad the Jazei is dead, wanting but a little time. But for you, it is not already determined that *you* must die; and if you make it so, then that is your choice. *Do not choose it!* Come to Inajaz, Jazei. Join me in preserving the seeds and memories of what is best in Jranjana. Come live and wait with me. When the Droálic empire falls to consumption and rot, we will emerge, and Order, and tell, and teach, so that Jranjana might be Jranjana once more."

Kenlin stood in silence, contemplating, for a very long time. He could feel the impulsivity, the emotional flippancy, lurking in his mind like a predator just outside the firelight; and yet, even though these thoughts lurked, they did not intervene. It was as though they, confident in their own judgements, had stepped back to allow Kenlin to come to their conclusion on his own. Very slowly, he began to nod his head in agreement—not with the Wanderer, but with *me*.

At last, after several thoughtful minutes, Kenlin spoke. "Wanderer... If you were asking us simply to come, without abandoning some other objective, I might respond differently. I understand your points—thank you for explaining them—and I might agree, at least in part, if circumstances were different. But as it stands, it doesn't really matter whether your reasons are sound or not. I will not do what you are asking. No."

The Wanderer was speechless. In a breathless, incredulous whisper, "After so much, still you do not see..." Then, gathering himself, he said, "What is it you refuse, Jazei? You refuse to come to Inajaz at all? Or refuse only to give up the hopeless idea of rescuing your uncle?"

Faery, don't be— No, let him; allow him his vexation. "Given what you think about our chances, those are both the same choice," Kenlin said wryly. "What we might have done if we weren't going after Klanjad is irrelevant. He's her father, Wanderer. She will never accept a plan that abandons him."

The Wanderer hesitated for several moments, and it was not difficult to imagine what he was thinking. *Don't try it, Faery.* "... I have never met your cousin, Jazei, though some little I have heard about her. She is, so I hear, of rare beauty and surpassing mind. But I know, as I am here, that she has not the magic of Jazeiz of legend. Nor, as I have heard, does she have the white-blond hair."

"Not enough Jazei for you?" Kenlin said acidly.

The Wanderer lifted his hands palms-out in a pacifying gesture. "Mistake me not: her presence here would be greatly welcome. I have no doubts of her exceptionality nor of your attachment to her; the Jazeiz have always fallen to extremes, either inseparable or fratricidal. But her absence... I am sorry if this offends you, but she will not inspire as you will, for she does not so nearly evoke the legends. If she will not come—if there is no way that you can convince her—then you without her..."

Ha! Had he said this to me on the beach... Taking a calming breath, Kenlin said, "You want me to abandon her, yes? I almost did, you know. Not even a day ago, I had fully prepared myself to leave her behind. She knew it. She almost killed herself trying to prevent it." The Wanderer did not answer. After a moment, Kenlin continued, "I'm not going to abandon her, Wanderer. She warned me yesterday that it wouldn't work. I tried; it didn't. I'm not going to try it again."

The Faery shook his head in disbelief. When he replied, his voice was dark, not as though astonished, but as though foreboding. "Even if she asks that you kill yourself, Jazei? Even if she leads you to certain death, still will you stand by her?"

Hahaha! Certain death? What, in these days, is certain? "I said I won't abandon her, Wanderer. I won't. I won't abandon either of them, and I think there's nothing you can say that will dissuade me."

"But I *explained* to you, Jazei! I told you why the Jazeiz must survive—"

"Yes, you explained, and you think your reasoning is unassailable, do you? You've thought it all out, and I'd be a fool to disagree?" *He didn't say that. Yes? But he does!* "You say the cities, when they rebel, will surely throw off the domination of the Droál; and yet, after what I hear is ten or more *years* of unrest, Jiánse remains occupied. You think Inajaz, your mountain city, will be strong enough to resist a small army and small enough to never merit a large army; and yet Natzut and Flunjat, mountain cities both, lie in ruins thanks to the Droál. And why did the Droál come to Natzut? I don't know for certain, but there is one obvious reason: because of the Jazeiz! I never would have believed it before, but ever since I met Klanjad, violence and ruin have chased us from the remotest mountains of the southeast to Ñaj-Gadan itself, the much-attested pinnacle of Jranjana. If you were to ask me for the surest way to *guarantee* that Droálic armies attack Inajaz, I would recommend that you send me, or any other Jazei, to reside there. We might not even have to reside! People who have helped us, spoken to us, people we've seen in passing... Even you, Wanderer, however many leagues away you are, should be wary. You've helped us now, but we are a curse." *I am a curse!* "It's death in these days even to speak in private to a Jazei!"

"Then we could conceal your presence," the Wanderer responded immediately. "You could hide in the rural mountains—"

"And they could try something, and we could try something, and so on, and so on," Kenlin retorted, "and sooner or later we would realize that we're only prolonging a game that they've *already won*. I see what you want me to see, Wanderer. Do *you* see? My point is not that there's nothing you can try; my point is that your plan is *uncertain*. It's probably even *unlikely*. And with that in mind, you ask if I will abandon them—both of them—for an unlikely idea? I'm sorry, Wanderer. *No.*"

He had counterpoints, as Kenlin had known he would, but the Faery refrained from blurting them out. *Back and forth, back and forth... He knows he can hope to be convincing, but nothing more, and I am not convinced.* After several minutes the Wanderer spoke, his voice thick with unwillingness. "And is there nothing I can say to you, Jazei? Nothing that will convince you otherwise?"

If one of us falls... Kenlin shrugged dismissively, but spoke gently: "What is there to say that you haven't said in this past hour?" The Faery said nothing, and one last time, no answer was answer enough. "For whatever it's worth, Wanderer, I am sorry."

The phantom had blurred again, and Kenlin could not clearly see its face; but even without seeing, he knew the Faery was shattered. *I can understand that. Or perhaps I can't. Ten years is half of my life; to what could I compare the loss of ten years of plans?* It was several long minutes before the Wanderer managed to gather himself. When he spoke again, his tone was lower and a little colder. He was no longer urging, trying to convince an ally; now he was negotiating as with a bystander, foreign and unpredictable—a stranger. "So you will throw yourself into this hopeless... And this is decided. Even your cousin could not dissuade you?"

Ha! As if she would. "When she wakes, Wanderer, she and I will talk about it. It will be a brief conversation."

The Wanderer sighed in frustration, but continued, "And what if, unthinkable as it may be, you survive? If somehow you endure this madness and emerge—successful or otherwise, but alive—will you then reconsider? Surely, unless there is some *other* Jazei to rescue, you will then have no cause not to come."

Wanderer... I still do not believe in your plan as you do, and I certainly don't think that my presence will bring anything but ruin. But...if you insist... "If we're still alive three days from now, and the situation has changed, then I will be willing to discuss it again," Kenlin said. "That's all that I can promise."

The Wanderer clicked his tongue, disappointed again, and his visage became more blurry and uncertain than ever. "Very well, Jazei. If this is your decision, then...I must do as I can to ensure you survive."

This caught Kenlin by surprise. "That's...generous. Are you certain?"

The Wanderer laughed bitterly. "I will give you knowledge of where to go; without it, you would for certain go to incorrect places, dangerous places, and fruitlessly die. I can try to hide your magic again, if needs be, for if I do not, you will surely be detected and killed. I need the Jazeiz to live, so if you *must* risk this rescue before coming to Inajaz, then my only choice is to help you survive it."

"Is there risk in that? Risk to you, I mean, other than my vague superstitions about disaster befalling everyone who helps us."

The Wanderer chuckled again. "I am a Faery, Jazei. There is no profane Droálic malediction that can menace me in magic, and I am far too distant for them to threaten physically. As for Misks, I say again: I am Fay. The March was long ago, but the Clans have not forgotten it. Even if they knew where I was, no Misk would dare approach me."

In spite of himself, Kenlin smiled. *He is fearless; that I can respect.* "Very well, then. For that, and for already helping us more than we could ever have hoped for, we thank you, Wanderer. So… Where is Klanjad now?"

The Wanderer paused as though thinking. *No, not thinking; Fading! Even as he remains here, he's gone somewhere else in magic to learn Klanjad's whereabouts!* After a moment, the Wanderer stirred and said, "Your uncle is yet where I sensed him last, near the eastern walls of Ñaj-Gadan. I suspect he is a prisoner in the Droálic encampment there. But you cannot be thinking of undertaking this tonight, Jazei."

Ha! Of course we will! No sense in waiting, what could… No! The impulsive eagerness had leapt so suddenly into his mind that Kenlin had to yank himself back from declaring something rash. *Not yet! Wait. Think.* After a quieting pause, Kenlin answered, "Perhaps not; that, too, I will discuss with Ranja. She's slept the entire day since we arrived here, so I doubt she'll be asleep for much longer. Give us time to talk; then, if you still wish to help us, come back again in a few hours. I'll tell you what we've decided, and we can discuss how to proceed from there."

The Wanderer answered gravely, "Very well, Jazei; I will return as you have asked. But even though you have dismissed it, I *beg* you that you speak to your cousin of what I have said: of chaos and Order, of Inajaz, and of the chance—and need—

for the Jazeiz to survive. Survive, Jazei! It is the nature of your kind. It is *all I ask* of you. Survive!" And with that, he disappeared.

Chapter XXXII:

Kenlin breathed out slowly, almost ponderously, as he at last released his magic. *One above! How long was I Faded? It was just after dusk when I woke, and now it's too dark to be sure. An hour? More?* And yet he felt nothing: no headache, no dizziness... He reflexively touched a finger to his temple as though to check that his senses weren't deceiving him. *No, not even a hint of strain. Ha! The magic was hardly intense, but to have sustained it for so long...* Inside and out, a satisfied smile crept over his face and echoed in his mind. *I think I'm becoming good at this. I think I like being good at this.*

"That was quite a conversation."

Kenlin started and turned. He hadn't known Ranja was awake; in fact, he'd nearly forgotten she was in the same room. She still lay on the cot where she'd collapsed when they had first arrived. "I hope we didn't wake you. How long...?"

"A little while." She blinked wearily for a moment. "Is there water?" Kenlin sat beside her cot, gave her a cup, and pulled a large jug toward her. When she had drunk her fill, she tapped the jug. "Did you draw this?"

He shook his head. "Like you, I slept almost the whole day through. Sorry, but keeping watch would have been..."

"Ridiculous," she agreed, nodding. Musingly, she continued, "Ataland didn't murder us in our sleep, then. And he didn't immediately run away either, but stayed at least long enough to draw water. Did he build the fire too?"

"No, I did that. I suspect he gathered the wood, though; it was piled up by the hearth when I awoke."

Ranja shook her head wonderingly, a small smile on her face. "I don't understand him, Kenlin. He didn't run away. If I wasn't one of us, even *I* would have run away."

Kenlin quirked an eyebrow. "From me?"

"From us." He narrowed his eyes skeptically. She met his gaze for a few moments, then gave a small shrug and conceded, "From you. You were strange on that beach, Kenlin. We've been through a lot together, and I know you as well as anybody, but that was...strange."

"I won't disagree. It was at least as strange for me as it was for you."

She gave him a long, unconvinced look. "You very quickly grow comfortable with the strange."

Hahaha! Yes? "And? You don't seem too shaken yourself, Ranja."

"I suppose I'm not. After all, we did make it out alive." She adjusted her posture on the cot, groaning and wincing as her sore body protested. She sighed, "Or maybe I'm just too tired to worry about it right now."

"Can you move?" he asked, concerned.

She shrugged. "I think so, but not well. Can you?"

"Stiffly and shakily." He hesitated, then added, "I'm probably not in good condition to fight again *very* soon."

She paused at this. "I heard some of what you were saying to the...Wanderer, I suppose. I heard what you said we would... Are we having the brief conversation now?"

"Yes."

"He told you we would fail?"

"Yes."

"He's right, you know," she said, meeting Kenlin's eye and speaking frankly. "There's no chance—none—that we'll be able to recover Father from the Misks. As soon as we're discovered, they'll know what we're attempting; and if we ever come close enough to even threaten success, they'll kill him immediately rather than risk his escape."

Kenlin nodded slowly. *I understand.* "They'll kill him immediately. But at least they'll kill him quickly. Yes?"

"That's the idea," she whispered. Then, as though in response to her own words, a pang shot through her: her eyes squeezed shut, her mouth drew back into a grimace of intense pain, and her entire body trembled and tensed. She rolled onto her back and turned her face away from Kenlin, and the moment passed.

Kenlin remained still. He did not speak and he did not reach out to her; he simply sat in silence on the floor beside the cot, his hands resting lightly on his knees. They remained like this, in silence, for many minutes. Ranja's mind was restless, filled with fragments of slowly-crystallizing thoughts. Kenlin's mind, by contrast, was at peace—simmering, incoherent peace—for he was sure of all he cared to know about the future.

Eventually, Ranja asked, "Do you suppose he's already dead?"

Kenlin shook his head. "The Wanderer said he's alive. He's being held in the encampment we rode through last night on the eastern side of the city, according to the Faery."

"And you truly believe that was real?" Ranja queried, turning again to look Kenlin in the eye. "I know there are things we can't explain otherwise, and I know what it would mean to you—for you, about you—if you say, 'No.' But I have to ask: do you truly, honestly believe it?"

Do I? "Truly and honestly, Ranja," he said, thinking carefully, "I'm… I'm not sure I care. When I was talking to him, it *felt* real, and he told me things that I don't think I could have—don't think I *would* have imagined. But if he isn't real, then…I suppose that means I can't tell anymore. Either way, it's all the same to me."

She nodded slowly. "I heard you say he wanted us to go to Inajaz. He claims he's made some sort of enclave there?"

"Yes."

"But even if you were sure he's real, you wouldn't go."

"No. Among other objections, his notion of escaping annihilation via obscurity is probably doomed from the start, and my involvement certainly wouldn't help. I don't seem to be very good at avoiding notice; these days, I bring disaster with me everywhere I go."

She chuckled at that. "So we do. His best option, ironically, would be to follow in Viarlin's footsteps and pledge fealty to the Droál, continuing Jranjanan traditions while disincentivizing the Droál from sending any army at all."

Ha! "Well, I can tell him that when he comes back, if you want me to. Although I'd be careful about giving him ideas; he just might listen to them."

She smiled, but had more questions. "He agreed to come back, then? He agreed to help us?"

Kenlin nodded. "Such as he can from where he is. He wants us to survive long enough to change our minds about coming to Inajaz."

"Good," she said, closing her eyes and nodding. "I don't understand him either. But if there's any chance he can help us get close to Father... Good."

"I thought that would be your reaction," Kenlin commented. "I asked him to return in a few hours, so we can include him in any plans we have by then. And, judging by your manner, I'm guessing the plan *isn't* going to be that we immediately leap to our feet and charge off into the night."

She raised an eyebrow curiously. "Would you?"

Now it was Kenlin's turn to laugh. *Why not?* "You know, I'd be willing to try it!" he crowed, laughing in and out and all around his head, freely and loudly until Ranja gave him a quizzical, slightly concerned look. "Oh, I might lurch a bit, and I certainly wouldn't sprint as far or as fast as I usually can. But I'll surely try it! Shall we?"

She smiled uncertainly and said, "I think we'll want to be a bit more methodical than that if we hope to succeed."

Do we hope that? That seems a dim light to hope by. Ha!

"But as for lurching," she continued, "I might do even worse than you would, Kenlin. Can you help me up? My legs feel like lead."

Wincing through his own soreness, Kenlin struggled to his feet and helped Ranja push herself up to a sitting position, her legs dangling limply over the side of the cot. She looked at her limbs in surprise as though she had expected feeling and energy to return to them just because she had sat upright. Tentatively, she leaned forward, put her weight on her exhausted feet, and slowly rose to standing. As she stood there wobbling on sore soles, she looked at Kenlin and said, "*Now* the Droál should be afraid." Kenlin laughed freely again, toppling back on the floor and laughing to the roof above and the sky beyond. Ranja, chuckling ruefully, plopped back down on the cot and rubbed her hands over her thighs. As Kenlin's laughter gave way to mirthful sighs, Ranja concluded, "I think we have no choice but to rest, and I don't think just an hour or two will be enough. Getting near Father will require both of us, and I'm useless right now."

I can't disagree, but, "How long, then? How long can we—and Klanjad—afford to wait?"

Ranja shrugged. "A day, maybe? They've had Father for a half-day already; either they've killed him by now, or we believe your Wanderer and they haven't. If they haven't, then there must be some reason for them to keep him alive, right? So as long as we act before their reason expires, then we have a chance to reach him before... You know."

"'...there must be some reason...' That's pretty nonspecific, especially for you. What do you suppose some reason might be?"

She tossed her head impatiently. "How should I know, Kenlin? Perhaps they want to display him to boost the morale of their armies, or to break the morale of their enemies. Perhaps they want to use him to further their position in negotiations, either as a bargaining chip or as a reminder of how powerful they are. Perhaps they want to torture him for information about his operations and contacts in the southwest. Or perhaps Skralade, or whoever, has some special plan in mind because of how long Father has been an impediment to them." With each new alternative her tone became quicker and sharper, and little hints of frenzy began to show through her manner. "Are you really going to make me continue?"

"No, I get the idea. There are many possibilities, we can't do more than speculate about them, and each is somehow worse than the one before."

"Precisely."

"And the longer we wait, the greater the risk one of those possibilities might become real. So... A day?"

She nodded solemnly. "A day. We'll recover at least a little, and then—"

At a sound from outside, both Jazeiz instantly whirled and tensed. Kenlin moved quickly and quietly toward where Klanjad's sword leaned against the wall by the hearth; Ranja, spying her glaive beside the sword, hissed for Kenlin to toss it to her. From outside, however, Ataland's voice called, "I'm sure you're still here 'cause I can smell you and hear you, and I'm sure you can hear me 'cause I'm not being quiet. So please, *please* don't try to kill me when I walk through this door. I'm a nice person. Look, I even brought you food!" The door opened just wide enough to admit Ataland's hand, which held two dead rabbits by the ears.

Kenlin, upon recognizing Ataland's voice, had immediately decided to let him in. Ranja, in contrast, had instantly recalled every suspicion she'd had of the half-Unnatilz. The rabbits, however, introduced a new and compelling reason for her to ignore her suspicions, at least temporarily. With a sigh that Kenlin guessed was at least partly theatrical, she said, "Oh, alright then. Come in."

Ataland pushed the door open and stepped in, blanching at the sight of the fire. He kept his right eye squeezed shut as he stepped forward and handed the rabbits to Kenlin. As he took them, Kenlin asked, "Is something wrong with your eye?"

"Nope," Ataland replied. "Just a few things too right with it. Fire hurts to look at for Unnatilz."

"But only with your right eye," Ranja noted. "Does your left eye not hurt?"

"Only if I poke it," Ataland quipped. He then explained, "It's one of the many wonderful benefits of being me. One in a glut of half-Unnatilz is born with mixed eyes. Most of us see either like humans do, lights and colors and such, or like Unnatilz do, hots and fasts and such. But a few, like me, are able to see both ways; and fewer still, again like me, have mixed eyes, meaning one fully Unnatilz eye and one fully human eye: in my case the right and left, respectively."

"Is that why you weren't afraid to swim?" Ranja deduced. "I wondered about it at the time, but there were more pressing matters. It's because you can see underwater like humans can, right?"

Peering at her dubiously, Ataland answered, "Right... Although, unless my eye is less human-ish than I think it is, humans can't really see underwater very well; it's pretty blurry. Between you and me, I think the Unnatilz-fear-water thing is more about smell and upbringing than anything else. When they really want to, Unnatilz actually can learn to swim, and a very few have. Don't go telling them that, though; diving into water is, by far, the best way to avoid getting thrashed if there's an angry Unnatilz after you."

"We have a little experience in that arena," Kenlin said with a vague smile. "Anyway, I apologize if it hurts your eyes, but I'm going to need the fire to cook these rabbits."

Ataland shrugged lightly. "Well, do what you have to do. I'll tell you, though, they are *exquisite* when raw."

Ranja made a disgusted noise in her throat but did not otherwise reply. Kenlin, having hunted for most of his life, had of course tasted raw game meat on a few occasions, though it was not a taste he preferred. For some time there was silence as Kenlin gutted, skinned, and portioned the rabbits. (Ataland declined to be given any of the meat, stating that he'd already eaten his fill; however, he did select a few choice morsels from among the discarded entrails, much to

Ranja's revulsion.) Ataland found another stoneware pot in a nearby building, whereupon Kenlin, lacking both ingredients and patience, partly filled the pot with water, added the rabbit, and placed the ensemble directly into the fire to boil.

Yet it would still be at least half an hour before the meat could be plausibly described as *cooked*. Kenlin, tending the fire and the food, was content to sit in silence, but Ranja still had doubts about their companion. After only a few minutes of thoughtful quiet, she said to him, "Let's talk about you, Ataland."

"Nah," he answered dismissively. "That's boring, I already know all about that. Let's talk about you two. You're cousins, right?"

"I think you know a lot more about us than we know about you," Ranja countered; though her words were unyielding, she kept her tone mild and courteous. "You grew up in Garna; why did you leave?"

Ataland shrugged. "Lots of little things. Mostly, though, I just had no reason to stay."

"Did you not have family there?"

"Still do, probably."

"I see. So family was not a reason to stay; was it a reason to leave?"

"I think you Jazeiz have a very skewed idea of what that word means," Ataland said, frowning thoughtfully. "In Garna, *family* doesn't really matter in the way you two seem to think it does. Unnatilz don't marry like humans do, so everybody's probably related to everybody else, but it doesn't make any difference. Kinship is a fluid concept in Garna."

Evenly, Ranja said, "You haven't answered my question."

"Hya! Well, would you believe—"

"Yes," she interrupted abruptly. "I will believe what you tell me. Even if I find it hard to fathom, I will try. So with that in mind, what will you say?"

Ataland was momentarily taken aback. "Oh, you're good," he said, a grin slowly spreading across his face. "What will I say? I think… Honestly, given the choice, I think I will continue to not really say much."

Ranja sighed wearily. "Please don't be difficult, Ataland."

"I'm not," he said very earnestly. "I don't think you really care about how many siblings I have, what it's like to grow up in Garna, or why a half-Unnatilz might leave there to go see the world of his other half. I'll tell you innocuous stuff if you ask me. But what you really want to know is whether or not you can trust me, and that's not so easy to answer in a sentence."

"Especially if the sentence contains only innocuous answers," Ranja muttered.

Ataland wagged a finger at her. "Except I don't think that's true. Because why *wouldn't* you trust me? It should be plainly obvious to everybody that I'm not a physical threat to you, given the Tower and the Channel and so on."

"As a rule," Kenlin said, "we don't need reasons to *not* trust someone."

Ataland acknowledged this with a nod, but pressed on with his thought. "So if I'm not a physical threat, then what are you concerned I might do? I figure your only reasonable worry is that I'll learn something about you and then, someday, somewhere, I'll tell it to somebody who shouldn't know."

"That's a bit vague, but the thought had crossed my mind," Ranja confirmed.

Ataland nodded, then slowly began shaking his head. "I don't do that, though. I don't share secrets that aren't mine to tell. And yet, how can you know that's true? You can't, not without knowing me for a long time. But if I immediately start blabbing recklessly about all sorts of things, you might get the impression that I'm loose-lipped at least, even if I don't mean anything by it. So, in short, ask me your questions, and I'll think carefully before I do or don't answer them. Left to myself, though, I'll share only what I think is appropriate, when I think it's appropriate, all in my own good time."

To Kenlin's surprise, Ranja didn't seem put off by this at all. On the contrary, she had listened with growing receptiveness to Ataland's explanation, and by the conclusion she wore an expression that seemed rather impressed. After a short pause, she gave a single accepting nod: "That all makes sense. Well said."

Ataland furrowed his brow uncertainly. "Um… Thank you? What exactly have we established here?"

"That you might choose not to answer our questions," Ranja summarized coolly, "and that while your reticence may not help us trust you, we shouldn't necessarily think worse of you for it."

That must be the most tepid, qualified admission of a lack of mistrust that I've ever heard; and even so, it's more than I thought she would say. To Ataland, Kenlin said, "I, for one, reserve the right to think worse of you at any time for any or no reason at all."

Ataland threw back his head in laughter. "Hya-ha! You'll have to queue up behind everybody else, then! So, anyway… Now that we all agree that I'm okay to not answer, was there something specific you wanted to ask?"

Ranja gave a sarcastic, though not quite sour, shrug. "Should I bother? Never mind. You're still here, and I don't know why. Why are you still here, Ataland?"

He replied with a matching shrug which was probably intended to be playful rather than mocking. "Where else would I be? I was in jail, I didn't exactly have ongoing business to attend to."

"You didn't have plans for what you would do after you were released?"

"Plans? I remember plans. I had a plan once. It was traumatic. I was nine."

"And you have no family you want to return to?" Ranja pressed him. "Is there nowhere that you wanted to go?"

"No," Ataland replied, restraining his humor for a moment. "I'm sure you plan things all the time and have a thousand and one ideas for what you want to do. I don't. If you want to know why I'm still here, the honest answer is, 'Why not?'"

Ranja struggled with herself, but she seemed almost incapable of accepting such simplistic rationale. "But, Ataland... You put yourself in danger for us. Why did you go back up the Channel to look for Father? Why didn't you leave us as soon as Kenlin started talking to phantoms? Don't pretend you didn't consider it; you actually mentioned it at the time. And later, under the cliffs, we two were staggering and floundering through the waves; you could have easily outpaced us there, then slipped past the Misks or scaled the wall and disappeared into the city."

"You're right," Ataland answered in a tone that was somehow equally serious and casual. "I could have easily outpaced you, or climbed something, or slipped through, or whatever. And that's just what it would have been: easy. See, I didn't really put myself in danger for you—not much, anyway—because once we got out of the Tower, there was never a time when I couldn't just jump to my feet and leg it, and not you nor anybody else could've done a thing to stop me. I got my own stupid self thrown into that prison, but even the guards in the Tower couldn't have caught me if I hadn't drunk myself senseless first. That's who I am: uncatchable. Always have been and always will be, until the one day when I'm finally not."

Ranja was frowning thoughtfully as though trying to remember something. "That's the 'prey god' alignment, right? Not Ondumazil's god, Andulaird; the other one."

Ataland started, clearly impressed. "Right, Nagelun. You've got some broad knowledge, Ranja. Not many humans know anything about Unnatilz culture, and nobody's heard of Nagelun."

Kenlin was completely lost. "What are we talking about?"

"The Unnatilz pantheon has a prominent pair of deities called Andulaird and Nagelun," Ranja explained. "Andulaird, the 'perfect hunter,' is the quintessential Unnatilz ideal, and by and large Unnatilz 'align' themselves with him. But his counterpart Nagelun, the 'perfect prey,' is much less well-known."

"The *other* god," Ataland said, nodding.

"I didn't even know the Unnatilz had a pantheon," Kenlin commented.

Ataland bobbed his head nonchalantly. "Many care a lot about that sort of thing, many others don't. Personally, I like the stories. But I've always figured that, if the hunt really is eternal and he still hasn't killed her yet, then Andulaird must be a lot worse at this than Nagelun is. I used to tell people that just to nark them up, and some would get so mad that they'd try to thrash me. Funny thing, though, that used to make them madder than ever: not a one of them could catch me."

Ranja's eyebrows rose. "Were these other half-Unnatilz that you were provoking? Or are you claiming that you used to voluntarily annoy, and then routinely outrun, angry *Unnatilz?*"

A broad grin had come over Ataland's face. He didn't answer directly, but said, "I think it affects your perspective, that. I don't worry about things the way other people seem to. I don't bother much about risks and plans and whatnot because in the end, if everything goes to shit, it doesn't really matter to me: I'll just jump up and leg it."

Ranja managed to not roll her eyes, though it clearly took effort. Kenlin, however, heard a note in the half-Unnatilz's voice that seemed familiar. "Does it make you curious," he said, "to wonder just what kinds of pursuers you can outrun? If you've never been caught, at least not without the help of your own carelessness... If you've never hit your limit... Does it make you want to know? Does it make you want to…do something crazy, maybe, just to see if you can get away with it?"

Kenlin hadn't planned to say that; the words had jumped to his lips unbidden, spurred by the same impulsiveness that had changed his mollifications to challenges during his conversation with the Wanderer. Ranja and Ataland both turned to him curiously, Ranja with a look of puzzled concern and Ataland with a look of… *Does he feel it? Or do I now hear my own thoughts in the words of others?* Ataland hesitated for several moments, frowning thoughtfully. At last, he said, "I don't…know. I don't think that way, but… I don't know."

"Then would you like to find out?" The look Ranja gave Kenlin was more concerned than before, but he ignored it. "Would you like to stay with us? We're making plans to do something reckless soon—something crazy. I suspect you've already guessed it: we're going to find Klanjad."

As Ranja sighed and swallowed her exasperation, Ataland said, "Hya! That's not a plan even by my standards. I assume there's a bit more to it than that?"

"Not much. The phantom, the one I speak to in magic, has agreed to help us. Beyond that, we have little information and no time to gather more. If we wait too long, Skralade will have Klanjad moved beyond our reach, one way or another. So we're going to take tonight, and probably the day tomorrow, to rest and prepare ourselves. Then as the sun sets, we'll return to Ñaj-Gadan, find out where Klanjad is being held, and see how close we can get."

Ataland furrowed his brow, confused. "You know that's not going to work, right? There are umpty-ump thousand Droál soldiers there, and Misks and Necromancers besides; and even if you did manage to get to him, they're hardly going to have him trussed up in ribbon and guarded by a housecat."

"We know," Ranja said. "We know we can't really free him—at least, not in that way. All we need to do is get close."

"Oh..." Ataland's eyes grew wide as he realized what she meant. "This is about the burning thing, isn't it? You *want* them to kill him?"

"I don't—" Ataland had chosen his words poorly, but Ranja stopped herself and let it pass. "Yes, it's about the burning thing. It's a long story, but I made a promise to Father. I won't let them do that to him."

Ataland looked to Kenlin. "Is this some kind of Jazei death pact? Did you make this promise too?"

Kenlin grinned incongruously, and a little of the quiet laughing in his head escaped as an audible chuckle. "No," he said dismissively, "but I have nowhere else to be. Do you?"

Ataland hesitated, thinking very seriously for rather longer than Kenlin had expected. After nearly a minute of silence, he asked Ranja, "Is this what he would have wanted? Your father, I mean."

Ranja opened her mouth to reply, then faltered. She took a long, shuddering breath and whispered, "This is all that I can do for him."

Ataland nodded very slowly, comprehending. "Okay. No promises about how far I'll go; whenever I want to run, I'll run. But at least to start with... Okay. I'll come."

The meal, at last, was fully cooked, and Kenlin turned from the silence that followed to remove the pot from the fire and the meat from the pot. As he worked with his back to his companions, he heard Ranja say quietly, "Back in the Channel, the first time I asked you why you were trying to help us, you asked if I would believe that you admired my father."

"That's right." After several moments, he said, "I'm sorry."

A few more moments passed. "Thank you."

CHAPTER XXXIII:

Kenlin relayed their decision to the Wanderer when the phantom returned. The Faery tried one last time to convince Kenlin to come directly to Inajaz, but without success. Disappointed again, he listened to the plan they had made and reaffirmed his agreement to help.

The plan, if it could be called that, was simple: they would use the horses and Droál cloaks they had acquired during their escape to try to pass unnoticed through the encampment west of Ñaj-Gadan. The Wanderer, unhappy with the idea, had suggested that they look for an alternative route, perhaps north around the lake; however, as Ranja pointed out, any such journey would take far too long, giving the Droál too much time to move or immolate Klanjad. Reluctantly, then, the Faery agreed to help them try to reach Ñaj-Gadan by masking Kenlin's presence with phantoms. This magical masking, along with their cloaks, might at best conceal them as far as the western gate, but not beyond. Inevitably they *would* be discovered, at which point Kenlin would use his magic to push forward as far as he could, then turn aside as a diversion while Ranja and Ataland continued in stealth. "And when you have drawn sufficient attention, then you will flee?" the Wanderer asked piercingly. "You will not wait to be overwhelmed; you will retreat once your companions are away from your diversion?"

"Yes, Wanderer. Once Ranja and Ataland are away from the danger, I will retreat in the opposite direction."

But he was lying, and though the Wanderer accepted his statement, Kenlin wondered if he knew. Ranja and Ataland would probably never be "away from the danger," so Kenlin would continue his diversion for as long as he could. He probably wouldn't be able to endure for long: the Droál had insurmountable force and would likely react to the Jazei incursion speedily and decisively. Neither Ranja nor Kenlin was expecting to survive. *Ha! But which is the fool who thinks that he'll kill me? I'll clean his blood from Klanjad's sword with the guts of the fool behind him!*

He dismissed the wavering, niggling parts of his mind that still fretted and hesitated. *Enough! There is no more place for hesitation; there is no wisdom in restraint. Tonight is the night to be eager and wild.* Before they had departed, while Ataland was busy elsewhere, Ranja had bid Kenlin a sincere and solemn farewell. The ride, the plan, the entire expedition was saturated with an air of deliberate finality that was *oh, so liberating!*

Their plan was to reach the Droálic encampment at dusk, or shortly thereafter. By the time they arrived, the Wanderer's phantoms would hopefully have sowed enough confusion among the Misks that Kenlin's un-Faded presence would go unmarked. So it was just before dusk that they donned their Droálic cloaks, mounted their horses, and left the cottage; then, as dusk mixed with true night, their horses brought them at last to the guarded entrance of the encampment.

Deep trenches had been dug on either side of the road and the dirt piled behind into an embankment, but whether for lack of trees to make an abatis or for lack of a threat to make it necessary, the embankments were not otherwise fortified. Likewise, no gate was built across the roadway, and protection of the entrance was solely the responsibility of a handful of inattentive, lazy-looking guards. From what Kenlin could sense, there were no Misks nearby to pose a threat— nor could he sense phantoms either. *Odd.* These guards alone, then, were to be the night's first trial, the very first place where they might be discovered and accosted. "Be patient," Ranja had advised earlier. "We know little of their customs and nothing of their language, but I know enough Misk that I just might be able to bluff our way through a few checkpoints before we have to fight."

Patience. Ha!

But there was nothing else for it: they must at least try to enter the camp without fighting, and he had no better idea. So he sat as calmly he could astride his horse, disguised by the Droálic cloak, as Ranja led the three of them right up to the encampment's entrance. Just beyond the embankment was a makeshift stables with several horses inside; and as the Jazeiz approached, though the bored and shiftless guards hardly glanced up, two hostlers stepped forward to take charge of their mounts.

Do they not permit horses to be ridden through their camp? Time for that bluff, Ranja, lest they expect us to dismount and explain ourselves. That would end poorly.

Ha! For them.

As the hostlers approached, one reaching for Ranja's horse while the other came toward Kenlin, Ranja looked down on him and said disdainfully, "Zale jalj-maz, joti. Maztiel idue tida, va daztidei kidiaiz." *Well, that didn't work.* Evidently her command meant as little to the hostlers as to Kenlin. The one near Ranja's horse looked over his shoulder in confusion, wondering if she was talking to someone else; the second, ignoring her, continued toward Kenlin.

Ranja, if you have a plan... She tried again—"Zatarshi! Taiei ma? Jiliei, zateta!"—but it was no use: the hostlers clearly spoke no Misk, and Ranja's unintelligible exhortations did nothing to dissuade them from their duties. *Get away from me, ass!* Both hostlers had now reached the horses. The one near Ranja babbled something in an unfamiliar language clearly requesting the reins, which she coldly refused to surrender. The one near Kenlin was more forward; approaching the horse's head, he actually took hold of the reins where they joined the headstall, tugging as though to pull them away from Kenlin.

Get away! As though on its own impetus, Kenlin's foot lashed forward viciously, catching the unsuspecting hostler in the face and smashing his nose. The man cried out in pain and fright as he fell backward, clutching his bleeding face. The other hostler stepped back in alarm, the shiftless guards started and scrambled to their feet, and even Ranja and Ataland rounded toward Kenlin in astonishment.

But nobody acted. A moment passed, and then another, and nobody said a word; the only sound was of the bleeding, broken-nosed hostler groaning through his hands. *Ha! They have no idea what to do, and neither do we. So...what now?*

As the shocked silence continued, Kenlin turned his hooded head toward the hostler who still stood beside Ranja's horse. Though the hood and the darkness hid the emerald eyes, the frightened man quailed immediately beneath Kenlin's shadowed gaze. *Hahaha! Yes, fear me, coward!* The situation was under no one's control, but Kenlin had the momentum. His reckless confidence rising, he spurred his horse to a slow, sauntering walk and continued forward with the air of one utterly beyond question. The terrified hostler fled before him, and even the guards, perhaps supposing that they were now in the presence of a high-ranking and singularly ill-tempered Necromancer, stood in nervous indecision, each waiting for someone else to raise an objection. Kenlin turned his hooded stare toward them; no objection was raised. *And that's well for you. Ha! You wouldn't have liked my next response. Hahaha!*

Ranja and Ataland followed Kenlin's example, and the three pressed on past the checkpoint at an irreproachable, unhurried walk. But once they were beyond earshot of the guards, Ranja quickly spurred her horse alongside Kenlin's. "That was different," she hissed in slightly disconcerted surprise. "Whatever possessed you to do that?"

"I don't know, there weren't many options," Kenlin answered lightly, amused by her tone. *Incredulous? Ha! That's fair; I wouldn't have thought that would work either.* "They did let us through, though; apparently my foot made an impression."

Shaking her head, she admonished, "That was too risky, Kenlin, much too risky."

Risky! You know where we are, yes? Risky! None of us will survive this night, Ranja. Risky? He turned to say some quip or other about the irony of her concern, but the reproach of being too risky was so preposterous that, when he opened his mouth, all that came out was a poorly repressed, incredulous guffaw.

As he laughed, she seemed to reconsider her reproof and nodded concedingly. "Alright, you've make your point," she said, and yet Kenlin couldn't stop cackling. "Don't laugh at me, Kenlin!"

"Sorry," he answered, still grinning. "It was just a funny comment, that's all."

"Well, ha ha."

Having managed to enter the camp without causing alarm, they did not expect to be challenged again until they reached the city gates, unless a Misk or magician became suspicious of Kenlin's presence. *As if! I can't sense them; it's unthinkable that they'd be able to sense me. And yet… No, I sense no one, no one at all. No Misks, no magicians, no Necromancy…and no phantoms. Where is everybody?*

From the horse behind them, Ataland said, "Am I the only one getting the feeling that this camp is just a little too, uh…empty?"

"What do you mean?" Ranja asked, though she was surely already considering this.

"Well, for one thing, where's the food?" Ataland pointed out. "Gobs of tents here, no imminent threats, the city's already taken, and the sun just set. This whole place should smell like the inside of a pub right now, and yet I smell less food than I would expect at a hog rush. There's nobody here, folks; or, at least, there's a lot less people here than there should be for a camp this size."

Ranja sighed. "I know. I was thinking something similar."

"That means you have theories," Kenlin noted idly.

She shot him a glance, annoyed by his insouciance, but she chose to overlook it. "Well, I think we can discount the possibility that this emptiness is due to attrition in the battle. There are simply too many empty tents here for that, and the casualties would have been concentrated in the east anyway. With that in mind, I can think of two places they might reasonably have gone. Their commanders might have allowed them into the city to ransack and pillage it; if so, that should be immediately obvious once we get through the gates. Alternatively, there's a chance that Jendraski actually succeeded in breaking through the siege here on the western flank. If he did that, he would likely lead whatever troops he had left northwest around the lake, and it's possible that the army encamped here might have given chase."

"That might explain where all their magicians went," Kenlin commented.

Ranja frowned. "There aren't any magicians here *at all?* No Misks?"

"None. Nobody."

She was taken aback. "Do you think... Were they all distracted away by the Wanderer and his 'phantoms?'"

"I doubt it. I don't sense any of his phantoms either."

Now she was alarmed. "So you really sense *no one*, then? Kenlin... Is your sense of magic impaired somehow? I mean, eyes can be dazed or blinded, and ears can ring. Can the magic—"

"My magic is better than ever," Kenlin declared, cutting her off. *Sometimes you think too much, Ranja.* "Why are you distressing yourself about this? We can see plainly, with our eyes, that the army has obviously gone somewhere. And if the army marched, wouldn't it want its magicians to go with it?"

"Yes, but if you don't sense the Wanderer—"

"And why *would* his phantoms be here? To confound an empty camp with no Misks in it? Assuming he came here earlier as a phantom, why would he stay once he realized there was no one who could sense him?"

His dismissiveness was clearly frustrating her—*Haha!*—but again she chose to ignore it. "So if he came here and found nothing, why didn't he alert you? Why didn't he try to contact you while we were on the road?"

"Who knows?" *Who cares?* "Maybe he didn't find out until near dusk. Maybe he's just having trouble finding us; I don't know how one navigates as a phantom. But again, why are you so worried about this, Ranja? There are no magicians here—no Misks, no Necromancy, no Unnatilz magicians... In short, we'll have a much easier time passing through this camp than we had thought, but you're acting like that's a bad thing. What was it you said to me once? 'Don't let yourself overthink it.'"

An angry retort rose to Ranja's lips, but she checked it. *Such needless self-control.* After a moment, she spoke quietly, but with heat still rippling beneath her voice: "If the Droál are moving armies about, then they might have moved Father. If that's happened, then we might be heading in the wrong direction. If you could ask the Wanderer—"

"But I can't. He's not here. So with *all of that* taken into consideration, we still don't know anything except that the next step of our original plan is going to be a little easier. So how—and on what basis—do you want to change the plan?"

She was very angry now. In a tense, dangerously low voice, she growled, "Stop interrupting me, Kenlin."

Haha! She doesn't have an answer. I—

He shook himself. Why was he interrupting her? There was no need for it. "I'm sorry, Ranja."

Ha!

She was not placated, but she let the subject drop, and they journeyed on in silence. As they continued, the encampment around them was so empty that, before long, the road became hard to see for lack of nearby fires. Thankfully, the horses still seemed to see well enough, and Kenlin and

Ranja simply allowed the beasts to carry them forward, step by step, toward the looming walls of Ñaj-Gadan. They were still on the main road that connected the outlying towns to the city's main western gate, but the encampment was so large that it seemed an age before the gate loomed at last before them. Visually, this gate was nearly identical to its counterpart in the eastern city. The road approached it only after passing through a narrowing gap between two outstretched arms of the fortifications. However, while the approach in the east had been naught but a killing field thickly littered with the newly dead, some effort at least had been made to clear the carnage away from this road. There were fewer corpses here, and a small number of living persons (presumably those tasked with removing the dead) had even pitched their tents beside or on the roadway. But whatever efforts were being made, they were too little and too late, for the entire area already reeked of gore and rot.

Yet the cleanup efforts continued despite the sickening stench; even at this late hour, there were workers loading corpses into carts and viscera into baskets. The workers looked up curiously as the Jazeiz passed. *Who would be travelling now, they wonder? What Necromancers would ride in a party of three? Take care, drudges, to ask only questions you wish answered—and pray that you never find out who I am.*

The gate, when they reached it, was opened wide. *And why not? These are the armies of the almighty, all-conquering Droál. Haha! What have they to fear?* However, a full contingent of twelve soldiers was guarding the entrance, and these did not seem half so lethargic as the ones guarding the camp. At the approach of the Jazeiz, the bronze-clad soldiers quickly leapt to their feet and formed a line across the road, blocking the entrance to the city. One of their number, a lieutenant of some sort, stepped forward and raised one hand in a firm but unaggressive challenge: "G'us iste kane kun nyalpaad."

That's easy for you to say.

Ranja, of course, couldn't speak so much as a word of the Droálic language; *such a shame that these cloaks can only effectively disguise us as Necromancers.* Nevertheless, she gamely tried again with the tools at her disposal: "Jaledi zalida. Maztida jaj tediril Skralade."

Even after so few words, the lieutenant was obviously surprised and concerned at being addressed in Misk. *Well, this is looking to be about as successful as it was an hour ago, and I'm not near enough to kick any faces this time. Do something, Ranja, before he becomes too suspicious and then...and then...*

And then what? Hahaha! What can he actually do?

The lieutenant, narrowing his eyes in concern and surprise, replied uncertainly to Ranja, "Uh... Jel-Misk. Jel-Misk." Behind him, his soldiers exchanged nervous glances.

And yet, doggedly, Ranja pressed on with her hopeless bluff. "Jaj zaztadesk? Maztalok kedrei ñaj-Eyjazinka, uien... Kenlin?"

For, acting on blind, reckless impulse, Kenlin had slid from his horse and walked wordlessly toward the bronze-clad lieutenant. *Still no one? There are these, and probably a few more somewhere to relieve them when their watch ends, and the corpse workers...* He was within a few steps of the lieutenant, whose alarm was growing with every step Kenlin took. *Is there really no one else? No Necromancers, no Misks, no magicians of any kind? No one who could stop me from doing, say...this!*

In a blur of magic, Kenlin threw off his cloak, ripped Klanjad's sword from where he'd tied it to his belt, and rammed the blade straight through the soldier's armored belly until his blood spurted and ran over the hilt. *Hahahaha! That's it? Is that all you're worth, Droál?* As the terrified, tortured man shrieked and clutched at the blade that impaled him, Kenlin looked back toward Ranja and, with a bemused shrug, explained himself: "No Misks."

Her jaw had fallen open in blank, incredulous shock. It was not a flattering expression, and for a moment she looked so funny that Kenlin couldn't help but throw back his head to laugh and laugh and "Hahahahaha!" He spun, Faded, slipped the sword from the gut of the dying lieutenant, and launched himself eagerly at the panicking soldiers beyond.

Slow down!

No, faster.

What am I—

Ha! Too many questions, too many hesitations. Not tonight!

There was no fight and there was no chase; the bronze-clad soldiers were slaughtered where they stood, most collapsing in butchered agony before they could even comprehend the foe they faced. As they wailed and retched in the dirt, Kenlin casually twirled Klanjad's sword, watching blood run down the blade and spray from the tip. *Well, this is just too easy! Oh, this is a good start; tonight will be a very good night.*

"Do you hear me, Kenlin? Get on the damn horse and ride before someone comes!" It was Ranja's voice, and *why so irate?* She had ridden forward, bringing Kenlin's horse alongside her, and now she threw the reins at his face before spurring her horse into a canter and charging away through the gate.

Ataland, who had much less control over his horse, had fallen behind Ranja and came up beside Kenlin a moment later. As Kenlin picked up his discarded cloak and mounted the horse, he noticed idly that the half-Unnatilz stayed a few arm-lengths out of reach. "What's going on?" Ataland asked with controlled alarm. "Is this a new plan? This doesn't seem like what we'd discussed before."

"New plan? Ha! Why? You don't think this is going well?" And so saying, he spurred his horse and followed Ranja into Ñaj-Gadan.

She had stayed on the main road but had only slowed down to wait after several hundred yards. *Giving space to see if I'll get caught by a Droál response? Not unreasonable; she hasn't accepted that the only strength they've left here is really quite pathetic. Or, rather, it used to be pathetic. Hahahaha!* When Kenlin reached where she waited, she seemed to expect him to stop, but he merely slowed his horse to a quick walk and continued past her. "Coming along?" he teased cheekily as he passed.

The night's darkness hid her expression, but Kenlin could imagine it. "Kenlin, stop right now. I said *stop!*" she suddenly yelled, leaning far out of her saddle and snatching the reins of his horse. "What are you *doing?* Were you listening at all, or have you completely forgotten the plan? Go as far as possible by *stealth*, try to *avoid* attracting attention and causing commotion...?"

Kenlin affected an affronted frown, but inside he felt *very easy.* "That's not fair, Ranja: I listened, I remember. But your plan wasn't working and they were getting suspicious. So I killed them, and thus far that seems to be a *much* more straightforward approach."

She was so shocked and unnerved that she didn't even acknowledge his point. "Have you lost your mind? You didn't consult me *at all*, you used magic against them, what in the *Depths*—"

Stop it, don't chortle. Why is her anger funny? But he laughed nonetheless; he couldn't help it. "I told you before, Ranja: no Misks. Nor were there magicians nor Necromancers; wherever the army went, they took *everybody.* So yes, I used magic against them. What could they do about it, scream for help? From whom? You think the corpse drudges would dare to come near me after seeing what I did to the soldiers?"

Ranja had listened with growing disbelief. "Who *are* you?" she retorted angrily. "Are you actually *enjoying* this? Kenlin, this is no time to suddenly develop a bloodlust."

He laughed again. *Don't! Why not?* "Why not, Ranja? 'Suddenly develop.' Would that surprise you? Haha! Why? I'm the one who recklessly shouted from a clifftop without a second thought. I'm the one who shot Skralade with an arrow that could just as easily have hit you. I killed the ambushers in Slionte, I was first to the bridge two nights ago, I broke through the Misk line——"

"I know all that," Ranja yelled furiously. "I was there. But this isn't like you! All of a sudden you're making unilateral decisions, jumping into fights without thinking, attacking people left and right and laughing like an *idiot* while you put our entire plan in jeopardy!"

Oh, enough about the plan. "Stop pretending you had a better idea," he countered dismissively. "As compelling as I find your impression of a Necromancer who only speaks Misk, the guards weren't fooled. And even if they had been, what I did didn't jeopardize anything. *No Misks*, Ranja. Nobody who matters heard them scream. Nobody's coming. Stop worrying."

She didn't answer, and it was too dark for Kenlin to read her thoughts in her face. *Ha! Well, she'll do as she pleases.* He took back the reins of his horse and spurred it back to a quick walk. Ranja followed, and Ataland fell in behind. After a few moments, Ranja asked warily, "You really sense no one at all? *Still?* Are you *certain* that nobody sensed your magic?"

Of course I'm certain. But, indulging her, he concentrated for a moment and, to his surprise, sensed a faint, flickering presence on the very edge of his perception. "Well, well! There *might* be someone who sensed me, but he's surprisingly far away, and he's no threat to us regardless."

She needed hardly a moment to parse this. "You sense the Wanderer? Where?"

"Back there," Kenlin said, gesturing pointlessly in the dark. "I can hardly sense him myself, so either he's very far away or his presence is somehow weakened. I think he might be on the western road, perhaps doing..." *Something. Does it matter?*

The night hid Ranja's thoughtful frown, but he could hear it in her voice. "And there are no other magicians you can sense, back there or anywhere else? Not even..."

Not even... Oh. "The Wanderer said he's on the other side of the city, Ranja. Even I can't sense things *that* far away. Don't invent reasons to unsettle yourself."

"You are *very* imperious tonight," Ranja chided acidly. "Then if you're so cocksure, why has the Wanderer sent a phantom behind us if there are no magicians there for him to distract? Too many strange things are happening, Kenlin, too many things I don't understand. If you understand them so well that you aren't concerned, then by all means enlighten me!"

Ah, Ranja! "Ranja, you know I haven't a clue what the Wander's doing; but I also know there's nothing I can do about it. So why worry? Unless..." *Hahahahaha!* "Unless you want me to try to ask him? I could ask him! I don't know if he can sense me at this distance; actually, he's in Inajaz, and I don't really know much at all about how his magic works. But if you like, I can try to Fade and shout as un-stealthily as possible, and maybe somehow he'll hear me and—"

"Stop it, Kenlin!" Ranja snapped, angry and upset, but lacking a real counterargument. "Have it your way then: don't question, don't think. Forget I mentioned it."

Feeling a little sulky, yes? But he thought no more of it; *that's what she asked me to do.* And after all, there *was* no better option for them at this point than to continue as planned. Any other choice would be to abandon their current course just because it was going too well. *And that would just be silly! Hahaha!*

Kenlin was careless, Ranja was resentful, and Ataland was wary and silent as they continued their journey deeper into Ñaj-Gadan. The surrounding towns had been nigh abandoned—uncounted thousands had fled upon the unexpected arrival of the Droál—but the city itself was far from empty. The start of the siege had been too unexpected for any sort of urban evacuation, so everyone living in Ñaj-Gadan had been trapped. Those in the eastern city two days ago had been caught between the fighting and the fires. The western city, however, had been almost untouched by either, for no major conflict had taken place here. In a single terrible night half the city had burned, the surviving garrison was gone, and everyone remaining in Ñaj-Gadan had been left defenseless, abandoned, forgotten. Yet the sun had risen after that terrible night, and there was food to be cooked and water to be carried, and people met each other in the streets to guess in hushed voices about what was to become of them now. Like a feebly twitching cadaver, the city continued to barely function in a ghoulish imitation of its former vibrancy, where purpose was replaced with mindless habit shrouded in a lingering, stagnant dread. The very streets and buildings seemed to hover in a limbo, uncertain whether the world was ending tomorrow or yesterday, and even the candle-lit windows gazed vacantly out with the haunted stare of the condemned.

As the Jazeiz and Ataland continued through the city on horseback, merely the sound of their hoofbeats was enough to close doors, dim lights, and send frightened urchins scuttling out of sight. As they passed, faint hisses of conversation leaked through drafty walls and open windows. When they were gone, the curious would peer after them and murmur together about what their passage could mean. But that was all; from the hushed buildings and dark alleyways, no sound came except these varied whispers born from many shades of fear. "I don't hear ransacking, I don't see pillaging," Ataland commented at last. "Unless they've already retired and taken up residence, I don't think the missing Droál army is in the city."

"Thank you for your insight," Ranja answered him coldly, "but we can see that for ourselves."

"And so you can," said Ataland lightly, unconcerned by her hostility. "But the fact that they're not here eliminates one of your theories for where they've gone, right? You said if they didn't come here to loot, then the Old Bold probably made it out and the Droál went northwest to chase him."

Blankly, she said, "That's the best guess I have."

Ataland paused for a moment—just a moment where he might have been frustrated by her taciturnity—before he said, "*I* see what's happening. You've already thought through all this, haven't you? One of your ideas is confirmed, and you've already moved onto how the next—"

"No, I haven't," Ranja cut him off, her own frustration boiling over. "I don't know, Ataland; I don't have enough information! Even if the army did march northwest, it doesn't make sense that there weren't *any* magicians at the western gate, not unless the whole army's on the march; but if that were true, they should be trying to rebalance from the east also, and we should be wading *right now* through an endless column of Droálic soldiers trying to get to the western city. So no, Ataland: I don't understand, and I don't like it one bit. I had *hoped* Kenlin might be able to sense something that could give us at least a little more information, but evidently he can hardly sense anything tonight."

How did this end up being my fault? Resisting the urge to laugh at her temper, Kenlin quipped, "I offered to Fade and shout at the Wanderer if you wanted me to ask him for information." She did not dignify this with an answer. *Ha!* "But if you'd rather I didn't, there may be another opportunity for me to speak to him, although I *will* have to Fade. A short while ago, his phantom changed locations. I sense him ahead of us now—and up."

He was going to continue, but she beat him to his own thought. "At the Tower? He knows we have to pass through it; is he waiting for us?"

Hahaha! "Sure! For all I can tell, why not? So far, he hasn't done any of the things we thought he'd do this evening, but I can definitely say that I don't know for certain that he's *not* waiting—"

"Kenlin!" There was anger in her voice, but also a note of hurt that, at least for a moment, cut through Kenlin's flippancy. "Can you...?" She took a deep, shuddering breath, flushing some of the emotion from her voice. "Maybe you've forgotten—or maybe you don't care—what we're trying to do tonight. Or, at least, what *I'm* trying to do. I know he's not your father, but—"

"Don't!" *Don't. Don't say that to me.* Kenlin physically shook himself as though to clear his head of the intoxicating, unwelcome levity. "I'm sorry, Ranja. I... I don't know why the Wanderer is doing these things. But if his phantom *is* at the Tower, and if he's still there when we arrive, that will be an indication that he's waiting for us, as you thought. If that happens, and if I still sense no one else around who would detect me, then I'll Fade. I'll ask him what you want to know."

Though she was clearly struggling to suppress it, there was still bitterness in her voice when she at last managed to answer, "Thank you, Kenlin."

He muttered something in reply, but his mind was otherwise occupied. He was frowning to himself—at himself. *What is coming over me?*

. . .

The fire had done its job: the great Tower of Ñaj-Gadan stood empty and silent, its white marble edifice visible in the night only as a looming void amidst the stars. Inside the stone exterior, the wooden floors and walls had all been catastrophically burned. Passage through the Tower was still possible via a bridge of scaffolding that the Droál had erected after the fire, but no real attempt had been made to post soldiers there: even after two evenings, the air still smelled of acrid smoke.

Instead, the guards responsible for securing the Tower—
a token force, no more than a platoon of bronze-clad
infantry—had pitched their camp in the western plaza near
the head of the Leaping Bridge. Their role, it seemed, was
simply to maintain a presence and discourage any belligerent
citizens from trying to occupy the Tower or sabotage the
scaffold bridge within. But this was hardly a threat worth
fearing, and so the soldiers were not watchful. The few who
weren't sleeping when the Jazeiz arrived paid no attention to
the cloaked, silent strangers.

When they reached the open Tower door, Kenlin
dismounted and tested the scaffold bridge. It swayed
underfoot, and none of them felt confident trying to ride
across it, so they were forced to leave their mounts behind.
"Stay close," Ataland instructed in a whisper. "Remember, I
can see in this dark. The walkway's pretty rough, so you might
trip if you don't step high. Presumably they marched people
in armor across this thing, but still… Better we don't find out
what'll happen if one of us falls and lands on it hard."

Imaginary sounds flitted through Kenlin's mind—a trip,
a curse, a crashing mayhem— *Hahaha! What a ridiculous way
to die!*

What? No! That isn't funny.

… Isn't it?

Shaking his head as though dazed, he followed Ataland
into the utter blackness of the Tower. *What am I on about?*
Falling from a collapsing bridge was nothing to joke about,
not a laughing matter at all. *And yet, after so much…it would
be rather a silly way to die, yes?* He smiled the smallest of
smiles, but it immediately gave way to a bewildered frown,
which was just as quickly swept aside by dismissive frustration.
*Damn this introspection. How purposeless. So long as I laugh
in my head, why care for how tasteless the jokes may be?*

"Kenlin, can you hear me?" Ranja had to raise her voice
a little to cut through Kenlin's reverie, but when he finally
heard her, he shook himself free of his thoughts and listened.

"We're in the Tower now; can you sense phantoms here? You said the Wanderer might be waiting for us. What can you sense?"

I can sense... He'd been so self-absorbed that hadn't even been paying attention. *Useless!* "Yes, there's a phantom here, or near enough. He'll come to me if I Fade."

"And can you? Will you?" The way she stacked her overlapping questions showed just how overwrought she was.

"I don't sense anybody else, if that's what you mean, Ranja. But I don't want to stop right here. Let's get off all these bridges; then I'll Fade for him."

She raised no objection—*Good.*—and the three of them continued in silence across the remainder of the scaffolding and out onto the eastern half of the Leaping Bridge. *After the dark in the Tower, the starlight seems brighter. There, that hole near the side, that's where Klanjad fell. Really, it's remarkable that a bridge like this could sustain such damage and remain sturdy. I wonder what it would take to bring it down?*

... I could do it.

What?! How and why in the Depths would I—

Oh, I won't. Hahaha! But I could.

In the privacy of darkness, he smiled to himself.

As they crossed the bridge to the eastern plaza, it became apparent why the soldiers guarding the Tower had chosen to camp west of the chasm instead of here. The western plaza had been nearly pristine, for no battle had been fought there, but the eastern plaza was littered with corpses. The dark masked the gruesomeness of the scene, and the dead had not yet begun to smell; even so, it was easy to understand why the Droál would choose not to lay their bedrolls in the blood of their compatriots.

As soon as the Jazeiz set foot on the solid ground of the plaza, Ranja made an involuntary noise. *Yes, Ranja, calm down! Stop hounding me. I told you I'd Fade for him; I keep my word.* He opened his mouth to say something unnecessary, but caught himself at the last second. *Enough.* He Faded.

As always with magic, he dismissed from his thoughts the stable clarity of the world he knew, and his perception began to waver. Then he called to mind the bleak, empty memories of the simple Strata used for Fading, and they condensed before him. Sight and sound melded and muddied, and reality churned around him as it always did. He did not see the Wanderer immediately, but mere moments passed before the familiar magical haze was cut through by the unmistakable sound of a death rattle.

A moment later, the visage of the phantom appeared as it had before, but tonight the apparition was ghastly. No longer was the vision indistinct: the Faery stood stark and clear, bleached with the pallor of death. Gone was the gentle glow, the soft golden light from unseen sources, and gone was the placid aura of his presence. The thing that stood before Kenlin tonight was as white as moonlit ice, his hair whipped about by unseen winds, his posture tensed with pain as his legs trembled, struggling to keep him upright on uneven ground. "We are undone, Jazei," gasped the phantom, wild-eyed. "It is already too late."

Kenlin's mouth fell open, aghast. He reached for words, but he had none. *What in the Depths…?*

Without warning, the phantom loosed a horrific, anguished cry of pain and despair—Kenlin flinched at the awful sound—but the Faery's voice warped even as it cried out, twisting into a memory, a telling, a babbling and inane echo of the art that had been the Faery's life.

> I remember for them all I am, all that was, that they may too remember and that *they* be not forgot. And they hear me in the commons, and they love to hear the stories, so I tell them, and I teach them, and I wander onward happy, for my words as tales stay on.

We are safe, Jazei! Strong, Jazei! We are sturdy in the mountains, for I sow my stories widely, and Jranjanan tales can flourish in the harshness of the highlands—

"Kenlin, are you alright? What's happening?"

"Ranja, I..." *One above!* As the Wanderer careened through his narrative, he slowly turned away as though half-consciously trying to show Kenlin... *Two wounds midway down the back, just to the right of the spine, the blade held at an angle... Somebody stabbed for his liver, then stabbed for it again. Whoever it was knew their knife: an assassin, or perhaps a healer. Someone has murdered the Wanderer.* As Kenlin looked on, the wounds, which at first had appeared unnaturally clean and clear, suddenly gushed forth a river of blood and gall that drenched the Wanderer's pallid flesh from back to heel before fading away to pool on unseen ground. *One above...*

—but lies! Lies! I lied to them, cheated them! I never intended— Perhaps it was chance? No! They're here; I knew naught of them!

A threat? Or a greed? Or a dare? Or a madness that drives him to murder. He takes him a knife from the house of his mother, the tools of his father, the toys of his brother; wherever he found it, he knows— Has he done it before? Ah! So true is his strike and so stealthy his treason— To murder the Teller! To silence the stories! He weeps for me, wails for me, stabs me again! Aaah! I flee up the mountain; he does not pursue me—

"Kenlin, what is—?"

"Ranja, *wait!*" Kenlin snapped. "Wait a moment! He's been murdered, but he's telling me..." *He's rambling, what...?*

"He's been *murdered?*"

—and *never* so vicious. To murder the Teller... To murder all tellers!

A summer of silence! They all will be hunted: my children, my protégés, murdered like vermin—

Like master like student, they'll silence the stories 'til those who remember wish only that they could forget. And all they who can tell, now *hate* they the Teller! Who tainted with knowledge forbidden by shadows—

"Kenlin—"

"Enough!" The angry shout resounded in mind, in magic, in Ñaj-Gadan, everywhere that Kenlin was. He lunged forward, grabbed the gibbering Faery by the shoulder, and spun him around so that they were face to face. "Ranja, hold! Wanderer... What has happened? Tell me plainly: is what I'm seeing real? Someone has killed you, yes?"

But the gibbering had stopped, for the Wanderer was suddenly speechless. Wide-eyed, he stared first at Kenlin, then at the hand still resting on his shoulder, then back to Kenlin's face. *Can he not answer? Is he too far gone?* After a moment, the Faery's shaking legs folded, and he began to fall; instinctively, Kenlin reached out his other hand and caught him under the arm. *But... I caught him? But he isn't really here!* Suddenly, Kenlin was as speechless as the Wanderer. He looked in astonishment at the hands which supported the phantom, touching the illusion, and he did not understand.

The Wanderer no longer had the strength to stand unsupported, so Kenlin gently lowered him to the ground. *How? How...?* But the shock of this strange magic, though it had completely disrupted Kenlin's thoughts, seemed conversely to have jarred the Wanderer from his franticness. "I have misunderstood, Jazei," he said in a ghostly whisper as Kenlin laid him on the ground. "I am wrong."

"What is happening?" Kenlin demanded in disbelief, staring at his hands. *What am I doing? And how?*

But the Wanderer, shaking his head in despair, answered only the questions Kenlin voiced aloud. "They have killed me, Jazei," he lamented. "As I slept, they killed me. As I *helped them*, they killed me. Jazei, I have failed! I have failed!"

"Who?" Kenlin was still staring at his hands, but his eyes and his mind no longer saw them. *Thoughts for another time.* "Who has killed you?"

The Wanderer continued to shake his head, shaking in disbelief, or rejection, or denial. "A boy—but a child, Jazei. The son of a butcher has butchered the memories! He—" But the Faery could not continue, for pain or despair overcame him and his words devolved into another horrid, sobbing scream.

But Kenlin, his shock fading, was beginning to see through the fog in his mind, to connect knowns with unknowns. *He was murdered...tonight. He helped us, and then this.* "This is because of us. This is vengeance for *me*."

Ranja and Ataland both reacted to this statement, but Kenlin only watched for the Faery's response. "No, Jazei! Do not think of it so. If this was done on Droálic orders, they must have learned of my efforts here, learned how I hoped to preserve—"

"They already knew," Kenlin interrupted savagely. "They knew all along; they've probably been watching you for years! If Skralade had cared what you were doing before, you'd have been murdered a decade ago. This happened because you intervened—because you helped *me!* Do you see, Faery? Do you see what I was saying to you? Skralade was at Guardél; I'll bet he encountered Faery magic there, then recognized it at Ñaj-Gadan and knew immediately—"

"Kenlin—"

"*Silence*, Ranja! And how many Faeries take interest in matters outside the Forest nowadays? If there are more than just you, then they're probably *all* dead—"

But Ranja refused to be silenced. Kenlin felt her hands fall heavily on his shoulders as though she had pounced on him. Instinctively he reeled back as though to strike at her, but she did not flinch. "Kenlin," she demanded, *"where is my father?"*

Kenlin watched her for a moment; her visage swam in the magic much as the Wanderer's phantoms did. *But she's right. If the Wanderer is dying...* Controlling himself, Kenlin turned back to the Wanderer. "It's over, Wanderer. I was right before; they've won. You've failed, I've failed, everyone's *failed!* But... Where is Klanjad? Ranja wants to know. There's nothing left, Faery, so if you can ease the pain of passing, if only for one man, then do it. I don't sense him to the east, at least not yet. Where is he?"

The Wanderer opened his mouth to reply, only to falter even as the words formed on his lips. "Jazei," he said, choking on a despairing, dying sob, "come to Inajaz. *Please,* Jazei! We cannot give up—"

"Give up!" Kenlin bellowed furiously. "You're beaten, and you always were; it's only now that you realize it. Only one thing remains: let us *end it,* Faery! Tell us where Klanjad is! I think I can sense far enough, and I still don't sense him here. *Where is Klanjad?"*

The Wanderer opened his mouth to reply, but another cough interrupted him as the weakness of his throat leaked into his last remaining breaths. Kenlin did not move. *This is how he will die—and a slow, cruel, incremental death it will be. His heart is beating much too fast, and his skin is already cold. It is many minutes away yet, perhaps as much as an hour, and yet he's already dead.* At last the Faery's coughs abated. Weakly, still struggling to catch his breath, the Wanderer whispered, "Your uncle is a captive of all of his greatest foes: General Disden of Zirgrad, the high priest Yenimag, the one known as Quedju, and Skralade of the Misk Clan Eyjazinka. That four such commanders travel together... It speaks of how strongly Jranjana's foes have committed to our ruin. Where they had originally planned to take your uncle, I do not know, but their plans have been disrupted and so for now they keep him near themselves. Jendraski—tireless, luckless Jendraski—has at long last managed to outmaneuver his enemies, if only in time to but sour their triumph. Such stories of failure... Who will tell of this, his last and most triumphant defeat? Alas for the tellers! Without them, his legend is lost."

Faery! "Enough laments; they waste breaths. Where is Klanjad? East or west?"

Another coughing fit wracked the Wanderer's lungs. Kenlin's hands were still gently supporting the Faery. *How is it that I can— No matter; he must breathe to speak.* Lifting gently with his right hand, Kenlin raised the Faery's shoulders off the ground. This caused his back to arc, stretching the knife wounds and compressing his blood-bloated abdomen. The Wanderer gave a choking, spluttering screech of agony— but his elevated shoulders were free to breathe again. *Use the first two breaths for screams; then tell me what I need to know.*

"East, Jazei," the Wanderer cried out pitifully as soon as he had air enough. "Your uncle is east." He screamed again as Kenlin gently lowered his shoulders back to the ground where the Faery's breathing would be more labored, but less tortured. As his pain subsided, the Wanderer spoke in an almost inaudible whisper interspersed with grueling, rattling gasps: "Two nights yon...what will be forever forgotten...Jendraski broke out from Ñaj-Gadan with many thousands of men, the last... They escaped onto the lake on a flotilla of fishing boats. Now, the bulk of this army sails for Skaj-Kraskedir...but the vanguard, led by Jendraski himself, has dispersed along the road from Ñaj-Gadan...destroying bridges and setting ambushes to harry...the Droál's reinforcements. Whether or not he may succeed—whether the siege at Skaj-Kraskedir will be broken, whether the Droál's reinforcements from Ñaj-Gadan may be delayed..." He coughed feebly, then resumed in an even weaker voice, "The Droál see it...as a risk. They march their eastern army...many, *many* thousands...toward Skaj-Kraskedir in haste." Another cough; Kenlin had to lean in close to hear the Wanderer now. "This army marches in a column...and near the rear...the commanders travel with guards...and wagons...and captives. Your uncle lies bound...in one of these wagons."

"Bound in a cart on the northeast road," Kenlin reiterated to confirm, "traveling around the lake on the path to Skaj-Kraskedir." The Faery's eyes had drifted closed, but he gave a barely perceptible nod. "Yes. Thank you."

Ranja, whose hands were still on Kenlin's shoulders, shook him slightly. "Is that it, Kenlin? Is that where he is? Can we go?"

Kenlin raised his head to answer, but as he moved, the Wanderer's hands lashed forward with the last of the Faery's dying strength. Kenlin was caught about the neck and pulled in close as the Wanderer whispered desperately, "Stand we now...in a high place of darkness..." At these words, Kenlin felt the air change. He heard the wind, felt a biting cold, and a vast emptiness opened up around him. He gasped. They—he and the Wanderer—were on a rocky outcropping high on the shoulder of a great mountain. High clouds hid what little light the sky could give. All about them was a black expanse of empty space filled only by the bitter wind. Every step in every direction would send him plunging down a different slope of the mountainside where every path was its own unique demise. "My sight leaves me..." the Wanderer said in a whisper that carried unnaturally through the howling of the wind. "No longer can I see...the future in the past... Jazei... Let not the past be lost, Jazei... The legends give you power...power to inspire...power to soothe... Condemn the world not to a future...forgotten before it begins... *Come*, Jazei... *Survive*—"

But in that instant, the dark focus that had held back Kenlin's growing mania— *Again! This again?! Hahaha-how?! Is his own death not proof enough?* "You're mad, Faery!"

Kenlin snapped wildly. "*Mad! How* can you still believe this nonsense? How can you not see you were *wrong!* There is no refuge, there is no survival, and *I don't save things.* '...the legends give power...' Here's power for you: I am *calamity!* Claim what you like about the dead, but *these* Jazeiz do not soothe, and we do not make safe. We kill, we destroy—when we don't create ruin then we are its heralds. I killed you just by *speaking* to you *from hundreds of leagues away!* So damn your enclave. Damn your safety. Damn survival. I *am* damnation, and I will bring my curse down on the heads of the *bastards* who place it on me!" *Hahahahahahaha!* He was on his feet. He had slapped away the Wanderer's grasping hands; the vision of the mountain had vanished, leaving the Faery lying crumpled and alone on the unseen, distant ground. "We're already dead, Wanderer, all of us, and all that's left is *how.* From Natzut to Ñaj-Gadan, for a *year* they've chased me, but now I know where *they* are. I will be their legend, I will be their damnation—I'll kill them all, and as they die they will know that *I am Jazei!*" He was screaming now, and as he screamed his voice cracked, for only an instant, into a keening screech that sent a bolt of ravaging energy through his body; his vision flashed red.

But the Wanderer, in contrast, grew weaker every moment. "Jazei..." he pleaded helplessly from the ground, too weak even to plaintively reach out. "Kenlin... Choose not this end... Let not forgetful darkness—"

But Kenlin ceased his magic.

CHAPTER XXXIV:

"Let's go!" He took off at a run, sprinting blindly through the dark across the corpse- and rubble-strewn streets of western Ñaj-Gadan. He'd half-expected Ranja or Ataland to shout some protest. But Ranja was as impatient to run as Kenlin was, and Ataland, standing warily many paces away, seemingly intended nothing but to cooperate—from a safe distance.

As he ran, Kenlin's leg smashed against something, and he fell. *Ha!* He was on his feet again in an instant, unperturbed, *damn the shin, who cares for a bruise?* His mind was alive with far too much energy—if he did not expend it, his head would explode—and so he sprinted, leaning back as he ran and closing his eyes, feeling the wind of motion, the pain of collision, the scratching and tumbling as he fell, *hahahahahaha!*

East through the plaza and straight down the main road he led them, never slowing his mad dash nor looking back to see his companions' progress. "Kenlin, slow down. Kenlin!" *Hahaha! Don't fall behind, Ranja; run faster, catch up!* But he managed not to Fade—he retained at least that much control—so despite his heedless headlong sprint, he never fully outpaced her.

Down through the city, over the canal, through the nearly deserted encampment beyond, Kenlin led them to run for nearly a league. Once they reached the encampment, Ranja had a chance to catch up as Kenlin swerved aside to *Die, Droál, die!* He didn't have to kill them: there were few, all human, left merely to oversee whatever materiel hadn't accompanied the marching army. *Too easy! Ha!* In total, he only killed five or six in the entire encampment, but each kill brought a tiny release of the wild energy coursing through him, forestalling—*Or beckoning?*—the moment when he could contain himself no longer.

And so, even though he ran almost without stopping from the high plaza to the far end of the Droálic encampment, with every step he gained more manic energy than he lost. He would have kept running, too, had Ranja not stolen horses from a stable, mounted one, and caught up to Kenlin leading a horse for him. *Hahahaha! Very well then.* Without breaking stride, he Faded—he didn't even pause to check that no one would sense him—and sprang directly into the running horse's saddle. The frightened animal snorted and tossed its head, but Kenlin merely seized its reins and spurred its flanks. *Onward, onward!* Heedless of the distance and the horse's stamina, he drove the beast to a full gallop as Ranja and Ataland followed him along the northeast road that led to Skaj-Kraskedir.

Within only a few leagues, Kenlin's reckless pace had completely exhausted the horses, but he did not slow. The road here led through town after town, some separated by mere minutes of road, but nowhere were there people to be seen. *If they're here and they're alive, then they're hiding. An army has passed this way.* He did not need his tracking skills to follow the fresh trail of ten thousand heavy, armored soldiers. The night was passing now, and light was growing in the sky; even from horseback, the innumerable footprints in the trampled dirt were clear to see.

There in the distance: magic at last! Misks, at least a dozen, and perhaps some humans as well. And other humans west of them? Why so many human magicians? Hahaha! And another; here I come!

The terrain in this region was low wetland crisscrossed by countless waterways, from brooks hardly worth noting to small rivers spanned by short wooden bridges. It was as they approached one of these bridges that Kenlin, still focused on the magic he sensed ahead, heard Ataland at last break his silence. "Kenlin, I smell— Hey, stop! Hold up!" *Haha! Never!*

He kicked his horse's flanks, and the weary animal struggled to run even faster. They were nearly on the bridge when Kenlin felt a hand grab his shirt's collar and yank him backward: Ataland had leapt from his horse in order to drag Kenlin off of his.

Hahaha! And now, at last, you think to betray me? He never even considered why else Ataland might have acted as he did. *He attacks? I'll kill him!* As the two of them tumbled to the ground, Kenlin Faded, twisted, slammed the half-Unnatilz to the dirt and drove his magically-strengthened fist through the traitor's— But he was gone! Quick as a caught fish, Ataland had squirmed through Kenlin's grasp and dodged away to the side. *Hahahahaha!* Jubilant, euphoric for a challenge, Kenlin thrust himself to his feet and whirled to face his erstwhile companion.

Ataland, too, was on his feet, but his palms were held outward, open and empty. "Kenlin, I smell them! They're—" But he stopped abruptly as they both sensed *Necromancy!* Ataland threw himself to the ground as the crowd-presence surged forward; it flung Kenlin backward and knocked Ranja, who had stopped her horse at Ataland's original warning, to the ground alongside her mount.

Damnation! Launching himself to his feet with the strength of magic, Kenlin wheeled back toward the bridge. A small force of Droálic soldiers, perhaps eight, had been hiding in the boscage on the other side of the river; they were led by a single violet-clad Dragluz like the one Kenlin had killed in Slionte. *Ah, some sort of rearguard left to watch the bridge. Then we're very, very near; hahahaha!* Though Kenlin and Ranja had both been knocked backward, Ataland's quick reaction had allowed the Necromancy to pass right over him; he lay on the ground exactly where he had dropped.

The Droálic soldiers had rushed immediately from their hiding place and formed a defensive line across apex of the bridge, but the Dragluz stood cockily before it. The Necromancer turned toward Ataland and raised his hand menacingly, but before he could conjure his magic, Ataland snatched up a rock and flung it with a flick of his wrist. The stone caught the Dragluz above the eye. He fell backward and yelped in pain and surprise, but nevertheless he swept his hand forward; this time the Necromancy caught Ataland off-guard and sent him tumbling backward.

But not me! Kenlin was already charging forward when the Necromancy began. Though Ataland had not been able to drop low a second time, Kenlin, learning from what he had seen, flung himself into a low slide that carried him underneath the brunt of the magic; he felt no more than a glancing blow to his raised shoulder, scarcely enough to raise a bruise. *And now for my turn!* When he regained his feet, he was Faded. Two steps later, his magic was as powerful as he had ever used before. *More!* By the time he drove Klanjad's sword through the face of the Dragluz, he had exceeded every previous limitation of his strength. The force of his strike burst the Necromancer's head like a cherry, and Kenlin's momentum carried him into and through the line of bronze-clad soldiers behind. *HahahaHAAA!* He wheeled and wielded, smashing through their weapons and tearing apart their defenses, their armor, their flesh and faces. It was *glorious!*

They were all dead too soon. *Too soon! I need more!* One still moaned and gurgled on the ground. He crushed the man's throat with his foot; then, in a frenzied surge of energy, he stomped and stomped and *splat! More, more! Ah, but there are more, just ahead. I sense Misks, and men—and now, even Necromancy. Oh, this is a good day! Oh, this is a good day! Oh, this is a good—*

"Kenlin?" It was Ranja's voice; she and Ataland had recovered their feet and come to the bridge to aid him. *Too late!* "Kenlin, what are you...? Are you alright?"

She was concerned. *Why?* "Of course I'm alright, Ranja." *Better!* At last, "At long last, I'm beginning to *be* as I always should have been," *strong*, "uninhibited!" *I was cowardly, hesitant, reserved, too* "weak before myself to *face* myself, but *not today!* for today I am *magnificent*," as if from an understanding, a *liberation from* "idiocy, all that *restraint* that I put on myself for such *pettiness*" that I couldn't even put to words," *but now I'm* "Unfettered, free of *this feebleness from* "fear" of true *strength!*" Yes, *ha!* now *I'm alright*, "I am wonderful, I'm *alive*, I am—"

"Kenlin!"

Her face was aghast, and it looked so *funny* that he could not help but to burst into raucous, manic laughter. "Come now, Ranja, you *cannot* tell me you don't feel it. We wanted this! We planned this! And *here we are now, yes?*" And he threw back his head and laughed, spun on light feet in a circle, raised his blood-soaked hands high in a jubilant *"Hahahahahahaha!* Come now, Ranja. Come! *Come!*" And with the bloody sword in his hand and the wild laughter still on his lips, he whirled and dashed northward toward where he sensed more, *more, MORE!*

Though he could not run fast enough for his own zeal, still he managed not to Fade. He was not trying to outrun them. *Ha!* No, he *wanted* them here, and he wasn't sure why, but surely he must share this *marvelous* liberation with them, let them revel with him in the *Brutality is the quintessence of nature, for a brute is a predator, and the greatness of man is as the greatest predator, the pinnacle killer, death-strong beyond even nature itself! So strong the strongest of brutes, yet so fearful the weak of brutality, they contrive a 'humanity' to idolize, a crafted demigod of gentle frailty to calm the quaking hearts of the feeble. Fie! A short, pathetic life upon the wolf who dreams of grazing! Yes, to fear the brutal is naught but a willful weakness: cowardice cloaked in self-righteousness born of a servile fascination with an empty, servile ethic. How 'right' for them! Ha! A fabricated rite! It is naught but to grovel and laud the inferior, a self-deception conceivable only in the pacified wake of the truly, rightly mighty. But when pietistic lies fall empty, and the monsters in the darkness are hungry, abandon, abandon, abandon! Damn restraint, unleash raw strength, embrace brutality, hesitate not to kill but savor the bloodshed, become you the monster that monsters all fear, relish the mad—*

"*Enough!*" He was sprinting headlong—it was long since he knew to where—but his mind was wild with voices that at last, at long last, he was not certain were his own, and he felt himself slipping and spiraling and *running faster and faster* until he suddenly feared *Too fast; I won't be able to stop!* Out of control, he jammed his toe into the ground as he ran and tripped, arresting his own rampant mind by throwing himself desperately to the ground. *Enough! Wait a minute!*

NO! Never again! But wait. . . What is happening to me? Are these thoughts even mine? Mine! Who are you? Who am I?

"Kenlin, get up! Get up now!"

His eyes were open, and they always had been, but as Ranja yelled to him it seemed as though a blinding fog was blown away, and sounds suddenly pierced his ears as if he had emerged from drowning.

They had crested a small hill, no more than thrice the height of a man; from here the road ahead descended slowly to small river a few hundred yards away. There was no village here, but the river was wide and deep enough that a wooden bridge had been built over it. The bridge, however, was aflame, and between the hilltop and the river, a vicious battle was underway. Someone—Jendraski's raiders—had hidden and waited as the Droál passed until only the very end of the column, which contained the commanders, remained south of the river. They had then set fire to the bridge and attacked with every soldier they had left. It was suicide, valiant, brilliant, and hopelessly ineffective. Though the fighting was intense and bloody, Jendraski's few elite soldiers were no match for the Misks and Necromancers that guarded and comprised the Droálic high command.

And they were screaming; everybody was screaming! Across the river to the north, Droálic captains were screaming at their soldiers, urging the heavily-armored men to try to cross the water and aid their commanders. Nearer, Jendraski's raiders were on the brink of defeat, some fighting, some dying, everybody screaming. The Droál were screaming too, shouting in victory or chanting their barbaric incantations. Even Ranja was screaming; as Kenlin clambered to his feet, she unleashed her shrill, piercing Jazei war shriek. But her voice was lost in the din of the battle, for everybody, *everybody* was screaming.

Like the blast of a gale, the urge to scream took hold of Kenlin; a consuming passion of limitless rage jolted him like a bolt of decadent, incandescent pain. His vision blurred, brightened, colored to a bloody crimson— *Wait!*—yet he fought for control of himself, suddenly terrified at precipice before his mind— *Yes!*—and he lurched forward, one step, two steps—*Stop!*—and the crimson in his eyes dimmed, then flared again as his gaze fell on the fracas before him, the dying men, the killing Necromancers, and the

Misks. On the battlefield, a group of Commune soldiers broke free of the fighting and began to rout in disarray, running by chance toward the hilltop where Kenlin stood. Behind them, the melee calmed for a moment and individual figures became discernible. There, standing with a small company of his kin amidst the corpses of the Commune's army, was Skralade.

And all else vanished. Kenlin did not remember a smashed friend, Ranja's bleeding shoulders, reaching hands in the morning, a burning homestead, or even Klanjad; the reasons were gone, and only the blood-red hatred remained. A vision seared behind Kenlin's eyes: Skralade's blood spurting over his hands, the Misk's face as the blade was wrenched left and right, anchoring him with pain while ripping out his viscera. In that instant, Kenlin dreamed of repulsive fantasies, knew them for what they were, promised them to himself, and laughed and laughed aloud and in his mind and with himself and all around. A cacophonous chorus he laughed, louder and higher and madder until, inside and outside, the laughter morphed into a Jazei scream that roared from every part of all he was. It flooded the air around him, easily drowning out Ranja, the Droál, the Commune, the very sounds of the battle. The scream chafed his throat, and he felt a rabid, raw, bestial thrill as louder he screamed, and his screeching cry echoed across the fields. He shut his eyes, and the world shattered at his screech; he opened his eyes to a new world that ran and rained a boiling red.

CHAPTER XXXV:

*What happened? One above, I've never felt so weary...
Why am I awake? I should go back to sleep. I should sleep...*

*... But no, still exhausted! What's happened to me? Am
I ill? Hurt? Weariness, stiffness, nausea... What have I done
to myself? Even my skin feels taut and crusted, but I can't see
what's... I can't open my eyes. Why won't my eyes open?
Why can't I open my eyes?!*

Kenlin veered from dazed lethargy to panic in a matter
of seconds; such is the process of waking up. Frantic, he lashed
blindly out with his hands, but there was no one there. *My
eyes! Why can't they open?!* His hands flew to his face, his
fingers probed his eyelids: a crusty coating of grime sealed
them shut. Vigorously he rubbed his eyes, and the grime
crumbled and fell away, and his eyelids flew open. *Day!* The
light of late morning stung him; his eyes blurred and blinded
in the brightness. He touched his face with his fingers, but
they, too, were crusted with a rough, grimy coating. As his
vision began to clear, he saw that his hands were stained a
blackish red. Not just his hands: his wrists, his arms, his
clothes, everywhere! Panic seized him for again; he yelped in
fright and began to slap at the filth that coated him. A few
chunkier bits fell away, but the streaks of blackish red clung
tightly to his skin.

"Easy! Easy!" In his frenzy, Kenlin whirled toward the
voice and struck out with a hand, but the speaker was savvy
enough to stand beyond reach. "Calm down, Kenlin!" the
voice shouted, sounding wary. As his panic began to recede,
Kenlin recognized the speaker: Ataland. Kenlin blinked and
tried to focus; slowly, the half-Unnatilz's face swam into view.
"Are you okay?" Ataland asked, watching him cautiously.
"You back?"

"I..." Kenlin began, but the mere act of speaking triggered a wave of dizziness. He staggered and fell to one knee.

Ataland did not step forward to help him. "Steady now," he said, his voice still tense with wariness. "Why don't you sit down and breathe for a while? There's no rush, no danger here. Nothing to get excited about."

Kenlin sat unsteadily on the ground and passed a hand over his eyes as though to wipe the dizziness from them. "No danger here... Where is here?"

"We're in a little ditch just a few hundred yards from the battlefield. The battle's over now, though; like I said, there's nothing to get excited about."

The battle's over? How? I must have been knocked unconscious. I only remember running, then screaming, then... "What happened?"

Ataland hesitated, then said unconvincingly, "Well, I suppose you might say we won. Or *you* won, I guess. All three of us are alive, so..."

All three of us...three... "Where's Ranja?"

"She's fine," Ataland said quickly, then corrected himself just as quickly. "She's alive. She's at... She went to find the cart."

"Cart?"

"Back near the Tower, you said Klanjad was being held on a cart on this road. When we first got here, there were some carts—"

"The cart!" Kenlin exclaimed, the possible implications of this suddenly galvanizing his dizzy thoughts. *I saw some of those carts. Didn't I? Or did I fail to notice? Wasn't I looking?* Hastily, he asked Ataland, "Then, did we manage it? Is Klanjad—"

"No," Ataland interrupted almost sternly, as though he were forbidding any misunderstanding on this point. "Whatever it is you think you managed, it didn't happen that way. Us three are still alive—somehow—but everybody else is dead. Klanjad, your uncle, was killed too...by fire."

A familiar instant silence filled Kenlin's mind like a blinding flash of darkness. "No."

"Ranja told me. I don't lie."

"How?"

"He was on that cart, a wooden cart. They might have put straw or oil or something in there to be ready in case they wanted to do this, but that's me speculating. Anyway, when we first saw them, the carts were just sitting on the road, and the fighting was mostly off to the left, away from them. But then Ranja screamed, and then you...happened. And the next time I looked back—"

"Where?"

Ataland hesitated again, but then nodded toward the sky to the north. Turning, Kenlin saw, climbing high into the clear morning sky, a pillar of oily black smoke. *No!* He was on his feet, scrambling over the muddy lip of the ditch; he was on the road, still unsteady, stumbling northeast toward the smoking heap ahead; he had reached the heap, lurched blindly into the smoldering wreckage only to stagger back with a cry as the hot embers burned him. But he would not believe it: *I have to see for myself.* He peered through the smoke, leaning as close as he could without being scorched. *He isn't there. Where is he?* Ataland had followed Kenlin; at the sound of the half-Unnatilz's footsteps, Kenlin snapped, "I see nothing in there, Ataland. Where is Klanjad?" He whirled angrily, but Ataland's head was turned to the right. Following his gaze, Kenlin saw a short track where something had been dragged from the ashes. Five or so yards away, Ranja knelt beside a burned and horrifically disfigured body.

There are odors, familiar to all who have shared a meal over a campfire, that are likewise associated with pyres. To Kenlin, the air now smelled of smoky autumns and fruitful hunts, a thousand merry nights with childhood friends and a hundred more with Ranja and... But now it *was* Klanjad that he smelled. He felt violently sick; dizziness and nausea doubled him over as he struggled to control himself, breathing open-mouthed so as not to smell... *I cannot believe it; I need to see.* Steeling himself, he straightened and walked slowly to the place where Ranja knelt.

Crusted black over red: the entire corpse was crusted black over red. Ataland had been right, the Droál must have thrown some sort of oil into the cart, for the inferno had been swift and incredibly hot. All over the wretched cadaver, the skin had been burnt black, cracked and crispy; but beneath this husk, much of the flesh was still moist, seared to a scarlet that was too bright for blood, too dark for meat. Black over red, everything black over red. There was no green: the eyes had been eaten by the fire. There was no white-blond hair either; the whitest place on this corpse was where the teeth, besooted as they were, leered through the face in a wide, horrid death grimace, for the lips had been burned away completely. Further down, the scorched skin had begun to slough away, showing glimpses of organs and bones underneath. The feet especially had been burned right through, and human ash was crumbling from the skeleton beneath. The same, however, had not happened to the hands; there were no hands on this corpse.

I still can't believe it... I can't believe it... I can't...

"It is him." She had not turned her head or even glanced in Kenlin's direction. She knelt beside the body on both knees, sitting on her heels with her hands resting on her thighs. Her back was straight, her shoulders were still, and her eyes stared unblinkingly forward, unseeing, looking past the horror before her to the nothing beyond it. She was turned away— he could not see her face well—but he could hear the unfathomable agony in her voice; it was rent and twisted, torn in all directions as the strain of her will shook and tottered. "Don't question me, Kenlin. This is my father."

"Ranja, I..." But he had nothing to say. She was not looking at the body, but Kenlin could not seem to wrest his gaze from it. At last, by closing his eyes and shaking himself violently, he managed to look toward his cousin instead. She must have leapt into the embers in order to retrieve Klanjad's body. Her boots had been almost completely burned away, and painful, bloody burns were visible where the embers had touched the bare skin of her legs. Her hands, by contrast, were merely badly blistered and scorched: she had grabbed her father's sizzling-hot arms and held on as she dragged his body from the dying inferno. *One above!* Kenlin was too shocked to think, but on reflex he stepped forward to look more closely at her injuries.

"Don't!" she snapped suddenly, hearing his footstep and knowing immediately what he was doing. He stopped. They remained that way, she kneeling beside her father while Kenlin stood to the side, for a moment while she collected herself. Gingerly, as though trying not to shatter her last shards of composure, she turned at last to look at Kenlin. Every muscle in her face was taut with anguish and tears ran unchecked down her cheeks; but she was not sobbing, and her eyes were wide, keen, and terribly bright. She looked him over for a moment, then gave the tiniest nod toward the north. "Go to the river," she told him. "Wash." Then she turned away again.

"Ranja, I'm—"

"Leave me, Kenlin."

"Ranja—"

"*Leave me!*" she screamed, and as the tortured sound escaped, her entire body convulsed once, just once. Her back arched forward, her head dropped, her jaw clamped tight shut—and she froze that way, tensed the point of breaking.

Kenlin heard two purposely-loud footsteps, then felt a hand fall heavily on his shoulder. "Come on, Kenlin," Ataland urged quietly. "She doesn't mean forever. Let's go."

He didn't want to leave her here like this. He wanted to say something, anything, there had to be something… *No.* He took a step back. Then another step. Then, turning, he followed Ataland away to the northwest. After twenty paces, he glanced backward. The very last of her will had collapsed; she had crumbled forward, thrown herself over her father's corpse, and freely wept her heart out.

Kenlin turned away and continued walking, but his stunned, plodding pace soon began to quicken. The shock in his mind was at last giving way to thoughts. *How did this happen? I remember running; I remember feeling...wild; I remember falling on the hilltop and seeing the battle. Did I see the cart? I don't remember. But Ataland said the carts weren't burning when we first arrived. After I tripped, what did I do? If I didn't immediately run to that cart...* To himself and aloud, inside and outside his head, Kenlin asked, "Did I cause this to happen?"

Ataland shook his head immediately. "That is definitely the wrong way to think about it."

Kenlin stopped in his tracks and looked piercingly at Ataland. "That's not a *no*."

"Then *no*," declared the half-Unnatilz. "You didn't light the fire, you didn't put him in that cart—"

"But I didn't run to help him either, did I?"

"Well, no, you didn't!" Ataland conceded, throwing up his hands. "You could have, but you didn't."

"Why not?"

"How the *fuck* would I know that?" Ataland demanded, flabbergasted. "Don't mistake me, though: that's a question I've been wondering myself. Why *did* you run to the fight instead of the carts, Kenlin?"

"I ran to the fight?"

"Oh, come off it!"

"Yes or no?"

"So, what, you're claiming you don't remember?"

Kenlin shook his head defensively. "I don't! I remember the journey, the fight on the bridge, and the running. I remember *seeing* a big battle with Droál and Commune soldiers. And then...I woke up in that ditch a few minutes ago."

Ataland obviously didn't believe a word of this, and he made no effort to hide his incredulity. For several moments, he stared intently into Kenlin's face as though trying to decide whether this was some sort of bad joke. Kenlin met his gaze evenly. At last, Ataland pointed to the open field to the south. "That over there. That was you."

Kenlin turned and looked in confusion. This was the field on which the Commune ambush had fought the Droál leaders and their retinue. The dead and dying were scattered throughout the tall grass. *But I didn't kill those people; they died in battle, they killed each other.* The only other thing on the field was what looked like a large, dark patch of mud away to the southwest. "I don't understand. What was me? The mud patch?"

Ataland snorted sarcastically. "Hya! Exactly. 'Mud patch.' You know what? Let's go see this 'mud patch,' shall we?" and he turned and marched off across the field. Kenlin, still bewildered, followed.

They had not gone far, perhaps a hundred yards or so, before it became clear that this was no ordinary patch of mud. The ditch where he'd awakened had been muddy; the soil in this area was of a mid-brown, peaty color. This patch, however, was tinted a very dark, rusty red, and it gleamed in the morning like a pit of moist clay. But it wasn't clay either; in fact, much of it wasn't mud at all. As they came nearer the patch, the bodies on the ground became more and more densely scattered. This place had been the epicenter of the battle's most intense fighting. He was still fifty yards away when Kenlin finally realized what the patch was; yet despite this realization, he was wholly unprepared for what he saw when they reached the edge.

When a wolf pack hunts an elk or deer, they do not wait for the wounded prey to die before they begin to feed. They tear open the belly first, seize the most succulent organs, rip them out, and ravenously scoff them on the spot. Then they grab the limbs, twisting and jerking until bones break and muscles tear away, and the chunks are dragged apart to be shredded and devoured piecemeal. The site of a wolf kill is a bloody muddle of bits and bones and viscera, and it is often difficult even to recognize what exactly it was they killed.

But never at this scale. Wolves will kill one animal, or maybe two, after which they must spend time creating their bloody messes. But dozens, many dozens, lay butchered in this tract of gore that Kenlin had mistaken for a mud patch. These had not been eaten—only a sparse few carrion birds had arrived yet—and so individual pieces were still easily recognizable: hands, trunks, legs, faces. But all these chunks were jumbled madly together and covered in a slurry of blood and guts that spilled from every piece to leak onto every other. Severed arms stuck up helplessly through the carnage where there were no dismembered shoulders near enough to claim them. Torsos had been hacked, crushed, eviscerated, and flung aside. Heads split down the middle faced two ways, or had been smashed and slathered over the bodies they once bedecked. And layer upon layer they lay, yard after yard, staining the churned ground and each other with their splattered blood and entrails... It was too much. Overcome at last, Kenlin turned away, collapsed to his hands and knees, and retched onto the ground.

Ataland, too, had turned his back toward the massacre with a queasy expression on his face. As Kenlin tried in vain to vomit up his empty stomach, the half-Unnatilz watched him somberly. "So you really don't remember that?" he asked quietly. Kenlin, still intermittently heaving, shook his head. "Wow. Well, I'll never forget."

"I did that?" Kenlin whispered, breathless with illness and shock.

"Yes. That was you. You'd been getting stranger and stranger ever since the sun went down, but you didn't *really* get weird until after you slaughtered that rearguard. Ranja asked if you were okay, and whatever you said back didn't make any sense at all. Then you just took off running—I guess you could sense magic from the battle and knew we were close—until we got to the top of that hill over there."

Kenlin had managed to calm his nausea, but not his shock. "That much I remember. But then I screamed, and..."

"That's when you did this. I think you saw the Misks, and suddenly nothing else mattered anymore. Ranja was doing that Jazei scream, but she stopped when you started; you can scream a *lot* louder than she can. She saw the carts, and she wanted to go toward them, but by that time you were already headed for...this."

Kenlin risked another glance at the carnage, then immediately turned away. He wouldn't have thought he would feel nauseous; no sight of death or gore had ever affected him so before. *But this...* "I can't do that," he whispered, able neither to believe it nor to doubt. "So many, and so *violently...* And there were Misks in there, several of them, yes? I'm not strong enough to do that."

"Well, you didn't seem much bothered at the time," Ataland replied coldly. "Misks, Necromancers, bronzy *and Commune* soldiers... You didn't hesitate. You didn't need to, I guess. I followed Ranja toward the carts at first, but we'd barely even started when somebody lit the fire. By that time, you'd been pretty busy, and people had just started running away, everybody. I ran too, once I saw you. Ranja kept going toward the burning cart, even though it was too late, but I was *gone.*"

He didn't run from the Droál, and he didn't run from the Misks, and he didn't run from a suicidal mission to ease Klanjad's death. He only ran...from me. "What exactly was I doing?"

Ataland shrugged and looked away, lost for an adequate description. "I don't know what else to tell you, Kenlin. You killed *everything.* The Misks were dead before they even had time to realize they were outmatched. You killed that first one, their leader, almost instantly, and I think you got several more after him. Then you just started racing around with magic, killing everything and everyone, *way* too fast and strong for any of them to stand a chance. I've never, *ever* seen magic like that, and I don't think I want to again. I'd always thought the tales of Jazei fighting were just stories."

But at one bit of news, a different, yet familiar, part of Kenlin's mind had become suddenly attentive. The nausea vanished, as did the shock, and a creeping thrill of energy began to stir in him. "Skralade is dead?"

"The chief Misk? He is *definitely* dead," Ataland confirmed, still looking away at nothing. "He was the first one I saw you kill, even before Ranja and I started for the carts. You were...thorough."

"Good. Good. And then I killed more Misks, yes?"

The tone, perhaps, of Kenlin's voice caused Ataland to turn to him in alarm. "That's right," he said with a curt note of something very much like fear. "Misks and everybody else, Droál and Commune alike. You didn't give a *shit*, you killed everything and everybody you could see. That's why I ran; and if you start that shit again right now, there'll be nothing I can do but run 'til I'm all out of world to run to."

Enough! Stop. Calm yourself. Restrain... Kenlin breathed deep, rejecting the energy. After a moment, the creeping thrill faded, and the nausea and shock began to return. Ataland watched him warily. When he had breathed away the last of the energy, Kenlin asked, "There were Commune soldiers there too? And I killed them?"

"At least a few, probably more," Ataland said. "I saw one that you killed near the end, when everybody was running away from you. You didn't have your sword, I guess you must have dropped it out there somewhere. You didn't need it, though; you just grabbed the guy by the arm and the neck and...ripped him up."

Why? Kenlin shook his head blearily. "Why did I do that? Was he attacking me?"

"Nobody was attacking you, Kenlin. You ran at them; by that time, everybody else was running from you."

"Yes, so I heard," Kenlin said. Though his voice was mild, Ataland nonetheless took a cautious step back. *One above, what I must have done to make him fear me so...* "I'm just trying to understand, Ataland. Was there a *why*? Did I kill him just because he was there?" Ataland did not answer. Kenlin shook his head again. "I could kill anybody at all for just being there."

"Hya! Don't comfort me." But a moment later, Ataland repented. "That wasn't called for. I'm sorry."

Kenlin shook his head again. "Yes? From what I'm hearing, you're well justified."

"Doesn't make it helpful," Ataland muttered. A long silence passed as Kenlin struggled to make sense of all he had seen and heard while Ataland stood by, chewing his lip in uneasy thought. At last, the half-Unnatilz said, "Look, Kenlin, I don't know you very well. If you truly don't remember and this is really all a surprise to you, then it's is probably the first time you've done this. If you'd done it before, even if you didn't remember it, someone surely would have told you. I've only known you a few days, and you're definitely odd, but this was different. You hadn't been like that before, and you're not— Well, you don't seem to be like that right now. That isn't you, Kenlin; that was...something else."

It was a clumsy but sincere attempt to console. Kenlin nodded his appreciation, though he was not consoled. Maybe he didn't need to be. *No. I won't think that way. Not now.* Forcing himself away from his thoughts, he asked, "And you? When did you come back? And how did I get off the field?"

Ataland sighed and shrugged. "I stopped running when I noticed you weren't chasing me, nor anybody else. Honestly, I got curious. When I got back, it was all over: everybody had either fled or died. Even the Droál soldiers to the north, the idiots who'd been trying to ford the river in full armor, had given up and gone away, though I don't know whether it was you or the current that scared them off. The carts were still on fire. They didn't burn themselves out until a while later, so

I don't think Ranja had been able to get very close. You'd collapsed out there in the carnage; when I arrived, she had gone to get you and was carrying you out on her back. I helped—I wasn't happy about it, I didn't want to get near you at first—and we took you to that ditch. Then, when the cart fires died down a bit, she went back over there. A few minutes later, you woke up."

A silence passed. Kenlin at last looked back at the blackish-red stains all over his skin, which he had long-since realized were grimy drying blood. "None of this is mine, then. This is all…that," he said, gesturing without looking toward the bloody massacre behind them.

"Pretty much," said Ataland. "You cut up your hands a bit, probably on other people's armor. But other than that, you were…"

Powerful.

But he did not let himself embrace that thought; he did not allow his mind to laugh. At least… *No. No. Enough for one day.* After many minutes of silence, Ataland finally said, "You should clean yourself up, Kenlin. The river's over there. Wash it all off, drink some water, take some slow breaths. I'll go try to find food or something, and then… I guess we'll figure out what to do next."

"Alright." It was easy to comply; he didn't really want to make decisions right now. Slowly, Kenlin rose to his feet and began to walk north toward the banks of the river ahead. After a few steps, he paused, turned, and looked his companion in the eye. "Thank you, Ataland."

The half-Unnatilz nodded; Kenlin turned once more and walked away.

Chapter XXXVI:

He walked northeast, intending to reach the river upstream of where the fighting had been. His path took him over a drainage ditch and into a field beside the road. With the last curious corner of his mind, Kenlin wondered what sort of crops might be grown here. Given the proximity of the river and the area's general flatness, this was probably a floodplain. Beans, maybe? Or barley? But this year, it didn't matter; whoever once tended this field was gone. Without a farmer to order the growth, the wild grasses had swarmed in to choke the crops, and the only things growing in this field were weeds.

At the next ditch, Kenlin turned north and followed the draining water to the river. It was not deep, and it was not cold, and it was not clean; no mountain stream was this, but the runoff of rain on the grassy hills to the east. But it was water, and as clouded and muddy as it was, *it's cleaner than I.*

He wore his clothes into the water, for they were as filthy as his skin. He hadn't realized, until he tried to wash it off, just how completely his body had been bloodied. The stuff was everywhere! He took handfuls of river mud and scrubbed his arms, his chest, his face, even his hair; slowly, the muck began to wash him clean. His clothes, however, were sullied beyond remedy. He took off his shirt, scrubbed it, kneaded it, scrubbed it again, but to no avail. Giving up, he looked pensively at the spattered, splotchy, red-brown discolorations that were now a permanent part of the weave, and he smiled a bitter smile. *Me too, shirt. Me too.*

As he dressed and sloshed back out of the river, he saw Ranja picking her way carefully down the bank, tottering on injured feet. He approached to help; she waved him away angrily. *No, I won't, Ranja.* Ignoring her dismissal, he stepped in quickly to catch her as she stumbled. She said nothing—

her head was bowed, her eyes were lowered, tears still trickled down the tracks on her cheeks—but she did not push him away again.

With only a little further help from Kenlin, Ranja sat down on a rock at the very edge of the water. The fire-rent tatters of her boots still clung to the bloody burns on her feet and legs. She didn't bother trying to remove them, but lowered both feet into the river boot-rags and all, wincing at the touch of the water. There was room for two on the rock; after a moment's hesitation, Kenlin sat beside her.

Neither spoke for many, many minutes. *Or only a moment?* Kenlin couldn't be sure: it felt like an eternity, but he was wary now of trusting feelings. However long it was, he waited in silence. *She came to find me. Take your time, Ranja. When you're ready, you begin.*

When at last she spoke, her tone was brusque, as though they were already mid-conversation. "Can you master it?"

Kenlin's tone, in contrast, was measured and deliberately calm. "Master...it?"

"The Rage, Kenlin. That's what it was, wasn't it? You passed into a Rage. Like Zadarj."

Kenlin did not answer immediately. Only a handful of stories featured the Rage of Zadarj; and of those few, none that he knew were clear on exactly what the phrase meant. It was said that, in his most intense battles, the great Jazei would become deranged, as mad and terrifying as a rabid wolf, after which... "I don't know, Ranja. I know little of Zadarj's Rages other than the term. I always assumed it was a just a poetical reference to his prowess on the battlefield. Is it something specific?"

"I wonder. Yesterday I thought as you've said, but today..."

"I don't know any more about today than you do, Ranja."

A quiet challenge: "Don't you?" But Kenlin did not answer, and Ranja did not press. After a silence, she continued,

"Legends say that Zadarj was by far the most powerful human magician who ever lived, but even he had his limits. The cost for overstepping your limits in magic is, as you already know, madness. For some, the madness makes them simple, or gives them a tic or a defect of speech. But other times, the madness takes the form of a berserk, primal fury."

Yes. "As it was for my father."

"As it was for you, too," she said; and for the first time, a faint, involuntary quaver tempered the hardness of her tone. "Or so I thought. You wouldn't have been the first, and neither was your father. It's rare, but at least a dozen Jazeiz over the centuries have paid that price for their magic."

Kenlin quirked an eyebrow. "At least a dozen? Can you name them?" When she did not answer, he shook his head. "I can only name one: Ranton. I know there were more, but... Well, it's certainly not a *celebrated* part of our legend."

After a pause, Ranja said, "I can't name a dozen, but I can name at least one more: Zadarj the Djinn-Slayer."

Don't be silly, Ranja. "Zadarj didn't die of madness," Kenlin said dismissively. "Zadarj survived the War and lived another four or so decades, yes? His reign ended when he disappeared, and no one has ever found his sword or—"

"Did I say he died of madness?" Ranja interrupted, her voice low and annoyed. "No. Zadarj, unlike anybody else in legend or history, paid the price of madness many times over. What few accounts I've heard of such madness are almost identical with the tales of Zadarj's Rage—except on one point. For everyone else, it was a final fury, a death throe. For Zadarj, it was a weapon."

"You think *that's* what the Rage of Zadarj was?" Kenlin asked skeptically. "You think Zadarj, the greatest human magician who ever lived, somehow overreached his abilities and drove himself mad; and then, by some *additional* impossibility, he was able to come out of it?"

Quietly, she noted, "*You* did."

No, I didn't. "It's not the same thing, Ranja."

"Why not?" she challenged, suddenly brusque again. "Because you have some notion in your head of what they must have felt, and that wasn't it? Because it doesn't match the words you expected? Or because you still cling to these fantasies of the old legends, convinced they were somehow *more* than the world that we see around us—that we create. You may imagine what they felt, or what they were, Kenlin, but I know what I saw, and I know what...F-Father told me *he* saw. '...a monster in my brother's body...' That's what he said. That's what I saw today. But Ranton's gone forever, whereas you... You came back."

"I didn't *come back*, Ranja; I didn't *go* anywhere. I wasn't..." *She doesn't understand, and she won't understand.* He clicked his teeth together frustratedly and said nothing.

But she waited. When he didn't continue, she prodded, "You weren't...?"

Ranja... He sighed. "You've given 'it' a name. You got that name from a story, which I suppose makes it easier to believe, but... You saw something on that battlefield that looked different from what you knew. So you've called it a name, and to you that makes it separable. If it has a name, you can talk to *me* about *it.*"

Again, she waited for him to continue; when he did not, again she prodded, "Yes?"

"... There is no *it*, Ranja. What I did on that battlefield... That was *me.* I don't remember it—not the last parts, anyway—but it wasn't an accident, and it wasn't an obtrusion by some sort of 'Rage.' I mean...it *was*, but it also *wasn't.* I would never have done the things that I did; and yet, *I* did them. I and I, but only me. Does that make sense?" She frowned. *No, I suppose it doesn't.* He sighed. "I meant to do everything I did—I truly believe that—even if I didn't really understand it. I was saying things that night, and the day before... Things that I would never say, I said; and if I wanted to—or, perhaps, if I wanted to want to—I could say them again. A part of me... You see? Even now." He shook his head, knowing his words were incoherent. *But then, so are my thoughts.* "... I was *ready* to do that, Ranja. At least, I was ready to do something. I wanted to see...just what I could do."

She allowed his words to hang in a silence. He wasn't sure what sort of silence it was supposed to be. Consoling? Empathic? She spoke at last: "Kenlin... I don't care."

What? "What?"

"I don't care," she repeated more strongly, and even though he hadn't been depending on her compassion, her heartlessness stung him. "I don't care what you think it is, or what I think it is, or whether 'it' is. However you prefer to describe it—as *it* or *you* or what have you—that doesn't matter. All I want to know is, can you master it?"

He was still wrong-footed by her sudden, callous dismissiveness. "I... What do you mean by, 'master it?'"

She closed her eyes, took a deep breath, and let it out slowly, though not quite steadily. In a more controlled tone, she explained, "The legends say that Zadarj's early Rages were a surprise even to him. In his first Rage—the massacre on the Kilgáire plains—I've heard it said he killed as many of his own soldiers as he did of the enemy. No one who caught his eye survived."

That sounds familiar. At this thought, something in the recesses of Kenlin's mind pulsed with just a hint of prideful satisfaction— *No.* He shook himself very slightly; to Ranja, it must have looked like little more than a shudder.

She saw it nonetheless—she must have—but she let it pass. "After Kilgáire," she continued, "there are fewer and fewer mentions of Zadarj killing his allies. Perhaps the human historians simply chose not to dwell on it; perhaps it became too unpleasant, or so commonplace that it became unremarkable. Or perhaps—as many have thought, and as I like to think—Zadarj began to master his Rage. Late in his life, they say Zadarj began to seek out impossible battles with fewer and fewer allies at his side. In such a fight, even an indiscriminate slaughter would be counted a victory."

And so, perhaps, might his own death. But keeping that thought to himself, he said to Ranja, "So that is what you call *mastery.* That's a bit unexacting, yes? He still lost control, he still slaughtered mindlessly. It sounds to me as though he didn't really *master* anything. All he did was refuse to give in until a convenient time, deciding only *when* to lose control."

"'Refuse to give in,'" she repeated, a tiny note of triumph in her voice. "And could you, too, 'refuse to give in?' Perhaps that's all the mastery that's needed; if you can resist it, you can control it."

Dammit, Ranja! "Stop talking about *it,*" he said to her, annoyed. "I can't speak for Zadarj and his Rages, but I didn't master anything and I didn't resist anything. Don't you see? There was no *it. I* wanted to do what I did, Ranja! I think I even said it once: I wanted to..."

Flatly and coldly, she completed his thought: "...to kill them all."

One above. Hearing her say it aloud, it sounded bizarre, like the ludicrous vaunt of an egomaniacal madman. *And yet I screamed out those same words, and I laughed at the challenge, and I burned to find out how close I could get. And then...I did. All.* Another pulse of sick satisfaction; another recovering shudder. *Enough! Enough.* Taking a deep breath, he said to Ranja, "If you ask me now about what I did... It's disturbing. Ataland showed me that battlefield, and it disturbed me—scared me, even. But that's only now, *after* the battle; that's not how fear is supposed to work. If you had asked me before—on the hill, on the road, maybe even as far back as when Klanjad first fell from the Bridge—quite honestly, I think I'd have laughed at you. You see? Even if I had understood where I was going, even if I'd known what I would do, I don't think I would have stopped. It scares me now, but I was different then. I. Me. *I* was different, and I *liked* it. I liked it very much."

Again she left a silence, and he again did not know what kind of silence it was until, at last, she broke it: "Good."

"*Good?!*" Kenlin said incredulously. "Good? Ranja, are you listening? What's 'good?'"

The heartlessness had returned to her voice. "You wanted to kill them all," she said icily, "and then you did. I'm glad you liked it, Kenlin; I want you to do it again."

"'It!' *It!*' What is *it*, Ranja? You want me to kill them all again? I can't; they're already dead."

"Good!" she snapped, louder, angrier, wilder. "They're already dead: that's what's good. You killed them all: *that's* what's good. And *it* is whatever happened—by you, to you, through you, I don't care! Whatever *it* was, it slaughtered them all. Good! So I want you to do *it* again!"

"Good, yes?" Kenlin snapped back, matching her rising wildness. "It was good, then, that I willingly—eagerly—*lost my mind*, Ranja? Good that I fought and killed blindly, like an animal? Good that I let your father die, and die horrifically, when we were so close that—"

"Don't you *dare*—"

"Don't dare me, Ranja! And don't pretend it isn't true: *I let Klanjad die.* I was so over-focused and so wild for a fight, I let the very thing we were—"

"No!" she shrieked, unfettered frenzy finally driving her to her feet, all her emotions glaring at last through the tattered pall she had thrown over them. "Don't you *dare* try to take that on yourself, don't you *dare* try to put Father's death between us!"

"It's true! If I had only—"

"*No! No!*" She had shut her eyes tight and clapped her palms to her temples, her fingers clutching at her head as though to hold her skull together, or tear it apart. "I won't hear it, *I won't hear it!* It's not true, Kenlin! You *didn't* leave Father to die. You weren't supposed to go save him, *I* was. Remember the plan? You were to fight, to draw attention from me while I went after Father."

Hahaha! "That's ridiculous, Ranja. You know perfectly well I'd forgotten about that plan long before—"

She screamed at him, "Did you, or did you not, fight and draw attention? *Exactly as we planned!* And even if that hadn't been the plan, *neither* of us could have reached that cart fast enough to save Father. They were ready for a rescue attempt, Kenlin! We always knew they would be; we were counting on it, even. I had hoped they would use a sword, or a knife, or a bow, but they...they..."

As her mounting grief and hysteria drove Ranja beyond words, Kenlin contrastingly forced himself to back down. *Calm! Calm. Don't do this to her.* She had turned her face away from him. He heard no sobs, but every muscle in her neck was tensed and her body heaved and jerked with barely-contained anguish. *I'm sorry, Ranja. Should we simply leave these thoughts unresolved, or...?* "They had oil in the cart," he said at last. *Better to say it and be done.* "And probably other fuel as well. Ataland told me. He said you couldn't have gotten there in time."

She still faced away, still convulsed with overpowering sorrow. She shook her head. "I... I couldn't..." She couldn't breathe; it was too much. Her head bowed, and her shoulders began to shake with the rhythmic, dry, silent sobs of one with no more tears to cry.

There was nothing Kenlin could say, so he let her cry in silence for a while. For lack of any better gesture, he lifted a hand to place it on her shoulder. She must have heard him move, must have guessed what he would do. "Don't touch me!" He pulled his hand back, and they sat and stood again in separate silence.

It was only a short while—or was it many, many minutes—before Ranja was able to quiet her silent sobs and wipe away the tears she couldn't cry. She took several deep breaths, only the first few of which caught in her throat. Back in control, she sat down again on the rock beside Kenlin, her blistered feet still resting in the river. "Why do *you* get to kill them all?" she muttered, resentfully stirring the water with her foot. "Why do you get to fight while I have to watch my f-father burn?"

'...get to...' "That's...not the way I see it."

"Well, see it that way," she retorted. Her snappishness roused Kenlin's ire for a moment, but he ignored it. But perhaps she had been expecting a reaction, for at his passivity, she checked herself. After another deep breath, she continued less provokingly, "I was shocked last night when you killed those soldiers at the gate. I was shocked at the way you were acting, at the things you said... Even later, though I didn't mention it, I was shocked at how you spoke to the Wanderer."

One above, I'd almost forgotten... "Well, you were right; I was pretty shocking."

Very slowly, she shook her head. "No. No, you were right. I was wrong. I shouldn't have berated you."

"Ranja, you were *wholly* justified in—"

"No, Kenlin, I was *wrong!* Aren't you listening? You did well while *I* failed. I couldn't get to Father—I couldn't save his life, I couldn't even save his death! But you wanted to kill them all, and you did exactly what you needed to do. You succeeded. And now...I want to kill them all too."

Silence. Long silence. *I already know, but I must ask:* "Who?"

"... *All* of them."

A pulse, a thrilling tingle, shivered down Kenlin's spine like a tempting caress. "All...the Droál?"

"The Droál, and the Misks, and the Unnatilz, and the traitors of Viarlin...every *dog* that ever hunted us, hurt us, chased us around and dragged us to this day," she said with a guttural, vicious snarl. "Every bitch-bred cur that brought this war to Jranjana, that invaded our homeland and ruined our lives: I want them dead, and their corpses rotting into the ground they sought to trample or thrown back into the sea from whence they came. We are the Jazeiz, Kenlin—you and

I, we are the last two. Jranjana is *our* land, and damn to the lowest Depths *whoever* would try to take it from us!"

Ranja... "You're practically rambling," Kenlin said, shaking his head. "You're angry—you should be—but you're not yourself. Take some time—"

"I don't *want* to be myself, Kenlin!" she shouted, wild again. *"Myself* failed; everything I believed in failed, and everything I cared about is gone. *Gone!* I want to make a new myself, and you will take the new *your*self."

"You're still rambling. You need to calm down—"

"No! *You* need to listen! Don't you understand? We are the Jazeiz now; the Jazeiz are *us*. We're not beholden to anybody anymore: not to the Commune, not to any cause, not even to F-Father! *We* control this identity now, Kenlin: the name, the stories, the *legend*, everything the Wanderer wished to exploit. It's *ours!* And *we* will make it once again as mighty as ever it was.

"Too much in these last centuries, Jazeiz have been painted with all sorts of phony ideals: honor, nobility, beneficence, and every definition of *heroism* embraced by any fool who could sit by a fireside and cough out his spin on a tale. But the Jazeiz rose to power in the War of Men and Misks, *before* the Age of Men, and our legend was founded on our ability to kill *anyone* who dared to oppose us. The cunning of Gealvind, the mettle of Karkéde, the incomparable power of Zadarj—*that* is what the Jazei name meant once. That is what our name will mean again, Kenlin; you and I will *make* it so."

"Would you be angry if I called this speech of yours grandiose?" Kenlin said drily. *"Rambling* was the wrong word; you're *raving*, Ranja. If that's... If you just need to rave for a while and want me to listen, I can do that. But when you say you and I will do things, it sounds as though you want me to agree."

"Yes!" she said, nodding a single enormous nod as though he'd *finally* understood. "Exactly, you must agree!"

"Agree to what?"

"I want you to say that you'll do it again."

"Oh, for— Don't go back to *it*, Ranja."

"Fine!" she shouted, once again angry...but this time, fully in control. "However you want to phrase it, I want you to agree that what happened on that battlefield today was a *victory!* I want to hear you say it was good. I want you to say that if you could do it again, you would do *exactly* what you did before!" Kenlin was stunned; his mouth fell open, but there were no words in it. Ranja pushed on relentlessly, "In the past year, I've journeyed halfway across Jranjana with a man who couldn't *ever* make up his mind: too eager to stay restrained, yet still always hesitant and unsure. But this morning I ran alongside one who saw clearly what he wanted to do, what he wanted to be, who he wanted to kill, and he *killed them all.* I want you to be *that* man, Kenlin; *say* you'll be that man!"

Kenlin spoke on reflex: "Ranja, that man scares me!"

"*Yes!* He scared me too, Kenlin. *You* scared me. But you didn't scare yourself. That's what you're doing now, and I want you to stop. You were right, you were strong, and you should be that way again. *Forever.* And I want to be right and strong, too. I will not be a scared little girl for long. We will become something new—we will make ourselves *the Jazeiz*— and our enemies will then be scared of *us.*"

I... Kenlin still had not recovered his wits; worse, her words rang raucously in the recesses of his mind, echoing louder as they were repeated and celebrated by the thoughts he now feared to give voice to. He shook his head, trying to clear it. "I... Ranja, I think our enemies are far beyond being scared of us."

She laughed—a bitter, mocking, cackling sound—and her laugh reverberated through Kenlin's mind like *No! Stop!* "There's no one alive," Ranja crowed scathingly, "who could have seen that battle today and *not* learned to fear you. Believe me, Kenlin, they're afraid of you; and if any of them aren't, they will be. And me as well! Probably none of them fear me yet, but they should. I will *be* someone worth fearing; even if I can't kill them myself, they will learn to fear the Lady."

Why?! "Why would they ever fear us? They've *won*, Ranja; how could we possibly hurt them now?"

Kenlin had asked this incredulously, certain there could be no answer. But it was a question of strategy, and Ranja, immediately in her element, leapt at it. "We can hurt them," she said, her wild emotions swerving to breathless zeal, "because their position isn't as strong as it seems to be. Yesterday, when you told me the specifics of your conversation with the Wanderer, I didn't believe most of what he said. In one thing, however, he was right: the Droál *do* depend on Jranjanans—particularly Jranjanan farmers—to sustain their empire, and their hold over those people is dangerously frail."

"So, what, you think we should adopt his plan now? Hide in the mountains and hope to survive long enough to—"

"No, Kenlin! Hiding is no good; we've been hiding for years, and it's gained us nothing. The Wanderer was wrong because all of his plans were about preserving, sustaining, surviving... He wanted to keep the existing Order alive. The entire Commune tried to do that. That fight is over; they lost. But just because the Droál destroyed our Order doesn't mean we can't also destroy theirs. The machinery of their war is enormous, and the cost to maintain it is high, and its operation depends on a steady influx of resources from vast numbers of people who hate them."

Kenlin had told Ranja the details of his conversation with the Wanderer the day before while they were resting and waiting for the evening to come. She had listened, he'd thought, very attentively, but perhaps she'd only retained what she wanted to hear. "I told you, Ranja, I discussed all this with the Wanderer. The dream that a city can successfully rebel against the Droál just isn't true. Jiánse has been rebelling for nearly a decade, and it still hasn't freed itself."

"Aha!" Ranja crowed in triumph. "But you're wrong! It *did* free itself, remember? Jiánse's rebelliousness began when Father took up residence there after the Commune's disastrous attempt to liberate it. In the year that followed, despite the *direct* focus of the Droál, the city became so violently unruly that, when Jendraski returned with a new army, the Droál simply fled rather than try to withstand a siege there."

"After which, as I recall, the Commune's army blundered into a trap, the Droál recaptured Jiánse almost immediately, and they've held the city ever since."

"And for nearly ten years *since*, that city has continued to be an enemy that the Droál have never, never been able to defeat. They can repress it—they can quarter soldiers there, and gather taxes, and inflict their hideous regime on the people—but they can only maintain their hold through the constant investment of additional force. Where do you think they get that force? Do you think it comes from the Droálic homeland? Do you think fleets full of soldiers and resources cross the sea every summer? Or does the force that keeps Jiánse down come instead from...?"

Ah. "...the other cities," Kenlin completed quietly.

Ranja nodded. A wide smile, not of happiness, was spread across her face. Though she sat nearly still, she almost seemed to vibrate with pent-up, frenzied energy. She panted through her mouth as though she was too hot inside, and what heat she couldn't vent in her breath burned wildly in her wide emerald eyes. She did not look pretty; she hardly even looked human. In her face was something primal, something eager and hateful and furious and triumphant, for which Kenlin had no true description. He had never seen that emotion from her before, but he recognized it immediately; he knew, without doubt, how *alive* it made her feel.

She said, "It isn't enough for just one city to rebel, for the Droál will simply leverage force from the other cities to subdue the rebellious one. And it won't be enough to hide in the mountains and wait for rebellions; even if they do happen on their own, the Droál would just crush the separate rebellions as they happened, one at a time. Someone will have to *start* the rebellions, Kenlin—everywhere, all at once. Someone will have to coordinate and strategize—to lead. Someone will have to ensure that, while the rebellions are starting, the Droál are not able to focus on repressing them."

Ranja, I don't know... "And how would we do that? And *who* would do that? Us? And Ataland, if we can convince him? Three is small for an army."

She dismissed this with a flippant wave of her hand. "There will be others, Kenlin. In time, the angry rabble rebelling against the Droál may become our army. Before that, we will use whatever allies we can find. Not all from the Commune will be ready to give up the fight yet; Merejor may still be alive, and Iaile of Iskena has always been a friend to the Jazeiz."

Ha! "The same leaders who just *lost* the war, yes?"

"To start with," Ranja retorted, unfazed. "Existing armies, but new approaches—and new commanders. For all his bluster against them, Father always supported the Commune whenever he could. They held him back. Now the Commune is no more, and its absence has left a void among Jranjana's powerful. The Jazeiz will fill that void, Kenlin. We will gather allies *to us*, we will be beholden to no one, we will fight under an emerald-eyed banner once again, and we will succeed where the Commune failed."

"How?"

"What, you want a detailed grand strategy?" she said with an annoyed toss of her head. "Here? Now? Obviously I don't know particulars yet, Kenlin; we will learn as we go and adapt as we learn. I'm not proposing any specific plan. But in broad terms this is how we will begin: we'll turn the hate they've inflicted against themselves, rally Jranjana behind the Jazeiz once more, slaughter these *savages* and drive them from our shores!"

But so many people have tried and failed, Ranja. Ha! Which people? Not us! Stop!

He shook himself. "Ranja, what you propose… You're depending very heavily on our personal ability to influence things, yes? As you said, we can't possibly know the particulars yet; we don't know what we'll face, and we've no idea how we'll overcome it. So your 'course of action,' for lack of specifics, essentially claims that we—you and I, and just because it's us—will succeed where many, many others have failed."

She did not hedge and she did not hesitate: "Yes."

Haha— Wait! Wait… "Perhaps you think more of our power than I…" *…let myself think?*

Very slowly and intensely, she nodded. "And *that's* why I need the man from this morning," she said, "the man who killed them all. You fret, and equivocate, and wonder if you can or you should. But the man from this morning wouldn't care. He might not be any stronger—he might be as doomed to fail as you would ever fear—and still he wouldn't hesitate. You didn't! Listen to me, Kenlin: I want to put us in terrible situations. I want to plan battles and wage wars. I want to send thousands of people to their deaths in the name of…anything at all, whatever I tell them is worthy." She stopped abruptly, as though she'd startled herself. In a quieter voice, she said, "I'm not ready to do that. I couldn't even tell you to kill Ataland back in the Channel. But you and I have seen this world now, and the way of the world is clear: savage strength prevails where heroism fails and dies. If we wish to destroy the Droál—to repulse the invader, to avenge our fathers, to free Jranjana, or whatever other 'noble' or 'selfish' cause—then we will have to be *brutal.* You've shown you can do that; I have not. But when the time comes, I promise that I *will* be ready, Kenlin. Will you promise the same?"

Kenlin was quiet. *Such truth... After all I've seen... More reluctance? More hesitation? I didn't hesitate this morning. And if I choose...never again.* He was quiet for a very long time. *There is always a reason to restrain. It keeps me in check, helps me not to commit to— Ha!* Ranja shifted impatiently; Kenlin remained quiet. *And what has all of that brought me? Hahaha! A trail of ruin, a black streak of ashes from Natzut to Ñaj-Gadan. To the Depths with it. Damnation! Damnation take it all!* And yet he was still, and still he was silent. At long last, Ranja spoke: "You know you want to."

Hahaha. Hahahahahaha! "You're wrong," he said, a faint hint of a cackle leaking from his mind into his voice. "I don't want to. And yet you're right: I really, really do." Another pause; she waited. *She's patient when she needs me.* He felt a quickening of his pulse and a coldness in his hands—a fading fear as a lifetime of guarded sensibilities felt themselves slipping away, losing their grasp. He gave them no voices; they could only call out to him in reflex, and he would not pay them heed. *Farewell. Farewell. But her patience is, at last, becoming thin.*

"Kenlin?"

"I am here... I am here." A thought struck him: *does she know?* "Taking this road... Becoming ready for those terrible situations... It will change you, too, you know. Yes?"

"Of course I know that, Kenlin. I said it myself. I *want* that change; I want what you have found."

"And it might be irreversible: if you change the way you think, you might never change it back. You know that too, yes?"

She opened her mouth with a quick and dismissive retort, then stopped. Uncertainly, she said, "Nothing is permanent, Kenlin. I can always change myself."

Hahaha! "Can? Perhaps. But will?" She still looked unsure. He elaborated: "When I sprinted onto that battlefield, I was wild and strong and unreserved; I was everyone you want me to be." *Ha! Everyone.* "Perhaps, even before I collapsed into forgetfulness, I *could* have chosen to stop, to change my mind and to think of things as I did before. But I *wouldn't* have done that. I didn't want to. Do you see?"

She did see, and she took a moment to formulate her response. At last, she said slowly, "To love what I am is a vanity, and to fear what I could be is cowardice. I am very, very vain, Kenlin; but I am no coward. What about you?"

The question was clearly spawned from impulse, but it was so blatantly, clumsily manipulative that Kenlin couldn't help but find it funny. He opened his mouth to reply, but all that came out was laughter. He turned away, shaking his head, but the laughter wouldn't stop. *And inside, too! Hahahahaha!*

"Alright, Ranja!" he said at last, stray cackles still stippling his words. "Very well! You don't have a real plan—Ha!—but on the other hand, neither do I. I suppose we'll figure it out, yes? And in the meantime... Alright, Ranja. Very well."

The feral, primal smile had long since faded from her face, but at his words a hint of it returned. *It's in her eyes; it burns there.* But she was not yet satisfied. "Say it."

"Say...?"

Her eyes burned brighter. "I told you what I want, Kenlin. I already said my part: what I will do, and what I'll become. I promised you that I'll be ready. Now you promise me, and let me hear in your voice the things that frightened me last night. *Say* it!"

Say it. He paused. Then he laughed aloud, inside and outside, caught up in the melodrama of the moment. He stood and strode into the river, turning back to face Ranja when the water passed his knees, and lifting his hands high as though exhibiting the world to her, he laughed again. "It's a different kind of *good,* yes?" he declared, his voice booming in and out and all around. "Good that I killed them all! Good that they died by my hand! And I can do so again, too. When I find more, I *will* again. Ha! Yes, Ranja, I'm not ready either, though I daresay I'm readier than you. You asked if I can 'master it?' I don't know; I don't know anything about it. But—*ha!*—I only know of one path to mastery: practice!" She nodded, satisfied at last. *Hahahaha!* But Kenlin suddenly sprang forward. *Did I Fade? I don't even know!* He grabbed her by the shoulders and looked straight into her eyes. Though she recoiled at first, startled, she met his gaze unblinking. "Then let us make our promises—the both of us, together, as Jazeiz! We will be as you have said: we will be different. We will be brutal; we will be strong. You will be implacable, and I will be unstoppable. We, the Jazeiz, will rise again to power, or else we will die on the ascent. We will outwit and overwhelm our enemies wherever we find them, and then..."

He paused. She understood. They finished the sentence together: "...and then we will kill them all."

He had nothing more to say, and she had nothing more to ask of him. Though he still jittered with energy, Kenlin sat down again on the rock beside her. They stayed that way, side by side, for a very long time as their fervor slowly, slowly cooled to calmness. At last, after many minutes, footsteps in the field behind them prompted both Jazeiz to turn. It was nearly midday now; the sun was high in a cloudless sky, and the greasy stain of the cart-fire smoke had grown faint as the last few blazes began to burn low. It had been more than an hour since Ataland had left to find food. The footsteps, however, heralded his return, and a few moments later the half-Unnatilz himself appeared over the bank. "Cheers, all!" he called, waving. His disposition had largely recovered since the morning, but his tone remained a touch more somber than it had often been. Nevertheless, he joked easily, "Once more, the Unnatilz hunter returns."

Ranja eyed his quarry. "I see you've hunted a wheel of cheese."

"Well, this is a populated region," said Ataland, unabashed. In addition to the cheese, he'd brought a skin of wine (he claimed he'd found it hiding in its den, and he'd had to quaff a bit to subdue it) and a loaf of bread, "picked fresh today from a bread tree." It was good to laugh—not wildly, inside and outside, but as a group—and the meal did much to restore their strength. At last, when they'd eaten their fill, Ataland eyed his companions. "You two aren't talking much. I suppose that means you've talked already."

Ha! "Some."

"You haven't left the area yet," Ataland noted, "so clearly you've decided to settle here permanently. Planning to become sheep herders?"

Ranja and Kenlin both replied at the same time: she said, "Rabble-rousers," while Kenlin answered, "Butchers."

Ataland glanced uneasily from one to the other. "Well, you took the whimsy *right* out of this conversation."

Ranja regarded the half-Unnatilz ponderingly. "You didn't run."

"I *did* run," he corrected her. "But then I came back."

She'd planned to say something else, perhaps to thank him for all he'd done to aid them. However, when she opened her mouth, she couldn't help herself: *"Why?* Why do you keep coming back?"

Ataland had a quip on the tip of his tongue, but he checked himself. "We've been down that road, I think," he said simply.

"But I still don't understand."

"Sometimes you don't need to." As Ranja visibly struggled with this, a crooked, half-sad smile came over Ataland's face. "Still can't manage to trust me, *huh?*"

"I should," Ranja murmured with a note of apology. "I *will.* But it's hard for me, Ataland. It's been a long time since trusting turned out well."

Ataland eyed her thoughtfully. "I guess you've had some hard times, probably a lot of them. Hard times teach lessons to those who survive. It's possible, though, to learn some lessons a little too well."

She nodded not in agreement but in acknowledgement of his point. "Learnings and unlearnings come in time."

Ataland nodded too. "True enough." He turned to Kenlin. "What about you? Do you trust me?"

"Yes."

"Well, that's much more straightforward. So I'm guessing you wouldn't mind if I continued to tag along?"

"I hope you will."

"Do you think I should?"

Ha! Should? Kenlin, paused, thinking back to their conversation in the house west of Ñaj-Gadan. Then, with a grin and a flippant shrug, he said, "Why not?"

Ataland grinned in return. "Compelling. Hard to argue with that." Ranja gave an exasperated *ugh*, prompting a chuckle from both men. Ataland continued seriously, "Same deal as before: I'll come as far as I want, and I'll leave as soon as I want. I don't tell secrets and I don't make commitments. If that's not alright, I'll get out of your way."

Ranja said nothing, but even Ataland now knew she didn't want him to leave. Kenlin smiled warmly. "We're glad to have you with us, Ataland."

The warmth of Kenlin's smile seemed to surprise Ataland. "I... Thanks. It's just for now, you know, but... Thanks."

A few minutes passed as they finished the last of their meal. When the bread and cheese was gone and only a few sips of the wine remained, Ataland broke the silence. "Well, this is cordial all around," he said merrily, passing along the wineskin. "We've fought, we've talked, we've eaten... Yet for all that, it's still today. What now?"

Ranja answered this. "We will take a few days to recover and plan, I think. We should probably return east and reconnect with what's left of the Commune. I have connections in Iskena, and Father had many allies who may be willing to help us. We'll need information if we want to understand what the Droál will do next and how those who still oppose them will react. But all of that will keep for at least a few days; if the world ends tomorrow, we couldn't have stopped it anyway."

"That sounds reasonable," said Ataland. "In that case, I suppose we'll need another abandoned house to squat in. Lucky us, this area seems to have quite a surfeit; funny thing about wars, that. Anyway, I'll scout around to see what I can find close by. Ranja, your feet look pretty bad; you need bandages or anything?"

"Liquor, if you find any," she answered drily, "for multiple medicinal purposes. The rest I can manage myself."

"Hya! Fair enough. If I stumble across any, I'll bring it by. Meanwhile, Kenlin, you...have somewhere else that you're going, apparently."

For Kenlin had risen to his feet, looking southwest. "I'm going back to the battlefield," he said. "The fighting's been finished for a while. I see the carrion birds are gathering; human scavengers will join them soon. Before they arrive, I need to go back to retrieve...my sword." He looked at Ranja as he said this. He did not ask for her approval, but with a single solemn nod, she gave it.

Ataland remarked, "I reckon your sword'll be where you dropped it, out in *that* part of the battlefield. If it's all the same to you, I don't want to come with."

"Yes, don't. What you said about finding shelter was good. Do that; I will find you when I've finished."

There was nothing more to say. Ataland, after a quick look all around, departed to the east in search of available shelter. Ranja, wincing, began the long and painful process of cleaning and dressing her many burns. Kenlin turned, climbed the bank, and proceeded west. Within a few minutes, he stood once again amidst the smoking ruins of the carts.

Only one last fire burned here, and it was small; it crackled instead of roared. Klanjad's body still lay on the ground where Ranja had left it. It wouldn't have been possible for her to bury it, but she had done what she could: a coarse tarp, only slightly damaged by fire, had been pulled over the corpse. Kenlin pulled it back. *Black on red, crusted black over red.* But the red was fading now to a pallid greyish brown. Even the heat of death was beginning to cool.

Without really knowing why, Kenlin drew from his belt the carved wooden kirsk he had taken from a dead man near Slionte. *Less than a moon ago? How many years to fill these days!* He held the dagger in both hands, blade and grip, as he gazed at his uncle's burned and blackened visage, memorizing it. *Crack!* With a sharp twist of his arms, he snapped off the dagger's blade a finger's width above the grip. Kneeling down, he gently placed the blade on Klanjad's chest, then covered the body again with the tarp. He stood, turned, walked away; and as he passed, he cast the broken, bladeless handle into the fire.

It was a few hundred yards from the ashes to the massacre, but Kenlin thought of nothing as he walked. A wind was rising; too weak to howl but too ambitious for silence, it sighed and hissed as it brushed across the battlefield. *Outside, and inside too.* The chambers of his mind were not railing or speaking or even laughing; just whispers of notions half-formed filled the vacancies where thoughts should be. He offered them voices, but *no.* They were content, for now, and that was enough. When they were ready, he would be.

Body and mind, he paused at the edge of the bloodstained massacre, and a vast silence fell over the expanse. *Onward.*

Squelch! When he stepped, the blood-soaked ground enveloped his foot in a vile embrace. *Ugh... No! No squeamishness, no turning back. I know; the way for me is onward.* He took another step—*Schluck!*—and the clinging muck released his foot with a sickening sucking sound. *Where is it? It is here somewhere—a weapon that can match my strength.* The swords made for Jazeiz were not like ordinary swords; they were crafted to withstand extreme forces, to weather and inflict extraordinary punishments. *Match me, weapon! Give me yourself; I will wield you with horrifying might.* He nearly stumbled as his foot came down on something slippery, fleshy... *No.* He pushed it aside and pressed on. *Even as I dismiss the sight of this slaughter, the scale of it! The brutality! And what else? They were weaker. I was stronger. And we will be stronger still.* He was nearing the center of the bloodbath now. A heaped ring of gore and carnage surrounded a sort of crater, perhaps three yards across, like the epicenter of a bloody blast. *This must be where I stood, at least for a time, standing and slaying. Their pieces piled around me as I cut them apart.* The ring of viscera had seeped and bled, filling the crater with a shallow crimson pool. *It's in there somewhere. But not a glint of it shines through the surface.* He stepped into the pool; his foot sank in the mud, and the sanguine slime rose above his ankle. *Down! Search! Dive! The weapon is here somewhere; what wouldn't I do to find it?* He knelt and stuck his hands in, feeling along the bottom. There were several other blades here, including one he recognized. *This is of Eyjazinka make, like the one I carried for so long after Natzut. Ha! What a feeble weapon it was! I need something better, something stronger. Where?!* On hands and knees he crawled, sloshing, searching. *Ah!* He cut his finger; *this one is sharper than the others.* Carefully, he felt for the hilt, found it, picked it up. *Yes! Here it is! Here is my weapon at last, steeped in a stew of scores of men. Still it thirsts; it shall taste a thousand more!*

He rose at last and, standing alone in the field of the dead, he claimed for himself the Jazei's sword. *Mine!*

THE END

ABOUT THE AUTHOR

Justin Murray lives in Las Vegas, where he can be found climbing mountains, singing in bars, and ceaselessly typing everything from software to sonnets. *Jazei* is his first novel.